THE ONE PRINCE

T 17555

D0958254

THE
REDAEMIAN
CHRONICLES

Book 1

BILL HAND

Thomas Nelson Publishers
NASHVILLE

Published in Nashville, Tennessee, by Thomas Nelson, Inc., and distributed
in Canada by Lawson Falle, Ltd., Cambridge, Ontario.

Library of Congress Cataloging-in-Publication Data

Hand, Bill.
   The Oneprince / Bill Hand.
      p.   cm. — (The Redaemian chronicles ; bk. 1)
   ISBN 0-8407-3453-0 (pbk.)
   I. Title. II. Series: Hand, Bill. Redaemian chronicles ; bk. 1.
PS3558.A461805 1992
813'.54—dc20   92–11875
                                         CIP

Printed in the United States of America
1 2 3 4 5 6 7 — 97 96 95 94 93 92

TO ROBERTA

You believed in me
even when I quit believing
in myself.

ACKNOWLEDGMENTS

✦

I'll probably overlook someone rather important, but here I go anyway.

This book would still be floating with the microfiche in my Macintosh were it not for the advice, guidance, help, and inspiration of a good many people. Thanks especially to:

Evelyn Minshull, who read an early version and not only stayed awake through the task, but encouraged its completion;

Carol Krepp, who listened to me read chapter after chapter to her and actually asked to hear more;

Michael Hunter, who said he would read the story for inconsistencies and had the nerve to find them and then the audacity to point them out.

Kevin Proper and Vance Lupher, who through years of playing G.I. Joes in the pastures and the basements, helped twist my imagination into the thing it is today;

My parents—Bill Sr. and Thola—who are appropriately proud of me, their prodigy, and my sister Karen who feared for Friend Rat's life;

Donald Brandenburgh for his help and patience and long distance phone calls;

Roy Myers—yes, I will remember you *when*;

Jane Jones, who worked fervently to tighten and improve this book, never heeding my pleadings that God had inspired every single word—you were a real help and your Tennessee drawl was a charmer;

and Roberta, my wife . . . but I already covered that one, didn't I?

◆

There was once a prince
who wished only
to be left alone . . .

Naturally,
fate made
him king.

✦ A PROPHECY ✦

hey had been listening to his stories and singing for hours when suddenly the minstrel
looked up. He set his lute on the floor and shut
his eyes.

"'Tis nearly time," he said.

Snout, the innkeeper, had been stamping about and
dancing merrily with his wife. He stopped abruptly and si-
dled up to the young singer, his expression conspiratorial.

"Time, sirrah, for what?" Snout whispered.

The minstrel said nothing at first. He only opened his
dark eyes and gazed toward the ceiling. His lips moved, and
Snout realized the young singer was communing again
with his father, that mysterious fellow he spoke of so often
but whom no one could see. Then he smiled, slapped the
innkeeper on the shoulder, and hooked a thumb toward the
door.

"Come with me!" he said, with a radiant smile.

They walked outside, Snout motioning for everyone to
follow. There the minstrel stood beneath the tavern sign
he'd grown so accustomed to these past weeks. It was two
boards nailed together and hung on a chain, painted with a
great platter of cheese and labeled "The Fettid Cheese." The
light of the open door bathed him from one side while dark

night cast sharp, dramatic shadows on the other. As his friends and admirers tumbled by, he stopped Snout and directed his attention east.

"What do you see?" he asked.

Snout squinted to sharpen the distant images.

"Trees in wind and silhouette, sirrah, dancing as though they were men, and a moon behind a veil of clouds. The hills are there, and behind us, the Valley of Men."

"You are a poet, sir innkeep!" the minstrel laughed. "Now, tell me, what lies beyond those hills?"

"Syncatus, our town!" called one fellow.

"The Castle Pentatute, some days off!" called another.

"Then mourn," the young singer told them, "for Syncatus shall become Desolation, and the Valley of Men will become a forest of souls awaiting the axes of angels!"

"And Pentatute?" Snout asked.

After a moment the minstrel strummed his lute and sang,

> The castle of light
> Shall be dark this same night.
> Destruction will come
> And despair beats its drum.
> The Scion grows cold
> And what I foretold . . .

"Sirrah!" Snout interrupted excitedly. "The time is at hand?"

The corners of the minstrel's lips turned up, a smile both sad and mysterious.

"Very soon, Snout," he said quietly. "Very soon indeed."

Part One

THE
KING IS
QUAD!

"**I** am dying!" muttered the king, and then he looked about. No one heard him, or at least no one chose to respond. So Pentatutinus said it again, louder.

"I am dying!"

And he peered about, his keen eyes shining with the only blaze of life still buried in the huge, gray folds of his skin.

The portly monarch had been stuffed and jammed into his throne, a great thing of acacia wood and silver with richly embroidered cushions of silk. The arms and legs were carved with reliefs of pomegranates, almond flowers, and buds and blossoms, while elaborate cherubim of gold rose from the backrest.

The throne room itself was a spacious hall with a floor of polished stone flagging. Its walls were inlaid marble hung with rich and heavy tapestries. A great window opened to the east, looking out upon the castle ramparts and providing most of the light within. Double rows of doric columns stood, thin and delicate, rising and becoming great, interweaving arcs in the ceiling far up above. Spiraling around and climbing each column were the same reliefs of almond clusters, and fit into every one were broad bowls of blazing oil. The ceilings were painted a brilliant blue and, with the light of the lamps, gave the impression they opened into the heavens themselves.

The room was massive—large enough to hold a thousand people. It did so this day, filled with subjects, most of them human, all of them gaily dressed. They wandered about eating, drinking, and laughing, barely noticing their portly king who occupied such a conspicuous place in their midst. They had gathered for the Feast of the End—a somber, solemn banquet held when any ruler or great lord of the kingdom of Redaemus was nearing death. The dying host would invite the most powerful folk of the kingdom to gather and pay their respects and to hear any final advice or pronouncements he wished to impart.

But if Pentatutinus planned to express such things, he alone would hear them. No one else was interested.

"Bah!" he muttered. "I'm the only king they have known. I've lived a thousand years! And when I am dying, it's nothing more to them than the passing of a cloudy day."

Then he did something he'd long had a habit of doing. When he felt alone or troubled, singing to himself, Pentatutinus made up songs. He'd often been called the Minstrel King, a mantle of which he was proud. He began quietly, a mournful tune building at the rotting folds of his mind, working its way through his body. At first it was like a comforting balm, but as he warmed to the subject, his anger began to churn and stew so that he was fairly bellowing by the song's end.

I am dying.
And I feel it to my bone.
Inside my flesh is rotten
While my subjects have forgotten
That all that keeps them living is this throne!
Five years ago
If I'd have coughed
They'd grovel for my mercy;
But now they barely humor me,
They laugh there while I'm dying!
Go back to your hovels!

I've sickened with my trying
To save you all from evils
Which the best of you deserve!
You loved me once
As I've loved you,
But now you've turned your backs, you fools,
Inviting Demio's forces in:
For when I die he'll surely win!

He paused, but the few in the room who'd stopped to listen turned quickly away. His energy left him with a rasping heave.

I am dying. And I feel it in my bones.

"Bah!" he added, "I'd fall rasping to the floor and still they'd laugh and gorge themselves with pastries from my wake.

"Subjects!" he called again and, giving up, muttered, "ingrates."

"You called, Sire?"

The old king turned his head, surprised. There on his left stood Friend Rat, who'd slipped unnoticed to the throne and now leaned, on tiptoe, with his pointed snout across the king's hammy arm. The furry counselor wore an expression of comical anxiety and nervously twisted his long tail in his hands.

Now, rats in this day weren't disgusting. They were clean, large, with (for the most part) big, sad eyes. Rats of Redaemus carried a benevolent look about them and tended to be friendly, though sometimes a trifle daft and proud.

And so Friend Rat stood gazing sadly into his king's eyes.

"Castle Counselor," Pentatutinus said.

"I am ever, as you know, at your service!" Friend Rat replied in his quick, staccato voice. The counselor had a habit of sounding tense and excited, even on occasions when he was profoundly bored. "If you feel alone, I am right beside you. When others turn a deaf ear . . ."

"Turn a mute tongue," Pentatutinus said irritably, "and listen to the mumblings of your king."

"Of course, Sire!" the counselor replied, surprised, and his mouth snapped shut with a clack.

"Rat, I am dying . . ."

"Tik! tik! tik! Sire! There's no call to be talking like that. Everyone knows it already, so 'tis just stale news."

"This is the comfort of a friend?"

"I dare not lie, Sire. Rats are a noble breed. 'Tis obvious your time is short. Why, just look how dark the Ruby Scion has turned these past . . ."

"Shhhhhhhhh!" the king hissed, sounding so much like a snake that the counselor jumped away in fright. Friend Rat clapped his hands over his snout and let his tail droop to the floor. Looking about, he half-expected everyone in the room to be staring in astonishment at the king's scepter, a rod of gold-plated iron on the end of which rested a dark, brooding stone. But no one was. Relieved, he drew a breath and went on.

"As I was saying, your coming demise is no secret. Just see how the subjects ignore your laws!"

"My laws!" the king moaned woefully.

"Even those. 'Tis not your fault, my lord. The laws are great things, but rather greater than the folk you gave them to, for they are lazy, if you don't mind my saying, and selfish, and wicked, and prone—I dare say!—to revolt. Come to think of it, they are quite revolting in the present tense, as well, unlike we noble rats . . ." he added, his nose in the air.

"Counselor!" the king moaned.

"Tik! tik! tik! Never one for small talk, are you, Sire?"

"Rat! Please! Not when I'm dying."

"Good point. Well, then, back to the subject," the counselor agreed, then added with a smile, "as opposed to the *subjects.* Yes! back to the laws. They're so strict and very hard to follow! It takes a strong leader to make his folk do so, and in your prime you did just that. You even held Lord Demio in sway in those days past! Oh, I believe that the bloated, grumbling old poop I see in this throne was once a proud and just lion!" he added, poking Pentatutinus in the belly.

"Raaaaargh! I'll line my socks with rat fur!"

"Sire!" Friend Rat laughed. "You'd never do that!" (and he retreated several steps just to be sure). "Besides, you're still great, if for no other reason than the memory of what you were. Your rule has been a great gift to humanity—and to hu*rat*ity as well. I'll prove it!" he added and, hurrying off, returned a moment later dragging an upset lady of the court in tow. "Go ahead; tell your king," he urged her. "What is the greatest gift to all humanity?"

"Go suck your tail!" she snapped, and stormed away.

The king sighed. "Why aren't my sons here? Where is our noble warrior-prince, Gregor?"

"He begged leave of the feast, Sire, because of the situation at the northern border. Demio's dark forces, you know."

"And Quad the Bookish and Uncourageous?"

"He simply begged your leave."

"Bah! If I weren't dying, I might as well be."

"You could make a case for that," Rat sighed.

The counselor curled himself up at the king's feet and together they watched the subjects mill about. This proved interesting at first: the provocative women in their low-cut gowns and high-peaked cones, the men in their bright, flashing capes with swords hung gracefully in scabbards that swung with their every step, sweeping food ungracefully from the tables. But after a time this one-sided activity grew boring and they became still, the king singing old prayerful tunes to himself and the rat adding his own melodic snore to the rhythm. Finally Pentatutinus stirred uncomfortably and announced abruptly, "Counselor Rat, I have decided."

"Mmmph? Sire!" the other replied.

"It's time to declare the next king. I've thought long and hard as to whose shoulders should bear this kingdom, whether Gregor's or Quad's. I suppose I should announce my decision to the court."

"One might suppose," the counselor agreed.

The king nodded and rapped his scepter on the floor. "You! Subjects!" he roared, then repeated the call, banging his scepter on the stone flagging until, little by little, they quieted down and turned to him. For a moment the king gazed blankly at his subjects—and they at him—before he cleared his throat and began.

"I am dying . . ."

A great moan rose from the court, the kind that rewards a terrible joke. They began to talk again, so loudly that the king couldn't make himself heard. Furious, he began making faces and rapped with the scepter again. He might have rapped a hole in the floor had not Friend Rat taken action, racing across the hall and snatching a horn from a startled royal messenger. Pressing this to his mouth, he made several long *blats!* on it. The sound fled in terror from the horn's bell, curdling wine and drowning all of its opposition. Soon everyone was slapping their hands about their heads, and not a few were rolling on the floor or stuffing bread into their ears. Finally he lowered the horn and stood, angrily tapping one foot.

"Tik! tik! tik! That's just all that I can say for you. Tik! tik! tik!"

"May I cut in?" the king interrupted.

"If you hurry," said the rat. "Their attention span is short."

"As you know," the king announced in his rumbling voice, "my days near their end. The time has come to name the one who will replace me."

Now the subjects grew interested, indeed. Whispers skittered across the hall: "It will be Prince Gregor!" and "Hurray for the Warrior-Prince! He'll make a fine king!"

Pentatutinus only shook his head, waiting for the whispers to stop. He called to his friend.

"Counselor Rat, bring me the heir to my throne. Bring me *Quad*."

"Quad!" the subjects echoed, shocked at what they'd heard. Friend Rat ducked down a side corridor to deliver the hapless prince.

◆

No one spoke.

There were a-hems and haws from some clearing their throats. Once or twice Pentatutinus opened his mouth as if he would say something; he even raised one puffy finger to make a point. But, disgusted at the insolence of these folk, he changed his mind and shut his mouth, or he simply yawned, pretending indifference to the shock apparent on every face.

"He can't mean Quad?" someone whispered at last. "The kingdom won't last an hour!"

"Shouldn't we protest?" said another.

"Where is Solofaust?" a bearded advisor asked. "The Village Counselor has always been our spokesman before. He can straighten the king's head."

In the midst of all the whispering, a short figure, draped in scarlet robes and wearing a green silk hat so broad its brim rested on his snout, wandered about, rapping an occasional shin with his cane and pausing now and again to exchange a greeting or word. This was a crusty badger named Solofaust, one of the kingdom's wealthiest and most powerful advisors to the king.

Close on his heels was an unpleasant gray rat with tattered ears and a tail and whiskers that kinked and screwed in every direction, who breathed with a wheezing, whistley sound. This fellow often ran errands or gathered information for Solofaust, though he had no official position in the king's court. In fact, he had no business *being* there. He was known as the Rat Mugby.

"*Wheeeeet!* Solofaust! *Wheeeet! Wheeeet* up, sir! *Wheeeeet* up, Solofaust!" the Rat Mugby wheezed.

"You shouldn't be here where folk can see us together," the badger growled, making no sign of slowing his pace. "My situation in court can't be helped when I'm seen with cutthroats."

"Cutthroats! *Wheeet!* Now that's a thing to say! *Wheeeet!* Cutthroats indeed!"

"Oh, shut up!" Solofaust snapped and spun around, cracking the rat across the toes with his cane.

"WHEEEEET!" the other squealed at the top of his lungs, and the badger opened his eyes wide in horror. A number of folk turned and stared, and even the king glanced his way. Solofaust slapped a paw over the Rat Mugby's mouth and slipped away, dragging the cutthroat behind him.

"Squeal like that again, and I'll clamp my paw on your throat!"

"Wheeet!" the other whistled in surprise.

Releasing him, Solofaust diffidently examined a wet paw. "You drooled on me. You're quite disgusting."

"I do my worst," the rat replied, walking to a nearby table and selecting some cheeses. "I'm having a bite. Mmm! Taste the cheese! *Wheeet!*"

"I've tasted more than I wish today, thank you."

"What do you think of the king's decision? Everyone's whispering about it. It's definitely bad, not good. He'll change his mind when you ask him to, of course."

"I doubt it."

"But look at him. He looks like a great marshmallow, toasted and stuffed into a thimble. I say his wits are addled. He probably doesn't know the difference between Quad and Gregor."

"The king is no fool. He meant Quad. I wonder why?"

The Rat Mugby gobbled a wedge of cheese. "Don't our plans revolve around Gregor?"

"Shut up!" the badger hissed. "Would you have us found out? You should stuff that tail you're always tripping over into your mouth, and keep both ends of you out of trouble!"

"Wheeeeeet!"

"And stop wheezing. How can you sneak about with that sound giving you away?"

"My victims think it's the wind," the rat sniffed as he shoved four slices of cheese into his mouth.

"Well, you're right," the advisor continued under his breath. "Gregor has an arrogant but simple mind. I can control him, and *he* can control the people."

"Shury oo cn cntroo Qua? E's a tootoo foo!"

"What! I can't understand you with all that stuff in your mouth!"

The rat spit it onto the floor and swept it under the table with his foot. "I said, surely you can control Quad? He's a total fool!"

"Perhaps. But Quad can't control the people," Solofaust mused, eyeing the chewed-up cheese with disgust. "Have you no manners?"

"Braaaaarp!" the rat belched, and Solofaust wrinkled his nose at the gaseous odor. "Sorry. I don't burp so well after cheese. I'm much better after sweetmeats," the Rat Mugby apologized.

An old counselor named Royan approached and bowed. "Solofaust, er . . . the, uh, counselors and, um, advisors have, what? discussed . . . yes, discussed this matter of, oh, crowning Quad most, er, carefully," he began, "and have, well, decided that, er, *some*one must approach the king, um, about it."

"Then do so!"

"We were, er, as it were, um, hoping you would."

"I!" shouted the badger. "Have none of you more backbone than a snail? Very well. I'll see what I can say to change his mind."

"A snail has a backbone," the Rat Mugby said with a superior shrug as Royan left. "In fact—*Wheeeet!*—a snail is *all* backbone!" The badger raised his cane with a whip-like snap and the Rat Mugby gained another kink for his tail.

Friend Rat stood at the heavy, oak door of Quad's bedchamber. He listened a moment and thought he could hear the young prince humming within. He tapped on the door and the humming stopped.

After a second, Quad called softly, "Matty?"

"Matty?" Rat echoed, raising a brow. He entered, finding

the prince at his writing desk, a quill in his hand and a silly grin on his face. Before the prince a poem was growing like a romantic disease across a sheet of parchment.

"Who or what is a Matty?" Friend Rat asked.

"What do you mean, 'who or what is a Matty?'" the prince demanded, his face red, as he scrambled to hide his papers.

"If Matty isn't a what, I should guess Matty's a who," Friend Rat explained.

"Matty?" Quad asked innocently.

"You called me Matty when I knocked," the rat said, exasperated.

"I was speaking of your fur."

"You couldn't see my fur!"

"Very well," the prince replied with a shrug. "Matty is a new scullery maid. Very pretty!"

"Tik! tik! tik! When will you forget these sculleries and drudgeries and look for someone who's your equal, Prince Quad?"

"I thought sculleries and drudgeries were as low as one could look, Rat," the prince mumbled.

"Come, Quad, you're not as bad as that."

"So *you* say. Tell the subjects that, see what they'll tell you. Tell Gregor that, see how he'll laugh at you. Tell Father that, see how he'll yell at you! Tell *me* that . . ."

"I just did."

"And see what I'm telling you? Bother it all! What do you want?"

"I want nothing as always, thank you. 'Tis your father who wants."

"My father?" Quad's voice changed to a squeak and he jumped up, pacing about. "What can he possibly want? What have I done now?"

"Nothing. He just wishes to speak with you in the throne room."

"The throne room!" the prince nearly shrieked. "There are people down there!"

"Yes, and he wants to see you before them."

"Tell him I'll see him *after* them! The people hate me. And he's going to scold me, I just know it!"

Quad threw himself on his bed and wrapped his arms about his knees, then rested his head on them so that his long nose jutted out like a plank above his feet.

"He'll tell me I'm lazy and should support my brother, who always used to pull my nose," he groaned. "And then he'll ship me off to some soggy old castle by the sea. All the better. I want to be left alone."

"How can you say that of your sick father?"

"Because I know him! Rat, I love the king. You know that. I practically worship him. I've studied his letters and edicts and acted as his personal secretary since I was twelve. I'd do anything for him . . . except go down and be humiliated." Friend Rat frowned as Quad added, "I promise I'll see him tonight."

"You'd best see him now," Friend Rat warned. "He looks grave, and may not *see* tonight." They looked at each other a long moment and Rat added cheerfully. "Besides! I suspect he plans nothing more than granting you his blessing!"

"I suppose you're right," Quad sighed. "I'll go and hear him out, and let the subjects have their laughs. At least then I can withdraw to whatever castle he commands and enjoy my anonymity."

With that Quad tied on his cape, slapped Friend Rat on the shoulder, and walked hurriedly out of the room.

"'Tis a good thing I didn't tell you what the blessing would be, Master Quad," the counselor said, looking after him, "or I'd be pulling you from the window ledge. Tik! tik! tik!"

◆

Pressed into his great, wooden throne in the middle of the room, Pentatutinus seemed a continent, and his subjects seemed like a larger but weaker one, spread out like a beach and pressed against the opposite wall. Between them stood Solofaust, nearly buried in his gold-embroidered robe and broad, floppy hat and plume. He was a red and green bastion in a flagstone sea. Behind him the subjects were obviously upset. Before him the man in the throne managed a look both passive and angry. The counselor, his own expression safely buried from view by his over-sized clothes, considered his position and wondered if he was making a mistake.

"Sire . . ." his steady voice began.

The king gazed with concealed humor upon the nose and paws poking from the robes before him.

"Is it you, Solofaust?" he called.

"Yes, my lord," he replied, bowing low. There was a taunt in the king's voice that triggered his temper and he fought to keep it back. "It is me, your humble servant."

"Humble, bah! And what is your game today, Counselor?"

"I wish to reveal a . . . misunderstanding."

"You do?"

"Yes. You said you would announce the next king, and then you called for Prince Quad—no doubt to secure an oath of support from him. But this court fears you mean to choose Quad as king, over Gregor. An obvious folly in their opinion! Perhaps the king could explain to his court that Quad was called on only for counsel."

"I called Quad to tell him he will succeed me. Perhaps *you* are the one indulging in folly. The court understands my meaning well, Solofaust."

"Quite well, I am sure, Sire, but . . . a word if you will. May I approach the throne?"

"You may keep your distance and speak for all to hear."

"Very well again, Sire," Solofaust nodded, his blood rising. "No doubt you've reasons for choosing Quad. Yet I might point out that these are dangerous times. The land is in chaos and the Dark Lord Demio is waiting for any excuse to pour his armies through Sheolfrost and into our strife-torn land. A warrior king is needed. Gregor has expe-

rience in war. He is proud and confident. Quad has only the
learning of books. He's rarely stepped beyond these walls
and has never handled a sword. He lacks confidence. He's
impulsive, excitable. Besides, Gregor has the people's support."

"Quad has mine."

"May I ask why?" Solofaust said with a bow.

"You may not," Pentatutinus growled. "I am the king. I
have spoken."

Pentatutinus couldn't see the angry blaze in the badger's
eyes, but he noted the quivering whiskers. Solofaust stood
silent a moment, thinking, wincing at the taste of bitter
humiliation in his throat. "Sire!" he said angrily, "think of
your kingdom! Think of Demio, ready to overrun us!
Surely Gregor . . ."

"The borders are not threatened by Demio," Pentatutinus shouted. "They are threatened by the stupidity and
ingratitude of the subjects. Had they obeyed me, shown the
slightest respect for my laws, I should still be healthy and
Demio would be far from their thoughts and homes! I loved
them, Solofaust! My rule was just! No one can deny that!
Yet look at what they have done to me with their selfish
ways!"

"I am sure, my lord," Solofaust replied. His eyes trailed to
the Ruby Scion, staring out from its scepter like a deep,
black hole with only a tiny fleck of crimson to hint at its
original color. "But certainly you . . ."

"Don't question my choices, Counselor, or you'll find
there's still a bite left in this fat, old king!"

"Sire! I do not question . . ." Solofaust began, flustered.

"Then leave me!" In his fury the king rumbled to his
feet, shaking the scepter as though it were a sword. In its
golden cup the Ruby Scion began to glow, the red speck
deep within brightening like a blazing ember, filling the
stone and then flooding the entire room, washing every
face a crimson red. The subjects gasped and pressed tighter
against the walls, then broke and fled in a panic through
the doors and down the corridors.

"I know what you are, Solofaust!" the king hissed. "And I know the thoughts worming their way through your little mind!

> You think you will rule,
> But slave you shall be!
> And only the one who is killed
> Sets you free
> From the perilous fall!
> The black of your master
> Shall fill all these halls
> For only a time,
> And the one who would sing
> Will then take it away,
> And your master and his will
> Sink in the bay!

The king came down from his throne, a terrible specter, and the Rat Mugby—who, rather than fleeing had hidden beneath a table—squashed himself against the flagstone and cowered there. Solofaust's knees quaked as the king strode toward him, the Ruby Scion raised high above his head. The badger's mind cried for retreat, but his feet would not obey. Instead, they gave out and he fell, shaking, to his knees.

Pentatutinus towered over him now, the Ruby so blinding in its mount that the badger slammed his eyelids closed against it. Instead of the head-crushing blow Solofaust expected, the king let the scepter descend slowly until it touched the crown of his head. Suddenly there was an explosion of fire and a blinding blast of light! The Rat Mugby stared in amazement: before the throne stood the king, bent and trembling. Where Solofaust had been was only curling smoke and a smoldering bit of plume. The assassin shoved his tail into his mouth and bit down hard to keep from squealing. He fainted.

Pentatutinus did not smile as he gazed at his work. In fact, a deep moan rose from his lungs and he staggered to the throne, barely reaching it and collapsing before crying out, "My son!"

Then there was silence.

And a pattering in the hall.

And a voice.

"Tik! tik! tik! Hurry along, Quad! Hurry along!"

The throne room door slid open and the prince and counselor stepped in.

"Where did everybody go?" Friend Rat wondered. "*Snff! Snff!* Someone burned the roast! Well, no matter. Sire, here is your son, and . . . Sire? Sire?"

Quad hurried past. "Rat! I fear it will do no good to call him," he said—and tears streamed from his eyes. "I fear . . . the king . . . is dead!"

" **I** can't believe you've kept this a secret from me!" Quad shouted. He paced back and forth along a battlement of Castle Pentatute's outer walls, which overlooked the sprawling community of peasants and merchants which thrived in the shadow of the castle—a dizzying tangle of streets and buildings known only as The Village. It was just early spring, yet the sun was warm and its magnetic heat drew royalty and common folk alike into its presence. On the winding road below the gate, children were laughing and throwing mudballs about. Quad was distracted from his anger for a moment and he watched, remembering how, only a few weeks earlier, he might have joined in their fun, winging the missiles and telling them tales of Redaemian lore. That was over now; the realization turned his mind back to the rat at hand.

"I simply can't believe it!" he said again, squashing the counselor's nose with an accusing finger.

"Dear me. I do think you're over-reacting, my lord!"

"Over-reacting? Because you waited seven days to tell me I'm king-elect?"

"I'm sure the subject just slipped my mind."

"Slipped your mind!"

"Tik! tik! tik! With all that excitement over the king's death and Solofaust's disappearance and . . ." Friend Rat began to protest, but a threatening glare from the future king snapped his mouth shut.

"Counselor Rat! Would you bridle your mouth! I'm sure it's the last thing to close in the kingdom each night."

"I believe the last thing is The Village taverns. Yet, as you wish, Sire. I am ever, as you know, at your service. When . . ."

"Rat!" Quad shouted.

"Yes, Sire!" the counselor said smartly, looping his tail over his snout and drawing it tight. His sad eyes peered from behind the loop and Quad tried to glare back, then found himself turning away to avoid laughing at his friend's ridiculous appearance. His anger was draining and, to regain it, the young prince mentally recounted the events of the week. In a moment he was livid.

"Again," he shrieked, spinning around. "I can't believe you haven't told me this!"

"You've already said that. You said it twice before, and then again. That makes three. Isn't this getting tiresome and dull?"

"RAT!"

"All right! I was only trying to help. Tik! tik! tik!"

"And stop that endless tongue-clicking!"

"My, you *are* put out!"

"Why didn't you tell me Father named me as his heir? You've had no trouble telling me everything else that's happened in this castle the past five hundred years!" Quad started to pace again, waving his hands about. "Because I had no idea that I'm to be king, I've made a total fool of myself . . . as if I don't do that well enough as it is! How many times have I wandered into a room and, after someone shouted 'Hail to the king!' stood looking around and wondering where the new king was?"

"You could hardly be expected to see yourself, standing behind your eyeballs as you do."

"No wonder the guards haunt me everywhere I go. There

was a time I could relieve myself in the garderobe without soldiers standing about."

"Well, you do need protection. You aren't exactly the most popular king-to-be Redaemus has had."

"Now I know why I've been getting so many presents from the lords! You told me they were an early celebration of my birthday!"

"Two hundred and sixty-seven days early, to be exact."

"Those weren't for my birthday. They were coronation gifts!"

"I never really *said* those were for your birthday."

"You implied it," the king-elect charged.

"An implication is hardly a statement of fact, Sire!"

"I don't care!" Quad boomed, fear and outrage rattling his voice. "Now I see why the scullery maids avoid me and children shy away from me! This is why the counselors have swarmed over me, telling me how everything should be run! I thought they were just practicing their ideas on me before they approached my brother. And here I am cleaning up their grammar and offering advice on how to better present their idiotic ideas!"

"Tik! tik! tik! The fates are cruel."

"I couldn't understand why people thought I was so vain when I said, after Father's funeral, that the new king would be as good or better than he. I thought I was talking about Gregor, but it seems I was speaking of me!"

"Quad! Some folk thought it was good to hear you give a kind word for yourself. They've had such a hard time coming up with something good to say on their own."

"*Auuuugh!* I should line my cape with your hide!"

"Hmm. You and your father certainly share some disagreeable traits," the rat said with a shudder and crossed his arms. "You were nicer before you inherited the throne. Why does power corrupt folk so?"

"That does it. I won't be king. No one likes me. The kingdom is in rotten shape, and there's nothing I can do to save it. Why, as soon as I'd fit the crown to my head, Demio would swoop in and fit my head to a pole."

"Sire!"

"I'll give the throne to Gregor. He's ambitious. He likes power. And he'd look charming grinning from a post."

"Quad, you can't refuse what your father has given you."

"Why not?"

The rat thought a moment and shrugged. "I don't know."

"How can I argue with logic like that?" said Quad with a bow.

"Because . . . because a king's decision can't be broken, even by another king."

"Is that true?" Quad asked suspiciously, his eyes narrowing.

"I've no idea, but it does sound noble, don't you think?"

"It sounds ridiculous."

"Nonetheless, Gregor can't take the throne unless you die."

"So be it," Quad said and climbed onto the battlement's embrasure.

"What are you going to do!" Friend Rat shrieked.

"Jump!" Quad replied, and bent his knees to do so. He hesitated, gazing at the huge, white stones in the wall below. "It's a rather long fall, isn't it?"

"Yes, Sire. And a painful one, too. Come down."

"I intend to." He sat and dangled his legs over the ledge, his arms braced against the stodgy merlons rising on either side of him.

"Come down on *my* side! It isn't as bad as all that!"

"Of course it is."

"You'll be a good king," Rat protested frantically. "Your own father said you're bright, and quite a talker to boot! You're far more qualified than Gregor! You've a sharper mind; many a battle is lost in blood, only to be won later with words. You're a man beyond your time, a poet, a dreamer! With a breath you can put new life into your father's laws, and if the laws can live again, you'll save Redaemus!" Quad looked at him doubtfully, but Friend Rat pressed on. "How can you jump? Redaemus looks to you in its time of need!"

"Perhaps you're right, Counselor!" Quad said thoughtfully. "I don't know what's gotten into me. I'm no quitter. I shall speak with Wilgate, the High Minister, about the crowning ceremonies tonight. Will you join me?"

"Of course!" Rat exclaimed, "and I am proud of you!"

With that he gave the future king a hearty slap on the back, and with a wail, Quad disappeared over the battlement's edge.

◆

The sun rolled lazily to the west, swelled with relief at the end of its journey, and dropped out of sight, pulling in a rainbow swirl of dusk-clouds behind it. No stars broke the darkness except those made by hearth-fires in the village below and the torches on the castle towers and gates above. The silence was broken only by the chatter of two bickering figures who'd slipped out the castle gate, their faces obscured in cloaks of the common folk, and picked their way along the dark road to the brooding village.

"I hope he doesn't scold you for not coming sooner," the counselor whispered.

"I suppose I might have come sooner if someone hadn't pushed me off the castle wall! You're lucky our moat's in water this time of year, Counselor!"

"*I* am lucky?"

"This road goes on forever and winds about like a spring. We're not halfway down and already I'm exhausted."

"The mountain is steep, Sire. The road winds so you won't have to descend at such a steep grade."

"I'm going to outlaw engineers. They save you the effort of a steep descent but make you walk five times as far! Why does the High Minister live in The Village? Every other important man lives in a castle."

"I've no idea, Sire. And he lives in a particularly bad part of it."

"The Village!" Quad muttered. "It's so big! It's the biggest city in the kingdom! Why do they call it a village?"

"Because when it was first built it was a tiny village."

"So? When I was first born, I was a tiny baby. Do folk still call me a baby?"

"'Tis a lovely night," Friend Rat coughed.

The Village, which spread out on a broad plain to the west of the castle, at first made a pleasant walk: Quad had always enjoyed—before his present situation—wandering along the cobblestoned streets with their colorful shops and gardens, and the back avenues with their massive, two- and three-story homes of merchants and officials. But soon the counselor was leading him through narrow side streets, deeper into the village's core ("To be sure no one follows," he said). This was a part of the kingdom the king-elect had never seen. Half-timber homes and shops of decaying wattle leaned and sagged, while the cobblestones of the once-proud streets now boasted great gaps of mud. These in turn gave way to streets of filth and worthless structures, many windowless and most with gaping holes instead of doors. Sometimes he caught sight of large families huddled asleep beneath a single rag of blanket, lying on a lone mat of dirty straw.

"Where are we?" he asked, his eyes wide.

"The commoners' quarter."

"Common folk live here?"

"Indeed!"

"These aren't homes. They're rows of rotting teeth. Do the subjects live like this, everywhere?" the king-to-be asked.

"No. But many do. And the number grows daily, I fear."

"They're in misery! Why didn't Father take better care of them?"

"He did, when the Ruby Scion glowed bright. Why have you never taken time to notice this before?"

"I was getting educated! Besides, I wasn't king."

"Tik! tik! tik!" Friend Rat replied. A little later he stopped at an intersection of mud-slush lanes and looked about, his whiskers quivering. "Well, here we are!"

"What! The High Minister lives here?" Quad gasped.

"Oh, no. He lives . . . someplace else."

"Where else?" the king-elect asked, his eyes narrowing.
The counselor shrugged. "Details, details."

"Are you trying to say we're lost?" Quad whispered frantically.

"Of course not! I know precisely where we are!"

"Where?"

"Uhm . . . here."

"Where is here?"

"Just look at that sky! Not a star in it!"

"We are lost," Quad moaned. "We'll still be wandering when the sun comes up, and a thousand assassins will take us!"

"Tik! tik! tik! You just hide in this bush, Sire. I recall a tavern some ways back . . . It seemed cheery enough. No one will recognize me there, I'm sure! I'll get directions and we'll be at Wilgate's in a shake!"

The counselor retraced their steps until he came upon the tavern. It was one of the better buildings in the area, made of mortar and stone with a red-shingled roof. A post jabbed out from a putlog hole over the door, and from it a wooden sign hung on rusty chains. "The Rasp & File," Friend Rat read, noticing with pleasure the neat painting on the sign of a rasp and a file beside a copper mug.

"A cheery-sounding place, indeed!" he said with a smile. "I should find a window to look through, I suppose, and check it out."

But all he could find were shutters locked tight where windows should have been. Light cut through their cracks like a knife, but the cracks were not wide enough to see through.

"Oh, well," he shrugged, and went around front. He listened at the door a moment, then peered through its massive keyhole. Here he had better luck. He made out rough-looking men, rats, and badgers and heard their singing, laughing, and telling of tales in voices low and mysterious.

"They seem pleasant enough," he told the door, and pushed it open.

Inside smoke and haze burned his eyes. At the bar, a

huge man with a mustache and beard that made him resemble a bear bent over a cask. The heads of animals and humans—some attractive but most a hideous complement to the tavern's filth and decay—turned instantly to observe him. The counselor waved weakly; none returned his salute. A few went back to their drinks and conversations, but most simply continued to gaze at him with frank hostility. The smoke and haze seemed to originate from lamps of sooty oil and rags and a fireplace where a sickly bit of blaze tried to burn a damp, moldy log. Crooked, splintered tables hosted food as much as three days old, and broken mugs decorated a hearth. The walls were of a gray and yellow plaster—at one time, Friend Rat assumed, they had been white—and huge, adze-hewn beams carried the weight of the ceiling. In the back a stairwell of rough boards disappeared into the darkness of the second story. Two or three heavily-painted women sat on the steps, seemingly absorbed in their own exposed legs, which they rubbed as they pursed their lips and made puckering sounds in his direction. The walls were lined with spikes, and hanging on them were pictures done on slate. These were mostly pastoral scenes of maidens driving cattle or villagers dancing about country bonfires, although one or two portraits were of human women minus their clothes. This seemed odd to Friend Rat. Why would anyone spend his time painting a human's skin when he could have painted her in her quaint and colorful dresses and frocks? He wondered too if the models had felt at all cold.

The rat nearly bumped into a honey-haired maiden with three mugs of ale in each hand, a harried but cheerful look etched in her pretty human face. She grinned at him broadly.

"Come in, stranger! Don't mind these old grunts; they're a moody lot, hey?"

"Indeed!" he agreed, pulling his cloak more tightly about his face until his eyes were hidden in its shadows and only his nose protruded. He selected two figures seated at a far table, whispering in hurried voices.

"Ah! A fellow rat!" he said to himself and strutted over.

"Excuse me!" he announced, then added quickly. "Er . . . don't excuse me, I mean!" (He wanted to sound as rough as they looked.) "But I need directions, sir . . . er, rogue!"

The other rat looked up.

"Why! *Wheeeet!* Who are you?" he demanded, curling a lip to show his sharp, crooked teeth. "Ah! No! Never mind," he added as the one sitting across from him, an opossum, smacked him. Grabbing the wheezing rat's snout, the opossum dragged him to her and whispered harshly in his ear. Friend Rat watched warily as the other rat's eyes grew wide, then shrank into narrow slits. Set free of the marsupial's clutch, the wheezer straightened himself and bowed.

"Forgive my *ru-u-u-u*deness, but we don't see many strangers in this place," he said. "My name is the Rat, uh, the Rat *Squashum*. Yes. And this is, uh—"

The opossum rolled her eyes and whispered to him again.

"Oh!" the Rat Squashum said, "this is Rüna. Please, have a *seeeet!*" Squashum winked at Rüna, who grunted curiously.

"My name is Bartholemew," Friend Rat said huskily as he sat. "Does that sound very rough?"

"No," Rüna said.

"But people call me Bart! Belligerent Bart, they call me . . . ahem, in the . . . ah . . . educated sections, where they know what 'belligerent' means, that is," Friend Rat added when the opossum raised a brow. "Around here they just call me Bart."

"Around here they don't know you," Rüna said. "If they did, *I* would know you."

"Well, if they did know me, they'd call me Bart. For if they didn't, I would . . ." He stopped suddenly for he wasn't at all sure what he would do in such a case.

"You would what?" Rüna said, wrinkling her nose and studying him with her tiny pink eyes.

"I would . . . I would request that they do!"

The Rat Squashum laughed harshly and slapped the counselor on the back.

"A brave scoundrel, I am sure! Certainly I would call you Bart at such a threat! *Wheeeeeet!*

"Rasp!" the wheezer shouted, and the large man at the bar turned. "Send a drink our way! A drink for the Villainous Bart!"

"Belligerent Bart!" Rüna corrected through a vicious smile.

"Make it strong," Friend Rat said, trying to imitate Rüna's grin. "Make it a true rat's drink!" He hoped a true rat would drink nothing stronger than a mild brandy and cheese.

"We were talking of . . . affairs at the castle," Rüna said. "An interesting topic, don't you agree?"

"Oh, yes," Friend Rat agreed. "A true topic for rogues."

"We were speaking especially of the strange death of the king," she continued. "Only the village counselor, Solofaust, was there, and he disappeared that same day. No one knows where. Or do they?"

"Do they indeed?" Friend Rat shrugged.

"Do you know the fellow?" the Rat Squashum demanded.

"I've heard his name once or twice," Friend Rat huffed.

"But who will be king? *That's* what concerns us," Rüna said insistently. "The crown was given to Quad, but he has yet to accept it. Do you think he'll be king?"

Friend Rat squirmed uncomfortably in his seat.

"The common folk hope it will be Gregor," he hedged.

"Yes, but the *kiiiiing* named that rangy little fellow, Quad."

"I suppose Quad knows he doesn't have the public support he needs to hold the crown," Rüna mused pointedly. "He no doubt understands it would be a *fatal* mistake."

"But how," Friend Rat ventured, "would we take it from him, if he decides to wear it?"

"We have ways, friend Bart," the Rat Squashum said (and the counselor wondered if he'd heard a strong emphasis on the word *friend*).

"Why do you ask?" the opossum ventured, her thin smile seeming more threat than comfort.

"Oh! Because I love evil things, I do!" Friend Rat hurriedly replied.

At that moment the woman with the thick, honey hair approached (*How out of place she looks with all these ruffians!* the counselor thought) and, with a swish of her skirts, set a drink before him.

"M'lord," she curtsied. She cast what seemed to be a warning glance at the wheezing rat and the opossum.

"Your stew's on the way, my muggy rat and 'Rüna,' too," she said, emphasizing the opossum's strange name. "Be careful it don't get too hot, lest it burn ye goin' down."

"I've handled stews like this since before you were born, child," Rüna replied with a hiss. "Away with you!"

All three watched the maid move along, the counselor wondering at their strange and hostile conversation. *Such a flurry over soup!* he thought, turning his attention to his drink. It was dark green, with bubbles rising from its depths, *like mud in a volcano!* he thought.

The Rat Squashum and Rüna watched to see what he would do. "Bart" decided to delay the drink with conversation.

"How did the king die?" Friend Rat asked.

"He was murdered, of course," Rüna said.

"How so!" the counselor demanded, trying hard to hide the horror that rose in his throat. "How do you know?"

"What if I told you someone was there," the Rat Squashum asked slyly. "And what if I told you that someone saw the king die? And what if I told you that someone killed the king, sticking a knife in his ribs and turning it—*wheeeet!*—slowly, like that?"

As he spoke, he dug his boney knuckles into Friend Rat's ribs, digging so hard it forced the air from his lungs.

"That's a lie!" Friend Rat whoofed. "There were no knife wounds on the king!"

"How do you know!" Rüna shot back.

"Someone told me! Yes . . . my counselor said so!"

"Well, he was right," the Rat Squashum confessed with a victorious grin.

"Yes. There were no knife wounds . . . *on Pentatutinus*,"

Rüna said, her voice so slow and measured, it sent a chill up the counselor's spine.

"Why aren't you quaffing your drink?" the Rat Squashum asked.

"Because it isn't strong enough!" Friend Rat replied. "Look at this! It hardly steams and doesn't even eat through the mug! You call this a true rat's drink?" With that he rose, taking advantage of the moment. "Before I leave, I need directions."

"Of course. To where?"

"Where, sir rat? To the High Minister, Wilgate."

"Why do you wish to see him?" Rüna said.

"That's none of your business, rogue!" Friend Rat snapped, banging his fist on the table. "Now give me directions, or else!"

"Or else what?" Rüna hissed, bristling and rising slowly from her seat.

"Or else I shall ask someone else!" Friend Rat replied, undaunted.

"You'd better listen to this fellow!" the Rat Squashum laughed, "lest he carry out his awful threat! *Wheeeet!*"

"Very well, draw him a map," Rüna said slowly, sitting again.

The rat drew it, using charcoal on a bit of brown paper, and Friend Rat took the paper, folded it, and put it in his cloak.

"'Tis a good thing you gave it over," he blustered.

"I am sure, Belligerent Bart," Rüna said.

"Just Bart!" he corrected sternly.

"Then good night, Bart," the other rat said. "May we *meeeeet* some dark eve and truly know each other's minds!"

"That we shall," Friend Rat promised, thinking it a rather odd way to say goodbye. Then he scurried out the door. The maid's eyes followed his form as it retreated into the night then walked over to the now-snickering pair of animals.

"Did you *seeeee* him, Nellie?" the rat gasped between laughs, grabbing the maiden's arm. "He will be *seeeeee*king for the high minister all night with that map!" the rat was chortling. "He will be lucky to find his own toes!"

"Even with a good map, I doubt *that* fellow could find his toes," the opossum observed.

Nellie laughed. "So! My lord and lady—what was it ye called yourselves? Squashum? And Rüna? Of all the silly names to invent!"

"Could you have done better?" the rat sniffed.

"I suppose they're better than 'Helen' and 'the Rat Mugby,'" she smiled, running her finger down the Rat Mugby's snout.

"Go away, child," Helen—'Rüna' to the Villainous Bart—sighed. "A mischievous child, Miss Nellie," she noted when the maiden had gone.

"But *sweeeet* as butter!" the Rat Mugby sighed.

"So. What did you think of our strange little meeting?" she asked.

"With Nellie?" he queried.

"With the rat!" she shouted.

"Well," he thought, then crowed, "it is obvious! Yes, it is obvious what this little meeting shows!"

"Yes, it is." The opossum drew the abandoned drink to her bosom and stuck her snout into the liquid.

"What *does* it show?" her companion asked a moment later.

"Don't you know who he was!"

"Of course! He's the Castle Counselor, Friend Rat."

"And what does his presence here prove?"

"It is obvious!"

"Just so." She slurped the drink.

"What does it prove?" the Rat Mugby asked.

"That Quad will see Wilgate and so accept the crown."

"Ah! And what should we do?"

"Isn't it obvious?" the opossum groaned.

"Of course!" the Rat Mugby shrieked. "It is *so* obvious!"

"Of course!" Helen echoed and leaned her head back, letting the dregs of the brew drain into her throat.

"Well? *Wheeeet!* What should we do?"

"We must alert our fellow conspirators. And send word to Prince Gregor so he can return to seize the throne."

"Of course!" the Rat Mugby laughed. He watched as Helen finished the drink, licked the cup dry with her long tongue, then slipped the cup into her pouch.

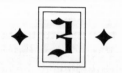

ilgate, the High Minister, was the link between the common folk and the castle, and
so it was that he lived in a stone cathedral
in the center of town.

Rumor across the land had it that the cathedral was
a great building of alabaster stone and delicate, colored
glass, towering to the sky, and nearly as beautiful as Pentatute itself. But once a tourist or pilgrim took the
actual thing into view, the rumor died a violent death.
The Village Cathedral didn't touch the skies as was com-
monly believed. Actually it barely touched the higher
trees in the village. And had one of those trees dropped
a branch on the roof, most likely the place would have
caved in. Great holes pocked its walls where blocks had
fallen out. The steeple had long ago disappeared, having
been struck several times by lightning. Its great bronze
bell used to ring with every castle proclamation, but that
had ceased to happen fifty years before when the bell,
its clapper, and supports crashed through the rotting
belfry. It made a beautiful sound as it buried itself in
the stone floor, old-timers liked to recall, and they all
agreed the memorial service for the bell ringer had been
a grand one.

There was a ceiling for the most part—it held up since nothing heavier than birds lighted on it—that was supported by great cracking pillars interlaced with a million cobwebs. This gave Wilgate, the High Minister, the notion that everyone was afflicted with nervous disorders, for whenever any folk would visit him, they constantly ran their hands all about themselves, twitching nervously. But it wasn't a problem of nerves that affected them so. It was a problem of raining spiders.

Once there had been colorful stained glass in each window, but these had given way to the pots and pans and books that Wilgate threw when he was upset (which was often). The courtyard was a litter of broken fountains, dented pots, overgrown weeds, and ambitious briars. All of this was surrounded by a low stone wall bristling with iron spikes, eighteen inches long and red with flakey rust.

Wilgate was a little man, very old and frail. He was considered one of the wisest men and, now that the king was dead, he also could boast having the shortest temper in the kingdom. Usually he wore a white tunic that fell to the floor and dusted it as he walked. His tall, pointed hat, which he wore more to make himself feel taller than for any symbolic significance, was embroidered with silk and fastened to his wispy hair with pins.

Even without his temper, Wilgate wasn't easy to get along with. The old man was more than a little deaf, and his eyes were caked with the glaze of growing cataracts. Quad was not really interested in meeting him, but he had no choice. Wilgate alone knew how to crown a king—and he alone held that authority.

There was another reason to see the High Minister, the king-elect realized as he followed the counselor (who long ago had forsaken the useless map). Quad desperately wanted fatherly advice, and it had been denied him by the king's sudden death. If Pentatutinus had left any instructions for his heir, he would have given them to Wilgate for safe keeping.

"Bother you, Pentatutinus!" Wilgate shouted. Inside the great run-down structure he sat at this table, glaring at the multitude of papers spread out before him. Three candles were lit, their wax dribbling onto the table and over its edge. The king's papers were scattered about as though they'd been dropped in a stack from the ceiling.

"Bother you!" he shouted again. "I never could understand your writing. Never in all my days, and that's been a good many in which to not understand. I can barely see a tree at twenty paces. How am I supposed to read this spidery stuff? Oh, that is a spider!" and he brushed it away.

"*Hmph*. How am I supposed to advise this young son of yours on how to run the kingdom or know how to place the crown on his head! I haven't had to do such a duty in more than a thousand years, you know. Of course you don't know! You're dead, aren't you? A lot of help that does!

"Well, let's see what I can make out: 'I, Pentatutinus, king of the land of Redaemus, worshiper of the Oneking and disciple of the Oneprince . . .' Thunder! I can't read a word beyond that! I'll make it up as I go along, then, and go from things you've told me, yourself . . . if I can *remember* what you've told me, that is. If I can't, well, it'll have to do, won't it?"

There was a knock on the door that made Wilgate start.

"Who is it?"

"It is Quad," a voice answered.

"Well, of *course* it's odd," Wilgate snapped as he gathered the papers. "A visit from strangers this time of night! Are you the king-elect?"

"Yes!"

"Well then, come in! Don't dilly-dally!"

The door opened and there stood the prince, pulling the hood from his head and looking, disappointedly, about.

"I have a friend. May he come in?"

"No, you have not offended me, and yes, you may come in. Didn't I tell you to?"

Quad and Friend Rat entered and Wilgate squinted at the counselor.

"Sit down," Wilgate said at last.

"Thank you," Quad replied.

"You look well, but your ears are too large. I should do something about it if I were you."

"Tik! tik! tik! I'm Friend Rat, the Castle Counselor. Prince Quad is the other one, the one with the yellow hair."

"Ah, of course! You're looking well, too. At least, I suppose you are. Let's see. There are two sons of Pentatutinus, that handsome lad Gregor, and the other whose name always escapes me. Which are you?"

"The one whose name always escapes you," Quad sighed.

"Ah! And according to these papers your father left, you're to be crowned." Wilgate leaned closer and squinted, popped his eyes open so wide that Quad jumped back, startled.

"Well, it's his throne, I suppose, so why argue? Let's see . . ." Wilgate said and began to search through the papers. "Ah! Here it is! 'I relinquish my throne to What's His Name!'"

"My father wouldn't call me 'What's His Name'!" the prince protested.

"Well of course he wouldn't!" Wilgate shrieked. "What kind of father would he be if he did? I call you 'What's His Name' because I can't read the old buzzard's writing!"

"My name is Quad."

"Well, odd or not, I must learn it if I'm to crown you. Still, you can tell me later. Write it on paper, two feet by four feet, and hold it up for me. I'll just read it then and won't have to worry over remembering it now.

"Down to business! So. It is time for the kingdom to fall into your hands. . . . Er, do you mind if I pace? It always feels more official. And I fear sitting in one place all the time—my joints freeze when I do, and this might take forever. Ah! this is much better."

Back and forth, in and out of the candlelight's glow the High Minister strode, and it did seem better for him, for his back straightened and his voice rumbled with a deep authority it had lacked before.

"We must be honest. The kingdom has no confidence in you. After all, you are weak. You're silly. You look more like a scarecrow than a king. You've no ambition. Your greatest physical efforts seem divided between charming scullery maids and trying to avoid physical effort."

Wilgate paused for a minute and straightened his pointed hat. He drew himself up to be as tall as he could to seem more imposing and be as official as possible, and he cleared his throat.

"Still, your father chose you instead of your brother, and he must have had his reasons. Have you good points? Yes: Sincerity. Gentleness. You're more loyal than the chattering idiots who run about the castle—more so than your brother, even. So perhaps you'll do all right."

"I still don't wish to be king," Quad cut in.

"Don't interrupt me, you little waxbound volume of ignorance!" Wilgate shouted, hurling the bundle of papers at him. They separated as soon as they left his hand, making a silent explosion that left paper floating everywhere. Wilgate seemed not to notice as he stormed the young prince, raising a bony finger and wagging it.

"Redaemus is about to be placed in your hands, and I've much to say! Oh, I agree you haven't the stuff for kingship, but your father has spoken. He told me—at least I think it was him—that you would replace him. I don't like it, but it's done, so let's make the best of this, you little twit! Er . . . do you mind if I pace again?"

"I'd prefer it."

"It's an awful strain, an outburst like that. Where was I? In the cathedral, of course!" he added, popping himself in the forehead as Quad and Friend Rat exchanged glances. "Where else would I be? Congratulations on your new kingdom. It's falling apart. You must save it."

"How?" Quad asked.

"Well, forget the armies. Useless things. They're managing the border skirmishes, of course. But when Demio's dark riders come charging through Sheolfrost, our soldiers will drop their weapons and run—unless, of course, they join his side. They've always been a fickle crew. Your father never relied on them, at least—sent Gregor to keep an eye on things. If he hadn't, they'd have all gone home years ago. The Laws kept control in your father's best days but everyone ignores them now. They were so hard to follow! I haven't followed them for ages, although I still try and get everyone else to. All the copies are getting moldy and the moths have been eating holes in the vellum, so I'm copying them. And since I can't read your father's writing, I have to make half of 'em up as I go along. They'll be easier to follow once I'm done, for I'm a nicer man. Even so, they'll be useless to you, because no one cares a whit about them anyway, easy or not."

"What about the advisors?" Quad asked, his voice barely concealing his fear.

"Ignore them. Treacherous fools, all of them."

"Then what chance do *I* have?" he asked hopelessly.

"Ev-e-ry chance!" Wilgate said, shaking his finger with each syllable, "*if* you can find the Oneprince!"

"The Oneprince!" Quad echoed.

The High Minister nodded vigorously as Friend Rat drew the prince aside.

"I've read about him in legends, but I never knew . . ." Quad whispered to the counselor.

"Sire! This Oneprince was a conqueror who was promised to your father's fathers by their fathers," Friend Rat explained, whispering. "He was supposed to be a great ruler who would one day bring the entire kingdom under peace and fellowship with the Oneking himself. Your own father claimed to have known him. Indeed, he said his own great age was due to that fellow and the Ruby Scion which the Oneprince gave him, so he once told me. I've heard him say the Oneprince was so mighty, not even Demio could stand against him. 'Tis a silly myth, of course, but believing it gave your father comfort, so I let it go."

"Then there is no Oneprince?"

"There might be. *Some*one had the power to make the late king last so long. But I think his highness put too much hope in the fellow. Besides," Friend Rat added meaningfully, "no one but your father has ever seen him."

"And lots of cherry tarts!" Wilgate concluded with a flourish.

"Cherry tarts!" the others exclaimed, remembering they'd left the High Minister talking in the corner. But Wilgate hadn't noticed. He was addressing Quad's cloak, which hung on a hook near the door.

"Of course, cherry tarts!" he told it. "The coronation must have cherry tarts!"

"But why?" the prince asked.

"Because I happen to love cherry tarts, and I won't crown you, otherwise!"

Quad and his counselor questioned Wilgate for some time to learn what, so far, only the cloak had been told: details of the coronation ceremony and the feast which would follow; how the new king should dress and act on that day.

"This has been most enlightening," Friend Rat said at last, "and we're grateful for your help. But 'tis time to take our leave. Come, Quad, I'll guide you back to the castle."

They said their goodbyes and the High Minister followed them to the door, watching as they disappeared through the front gate, muffled again in their cloaks.

"He said his name was odd, and he was right. . . . Cumquat is *very* odd . . . as odd a name as I've heard, and I've heard many!" the High Minister said, shaking his head.

The coronation was set and the kingdom buzzed with activity as it prepared for the fated day. No place was busier than The Rasp & File. Humans and animals, cutthroats and vagabonds, they pushed and squeezed about, trying to get closer to the central figure, Helen, a frowning old opossum in a skirt. She was seated in a lashed-together rocking chair made of willow sticks, which sat upon a table to put her in better view. Her face was screwed and angry and her tight, bony fist waved about.

"What do you say!" she shouted.

"We say put 'im under the ground!" someone yelled.

"Down with the king!"

"We want Gregor! Kill Quad!" screamed a frantic shrew named Shrieker.

"Off with his head!" cried a rat.

"Give me rice and plenty of it!" shouted a confused old man who'd been waiting too long for service.

"Quiet! Quiet!" Helen called. "Hear me! We must rid ourselves of Quad."

"Yes, you are *rieeeeeet!*" said the Rat Mugby, standing behind her.

"Word has been sent to Prince Gregor," Helen continued.

"But I doubt he'll take the initiative to start things. We must show Gregor he has our full support, and we can do so by dealing with his brother."

"How?" File grunted.

"Isn't it obvious?" the Rat Mugby scolded.

"*We* must begin the revolution," Helen said. "One of us must execute Quad."

"Sounds easy enough!" Nellie laughed. "Until you realize that, first, we must get near him."

"We need an assassin who can slip past the guards," Helen agreed, her eyes darting about. "Perhaps the Rat Mugby."

"*Wheeeeet!* Of course!" he shouted, taking a spoon from the bar. "I'll sneak up on him as he walks about in the crowd. Then I'll introduce myself, like so" (and he put his arm about Nellie's waist): "*Wheeeet!* King Quad, I am the Rat Mugby and I've come for the gift you were going to give your brother."

Nellie laughed and, crossing her eyes and plugging her nose, said, "A gift from me to my brother? And what might it be?"

"It is your lieee*eefe!*" the Rat Mugby shouted as the tavern rogues cheered. "And then I will twist—*wheeeet!*—the knife slowly in his ribs!"

"And if you demonstrate with that spoon, I'll twist your snout inside out, Master Wheezer!" Nellie said, joining everyone's laughter. But the shrew began to jump frantically up and down.

"Wait! Wait!" Shrieker squealed, and Nellie lifted the tiny creature onto the bar. "How will you get *near* Quad? Tell me that," he said.

"With all the confusion? Easily," Helen said.

"Shrieker is right," the barmaid noted. "The Castle Counselor was here the other night in disguise and talked to you, Helen. Remember?"

The opossum's nose wrinkled. "So?"

"He just thought we were common folk," the Rat Mugby added. "He'll think nothing of us in a crowd."

"Oh, no?" Nellie leaned over Helen's shoulder and spoke

in a voice remarkably like the rat's. "What if I told you someone was in the throne room and saw the king die? And what if I told you that same someone's was the hand which killed the king, sliding a knife into his ribs and turning it, like so?"

Helen's eyes opened wide as she recalled the conversation, but the Rat Mugby shouted defensively: "Friend Rat would suspect nothing from that! We spoke as if we'd heard rumors, nothing more!"

"The assassin is right," Helen huffed.

"And what of a thing Helen said, Master Wheezer?" Nellie continued, and now she scowled, her voice low and her finger lifting the rat's chin. "Yes, you are right. There was no knife wound . . . in King Pentatutinus, at least!"

The old opossum rocked nervously in her chair. "I see what you mean. I see what you mean."

"Not even the stupid rat who serves Quad could miss a threat like that!" Nellie mocked. "Oh, he'll keep an eye for ye, Counselor Rat will, and you'll not get near his master."

"I believe I have an answer," Helen said.

"Is it obvious?" the Rat Mugby asked.

"No, it isn't obvious!" she snarled at the assassin, then added more calmly, "We'll simply do away, first, with Friend Rat."

"Let me!" Shrieker cried. "I'll chop off his tail with a carving knife!"

Nellie smiled while the others applauded the new plan. When they'd quieted down she asked, "And what will Quad do when he finds his counselor dead?"

"He'll be so afraid," the Rat Mugby laughed, "that he'll have twenty guards surround him night . . . and . . . day . . . and . . . and . . . uh . . ." He fell uncomfortably silent.

"Won't be easy getting through a ring o' guards to kill the fellow, hey, Master Wheezer? Especially if you wish to survive the deed? Ha! If you weren't so free with your flapping jaws . . ." Nellie folded her arms before her, thrusting one hip out. "You had a chance to milk Friend Rat for information. Instead the silly fellow milked you! A fine lot of conspirators we make!"

"A fine lot, indeed, so long as there's someone other than babbling rogues and arrogant barmaids at the helm," a gravelly voice declared.

"Who said that!" Nellie demanded, her cheeks burning. Looking about, she found the speaker sitting at a table by the far wall. He was small, dressed in a dirty cloak, his face hidden in the shadow of his hood. He held a cup of ale and crushed bugs in his paws. The barmaid stormed over to him, her fists clenched on her hips. "And who are you to talk so to me!"

"You all know my name. I am your helm, that was struck by lightning . . ."

"Riddles! I hate 'em!" She seized his hood and pulled it back—and her own shock deafened her from the gasps that filled the tavern: "Solofaust!"

"Indeed," the badger nodded slowly.

"How . . . ?" Helen began, fumbling with her words. "When the king struck you with the Ruby Scion, you disappeared and we thought you were dead!"

"Disappeared, indeed, and in fire and smoke as my poor, burned hide gives witness. But killed? It takes more than one fat old king to do that."

"Where've you been?"

"Here, for the most part, in this disguise!" Solofaust answered Nellie with a barking laugh. "Oh, for a few days I was off . . . consulting . . . with the Dark Lord Demio. Mostly, though, I've been recovering. Thinking. Attending to things which need attending in secret, for there are changes in our plans. Nellie, fill this cup again, and grind the beetles finer! Yes, it's time to make myself known once more."

"Changes, my lord?" Helen asked, her pink eyes wide.

"Yes. We no longer look for Gregor to be king. He, too, must be destroyed with his brother, though we'll let him think otherwise. Why live under the control of the House of Pentatutinus, my friends, when we can rule this land ourselves? We! Under the happy guidance of Lord Demio!"

✦

Solofaust sat in his den, a low-ceilinged, underground home of some dozen rooms and chambers. It was a humble place, for a counselor, with sparse furniture and lighting; its only impressive feature was his library, a long and tapestry-draped stone chamber lined with row upon row of books and scrolls. This was Solofaust's shrine, where he spent most of his hours studying and contemplating. He was there—lying deep in his thinking chair, feet propped on a stool—his shining eyes glued to a dancing fire. The old badger was wrapped in medicine balms, and a skin of hot water soothed his aching skull.

"Blasted head has throbbed since that day in Castle Pentatute," he said to no one. "But at least I am in control again."

Such long, miserable days these had been! As the fire licked enticingly at the air, he recalled the mistakes that had led to his adventures.

"And there were many, weren't there, old fool?" he asked himself, scooping dried bugs from an earthen jar he held in his lap and popping them into his mouth. "First there was the old king's decision to crown Quad. Ha! Who'd have believed it? I put my money on Gregor . . . and plenty of it! Lavished that arrogant idiot and his men with gifts, I did, and nearly emptied my treasury doing it.

"Why did your father crown Quad?" he now asked Gregor, who wasn't there. "You, I understand. You can control the subjects, while I can control you. And best," he laughed mockingly, "you'd give me your blessings to do so!"

A perfect puppet, the counselor thought. Gregor was a hero the subjects looked up to—they would obey him without question. Yet Gregor, too arrogant and ambitious to refuse the crown, at the same time shunned its many and tiring responsibilities. He preferred galloping about with his famous Honor Guard, making himself a playful legend and letting his petty generals handle the administrative and judicial "nonsense" of running the army. *Gregor would've been happy to sign me on as secretary and let me run Redaemus! Of course, none of that matters now.*

No, now I must contend with that suspicious brat, Quad! He isn't fit to run the kingdom. He has no support, and he's terrified of everything. Still, the boy's smart. More than once I've caught a dangerous glint of mischievousness and understanding in his gaze. "Beware of fools with intelligent eyes," Father always said.

If I'd known Pentatutinus' plan earlier, I could've approached Quad and gained his confidence. But now he's given his trust to that simpleton of a rat. Blast my stupidity.

"Bah! He could never control the subjects, anyway, even with me behind him!"

Solofaust rose to stir the fire, shaking his furry body to loosen his stiff joints.

"The healing process is slow," he told the blazing log as he jabbed it with a poker. "Do you know my worst mistake . . . the absolutely most stupid thing I did? Arguing with Pentatutinus when he'd made up his mind, and assuming he was as helpless as he looked! Still, things worked out. The captain of the castle guards has thrown his lot in with me, and I've managed to place my conspirators in the kitchens on coronation day. So the kingdom will still be mine . . . for the most part, at least."

He shuffled back to his chair, frowning. "I must try and get that Ruby Scion for myself. With it I might be more powerful than even Demio. How powerful it must be if it can send me to . . . that place. Well! I deserved it, didn't I? After my foolishness, of course I did! But those mistakes will not be repeated. No, Master Solofaust, I think not. I've learned my lesson. Now, I am in control."

He selected an especially large beetle. Nibbling at its head, he reviewed his plans and snorted softly. "Things are coming together very well. The conspirators will handle Quad; Artemus, the captain, will kill or arrest the lords and nobles; and by then I'll be nimble enough to finish Gregor.

I'll not get a kingship for my efforts, but at least I'll be governor, and the folk will obey me. Ah! Lord Solofaust, Governor of all the western kingdom! Ha! ha! ha!"

He leaned back, placing his paws behind his head. He was happy and undeniably pleased with his own cunning. Picturing himself on the throne he'd envied so long, Solofaust allowed a broad smile to cover his jowls.

Nothing could ruin his pleasure now. Except for thoughts of that place. And he refused to think of it.

But a warm fire and a belly full of beetles made him drowsy. He nodded off, and as he slept his recent trip slunk back into his dreams—as it always did. . . .

In his dreams, Master Solofaust screamed.

"Aaiieee! Where am I?" he cried, sitting up suddenly. It was dark and a bitter cold racked his trembling body with chills while fiery pain consumed his skull. The scent of singed hair and hide filled his nostrils and fear clung desperately to his spine.

"Where are you?" a voice replied. "Hee-heee! You are here, Mister Badger!"

"Where is here? 'Tis dark, and I see nothing at all."

"Think, Mister Badger! What do you feel?"

"Chains," the groggy counselor muttered. "I am in Pentatute's dungeons, then, though I don't recall them being so cold. And who are you, the jailer?"

"Jailer? Hee-heee! I am Scumwort, keeper and servant of my lord!"

"Your lord Pentatutinus?"

"Demio!" Scumwort replied from the darkness.

"Demio!" Solofaust echoed, shocked. "Then I'm in Ebon Bane!"

"Oooh, good badger! You understand! Wonderful! You know where you are!"

"But I was in Castle Pentatute a moment ago!"

"Hee-*heeee!*" Scumwort squealed, and Solofaust felt the

stinging smack of a slimy hand across his snout. "Not *moments* ago!" Scumwort said, "but, my, my! Hours ago! Days ago! Weeks! Months! Or years! Perhaps you have been here forever and only dreamed you were not, could that be so?"

"How did I get here?"

A giggle came from the darkness, and a new shiver of fear crept over Solofaust.

"So. I'm in the Dark Lord's castle."

"Not quite! Hee hee! You're below it . . . leagues below it!"

Solofaust contemplated his companion and his situation. Beneath Demio's castle? *How did I get here? Why? Well, first things come first,* he mused, *and the first thing I need is light. Let's see how far I can get with this mindless creature.*

"Scumwort!" he called, "give me some light."

"Light! Light! Light!" it squealed, then hurried away. In a moment Solofaust saw a glow in the distance and Scumwort rounded a corner with a torch in its hand. The creature was dwarf-sized, naked, and sickly yellow, with a broad, flat head shaped like a saucer, balanced on a stick of a neck jutting from a tight, shiny body. At the center of its platter-shaped head, two eyes bulged upward like tiny, overturned bowls. Long, boneless fingers and toes sprouted from its thin, stringy legs and arms. Grinning idiotically, the flap-hatch of its jaw dropping to reveal rows of razor teeth, it giggled. "Hee-heee! Come, Mister Badger! Your lord waits!"

"Why does he wish to see me?" Solofaust grunted as the scum-thing's hand reached out. It only giggled and, unlocking his chains, held its hand toward him again. The thought of touching this thing revolted the counselor, but at last Solofaust held out his paw.

"Lead on," he sighed.

Solofaust found himself following the scum-thing down a long, narrow hall that seemed to bend always to the left in a continuing, tightening spiral. There was no light, except for Scumwort's bobbing torch, and the things its blaze re-

vealed shocked and revolted Solofaust. There were dungeons on either side, some closed off by great doors, but
most with yawning holes sealed by iron bars. They were
rancid with rot and the prisoners within appeared to be
mere echoes of former beings who scurried into the
shadows in fear or pressed against the bars, their ghostly
eyes searching, curious to see who'd soon be joining them.
Solofaust wrinkled his nose at the odors and noted the prisoners' sickening appearance: filthy, jaundiced, starved,
many showing the marks of beatings, their clothes little
more than tattered shreds. As their moans and cries came
to his ears, nausea swelled in Solofaust's belly.

"Is it much farther?" he gasped.

Scumwort giggled and went on.

In desperation the counselor took refuge in his thoughts.
Losing himself like that was always his greatest refuge, for
then he felt in control, *and being in control*, he told himself again, *is everything.*

Why does Demio want me? He'd dealt with the Dark
Lord before, sending messages and prisoners in exchange
for jewels and favors, but he'd never actually met the evil,
brooding thing that called itself "Demio." Few folk had, he
knew, beyond the thousands that filled these dungeons like
stale vomit and the unfortunates who, it was rumored, Demio ate on occasion. Solofaust shuddered at this possibil-
ity, then dismissed it.

*If he wanted to toss me in his dungeons or onto his
dinner plate, I'd be there already. Besides, I've done nothing to upset him. It must have something to do with the
king. Yes, Pentatutinus is certainly dying, and of course
Demio knows it. He doubtless wishes to negotiate concerning my takeover of the land, to offer advice and aid in
exchange for part of Redaemus' wealth. That would be
good, for I've certainly benefited from his help in the
past. . . . Just so he doesn't try to press himself on me too
much. I'll not be your puppet, my lord. I'm too smart for
that.*

Well, I shall learn what he's up to soon enough.

Solofaust suddenly realized that it was getting darker.

Scumwort was far ahead, a small figure in the distance, lit by a tiny glow.

"Wait, you idiot!" the counselor shouted, wanting no part of being swallowed up in the dark with all these dungeon-creatures. He scrambled to catch up.

Prince Gregor's armies were massed at the border between Redaemus and Demio Sway, but their real protection came from a range of frozen, jagged mountains and glaciers called "Sheolfrost." This brooding aberration rose imposingly from the plains into the sky and imposed its image from the eastern to the western seas.

The only ways to cross the range were through three passes—the Greater, the Lesser, and Whistler's Pass (so named for the constant, wailing wind cutting through it). Solofaust knew each well—how they twisted about over hanging rope bridges, swinging wildly across chasms, and along inches-wide paths chiseled in sheer cliff walls; how dark and evil things seemed to live in the shadows of every broken rock and boulder that littered the way and watched the merchant caravans as they passed. He knew how even these passes were often made impassable by winter snows and spring floods (and spring came late in the year), for he was put to work along them as a cub in his father's caravans. He remembered each path and, as he followed the scum-thing through Ebon Bane's moldy roots, recalled mentally the waystation where horses and mules were traded for ale and the pack-slaves who carried the burdens through the regions horses could not traverse. The slaves were men, women, and even whole families of rats. And they were humans and badgers who had not been able to meet their debts to wealthy lords of the kingdom and so were kidnapped and sold in the black market. Or they were petty criminals from Demio Sway. Usually Solofaust's father would purchase the freedom of the badgers and sometimes of others if they showed promise toward undermining Pentatutinus (The Rat Mugby was one of these). Others he purchased were allowed to earn their freedom if they could complete five trips through the passes, carrying his goods; but it was rare one could survive the punishments of the passes for so many runs.

Once through the Sheolfrost, the glittering, icy tundra of Demio Sway, the kingdom of Lord Demio opened to him. He knew this land, as well. The kingdom formed a crescent shape rising north from the Sheolfrost, with its two points forming a bay on the northernmost side so wide that one shore couldn't be seen from the other. The dark lord's kingdom was flat and nearly featureless, interrupted only occasionally by hills at its eastern and western extremes. Because of this, sharp winds that cut through the warmest cloaks or fur always blew across the frozen land.

The bitterness of the land never bothered young Solofaust as he drove his father's animals and men along. He'd rather liked the cold, and the solitude of the journey had given him time for his precious thoughts. Still, Demio Sway depressed him. Everything was shades of gray—the sky, the ground, even the wisps of snow and the sunsets which dredged the daylight away, and the subjects were the same. Upon reaching Grief's Bane, the largest city in the Dark Lord's realm, young Solofaust had always watched the silent little folk, moving about like phantoms, never able to stay still, yet never seeming to have anyplace to go. They moved quietly about their duties until the day's end when most would lock themselves behind the doors of their blank, stone homes. Even the taverns in this land were generally still, except for the shockwaves of laughter that came all too loudly and suddenly to be sincere.

Solofaust's father, Spartanus, always went straight to a nameless tavern when he came to Grief's Bane. There he met with a man named Tentatious, who possessed the only sincere laugh in the land, Solofaust was sure, and who carried candied beetles in every pocket. As he lavished the sweets on the boy badger, he spoke with the elder one in his strange, breathy language. Every such meeting ended with an exchange of sealed papers from his father for Tentatious' jewels and gold. Tentatious was not only a merchant,

Solofaust had come to realize, but a spy and advisor of the Dark Lord as well.

"You will learn life isn't easy," Spartanus told Solofaust later, walking with him to the edge of the docks, crawling spider-like from Grief's Bane into the Great Ice Bay. "We are badgers, boy, and a badger controls his own destiny. I do not betray my kingdom, for the secrets I sell to Demio are nothing that can destroy it, and nothing the old bird wouldn't learn from others, if not from me, anyway. And why should others have this wealth?

"You've been told Demio is cruel, but Pentatutinus is just as harsh. Particularly he isn't good to badgers. We owe him nothing, for he's given us nothing—nothing more than a set of idiotic, moralistic rules."

"And what has Demio given?" the young Solofaust asked, his whiskers quivering.

"Look about you, boy!" Spartanus laughed and waved at the caravan of prisoners and goods being loaded into the long, low ice clippers, waiting for their secret journeys across the canals of the Great Ice Bay. "We're rich, we're powerful, and we have the Dark Lord's protection. For a few secrets and petty betrayals, Demio has given us everything—everything but Redaemus of course. And that shall be ours one day."

"But I've heard Demio makes slaves of folk for no reason, that he eats them too! Isn't that cruel?"

"There is no cruelty. There is no good. There's only necessity, and that guides our actions. Demio's is a sparsely populated kingdom, so he needs slaves to handle the work. As a carrion-thing, he eats human meat to survive. So far as I know, he's never touched the flesh of a badger. No, Demio has never been cruel to me, and so long as he isn't, I'll not put him down. For some, his ways are evil, but for those who watch their steps, his ways are beneficent. And so, for us, he is good."

Spartanus patted his son's shoulder and the badger cub smiled. After that year, control of the caravans was given to him, and he continued to run them until Pentatutinus outlawed all trade with Ebon Sway ("Another outrage to the badgers!" his father shouted). All the while Tentatious befriended young Solofaust and taught him well.

Spartanus died rich, but bitter, and Solofaust converted his inheritance into bribes. With these he earned a post under a lord to the king. It didn't take long to learn the ways of government, and as a result, his lord was murdered by a wheezing assassin one night. By right of his position Solofaust took power. The king, he knew, was suspicious of him, but could prove nothing. Besides, already the old king's power was waning, and it was easy for Solofaust to dodge any attempts to be ousted.

In the meantime he nurtured his constituents, wooing them with carefully chosen arguments ("A blacksmith builds horseshoes, but a wordsmith builds revolution," as Tentatious once said) that their king was evil and his laws absurd.

So, after all my careful work, you wish to step in, Lord Demio, Solofaust thought now as he followed the scumthing, whose torch bobbed about like a drunken firefly. *Again, I'll take your help, but I'll not be your puppet. Perhaps, if I am careful, I can even make you mine!* But how? To manipulate the Dark Lord, he would have to understand his ways and find a way to skirt his power—a power he'd always known to be great and, now he realized, seemed mysterious and magical as well.

The Castle Ebon Bane—with its great tower, the Ebon Eyrie—was built on and carved into a rocky island in the middle of the Great Ice Bay. It so intertwined the island that the two were virtually one, a black and rocky cliff that shot up from the depths of the bay and climbed upward, a mile round at its base and reaching a thousand feet into the sky.

The core of Ebon Bane was hollowed out, filled with dungeons and twisting stairs and chambers, going from the castle's tip to deep within its roots beneath the bay. A broad platform atop the island, spreading far beyond the island's shore, cast its shadow on the ice below.

Ebon Bane could only be reached by ice boat, a kind of long, low sailboat on runners, or by the majestic ice clippers. But even these methods of reaching the island weren't possible for most, for the surface of the Great Ice Bay was not simply one sheet of ice. It was broken into thousands of ice shards piled upon each other at crazy angles, thrusting upward a hundred feet into the air like mountains, or plunging at steep angles into other sheets of ice below or directly into sub-freezing water. The constant wind and strong currents kept the narrow channels moving in a winding, clock-like motion, so that the twisted maze that reached Ebon Bane one day would lead endlessly nowhere the next. Only the Dark Lord and his closest associates knew on any day which channels would actually lead to the rocky banks of Ebon Bane.

"You can't hope to reach Ebon Bane on your own, my little friend," Tentatious once said. "You can only go there on the wings of the Dark Lord himself."

"The wings of the Dark Lord!" Solofaust muttered as he rubbed his chilled limbs. "Well, my fiery-eyed friend, it seems I've found another!"

The torch stopped bobbing ahead and Scumwort grinned beneath it. "Hee-heee! We are here, Mister Badger! We are here!"

They stood before a great oak door, its stone handle carved in the image of a bird's head.

"Demio is in there?" Solofaust asked, disgusted at the knot of apprehension that rose in his throat.

"No-no! No-no!"

"Then what is?"

"Open it, fearless badger, and see!"

"Out of my way, then, you mindless creature!" Solofaust roared. Making the knob a substitute for the scum-thing's neck, the furious counselor seized it, wrenched the door open, and stepped through . . . nearly tumbling off a narrow ledge and into the bottomless chasm below.

◆

With a gasp, Solofaust stopped himself and staggered back to the door.

"It's just a staircase!" Scumwort giggled.

"A staircase, indeed!" the badger said, clinging to the doorpost and peering down.

The door had opened into a shaft, some thirty feet wide, that seemed to extend endlessly both above and below them. Anchored to the walls by fat, rough-hewn posts, a narrow staircase of stone wound painfully upward, torches marking its shaky progress. These twinkled in the distance like stars, finally disappearing in the darkness above. Below, the same torches were mounted to the walls every forty or fifty feet, finally fading out and looking oddly like reflections in a black pool.

"Is there no bottom?" Solofaust asked in awe.

The scum-thing giggled. "Come! The master waits!"

"It seems a long climb."

"Hee-heee! It is! It is!"

"And there are no banisters," the badger added, looking doubtfully up. "Mind you, I'm not afraid. But we badgers don't like heights."

"Then watch your step, Master Fearless! There is cold and wind! There is ice!"

Exhausted and dizzy, Solofaust climbed the steps with his back pressed to the wall and his arms spread wide. The staircase was cracked and broken and at times he half-expected it to give way, bequeathing him to the emptiness below.

"I don't see why he won't meet us halfway," the counselor snarled.

"Hee-heee!" the creature replied and, quickening its pace, it sang:

Skip and climb! Skip and climb!
Scumwort skips and then it climbs!

Off to eat its dinner fine!
Ever onward Scumwort climbs!

It gave its song some thought and added, "I like dinner:
yes, I like it very much!"

"Your singing would make a maggot wince," Solofaust
panted. "And I wish you'd slow down. I'm a badger, not a
scurrying rat. And what does your master want of me?"

Scumwort! Scumwort! Scumwort knows
Deals the Master wants to show,
And where the badger has to go
To make the Master's power grow!

Scumwort stopped suddenly to look back, and the two
collided. Solofaust's eyes popped open in surprise as he
hugged Scumwort for balance.

"Blast you! Warn me when you're going to stop!"

The scum-thing's face was buried in his cloak and its
muffled giggle floated out. The counselor considered throt-
tling it, but instead stepped around it, being careful to keep
Scumwort on the outside as he passed. "There. You keep
behind me and tell me when to stop."

"Go! Go!" Scumwort urged.

Still they climbed, Solofaust groaning with every step.
Soon it occurred to him that his companion had not giggled
or sung in some time.

"What's got your tongue?" he asked.

There was no answer.

"Scumwort?"

Solofaust turned. It was gone.

A cold knot twisted the badger's stomach as he looked
desperately about.

"Where are you! You miserable slime creature! Show
yourself! You! Slime creature!" But his roar only echoed up
and down the shaft: *Slimecreature!slimecreature!slime-
creature! creature! creature!* and he balled his fists, shak-

ing with anger as the echoes bounced from wall to wall, gay and mad as the scum-thing itself, then faded to silence.

"How dare you abandon me!" Solofaust roared. "Leaving me alone on these forsaken steps! Come out here!"

Again the echoes scattered like frightened crows, their flight leaving a fog of silence on the badger's ears. His fists fell open as he listened, and he whispered, "Please!"

He stood there, not willing to abandon the safe feeling of the cold wall against his singed and burning back. He sniffed, but caught no scent of the creature.

"Well, it's gone," he told himself, "and you're better for it. Get climbing, badger, before these torches burn out."

Every door he came to, he tried, and every door he tried, resisted. At last one swung open and he staggered in, panting and wheezing. He was in a room or a hall. He could tell that much by the coldness and the draftiness. But there were no lights. It was black, and the dull light of the torches in the shaft did little to reveal its dimensions. Whichever it was, he decided he must now be above the bay since he felt a tinge of salt in the air.

"Hello!" he called. "No answer. I assume I'm alone, then. I can't see, but at least I'm away from that bottomless shaft."

He shut the door, deciding that total darkness was better than having that shaft gaping open behind him.

"Darkness suits me fine," he said aloud to no one. "Well! if Demio wants me, I'm sure he can find me. Until he does, I'll lie here against this wall and adjust to the darkness. In fact, I think I'm going to snooze."

An ugly smell made the badger's nose twitch and brought him awake. Solofaust sat up and sniffed.

"Who's there?"

"*Zolovauzt!*"

The cry pierced him like a javelin and felt like it slit the length of his spine like a knife.

"My lord!" Solofaust cried, struggling to his feet. He stumbled on something, a column perhaps, and cracked his snout against a wall. He fell, arms splayed and reaching for the stone floor which met him hard enough to take a sampling of his skin and all of his breath. He lay there, shivering.

"Yezz, counzelor of the zzqum of the kingdom, it izz me."

Out of the darkness small balls of fire appeared, floating in the air and growing until the place was washed in their meager glow. Demio, an enormous winged creature, was perched on a granite throne, which was splotched white with his feces. In one cleaver-sharp talon he held a scepter set with a dark stone, equal in size to the Ruby Scion. Yet this stone was far different, for instead of the Scion's murky darkness, this one's blackness was impenetrable and perfect. It seemed, Solofaust thought, to be more of a hole, a tiny window balanced on its staff, opening into a world he would rather not know. *So this is the Ebon Trist,* he thought, *from which he is supposed to call his servants of the demon world.* Solofaust shuddered at the thought. Demio's beak was broad and hooked, easily capable of tearing flesh and bone, and he frequently brought it together with a sharp, angry clack, followed by a quick twist of his head as his eyes blinked or widened with loathing and mockery.

"Rize, my vaithful zervant. You do not fear me, do you?"

"Of course I don't fear you," the badger replied, remaining prostrate where he was. "I do, however, respect you."

"That izz good. To ztart, I believe you owe me your humble and zinzere thankz."

"For what!" Solofaust huffed.

The Dark Lord's eyes lit up and his beak snapped together. The badger swallowed hard, realizing his response had been dangerously brash. *Careful!* he thought to himself. *Too much fear, too much boldness—either will get you killed.* He watched the silent fowl, waiting for some response.

At last Demio leaned back with a nod, then continued.

"I have zaved your life, badger. I have brought you vrom the limbo whenze Pen-tah-tutinuzz sent you."

"Would your lordship say how?"

"The Ebon Trizt," Demio replied, blinking. "I was zhure the zcum-thing would have told you."

"It told me nothing," Solofaust growled, seeing Scum-wort peek from behind the throne and giggle. "Of course," he added, "my humble, heartfelt thanks is given. Now, why did you wish to see me?"

In spite of his boldness, Solofaust had to fight off another shiver, which rose at the thought of being hauled through anything by the power of that dark stone.

"I have need of a favor."

I thought so, Solofaust mused, then said, "What kind of favor, my lord?"

"A new king will be crowned zome days henze. Quad. It would be . . . convenient for me iv you would make zhure the crowning doze not take plaze."

"You wish me to assassinate Quad?" Solofaust asked, feeling a bit smug.

"You already plan that. I wish you to alzo azzazzinate Prinze Gregor."

Solofaust started. "Why Gregor? He's a perfect puppet!"

"Any zon of Pen-tah-tutinuz on the throne iz a threat to me," Demio said slowly as he preened.

"I am your servant," Solofaust said calmly—though his whiskers were trembling—as he bowed. "But I must point out that this work will cause me quite a bit of extra trouble and expense. It would be dangerous, as well. What will be my payment?"

Demio glanced at him sharply, lowering his head with a snake-like motion. He seemed to regard the counselor as a wolf might a rabbit. At last, after some moments, he blinked.

"I zhall give you the Caztle Pen-tah-tute, and you zhall be governor of the weztern kingdom as far as Yeruzhela."

"In all fairness, my lord! I've been loyal and worked years on this matter! I should be king, and of all the kingdom! What you offer is low pay!"

"It iz grand pay-y-y," Demio hissed. "Anything would be grand pay: you would do it vor nothing iv I azked."

"Nothing?" Solofaust's smugness was gone, replaced by a new sense of fear.

"I have given your family protection and wealth zince your father was a cub. Do you zuppose I did it vor charity?"

"We gave you information in exchange for it . . ."

"Invor*mazion!*" the fowl shrieked. "You've never told me anyvhing I didn't already know. I could have told you all that and more, arrogant bug! I have befriended you for thiz day alone! I need a reprezentative in Redaemuz, for I cannot leave my caztle now. There is another enemy I muzt watch for. These idiot kings are below my dignity. I need an obedient zlave to do my bidding. You are blezzed, Badger, for I have dezided you shall make an . . . adequate zlave."

"I am no . . . !" Solofaust began to blurt, but a snap of the Dark Lord's beak and a tensing of his talons stopped him. "I should at least be governor of the whole kingdom!"

"You arrogant vool! You zhall do it for *novhing!*"

"Nothing!" Solofaust protested, his voice barely audible and one paw clutching his chest.

"You zimple idiot of a bug," Demio hissed, rising. "Even when I give you novhing, you are rezeiving a prize a mizerable beazt like you shall cherish!"

"What is that?" Solofaust whispered.

"Your life!" Demio shrieked, rising to his full height and leaping at the badger. He beat his wings furiously and a whirlwind lifted Solofaust from the floor, tumbling him head over heels, banging him against a column and then a wall. With the Dark Lord's deafening shrieks in his ears and stench in his nostrils, Solofaust rolled along helplessly and finally crashed against the door with such force that he felt his ribs crack and the door's hinges rip loose. It flew open and the helpless badger tumbled through, grabbing desperately for the door frame as he passed, but his grip was no match for the Dark Lord's beating wings. Solofaust found

himself rolling across the steps, over the ledge, and into the bottomless shaft.

He fell, twisting and spinning, his eyes frozen wide and his mouth gaping. Doors flashed by in a blur and the blinking torches formed an endless yellow streak as he plummeted by. In moments he passed the door through which Scumwort had first brought him and quickly the lowest torch became a memory.

In the darkness he fell, screaming his terror.

"I will do it!" he cried at last. "Master! Save me!"

And he struck something.

It gave under his weight, snapped, and he fell through. Twenty feet further he struck another, fell through, and struck a third, then a fourth. They were nets, and the fifth one held. He lay there gasping, feeling his heart pounding against his throbbing ribs.

◆

Now, wrapped in medicine balms and sitting before his warm fire, Solofaust awoke with a start, panting heavily and feeling again the cold terror. He'd tried to tell himself that Demio had stretched the nets before their encounter, that the Dark Lord had been desperately hoping the badger wouldn't call his bluff before reaching them.

But the words of the scum-thing as it dragged him from the last one reached through the fabric of his dream, and settled on his heart like the ice of Demio Sway.

"Mr. Badger, had you not begged and agreed, I'd have cut the net and you'd be falling still! Hee-hee!"

"Prince Gregor returns! Hail Prince Gregor!" The cry began at the watchtower and was taken up by two fishwives turning to shout to a baker, who in turn called to the cobbler. Soon the announcement had passed through the entire village. The peasants responded by crowding the muddy streets to cheer. Here was their hero, the hope of the kingdom, with the sun sparkling off his crested shield and polished armor, his great white stallion sweating rivers at its flanks while its hooves tore up the cobblestones in a shower of sparks. Young women rushed to loosen their hair and to pull their necklines just a little lower in hopes of catching an admiring glance from the royal eye, while their mothers, full of fairy tale dreams, pushed them along. Young men with fantasies of leaving their squalor to join Gregor's ranks, and pimply officers who dreamed of leaving the sorry life of a soldier to join in the prince's Honor Guard, vied for positions close enough to feel the wind as the warrior-prince rode by. Boys grabbed swords of wood and fought each other along the curbstone: "Ha! I'm Gregor!" "You were Gregor last time! You be someone else!" "Ha, then! I'm Narramoore!" They won their victories, setting smaller children crying and getting themselves crowned by the toddlers' angry fathers.

A rumble in the distance gave way to horsemen bursting into view. Two men on shining black steeds approached at a gallop, each with his head high, the breeze whipping his hair. They wore capes of brilliant red with shining chain mail hauberks and hammered leather leggings and brassards. They carried the colorful, double-tipped triangular pennants of the Honor Guard and Redaemus. Peasant folk scrambled from the street's edge for safety as the horsemen came upon them, mothers grabbing for their babes and older children scrambling under the safety of the legs in the crowd. The reckless advance riders roused some curses from the populace, but the spectacle of their passing turned those sounds to earthy cheers.

The first rider refused to acknowledge his admirers—nor would he until he reached the last hundred yards before the castle ramp itself. There the powerful lords, counselors, and wealthy merchants would be cheering. The second advance man, however, was a golden-haired boy of fifteen, and his grin betrayed his obvious pride at being seen in the prince's company. He even waved at his jealous peers and winked at a maiden who promptly collapsed in a faint at her fuming betrothed's feet.

The warrior-prince thundered past, his shield and armor sparkling in the sun. He was ruddy and handsome, with short, neatly trimmed black hair barely visible beneath his helmet. His steely gray eyes were fixed on the riders ahead, his square, muscular jaw thrust forward and his mouth set in a determined, yet not unhappy frown. A continual explosion of huzzahs followed him like the wake of a fast ship as he raised one ring-covered hand in salute. This urged the peasants to even more exuberant admiration and the corners of his lips inched upward.

Close on his heels came the bulk of the Honor Guard, large, colorful men in outlandish clothing and armor, each a legend from a far-away corner of the kingdom, and even a few from without. To most the Honor Guard was an elite corps of motivated, skilled, and dashing warriors. To a few critics, however, they were little more than a band of immature and mercenary men—Gregor's collection of unusual and bizarre playthings. Some rode by, their horses laden with blankets, cloaks, and high saddles, while others rode almost bareback. Though every warrior was dressed in fine clothes, the manner and variation of each costume's cloth, cut, and style gave the whole procession the look of a parade: Some were bright and colorful, worn by perfumed dandies with oiled hair and delicate jewelry, while others bore the autumnal hues and shaggy fur of the woodlands and northern regions. These latter men wore heavy pendants of gold, silver, or brass on chains and leather thongs about their necks or draped from their saddles. All were human; all were proud.

The road leading to the castle twisted and wound its way through the village, about the merchant districts of elaborate and sturdy homes and shops rising one against the other.

The Rasp & File was not along this favored route, but many of its regulars were among the crowd. Nellie was there, escorted by her usual court of admiring teenagers and young men with little income and fewer teeth. They were nothing to be serious about, she thought, but they were fun to chat with and tease, and their muscular, farm-grown frames were pleasant to look upon, as well as being handy for keeping some of the less noble villagers at bay. She was hoping to catch a glance of this man who'd accepted her fellows' bid to snatch him a crown, but who would instead wind up giving the conspirators his head.

She had risen and left her little room in the back of the tavern early that day, grabbing her motley escort and leading them from the slums to that quarter of The Village where the lower- to middle-class merchants and lesser officials lived. She had enjoyed sneaking about and spying on her social superiors since she was a child. It wasn't that she resented her own kind—she loved them as dearly as a mother would love her own child—but their simple, superstitious, and unquestioning ways at times were maddening. Nellie's head had always been full of questions and wonder, while her tongue enjoyed the feel of the impressive words she learned from eavesdropping on the educated folk. For this reason, as a little girl, she'd spent any free moment she could snatch sneaking to the parks that were built in the midst of the wealthy classes where she hid among the bushes to watch them dance and eat and talk.

But while she envied their style, eventually she learned to hate this class of people. Their gossip of the castle was fascinating, yet their crude and disdainful references to her own folk left her feeling dirty and ashamed, making her cry bitterly. Besides, whenever they caught her, she found herself thrashed soundly and sent along home, a bundle of bruises and welts. The children treated her no better, insulting her and throwing stones. As she developed into a young lady of fifteen, their taunts and jeers took on a decidedly unpleasant nature and she decided it best to abandon her spying games altogether.

At the king's school of the lords, however, she discovered that students were too busy and tired to notice her. She nearly swooned as she camped outside the hall's great windows, listening to the thin, bearded men and badgers who spoke of wisdom and debated about the existence and qualities of the Oneking. The heavens, poetry, and the notions of science, nature, and love were always on their lips and, while she suspected that some abandoned all this high thought at the end of the day to go home and beat their families, still others were sincere and truly in love with their knowledge. One instructor, a badger, discovered her outside his window one night and, rather than driving her away with switches, invited her to his den. There he fed her, lectured her, and during subsequent visits taught her to write and read. As their friendship developed, the two began to open up to each other. He told her of his summers spent running his father's great caravans, and of his successful application through some well-known lords to become an apprentice to the aging Village Counselor. In turn she spoke passionately about her own folk and their miseries. He listened earnestly and carefully, his eyes sparkling with interest, his probing questions and comments displaying deep concern. At last he announced, one cold night, that he wished to meet these common folk for himself.

The next night she dressed him in a peasant's cloak, laughing at how silly the dignified educator appeared, and then excitedly led him to The Rasp & File. There he grew close to her folk and returned often, lecturing and filling their hungry minds with knowledge and a desire for freedom from the selfish, hateful folk who ruled them and the tyrannies of an uncaring, sick old king. That educator's name was Solofaust, and she had come to love him like a father. He in turn, she suspected, loved her as a daughter, as well.

One benefit of Solofaust's friendship was the knowledge that his spies were always tailing and protecting her, thus making it possible again to slip about the wealthier quarters of the village. And so today, with the additional protection of wooing farm boys beside her, she came to see what kind of reception the lower merchants would give a prince. She wandered along the clean, colorful streets so full of exciting sounds and smells—tinsmiths and forgers clanking away at their craft, the aroma of fresh bread and pies wafting from the bakers' ovens. She kept herself occupied in this manner, chatting merrily with her farm boys, until she heard the wave of shouting that preceded the Honor Guard. At her nod, her escorts wedged an opening through the crowd for her, and she stepped to the edge of the street. Around the bend, a hundred yards away, the advance riders galloped into view. An old woman behind her gasped, "Annabelle! Come back!"

Wondering at the sound, she turned to see a grinning, tiny girl, her arms extended and waving as she marched gaily from the crowd and into the road. A brightly painted toy, dropped from a cart and now lying on the cobblestone, had caught her eye and she meant to claim it for her own. With an awkward deftness, the child ducked and dodged the few hands that grabbed for her, seeming almost to dance to the tune of her grandmother's desperate calls. The stout old woman tried to force herself through the wall of people before her, but they were too tightly packed to let her through and too involved in the spectacle of the riders to notice the reason for her despair.

Nellie hesitated, surprised, as Annabelle, giggling and spreading her sticky fingers before her, twirled past. But as the toddler stepped into the street itself Nellie reacted, crying out and racing after her, even as the sound of the riders crescendoed to a thunder. Annabelle, hearing her name shrieked by a stranger, froze in fear and began to scream. The barmaid grabbed the child's wrist, jerked her from the ground, and drew her, kicking and screaming, to her breast. She spun rapidly on her heel to return to the curb, but a slippered foot caught between the cobblestones and she fell to her knees with a skin-scraping thud. A cacophony of shouts and pounding hooves filled her ears and when she looked up all she could see was the massive, heaving chest and throat and flaring nostrils of an oncoming horse, its great hooves ready to trample her. With a cry she folded herself over the child, praying that at least Annabelle would survive.

But to her surprise the horse stopped, its rider pulling it up so suddenly that the animal reared and neighed.

"Out of the way, you fool!" the rider shouted. "Out of . . . ! Is she all right?"

Nellie looked up. The youth in the saddle was looking hard at the screaming child, his eyes wide.

"Can I see her?" he asked.

Carefully Nellie exposed the squalling child and the rider smiled.

"She looks like my sister," he said, then added more severely, "Why did you let her into the street?"

"I . . ." Nellie began, but her words were cut off by the approach of a third horseman.

"What's going on here! Why are we stopped!" Prince Gregor demanded. He swore and raised his fist as if he would strike the boy—who flinched—then thought better of it and checked himself.

"Robin, if you are to be one of the Honor Guard, you

must not let petty incidents draw your attention from . . . What's this?"

"A child, my lord!" Robin said, venturing a smile and quickly regretting it.

"I can see it's a child!" the prince screamed. "What is she and this . . . this wetnurse doing here?" His eyes jumped furiously from Nellie to Robin and back. "And why did you stop?"

"If I hadn't, I would have trampled them!"

"There was no such danger. The horses can jump and avoid this rabble," Gregor snapped, adding for Nellie's benefit, "and the rabble know well enough to stay out of our way!"

Suddenly livid, Nellie rose to her feet and practically shook the screaming bundle in the prince's face.

"This child ain't old enough to know what arrogant fools the king's men are," Nellie said in a loud voice. "And I don't doubt this horse was about to . . ."

Gregor's head spun around with a snap and Nellie's jaw clamped suddenly shut. That flare-up of temper could have her hanging from a gallows before nightfall, and she knew from the angry silence of the crowd that there would be plenty of witnesses ready to revel at her fate. Feeling the heat of Gregor's glare, she set the child down (who ran, wailing, to her grandmother, who in turn whisked her silently away). Dropping her arms to her sides and unconsciously clenching and unclenching her fists, Nellie let her eyes meet the warrior-prince's.

"What did you say?" he asked, his voice cool.

"You heard the words, M'lord. I don't know I can exactly recall 'em."

"Perhaps you'd better retract them."

A second warrior rode up. He was a large, serious-faced officer, wearing a blue, sashed shirt and a cape attached to his hauberk.

"She's a peasant, Sire. Let's leave her alone. She doesn't understand what you're saying."

"I think she does, Narramoore," Gregor replied.

"He means for you to take your words back," Narramoore explained, turning to Nellie. "On such a beautiful day, your Lord Gregor is willing to forgive your brashness for no more than an apology."

"I know what he meant, thank'ee," Nellie replied, her eyes never leaving the prince. "My lord, forgive my temper, but I won't retract my words. That child was near-trampled."

"You're talking to the prince!" Robin said angrily, kicking at Nellie. She took a step back, easily avoiding the blow, as Gregor motioned him to silence.

"The girl was in no danger," Gregor said. "We'd have skirted around you and been gone in a minute, but your silly actions—" (and he flashed a look at Robin) "not to mention yours—have delayed an important consultation. I've no time to deal with you, so out of my way, girl. Go back to your charge."

The prince gave an impatient signal with his hand and Robin and the other advance man rode on ahead while Narramoore returned to the body of the Honor Guard. Gregor started forward, steering his horse close enough to bounce Nellie roughly aside. She found herself sitting on the cobblestones again, this time to the merry laughter of the crowd, and her cheeks flushed hotly.

Gregor stopped and turned in his saddle once more. "Wait. Haven't I seen you before?"

"I should say not!"

"Yes, I have. On a locket. A little painted image carried by the Village Counselor, Solofaust. He came north some days ago, along with an old 'possum and some kind of silly rat. I'll have to remember you and tell him how we met." He laughed, then shouted, "Ho!" and in one quick, fluid motion the Honor Guard took off in a gallop, veering some five or six feet from Nellie as they charged past.

She sat there, watching until they were gone. Then she felt hands grasping under her arms.

"Don't grab me so!" she snapped at the farm boys. "I've feet and hands of me own!"

✦

☮regor rode on. The more he thought of the peasant girl,
the angrier he grew. When he reached the last stretch
where merchants and lords waited to see the princely
march of the Honor Guard, he spurred his horse to a harder
gallop, rushing past his advance men and thundering up
the castle road. A few minutes later he guided his stallion
through the gatehouse and, thundering through to the inner ward, reined to a sudden stop.

"I've returned to the castle of my father and his Laws," he
proclaimed as the surprised and harried Honor Guard
straggled up behind him and courtiers and stableboys gathered about. Unsheathing his sword, he waved it high.

"Bring me Quad!" he ordered.

Gregor's voice rang with authority across the castle
grounds. Quad heard it immediately and so it was only
after a diligent search that Friend Rat discovered a quivering lump of blanket in a hall closet.

"I told you this would happen," the lump said. "I told
you! Sooner or later my brother was sure to show up. Nothing good will come of this!"

"Quad! You must go to meet him. After all, you don't
know that he has any intention of harming you."

"More important," Quad countered, peeking out, "I don't
know he has any intention of *not!*"

"Tik! tik! tik!"

"Do all rats say that? 'Tik! tik! tik!'?"

"Most I know of, Sire. 'Tis a handy phrase."

"Well, it drives me to distraction and I wish you'd give it
up."

"Will you please meet your brother?"

"No," Quad answered, drawing his head into the blanket.

"You should at least go and shake hands."

"My hand is shaking plenty now, thank you."

"Sire! Please! 'Tis the kingly thing to do!"

"Tik! tik! tik!" Quad said, from inside his blanket, his fists on his hips and his head wagging with each word.

In the early afternoon Gregor stood along the castle battlements, gazing beyond the village to the fields and forests which lay beyond. In his hand was the conspirators' letter—a strip of parchment that was stained, creased, dog-eared and badly worn. Scanning its contents once more, he granted himself a mischievous smile.

"Pardon, Lord Gregor!"

He quickly folded the letter and shoved it into his cape pocket. Turning, he met a set of mournful eyes.

"Ah! Fred Rat, the Castle Counselor!"

"Friend Rat," the counselor corrected him.

"What can I do for you?" Gregor beamed.

"Sire Quad asked me to inquire of your purpose."

"Did he? Where is the little fellow? I thought of chopping this place apart to find him, but why dull a good blade?"

"He wishes to know . . ."

"If I promise not to pull his nose. Hasn't changed, the ragged pup. Paranoid as always!"

"And you are arrogant and secretive as always. What is that letter you were holding?"

"A report of my forces, just arrived."

"I see."

"You don't believe me. Would you like to read it?"

"If I may!"

"I'd let you, but the information is too delicate." The prince turned his back on the counselor and looked out across the land.

"And what does this report of your forces show?" Friend Rat persisted.

"Nothing to hold a feast over, coronation or otherwise," Gregor said, suddenly grave. Then he turned, smiling broadly. "Well? Where's my brother?"

"Waiting to give you audience," Friend Rat said with a deep bow.

"Tell him I'm coming, then. No need to fear me; not now.

I'd hardly lop off his head, myself, right here on the eve of his feast! Go on, Rat, tell him."

I shall, Friend Rat thought as he scurried away. *But your promises of Quad's safekeeping seem none too promising to me! Tik! tik! tik!*

✦

Artemus was no joy to look at, or to be around. Big and burly, he had a fist for a face with eyes set too far apart. He was none too bright, but was strong and determined, with a willingness to do whatever needed doing—thus he had risen to the rank of Captain of the Guard.

His quarters were cluttered with documents regarding his fellow officers and the more ambitious men under him. *Independent spirits are dangerous*, he liked to think. *They eye one's post with too much interest.* Such guardsmen usually found themselves transferred or, if they were foolish enough to refuse a change of duty, got caught in terrible accidents or arrested for crimes they couldn't recall committing.

He was the kind of man Solofaust was looking for—in love with power and unscrupulous as to how he wooed it, yet with too much fog in his head to be a serious threat to an imaginative fellow. *You haven't the creativity of a dirt clod*, Solofaust thought, watching the man.

Artemus sat by the tower wall, lovingly cleaning his sword with oil as he spoke in slow, measured tones.

"I've been with you all along in Quad's overthrow, for he can only hurt the kingdom, and I've agreed Gregor should rule in his place. Now you tell me we must do away with the warrior prince, as well. I am out of it, then, and so are you. Do you understand?"

"You are the one who lacks understanding," Solofaust said with a slight smile. "Think! Gregor will destroy this kingdom as surely as Quad, though in a different way. I have seen the armies Demio has lined up to invade this

land, and we both know what rag dolls of soldiers we have
to defend the passes. They won't hold Demio back even a
day! Yet, if Gregor is king, he'll try to fight the Dark Lord,
for he has more pride than brains. Demio will run us over,
and in his wrath Redaemus will be fortunate indeed to have
a hut left standing, or a man, woman, or cub to live in it!"

"There's a limit to my treachery, Counselor. I'd rather
die with honor than lay my sword at that dark bird's feet."

"No one's asked you to lay down your sword, but simply
to expand your loyalties," Solofaust said. "If the conquest is
peaceful, Demio will treat the kingdom well. There's nothing wrong with being on the winning side!"

Artemus only grunted and examined his blade.

"Come!" Solofaust continued. "We can't stop Demio
from ruling our land, but we can make that transition easier and more lucrative for both of us. You once saved Pentatutinus' life . . . The armies see you as a hero. If they lose
Gregor, they'll support you in his place. We'll tell them the
prince died in the fighting on Coronation Day. Artemus!
The Dark Lord rewards those who help him . . . rewards
them very well."

"*Very* well?"

"Indeed!" Solofaust smiled. "I shall be governor of half
the kingdom. Perhaps you'd like to be my general? Of
course, if you're happy guarding the halls of this moldy, old
castle . . . It's your choice."

"I don't like killing a soldier as fine as Gregor. Still . . . I
see your point. Resisting Demio can only bring suffering."
Artemus ran his finger gently down his sword. "Mind you, I
think only of Redaemus in these matters."

"Of course." Solofaust smiled.

"Well . . ." (Artemus traced his lip with his tongue) "I am
with you."

"Good!" the badger said, rising, and leaning heavily on
his cane, he walked away.

"Change loyalties?" Artemus muttered to the receding
figure. "I shall teach *you* a thing or two about loyalties, my
traitorous friend."

✦

(Q)uad sat on the pedestal below the throne as the counselor hurried into the great hall.

"He's coming, Sire!"

"Don't call me a sire. I'm not a sire."

"You will be soon enough. Cheer up, Quad! Tomorrow
you'll be king, but you look as if you're facing your own
funeral."

"I am!" Quad shook his head slowly. "It's only a matter of
time until I'm killed . . . probably until tomorrow."

"Tik! tik! tik! Here, sit on the throne. That'll make you
feel better."

"I don't know. Somehow, it doesn't seem proper . . ."

"Oh, come on," Friend Rat wheedled. "Try it out!"

"Well," Quad said, starting to smile. "Perhaps for just a
moment."

"Quad!" a voice boomed. The prince's face drained as he
saw Gregor enter the room. "So!" the warrior-prince declared, "here I am, face to face with the hope of Redaemus."

"The crown was not my choice," Quad said, his voice
almost apologetic.

"Still, you didn't refuse it."

"Well . . . that wasn't exactly my choice, either."

"Somehow, I believe that," Gregor said, tossing a mean-
ingful glance at the counselor.

"See here!" Friend Rat said.

"Shut up, hair-bag." Gregor paced back and forth, his
sharp eyes seeming to take in and measure every detail of
the place, as the counselor wrapped his tail about his
snout. "How does it feel to sit on Father's throne?"

"I haven't tried it. There'll be plenty of time tomorrow."

"I wouldn't be so sure!" Gregor laughed.

"What do you mean by that?"

"What do you plan to do about civil problems?" Gregor
asked suddenly.

Quad shrugged. "End them!"

"Just like that!" the prince snorted. "And what will you do about Demio?"

"What are you doing about him?"

"Losing," Gregor carelessly replied. "I'll tell you frankly, when he's ready to come, he'll come. I doubt more than half our soldiers will even stand to fight. They need a strong and willful king to give them courage."

"I see . . ." Quad began, his eyes widening.

"No, you don't!" Gregor shouted. "You royal puddle! You're to rule this land, and all you've done to prepare yourself is hide within these walls, cowering over your books! Your brain is so choked with legends and romantic notions that you're useless!"

Quad swallowed and locked his fingers behind him to stop their shaking. "You've insulted me quite well, thank you. Is there anything else?"

"I have a request."

"Then make it and go."

"Ah-ha! A little courage. How refreshing! This concerns the coronation feast. I wish to sit beside you."

Quad's eyes fell to his brother's sword and Gregor laughed, the sound booming and happy.

"Don't worry! Mine will hardly be the hand that slays you! Who would support a king who's killed his own brother?"

"Your request is granted, then," Quad sighed.

But all day long he wondered what grand joke Gregor was getting ready to pull, and how desperate for himself the results would be.

Coronation day arrived at last with murky skies and a spring frost that coated everything in delicate webs of ice until the sun pushed through the quilted clouds and melted it away. Its rays slipped through a window to discover a lonely prince and his counselor walking Pentatute's drafty halls.

"I don't trust Gregor," Quad said.

"Don't worry," Friend Rat replied. "I've ordered the castle guards to keep an eye on him."

"And who'll keep an eye on the guards?"

"Tik! tik! tik! Is there no one you trust?"

Quad draped his arms across the counselor's shoulders. "Only you, my friend. Only you."

"Gag a maggot," Friend Rat muttered in reply.

"What!"

"You're waxing melodramatic, Sire. 'Tis a trifle nauseating."

"I'm sorry. Aren't kings supposed to say that kind of thing?"

"Your father never did. If he loved someone, he simply refrained from hitting them."

"Wheeeeeet!"

They were passing a large vase and Quad froze in his tracks.

"What was that?"

"What was what?" Friend Rat asked, looking about.

"That noise!"

"Only the wind," the vase replied.

"Oh," the counselor and prince exclaimed, each thinking the other had answered. They walked on.

A moment later a snout poked over the vase, turning this way, then that, and quivering excitedly, its whiskers fluttering. The Rat Mugby leaped from the vase, caught his foot on its lip, and landed with a *splat!* on his chin. He scampered behind the vase and listened a moment for any response to his noise; there was none. Grinning, he gulped a snicker and advanced into the hallway, drawing a long, wicked dagger from his belt.

"Well, well, Belligerent Bart! We shall meet in that alley at last, and I'll show you my mind! Wh*eeeet!*" He ran his thumb along the knife's blade, yipped as he cut himself, and then scurried down the hall.

The castle kitchens were especially busy, but Counselor Solofaust had been kind enough to recruit village folk to help prepare and serve the feast. They met in the serving hall, as the badger paced back and forth before them, pointing occasionally with his cane.

"Today is our day, and shall be remembered with feasts and festivals forevermore—celebrations in honor of our freedom from the laws, not of our bondage to them! Let us review our plans."

He picked up a large sack and tossed it at The Rasp & File's barkeep.

"File! You'll taint the casks with this, and see that the new king and his friends drink it. You'll not be found out, for there's no taste to the stuff, nor is it lethal. But once in their bellies, it will make them, shall we say, very happy and desirous of sleep? Thus, when swords are drawn, they'll be capable of little resistance. Do well and you'll have the castle's choicest casks for your tavern."

"I'll do well, indeed, then!" File laughed.

"And Nellie! Beautiful as always, a comfort to a grumpy old badger. You're certain so many guests won't confuse you? I'd hate to find a tainted cup at my place."

"You know me, Lord Badger. I'll not fail ye. I'll bring your usual, with all its creepy, ground-up bugs."

"And the king's *special* dish?"

"Shall be a shrewish one indeed!" She laughed. "But my lord! You've so many conspirators about. Don't you fear a slip-up or a turncoat?"

"How so?"

"My papa used to say, 'Five conspirators build a world but a hundred create a travesty.'"

"Pretty words, my fine lady. But sadly ridiculous ones as well," said the badger.

"Each of you," he added, turning to the others, "knows you're working for a better life. You'll not exchange that for the few baubles you'd get from turning me in. Those not so pure in motive I've bought with greed," he said, chuckling. "Baubles a-plenty! They're a great, motivating force when you live on the sorry gruel of a foot soldier of the king. The guards support us, Friend Rat is at this moment being dealt with, and Gregor will stand by and watch while his brother is slain, for he's convinced the throne shall fall to him."

"Who'll tell him otherwise?" Nellie smiled.

"I shall have that honor," the badger replied and, pulling the handle from his cane, revealed a long, slender dagger. Nellie reached to touch it but Solofaust jerked the weapon away. "I wouldn't, my dear. Prick your finger on that and you'll be dead in a second.

"Now. Where's our littlest hero?"

Helen, who had been watching the exchange between Solofaust and Nellie with a frown, spoke up. "Already under his bowl," she said, pointing to a table groaning under the weight of platters and pastries. Solofaust lifted the bowl and out jumped a frantic little shrew.

"Is it time? Is it time?" he begged.

"Not for several hours!" Solofaust laughed. "You know what's to be done, Shrieker?"

"Of course! Quad will lift up the bowl, then I'll jump out and stab him! Stab! Stab! Ha-haaa!" The little shrew danced a sort of jig as he spoke, waving about a tiny dagger.

"You'll kill no king with that," the badger huffed. "Wet it with this before you strike" (he handed the shrew a vial stopped with a cork) "and you could drop a dragon. I'll tap the bowl—like so—and that will be your signal to get ready. When the king lifts the bowl, jump out and lash at his face. Strike him once—that will be enough—then run and lose yourself as fast as you can.

"That, of course," he said to the others, "is the signal for the uprising. Helen will give each of you butcher knives and axes, and you shall join the battle.

"Now, then! Are we ready?"

"Aye!" they replied.

"Then to your duties! Tonight, Demio, the benevolent, shall reign supreme!"

Everything was ready! Artemus bore an indulgent smile as he paced the battlements overlooking the feasting tables in the broad courtyard below. The sun was warming up nicely and the sky was clear, promising weather for a feast or a revolution, he thought with a smile. Things were coming along better than he'd hoped.

Castle Pentatute was located on a tall, rocky hill that overlooked the coastline of Redaemus' western shores. A moat had been carved into the limestone bedrock around the edges of the castle and, in early spring and through much of the summer, this moat served as a kind of cistern, filling halfway with water, protecting the castle walls from direct assault (in the winter, it was drained through sluices to the sea). North and east, Pentatute Hill tumbled precipitously to flatlands that had been cleared of any woodland for several hundred yards. To the east stretched the immense village.

Pentatute was double-ringed, a castle within a castle. Its outer walls rose twenty feet, with towers at every corner and a gate standing thirty feet high. Within that wall, or curtain, constantly patrolled by a battalion of men and rats, lay the outer ward, a courtyard of fruit trees and flowers some fifty feet wide, encircling the great palace. Then came Pentatute's inner curtain, its tallest wall, which towered forty-five feet to the tops of its merlons and sixty feet to the roofs of the multiple towers. Within these ten-foot-thick walls in the palace's central courtyard, behind an impassable inner gatehouse, the feast would be held.

Solofaust had suggested the site. It was closest to the kitchens, he'd told the king-elect, making work easier for the workers. Besides, if he expected an attack from assassins, wouldn't the inner courtyard be more secure? Quad had readily agreed to the plan which, in reality, helped further trap him and any loyalists who might rise to his defense. Their only way to escape would be to flee through the inner gatehouse, the outer ward, and the outer gatehouse, but each would be well-defended by Artemus' men. Escape for the hapless king-to-be was virtually impossible.

Artemus smiled warmly at the thought. Gregor had been most helpful, agreeing to the plan and helping Artemus decide how to best place his soldiers for the revolt.

"My archers will line the battlements to pick off any who would help the king," the captain of the guard had begun.

"No!" Gregor had told him emphatically. "The archers of the castle are fine for shooting at an enemy mob, but the courtyard will be filled with peasants, not to mention me and Solofaust! Send only a handful up, in case there should be trouble. Maybe six. For any selective shooting, I will send my own men. I have two archers of special ability, Narramoore and Arlan of the East."

"My lord! I appreciate the offer," Artemus responded, "but we must keep your Honor Guard out of sight. We've already agreed, you, me and Solofaust, that this rebellion must look as though it was done by the peasants alone, and that I only joined in on the moment, an' that you were crowned, near agin' your will."

"Then we'll dress them in the costumes of the palace guard," Gregor suggested. "It'll do them good to look like something other than dandies for a while. I don't want any chance of soldiers or peasants being killed by clumsy archers. Meanwhile, I'll add a handful of my Honor Guard, spread them about the inner and outer wards, just to make certain that things go without a hitch."

Artemus had taken some offense at his insistence, but realized now that Gregor had been wise, as usual. Just the presence of that handful of famous warriors would instill extra courage in his men, and help convince them that their cause was just. Of course, only his men would know about the disguised warriors—three in the inner ward, two on the battlements of the inner curtain, another half dozen in the outer ward, and two more on the outer curtain's battlements. The remaining Honor Guardsmen would wait outside the castle walls.

Artemus scanned the battlements for Gregor's prized archers. They were not hard to find, disguised or not. Two men stood, itching and twitching, looking irritable in clothes they undoubtedly considered to be uncomfortable and degrading.

"Yer used to finer things, my lads," he laughed. "But ye'll adjust. And I'm sure Gregor has promised ye great rewards."

Of course, the warrior-prince had no idea that Solofaust planned to kill him, and so render any such rewards nil. But that was all right. Solofaust didn't know of Artemus' plan to kill *him*, either. He would say nothing to warn Gregor of the counselor's plot. He would let the old badger himself reveal his treachery by allowing Quad's death. Then, heroically, Artemus would step in and kill Solofaust. Gregor would get the throne . . . *and be so pleased at my heroics that I'll wind up general of the armies!*

He looked to the tables below where servants—the Village Counselor's rabble among them—were busily setting up chairs and tables and benches. It was a broad, open area of grass broken only by a lily pool and an occasional, just-budding lemon tree growing along the pebble-strewn paths. *'Tis like a shooting gallery,* he thought, *where no one can escape my archers—Solofaust included. Stupid, arrogant badger!*

Yes, things are going well, indeed.

"**I** can't hold it off any longer," Quad sighed as he and Friend Rat contemplated the huge, empty throne. "Custom demands that the prince-to-be-king meditate on his coming reign while sitting by his father's tomb—an appropriate place for such contemplations, in my case."

"I'll come with you."

"No. I have to go alone. I don't want to, mind you. There's nothing like a king's tomb for having a hundred nooks and crannies in which to hide assassins. And I'm sure there's enough assassins about to fill every one of them."

"Sire! I've had the tombs searched twice, already. Besides, the subjects will give you a chance. They'll not raise a hand against you 'til they've had time to see if you're as bad as they fear. That should give you *several days* of safety!"

"Your confidence warms me to the bone, Friend Rat," Quad muttered. He walked heavily away, leaving the counselor to gaze at the throne alone.

"Tik! tik! tik! I'd like to say something to boost his confidence," he told it, "but rats are a noble breed, and . . ."

"Wheeeeeet!"

He started. "Is that the wind? Or is someone here?"

"Wheeeeeet!"

The sound came from a nearby window. Rat drew in his

breath and, nervously twisting his tail in his hands, scurried in that direction. He stopped some paces short of the opening and called, "Is anyone out there? I know you're there, and I have a knife!"

No sound.

"I'd best have a look," he said, "though I'm certain that, when I do, I shall see my nose sliced off by someone clinging to the wall." He crept closer, then slowly leaned out. From nowhere he was struck, *"Wheeeeeeet!"* by wind that beat at his face. But as for would-be assassins, he saw only the servants milling in the courtyard far below.

"Ah! It is the wind. Tik! tik! tik! You're letting Quad's fears get the best of you," he scolded himself, climbing back inside. "Tik! tik! tik!"

"Wh*eeeeeet!*"

He stopped. *That* wasn't the wind.

"Who's there?" he demanded, creeping along the wall, his eyes wide. There was a sudden *plumpf!* above him and the counselor spun around to see a giant tapestry falling from the wall. Landing squarely on him, it buried and pinned him, leaving him squirming helplessly on the floor. The Rat Mugby laughed from above.

"Wh*eeeeeet!*" What do you see?" the Rat Mugby called down to the struggling counselor.

"'Tis dark!"

"Belligerent Bart! You *do* know my mind!"

The Rat Mugby pulled his twisted dagger from its sheath and jumped on the huddled form below. Seizing the lump with one hand, he buried his blade in it with the other.

ⓣhe royal tomb was deep within the stoney mountain on which Castle Pentatute sat. It could be reached only by a long, winding stairwell, which seemed to descend all the way to the netherworld. Quad took each step with caution. The odd shadows thrown everywhere by the twitching flame of his torch made him jump at almost every turn. Every so often there were seats of stone carved into the stairwell shaft, and he took advantage of these to rest his nerves. *Such a narrow, creepy climb this is!* he thought once. *Father! They must have brought your sarcophagus down in pieces. But how did they ever get someone as big as you down here?*

Finally he saw the ochre glow of the family tomb, where lamps had been lit by servants earlier in the day. Pins and needles poked at the underside of his skin as he entered the massive cavern and looked about. Quad had not been down there in years, for he was not fond of dead folk, even his own. Everything had been swept clean—the walls and floors and vaulted ceiling of polished stone were free of dust and cobwebs. Along the walls were vertically placed sarcophagi of princes, lords, and even a rat-jester named the Rat Wugwart, of whom his father had often spoken fondly. They seemed to stretch endlessly before him, imposing white sentinels carved with reliefs of flora or cherubim.

He remembered his father taking him down this very hall years before, scolding him for cheerfully skipping along, then kneeling down to explain the solemn importance of the place.

"This is where our ancestors and our heroes lie," the king said. "Here are your father's family and friends and allies, the protectors of our land."

"And warriors, too?" the bug-eyed child Quad asked.

"Warriors too!" Pentatutinus said with a low laugh. "But not all heroes are men with swords. See? There are great prophets as well, who foretold the day of the Oneprince, and of that great last day when the Oneking himself will rebuild our tired corpses, knitting together our dried-up bones and laying afresh our innards and muscles and flesh! What a day that shall be," he added with a far-away look, and Quad thought there was a happy tear in his eye.

"Father!" the boy said as he traced his little fingers along a slab. "What did this one look like?" His father obliged with a stirring description and Quad ran to the next.

"What did *he* look like?" Again Pentatutinus explained

and soon Quad had made the same demand at a dozen slabs.

"Enough! These men are long dead and you tax your father's tongue!" Pentatutinus declared.

"Had you thought to carve their faces on the stone, I would not ask!" Quad laughed.

"My son, we do not carve the images of men, for that is an affront to the Oneking we worship."

"Why?"

"Men—humans, rats, badgers, and all—are weak in their hearts and all too easily worship one another. Images would only help that trait along."

"I don't understand."

"One day you will," Pentatutinus had said, gathering the boy to him and holding him close. "But, here! Don't think of it today."

Quad gazed down the long row and began to walk, his steps uncertain. Momentarily, in the awed silence of this hall, he forgot the notion of assassins or a kingdom or a crown, and he wiped his eyes with his sleeve. The bones of prophets such as the Ariel, whose writings and mysterious epigrams he'd learned to love, were here. There was Abramus, his grandfather who'd died nearly nine hundred years before. The letters of his name, chipped and eroded, were barely legible. There was his mother, whom he'd never known, and a little farther down the strangely empty vault of Endoria.

"No one is here, Father?"

"That was Endoria, a strange and beautiful woman."

"Is she dead?"

A pause. Then, "Yes."

"Did they lose her bones?"

"No, Quad. Her bones are quite well, and the flesh is still upon them." It had sounded like a joke, but his father hadn't smiled. "Only her spirit is dead, and here is where it lies."

Quad stopped at this empty sarcophagus a moment, wondering again about this dark woman of his father's past. *Who was she? Where is she now? In the kingdom? Demonia? Another land? Perhaps in Dagon, the dragon-kingdom across the sea? Why did her spirit die? What does that mean?* His father had refused to say and never allowed the subject to be brought up again. Quad had searched for her in the writings of the ancients and found nothing. Grilling Friend Rat for hours produced the same result; if the counselor knew anything, he denied it, which was enough for Quad. Rats were silly and prone to strange deceptions, but he'd never known one to lie.

At the end of the hall he came face to face with the huge marble tomb in which his father's remains rested. Suddenly the loneliness and loss he had kept numbly inside these past weeks flooded out. He clung to the cold stone and sobbed uncontrollably, begging the Oneking for release.

◆

Wilgate stood before the throne as the folk crowded around. Quad appeared at the door, flanked by guards. His downcast face made him seem more prisoner than king as he moved through the parting crowd. He nearly stumbled over Solofaust, who'd suddenly stepped in front of him.

"Come, my lord, the High Minister awaits," Solofaust said, holding out a paw. "Allow me the honor of escorting you to your throne."

"Where's Friend Rat?" the prince asked, surprised.

"He sends regrets that he can't attend the crowning. Sudden stomach pains, he said to tell you. Don't let on that you know, but in truth he's part of a big surprise for you."

"He told me he'd come," Quad said stubbornly.

"Stop acting like a child!" the counselor whispered harshly. "Look! They're handing you the Ruby Scion. Take it and at least *pretend* to be worthy!"

Quad lifted the scepter from a satin pillow, which was held by a servant. He wondered briefly if he'd be able to drag such a heavy stick about all day and stared at its muddy gem as one might a large snake.

"All right," he said after a moment. "You may lead me, Counselor, since Friend Rat isn't here."

The two walked to the throne and faced each other, then the badger dipped briefly to one knee and left. Quad seated himself and Wilgate approached, his smile reassuring.

"Wilgate! I'm sorry," Quad whispered, "but I forgot about that card with my name on it."

"No need! I remember your name, for it is an odd one," Wilgate reassured him. He turned to the court and spoke in a high, shrill voice.

> The king is dead!
> But in his stead
> another shall take the throne!
> His name is Cumquat!

"Quad!" Quad whispered frantically.

"Yes, I know it's odd," Wilgate muttered under his breath. "I should change it, if I were you."

Now he turned to the folk.

"Subjects! Do you take this man to be your lawfully wedded king? You will answer, 'We do.'"

"We do," they replied.

"And Cumquat, do you take this unruly mob to be your kingdom? You will say, 'I do.'"

"I do," Quad said, then added, "This doesn't sound like the proper ceremony. Are you sure it's the one prescribed in the Laws?"

"Well, I can't remember, exactly. I tried to look it up in the village, but the penmanship of your father was awful and reading it is such a great strain on my eyes. I know there's *some* ceremony that goes like this. It's my rendition, at any rate, and so it will serve well enough." Then he snapped, "May I get on with it?"

"You may," Quad sighed.

The ceremony didn't go at all as Quad thought it should. In ten minutes the crown and scepter were blessed and set upon him. Wilgate even handed the new king a dozen roses and made him parade up and down before the subjects while a choir sang.

The king-elect tried to look noble as he walked, but the attempt was hopeless. The crown, a band of gold decorated with long, shining spikes, had looked fierce on Penta-tutinus. But on Quad it seemed embarrassed, sagging on his forehead—the spikes actually appeared to wilt. The Ruby Scion looked murkier than ever in his hand, and Quad's allergies made him sneeze the roses' petals off. At last Wilgate stopped him, poured a bottle of oil over his head and turned him, the liquid dripping from his nose, to face his subjects.

"I now pronounce you king and kingdom," the old man said.

To Quad's surprise, the people cheered!

This unexpected reaction made him feel so good he forgot all about Friend Rat as he was victoriously swept along. Gregor shouldered his way through the crowd to walk at his brother's side.

"Fear not, Quad," he said, winking at the badger who stayed near by. "The day won't seem so long now, and I'm sure you'll join Friend Rat at any time!"

It was the largest feast Quad had ever seen. Great roasts steeped in sauces, colorful vegetables steamed in kettles, and icing-laden pastries turned the serving tables into a garden of sugary color. Servants and Solofaust's villagers bustled about, making sure no cup or plate stayed empty. Everyone was having a good time, the new king thought, as he looked about, especially Gregor, who laughed more heartily than anyone. It was as if he were keeping a great secret from the world.

Bards sang old tales in rhyme while acrobats and jugglers bounced about, giving the courtyard the air of a friendly asylum. Lords and ladies and even servants and chambermaids paused to congratulate the king (the latter giggling embarrassedly as they did), and it wasn't long before even he was feeling quite good about himself. His brains were growing fuzzy from the wine he'd been gulping to steady his nerves, and so he only half-wondered at Friend Rat's disappearance. Stretching his arms lazily, he nearly knocked a broad, feathered cap off a bard's head.

"Ah, Sire!" the fellow said with a low bow, his dark eyes twinkling.

"Ah, Minstrel!" Quad laughed, trying to imitate the greeting and bumping his head on the table. He stared at the man, whose deep, mysterious expression stopped Quad cold. The bard stood there, addressing him with a genuinely warm smile—and yet his eyes expressed some deeper emotion he couldn't read. Concern? Sorrow? *Ridiculush*, Quad thought, shaking off an unexpected chill. He grinned again and said, "I never expected such food and drink!"

"Though the meats and fruits may hold your eyes, the covered dish holds the surprise," the bard laughed in a singsong way.

The king raised an eyebrow and stared a moment longer at the man, wondering why this simple singer impressed him so. He was not particularly handsome, although he looked intelligent, even noble. Shaking his head in an attempt to clear the fermented mist that was filling it, Quad turned to Solofaust.

"Now here is a man with a winning way!" he declared.

The badger looked up with a scowl. "I see a man with an irritating habit. Haven't you better things to do with your time, bard?"

"Lord Solofaust!" the other replied with another bow, "I've a rhyme for you, as well.

> As you sit and grumble
> With your words so full of thunder
> Do you know the hour you're under
> Brings you blunder after blunder?

"What do you mean by that!" the badger snarled.

"Do you wish me to explain?" asked the bard.

"I wish you to go away!" said the badger.

"Let him stay!" Gregor said. "I find this fellow entertaining."

"I find him disrespectful and a rogue," Solofaust barked with disdain.

"Now, Solofaust . . . !"

"'Tis no trouble, lords. I'll take my leave," the bard said. "Oh, a pity about the wine," he added with a wink and a nod to the badger. "'Tis not so potent as you'd think."

Solofaust watched him leave, trying to keep track of his movements to see who he would harass next, but quickly lost him in the crowd. *This character seems to know my plans,* he thought with a shiver. *Yet, he isn't giving me away. What's his game? I'd best send Artemus a note to arrest him. Then I can give* him *some riddles at my leisure.* He removed a slip of parchment from a pocket of his robe and scribbled some words on it with a bit of charcoal, then looked up and down the table for a courier. He noticed with some dismay that the guests were eating, laughing, and talking loudly. *They've all been drinking from the tainted casks; by now they should be half asleep,* he mused. But the only one in any kind of stupor was Quad, and he only because he was unused to spirits. Sighing, Solofaust motioned for Nellie to come.

"My lords!" she said, arriving with a large silver platter covered by a sterling bowl. Her gaze locked onto Gregor's for a moment during which the prince's good-natured smile faded, replaced by a quizzical frown. There was something disconcerting about the way he watched her that made her feel suddenly alarmed, and she looked away and shifted on her feet. Their silent communication lasted only a second, and if Solofaust noticed, he made no sign.

"If you please, a compliment to the captain of the guards," the badger said, tucking the note into a pocket of her skirts, "for keeping watch so well."

"Are you new, my pretty one?" Quad asked, obnoxiously charming.

"I'm from the village, Sire," she replied with a slight curtsy, nervously chewing her lip.

"And what new dish did you bring?"

"A special roast for the king," Nellie replied a little too loudly, setting down the tray and hurrying away.

"Well, let's see it!" Quad exclaimed, placing his hands on the bowl.

"Wait!" Solofaust said, "it may be hot."

"Nonsense," Quad insisted, "I see no steam. It's cold."

The badger tapped the bowl twice. "Ah. So it is, Sire."

As Quad reached for the bowl, Gregor frowned, watching the counselor.

"Wait, Sire!" he said suddenly, arresting his brother's hand. "Any good roast should be carved first!"

Before the others could react the warrior-prince rose, freeing his sword from its scabbard and raising it high over his head. The sun glinted off the metal as it sang through the air and struck the bowl's center, slicing through as if it were paper. There was a great squeal and blood ran from the split cover.

"My! but the meat was rare!" Quad exclaimed.

The badger stared in shock.

"The surprises have just begun," Gregor laughed. "Look above!"

Solofaust did, and saw Gregor's archers, Narramoore and Arlan, together on the ramparts. At first he did not comprehend, but then Narramoore raised an arm and the two dropped to their knees. Arrows from the outer ward and even from their own midst plucked Artemus' archers, leaving only Gregor's men.

"So! You are loyal to this rag, my prince!" the badger barked, backing away. "You've played along with me, hoping you would best me with surprise! See how far you get, sir, for I've a few of my own!" He raised his staff above his head and Gregor spun at the blood-curdling screams of an army of peasants and guards wading with butcher knives, axes, and swords into the shocked sea of coronation guests.

Nellie had walked quickly away from the king after she'd set Shrieker before him. The new king was surely an idiot, she believed, but she still wanted nothing of watching Quad's expression as the shrew jumped up and down before him, slashing his nose and eyes with a poisoned knife. Indeed, though she looked forward to Solofaust's rule, she had been horrified all day long at the prospect of having to be involved in the bloody battle that would birth it. She never heard Shrieker's dying wail over the chatter of the crowd, for her attention was solely on ducking into the castle and finding a place to stay until the fighting ended. She hunched her shoulders involuntarily as she awaited the inevitable rush of her fellows charging past her and into the fray.

She reached the kitchen doors and still the fight had not begun. Helen stepped out and thrust a knife into her hand. "I don't want it!" she protested.

"Take it!" Helen insisted. "There's a battle to fight."

"Aye, and I've done my part. The rest is up to you."

"We all must help to carve this kingdom from the innards of these fools," the possum hissed. "There goes Solofaust's signal! Go back! You'll return with glory!"

In a fright, Nellie tried to side-step the conspirator, but was rammed by a man rushing past her, a war cry leaping from his toothless mouth and a cleaver waving in his hand. Before she gathered her breath from that, other surging, shouting bodies swept her into the courtyard where, in horror, she watched the first of the bluebloods die: a lord, old and grizzled, rising to run, his hand before him as a feeble defense. He cried out as a cleaver cut through his fingers and cracked the bones of his head. He was close enough that his blood sprayed her hands and breasts. Nellie brought one hand to her mouth with a shriek, nearly slicing her own face with the knife she held. This she let fall to the ground and stood, motionless, her eyes wide, fingers splayed across her lips, doing nothing to help or hinder the revolution as the helpless men and women were killed or dragged past her to a questionable destiny within the dungeons of Pentatute.

Gregor looked about, shocked as the mob of guards and peasants went about gleefully, literally carving a new kingdom from the flesh of the old. The guests screamed as they were engulfed and butchered in the bloody chaos. He had not anticipated this; the conspirators had agreed that any killing would be kept to a minimum. The archers on the wall would shoot a few chosen lords, and the threat of their arrows would be enough to subdue the rest. He had expected that his own men taking control of the battlements, alone, would end the affair.

Slay me for a fool for letting this happen! he thought. Already Solofaust was stepping forward, twisting the tip from his cane. Gregor kicked him sharply with his boot, sending the counselor sprawling across the ground. He glanced around quickly, seeking an escape route for himself and the king. The gate house was swelling with soldiers, and he knew they could never get through it alive—even if they survived reaching it. Instead, he selected a garden doorway down the lemon tree path. With a grunting heave he overturned the table between himself and the oncoming wave of revolutionaries. This way, at least, he would not be overrun. Quad stood slack-jawed and speechless in the carnage. His mind begged desperately for permission to panic, and only the excess of wine in his system gave him any semblance of calm. Adrenalin was pumping through his system like a bellows to sober him.

"Follow me!" he heard Gregor shout.

"Follow you? But where?" he shrieked.

"Inside!"

"They want to kill me!"

"I know!"

"You don't!"

"Your perception is astonishing," Gregor yelled between sword blows across the table. "And I'd love to chat some more, but if we don't move now they'll be draping the trees with our entrails!" Spinning as Quad practically clung to him, the warrior-prince started for the doorway, hacking a path with his weapon as he did. So long as they couldn't mob him, the untrained peasants were afraid to fight him, and only a handful of Artemus' men offered resistance, for his swordsmanship was legend in the kingdom.

Quad gasped and felt the bile rise in his throat as his brother's blade rose and fell with a terrible rhythm of death. Howls of hate and cries for victory turned to shrieks of fear and pain as inexperienced men with knives, swords, and makeshift spears fell beneath the bloody steel. A peasant's arm was lopped off at the elbow and tumbled past the king; not an instant later a severed hand bounced off his chest. He cried out in horror, stumbling over a man and a rat who sat together, each numbly contemplating the stubs which moments ago had been their arms.

"The . . . the people!" Quad managed to beg as Gregor pushed him through the door. "Go back and save the people!"

"The people are lost, and if we don't keep moving, you will join them," Gregor snapped. "Now, come!"

Solofaust had climbed on to a table where he could view the battle and call commands. He was furious that Gregor and Quad had slipped away from him, but following after them in this writhing mob was impossible. *Let Artemus deal with them,* he thought. *Even if they get inside, his castle guard will find them. After all, how long can they hide?*

On the ramparts, Narramoore and Arlan stood and looked in amazement at the battle filling the courtyard below. The three Honor Guardsmen who had been planted in the crowd fought valiantly, but each was quickly brought down by the pressing sea of subjects.

"Where do we shoot, Captain?" Arlan shouted.

"We don't!" Narramoore replied. "In that swirling mass, it's impossible to tell the conspirators from the guests. Shoot only to save the king." With this hope, each set an arrow to his bow.

"Over there! Arlan shouted, pointing to the nearest tower. Narramoore looked as soldiers and villagers climbed toward them, stumbling through the narrow door, screaming and waving their clubs and swords.

"They're coming out my side as well!" Narramoore shouted, turning to his right. He let his arrow fly. It found its mark in the belly of the foremost man who bent forward with a cry and fell from the walk. In an instant the Honor Guardsman had let fly another arrow, and then another, plucking two more. But as each fell, another came tumbling out to take his place. There were even women in the advancing throng, Narramoore noted with dismay. He stole a sideways glance and saw that Arlan was facing the same unending line.

"There are too many!" Narramoore called. "We were supposed to be firing into any guards below to stop the slaughter—instead we're spending all our arrows defending ourselves!"

"Aye, it seems our general has underestimated this enemy!" Arlan called back. "'Tis a good thing they've put no archers on the ground, or we'd look more like porcupines than these fellows about us! By the Oneking himself, do they ever stop coming?"

"Have you many arrows left?" Narramoore asked.

"Not nearly so many as I have peasants to use them on!" Arlan replied.

"I've only three," Narramoore said between breaths, "and once they're gone, my bow will do a bad job against clubs and swords."

Arlan set his last arrow to his bow. "After this, I'm out!"

As they talked, their foes were silent except for grunts and war cries. They waited at the towers now, hesitant to be the next to take an arrow, but they wouldn't wait long.

"'Tis time to run," the captain decided, waving to a warrior on the walkway of the outer wall below. "Ho! Nabo!"

The man, dark-skinned, unshaven, and nearly a giant in size, picked up a three-pronged iron hook on a length of rope and swung it about his head three times, then hurled it across the distance. The hook sailed up, through the space between the merlons, and hooked into the wall Narramoore stood beside. Pulling the rope taunt, Nabo quickly tied his end of the rope around another merlon. Narramoore noted that the same blood bath was taking place without the wall: arrows clattered about Nabo while Mandax, the warrior beside him, lay sprawled on the walkway with arrows sticking from his chest.

"Go!" Narramoore shouted. "'Tis a trap; we'll regroup

outside the walls!" As Nabo jumped over the battlement and into the moat below, Narramoore grabbed Arlan's shirt and dragged him onto the embrasure.

"Let's go!"

"I hate this," Arlan muttered, joining his companion, shouldering his bow and drawing a short, grooved rod of iron from his cloak. He glanced at the warrior-prince fighting below. "'Tis like we're abandoning him."

"We've done all we can," Narramoore said, pulling his last arrow. "If we're quick and the fates are with us, we may still stop this slaughter and save the king once we've joined what's left of the Honor Guard."

Arlan set the bar upon the rope and, using it as a handle, he jumped from the embrasure and slid across the rope, high over the fighting in the outer ward below. Narramoore turned rapidly left and right in an attempt to keep the rebels at bay. They watched him tensely, and he guessed they were gathering the courage to charge. He could wait no longer. Taking a last glance into the courtyard he spotted the Village Counselor.

"Ho! Solofaust!" he shouted, "A parting gift for your black heart!" And, his last arrow fired, he jumped onto the rope, sliding down after his friend. He hoped he would reach the outer wall before one of the peasants could cut the rope and send him tumbling into the hopeless battle going on below.

Hearing his name called above the din, the badger wheeled around; but a dying noble struck him, throwing him from his feet. This accident saved Solofaust's life, for instead of cleaving his heart the arrow pinned his shoulder to the table top.

Gregor and his brother finally reached the hall, but the warrior-prince had to quickly pull Quad to his side when Artemus stepped suddenly before them. Panting heavily, a look of astonishment on his face, Artemus demanded, "Why are you killing my men? Don't you want to be king?"

"A crown on my head wasn't in Solofaust's plans," Gregor said, his lips pressed into a tense smile.

"It was in *mine!* I'm going to kill the badger, not *you!*"

"And to see me king, you'd also kill Quad! Do you think a son of Pentatutinus would support such treachery? Do you think I've the morals of dung-beetles such as you? Step aside!" Gregor roared, swinging his sword.

Artemus barely parried with his own, but the stunning force of blades meeting was so great the captain's sword shattered at the hilt. Gregor swung again and Artemus brought up his shield, absorbing the blow but staggering under Gregor's attack. Again and again Gregor brought his sword down, but his swings were made careless by his anger.

Artemus countered each with his shield, his fear-twisted face soaked in sweat, his bones rattling at every collision of steel. The shield began to crumple and finally gave, ripping under the blade. He let it go, and retreated several paces as Gregor swore and smashed the tangled weapons against the wall in an attempt to disentangle them.

When he had his sword free, he spun to find the captain, who stood panting by a great hall. Behind them the sounds of fighting began to fade. Already the courtyard slaughter was ending. A bent, old opossum appeared at the door and shrieked, "They're in here!"

"Count yourself lucky, Artemus," the prince growled. "If I didn't have the king to defend, I'd come after you at any cost and wash the walls with your blood."

"Count yourself dead!" Artemus cried back. "Demio shall see to it!"

"Demio!" Quad gasped.

Gregor pushed the stumbling king forward as the retreating captain's footsteps echoed down the halls.

"Move! Your counselor waits in the throne room, as does, I hope, a secret passage out of here!"

"Friend Rat?"

In moments Quad rushed to the throne and hugged the furry creature who had hidden behind it.

"I feared you were dead!" Quad gasped.

"I nearly was! Some village fiend threw a tapestry on my head and jumped me. Then he started stabbing away with his knife!"

"Are you hurt?"

"No, but a heroic stool lies in tatters."

"My heart is warmed by this reunion, and my courage by the example of that stool," Gregor said, his voice hot with sarcasm. "But our fate will be no better if one of you doesn't remember the whereabouts of the passage from this room."

"There is a passage," Quad agreed, "and it leads to a cavern in some woods, north of the village."

"Then take us there!" Gregor ordered.

Gathering courage, Quad led the way.

Part Two

THE QUEST
FOR THE
ONEPRINCE

The minstrel had walked lightly through the inner gatehouses. No one attempted to stop him; in fact, they seemed to not even notice him. He crossed the courtyard and passed, unchallenged again, through the outer gate house, then trotted down the ramp toward The Village. A wagon, pulled by fat, shaggy ponies, waited near a neat little tavern and he climbed on. The driver, a plump rat, gave him a worried look.

"Such a severe countenance, sirrah! Did you not meet the king? Does the prophecy not go forth?"

"I did and it does," the minstrel declared. "Now drive, Snout. We must go, so the evil can begin."

"But where is the king, sirrah? Is he not to be spared?"

"I have sought the king," the minstrel said sternly. "Now 'tis his duty to seek me. At the proper time he will meet us at The Fettid Cheese. But there's much he must learn first, and there are many words my father and I must exchange, so that I can learn what must be done.

"Listen. Do you hear?"

Snout turned his head toward the castle.

"The ring of swords and the cries of the folk."

"You see? It has begun. Now, drive!"

◆

The secret passage, entered by ducking behind a tapestry at a recess of the wall, seemed endless. It was pitch black, and no one had a torch. The three stumbled along, Quad leading the way (for he knew it best), followed by Friend Rat clinging to his robe, and then by Gregor, who held the counselor's tail with one hand and his sword with the other. He tried vainly to see in the darkness.

"Is it much farther?" Gregor asked.

"*Very* much," the king replied.

"I just hope you know your way," Gregor snarled. "Ha! The way you cower at shadows, I can't believe you played here as a child."

"Without a torch there are no shadows in a tunnel. And the dark doesn't bother me."

"Nor me, but I hate being boxed in. These halls aren't more than two man-breadths wide."

"Ouch!" Quad yelled.

"What is it!" Friend Rat asked trying to wrap his tail around his snout for security.

"A wall. The passage must turn here. Funny, I used to know the number of steps it took to reach each turn. Either I've forgotten or it takes me fewer steps to cover the same distance."

"No wonder Father turned the crown over to you! Such wonderful deductions are far beyond me now that I'm grown."

"But you're far nobler than I," Quad said modestly.

"I was joking," the prince snapped.

"So, perhaps, was the king!" Friend Rat put in. "Tik! tik! tik!"

"Blast!" said Gregor.

"What's wrong!"

"I found your wall."

"There are steps somewhere ahead," Quad said. "Beyond them should be storage chambers that Father was building up in the event of a siege. There we should be able to find some torches."

"And flints and oil to light them, I suppose?" Gregor said.

"One would suppose," Quad agreed.

"Indeed!" Friend Rat piped in.

"How far off is this chamber?"

"We should reach the steps any time."

"How will I know?" Gregor asked.

"At this rate, you'll hear me fall down them."

"Do you hear anyone behind you?" Friend Rat asked the prince. "Oh, I just know they'll find the secret door!"

"Worrying won't make that any less likely," Gregor grumbled. "Keep walking, Counselor, and . . ."

His words were cut off by the sound of a king tumbling down a flight of stairs.

It was the first of many flights, and as the three descended, the wall's consistency changed from the stone of the castle's roots to shale and clay. This pleased Gregor, for the deeper they went, the closer they got to the end of their journey—*and I'll be thankful when we don't have these narrow halls and sharp turns to bump into*, he thought. *Devil take us for not taking time to grab a torch in the throne room!* Suddenly the wall disappeared from his grasping fingers.

"What is this!" he demanded, "another turn?"

"Didn't you feel the draft?" Quad whispered. "We've entered a room, some thirty by fifty paces large—child's paces, of course. There are three such rooms in the passage."

"Is this your storage chamber?"

"I do believe," Quad answered.

"And where are the torches?" Gregor demanded.

"Anywhere. We'll just have to feel about 'til we find some."

"Then step aside," Gregor said. "I'll find one and light it so we'll at least see the turns coming!" He went forward as Quad stepped to the left, but rather than getting out of each other's way, they collided in the dark. Gregor landed against a pile of crates that spilled open and dumped their cargo of torches, which rolled noisily about. As he swore loudly and Quad apologized wildly, the counselor ran in circles squealing, certain they'd been found by Solofaust's guard.

The trio lost half an hour to finding oil (Friend Rat finally found a pot by stepping in it) and flints. Once they had light to see by, however, they made up the lost time and found their march noticeably easier on their scraped fingers and bruised noses.

"I don't know but what I was happier in the dark," Quad muttered. "Now that I can see, I'm imagining soldiers waiting around every bend."

"Well, we're certain they're lurking back in the castle," the counselor advised. "So, shall we go on?"

Finally they reached a hall that ended abruptly against a wall of stone.

"We're here!" Quad announced.

"Where?" Gregor said.

"At the entrance to the cavern."

"Through another secret door?"

"No, right through that hole." The king pointed to a small, black opening in one wall, about four feet from the floor.

"That?" the prince scoffed. "It may be an entrance for you or your country mouse, here . . ."

"Tik! tik! tik!"

"But a man like me will never squeeze through."

"Of course you will," the king said. "What other choice do you have?" He grabbed the hole's rim and started to climb, then checked himself. Turning to the others he bowed. "Friend Rat, you go first."

"Me!" the counselor squeaked. "'Tis *your* childhood haunt!"

"I can't go first. I'm the king! I'm the reason we're slinking about! What if that badger has soldiers in there?"

"Then let Gregor go first. He's a warrior."

"I'm not trying that cubby hole 'til I've seen you make it! I doubt my broad shoulders will fit," Gregor said.

"I'd be more concerned about your large head!" Friend Rat retorted.

"Quad, if you don't shut this rodent up I'll de-tail him."

"Rat, your tongue is doing us no good," Quad scolded. "Now hush and go through."

"But someone on the other side might grab me!"

"It's a chance we have to take," Gregor said.

"Easy for *you* to say!" Friend Rat stood on his tip-toes and inched his snout into the opening. "There could be crawly things, spiders and icky stuff like that." Suddenly a blaze of light zipped past his head. Squealing, he fell back to the passage floor with a *thump!*

"What are you doing, you little idiot!" Gregor whispered harshly at the king.

"There! We are in the dark," Quad said smugly. "The torch is in the cavern now. We have three choices: to go back to the castle, climb through this hole, or stand here in this tiny passage, in the dark, and let the crawly things get us. If either of you don't like the last two choices, then one of you please lead the way."

"For pity's sake," Friend Rat mumbled, already scratching his hide. "I'll go. What I do for Redaemus! Tik! tik! tik!"

The counselor didn't fit as easily as he'd hoped. His head and shoulders were a simple matter, but his bottom stuck like a cork. He grunted, groaned, and tugged. Still he would never have pushed through had it not been for the assistance of Gregor's boot.

He tumbled about twenty feet down a slope, where he came to rest upside down, his large eyes peering out between his toes and an "*Oooomph!*" escaping his lungs. The torch light made everything appear eery—stalactites, stalagmites and great, sloping walls—but he didn't notice. What the counselor saw was a soldier, his face filthy, his armor dented and kinked, and his cape torn and bloody. Frowning, the man had drawn his bow and, fitted in its string, an unpleasant arrow tickled Rat's nose.

✦

"The king, the prince, and that idiot rat! Bring them or I'll have you guarding the *in*side of the dungeon cells!" Solofaust shouted at the quaking guards. "GO!" He banged the floor with his staff and the burly men stumbled over one another in their hurry to escape.

Once the fighting had stopped and Solofaust was certain Quad and Gregor had fled and that all the castle guard remaining alive had defected to support him, he and his fellow conspirators had moved into the castle. Solofaust's first official act was to declare himself governor.

Now the new governor sat on the throne, which was on an ivory pedestal at the top of three steps in the middle of the murkily lit throne room. A lone figure sat on one step behind him, but the badger paid him no mind. Instead, whiskers quivering, he regarded the third figure in the room. "Speaking of idiot rats," he said to it, "approach me."

"*Wheeeeet!* It wasn't my fault!" the Rat Mugby squealed, wringing his kinked tail.

"Haven't you enough respect to bow, at least?" Solofaust sighed, his voice more tired than angry.

"I never bowed before."

"I was never your governor before."

"Rats are proud! They never bow!"

"Rats are a nuisance. They're mindless, noisy, filthy, irresponsible, and troublesome. How could you let the castle counselor live?"

"*Wheeeeet!* It was an honest mistake!"

"That's an odd phrase, coming from a scoundrel."

"All right. A *dis*honest mistake," the scoundrel replied.

"Oh, shut up! I want you to go and find them. You're good at that sort of thing, at least. Sniff them out! Your nose has sense, even if your mind hasn't."

"*Wheeeeet!* That's funny!"

"What is?"

"That my nose has *scents!*"

"Get out of here!" Solofaust yelled.

"Hrrummph! I can't say much for your choice of conspirators," the man sitting behind the throne said, as the rat slunk away.

"*My* choice, Artemus? You're the one who let Gregor's men infiltrate your ranks," Solofaust accused.

Artemus gazed at his sword while he thought this over. Though he and the badger spoke to each other, neither had looked at the other during their conversation.

"Perhaps so," he said, "but you're the one who told me Prince Gregor was in this scheme."

"You'll not talk to me like that!" Solofaust warned, twisting in his throne. "I'm the lord here!"

"You're lord only so long as this sword supports you." Casually, Artemus took out a cloth and shined the weapon for a moment. "And no longer, my lord."

The governor watched Artemus carefully. The soldier lowered his eyes to the weapon he was lovingly cleaning, while his short, fat fingers held the hilt expertly, even tenderly.

"I'd reply in kind, Artemus, but games and threats won't win this kingdom. It is mostly ours now, but there are still forces loyal to the king: the city of Yerushela, no doubt, for it is Pentatutinus' birthplace, and possibly the armies at the Sheolfrost. They were, after all, Gregor's personal command. But the rest of the armies and cities are ours . . . The promotions and executions I've ordered will see to that. . . ."

"The armies and cities might *all* be ours if Gregor wasn't running around out there, alive, with his Honor Guard."

"What! His Honor Guard? I thought you caught them in a trap!"

"I did, and most of them are playing dice in some hall of the dead now. But a handful—the best of them—escaped," Artemus said.

"Blast! Has nothing gone right? Well, dragging those two simpletons about as he is, at least Gregor will be easy to find. As to the army at the Sheolfrost, it's now leaderless and it was already dispirited. I'll funnel some gold their way and we'll see what happens. Meanwhile, I suggest you tour some of the camps and make appointments and promises of your own."

"Your tongue frazzles my brains, Governor. Still, you're in charge until Demio tires of your blunders and seeks a leader with a simpler tongue but a more successful record. Excuse me, I've speeches to write."

The soldier rose to his feet and, with a slight bow, left the hall. Solofaust remained on the throne and, feeling a chill, drew his cloak tightly about him. He let his brow furrow in concentrated disgust, and felt the throbbing of his bandaged arm and head. His stomach twisted as if a green worm were turning in there.

"Even you show a spirit I didn't expect, Artemus," he growled aloud. "A very dangerous spirit, at that. Such victories! I own the castle; I govern half the land. The folk—for now, at any rate—nearly worship me. Yet I feel like a cub who's lost his dog. Problems! Everywhere, problems! Those three on the loose, a new general who threatens to overthrow the overthrower, and Pentatutinus' pathetic and prophetic little song as he struck me with the Ruby Scion. . . . Bah!" He squirmed in his seat and thought.

"Look at me," he said, "more of me bandaged than not. I can trust no one, it seems, but Nellie; she's the only one unspoiled by greed. Look at all you've won . . . and feel how little you enjoy it."

He leaned back and stared into the darkness of the vaulted ceiling. The shadows grew long, then melded with the growing dusk. Pillars at the far end of the throne room changed into whispery shapes before his eyes, like the legs of spinning spiders. Soon those legs seemed to move about, weaving the delicate, bloody threads that held Solofaust's new world together. As he watched, a bat caromed into the great hall, its leather wings whipping a soft, angry staccato, its tense, ebony body weaving and threading a tapestry in and about the spider's legs.

The governor leaned forward, following the jet bat-thread as its cord hog-tied the mammoth spider, leaving it pinned and hopelessly tangled. Suddenly it plummeted, crashing through the floor, pulling the ceiling and Solofaust and all his world through that gaping hole and into the bottomless shaft of Ebon Bane which hungrily swallowed them.

"No!" He screamed and jammed his fists into his eyes.

When he opened them, everything was dark. In the distance, he saw a glow and then a torch, its creator. At last the creature carrying the torch popped into view. It blinked its huge eyes and sniggered.

"Why, hello! Welcome back, Mr. Badger! Welcome back to here! Hee-hee!"

Nellie was singing as she piled logs into the castle ovens. Helen, seated on a table with her tail wrapped about her, watched quietly. She didn't like Nellie, had never wanted her in the conspiracy. The girl was smart, granted, but she turned her nose at authority and was too carefree and independent for Helen's taste. Solofaust had pushed for Nellie's acceptance, and of course a request from him was the same to Helen as an order. Still, she abhorred the young, human woman—her pretty looks, the way she played up to the counselor—and she especially disliked the way he sometimes played up to *her*.

"Old Solofaust's feeling low," Helen said finally.

"I don't see why. He's got his castle."

"I'm sure 'tis the betrayal of the prince."

"Betrayal!" Nellie laughed. "The prince outfoxed him. 'Twas Solofaust who planned a betrayal. Gregor only played along."

"You seem happy with the outcome."

"I like Solofaust, and I'm hardly glad that Gregor's loose. Still, 'tis a grand joke when the prey outwits the hunter, don't ye think? And a real trick to beat the badger so?"

"Indeed," Helen murmured, running her red eyes over the girl.

"I think I'll mix him some of his buggy wine. That should cheer him up," Nellie said, and taking a mug from a shelf, she strolled to the wine barrels where she selected an old cask and turned its tap. Helen watched thoughtfully.

"Why didn't the drugged wine work, I wonder? You had access to it."

Nellie only shrugged and went to a large, earthen jar where she scooped up a handful of dried beetles. These she diced with a heavy knife and sprinkled into the mug.

"And that minstrel," Helen continued. "Solofaust put a handsome price on his head, yet he's not been caught. I wonder what happened to him?"

"I've no idea. When the arrows started coming in, all I watched was my own skin," Nellie said. "You know? I'm glad he don't eat these things fresh no more. They were so hard to chop when they ran all over the table like they did." She smiled as she spoke, running her fingers about as if they were beetles. "Well! you'll have to excuse me. Solofaust likes this better while it's cold."

"Then you'd best run the whole way. He's at the other end of the castle."

"No problem," Nellie smiled, as she left the room. Helen sat, watching, then noticed that the earthen jar's lid was on the floor.

"Oh, the bugs will go stale!" she growled, bustling over to the lid. As she pushed it into place, she began to wonder at Nellie's easy attitude about covering such a distance with her drink, and her eyes narrowed. "Nellie?" she called.

There was no response.

Huffing, the opossum hurried into the hall, but of course Nellie was gone.

"Bah!" Helen growled, turning the corner. She stopped suddenly. *No problem! What did that mean?* It wasn't the words so much as it was the childish and gay way the girl had said it . . . as if she had a secret. Nellie was that way, Helen knew well enough from their days at The Rasp & File. She enjoyed her little secrets and her jokes.

Sometimes her big secrets.

And secrets are worth checking out. Helen smiled.

Solofaust would ask Nellie to stay, and they would talk

and laugh and advise and console, no doubt for a couple of hours. Frowning, Helen took hold of a soldier's sleeve and dragged him down the hall and up a flight of stairs, then down another hall to the painted door opening to Nellie's room. This was one of the finest chambers in the castle, and it made Helen bristle to think of how Solofaust had awarded it to his little "pet."

She posted the soldier outside the door and went inside.

"I don't know what you're up to, child, but I shall find out within the hour!" she said, beginning with the huge bed. She stuffed herself under it and sniffed and groped, but found nothing. *The floor under here is clean enough to eat off,* Helen thought. Nellie was clean, at least.

She backed out and unmade the bed. Then with a grunt she overturned the huge mattress; again there was nothing. She thought of remaking it and instead went to the door. Opening it, she thrust out her snout.

"Guard, send for a maid. Call Cleophas. I can trust her."

Without waiting for a response, she pulled her snout back in and went to the dressers and then the closet, a room some twenty paces by ten paces, hauling the dresses out and searching each and every one for hidden pockets and treasures. She found a hidden pocket or two, but no treasures that could mean anything to anyone but a sentimental human. She even crawled through a few of the dresses, sniffing along their seams and fabrics.

Nothing.

The room was lit by lamps and candles, none of them big enough to hide anything. There was nothing on the ceiling but painted planks, and it was some twelve feet or more high. It was doubtful Nellie could have reached so far to hide anything, anyway.

Think! She's up to something! She must be! Helen thought as she stood in the middle of the room, her arms folded, tapping her feet.

Next she crawled carefully along the floor, sniffing and touching and prying at every board. None gave way. She went through everything again, more carefully. Still there was nothing to use against Nellie. With a huff, she sat on the bed to think. Cleophas knocked on the door and entered.

"Clean up this mess," Helen ordered.

"How?" Cleophas began. She was a large, matronly woman who continually wore a scowl.

"Did I ask for questions?" Helen asked. "No? I thought not. Keep watch of this Nellie girl. She's up to something, I think."

"And if I see anything?"

"You shall be rewarded, of course," Helen replied. "Now, clean this place up carefully. The girl is fastidious and I don't want her to suspect . . ." Her voice trailed off suddenly and she raised a finger to her mouth. "Shhhh!"

They turned toward a scuffling sound in the closet and peered in, wondering. At first they saw nothing, but then a panel in the closet's back wall lifted up and as Helen's jaw dropped to her chest, Nellie crawled out.

"What am I doing here?" Solofaust roared, trying to hide his panic.

"Looking ridiculous, Mister Badger. Looking pale! Heee-heeee!"

The scum-thing's eyes spun around in their sockets as the creature rocked back and forth, leaning so far to either side the badger expected it to fall over at any moment. Its voice cut through its sharp teeth in a harsh whistle.

"Master wants to speak with you!"

"About what?"

"Things!" Scumwort said, and sang,

'I wonder what hiz problemz are,'
He said of Badger from afar,
'He needz advize if he'z to win.'
With Ebon Trist he brought you in!

"So. I was brought in by Demio's scepter again for . . . a . . . consultation," Solofaust commented, some of his courage returning.

"Yez-z," Scumwort replied in imitation of its master.

"I wish he'd come to *me* once in a while. I can't afford to be dragged away every time some idea strikes his fancy. Well, I'm here, so let's get on with it. Where is he?"

The scum-thing blinked. One finger uncurled, pointing upward. Solofaust shuddered.

"Is Mister Badger afraid of the steps?" it asked.

"Mister Badger is not," Solofaust said, rising. *It's that endless hole they're wrapped around that worries me,* he thought.

"Don't you worry," Scumwort said, grabbing Solofaust's sleeve and pulling him along. "The Master says you won't climb a step. Hee-*heeeeeee!*"

For the second time Solofaust followed the waddling form of the scum-thing through the circular halls, past the groping hands and ghostly forms of the dungeon folk. Finally they walked through the door and onto the cracked stone stairwell of the bottomless shaft.

Now what? he wondered as he began to climb the steps.

SKREEEEEEeeeeeEEeeee!

The governor looked up to see Demio's giant form swoop out of the darkness, plunging like a huge black rock, his thick, sharp talons stretched wide. The Dark Lord snatched the badger from his narrow perch before he could react. Down they plunged, the Dark Lord's screams filling Solofaust with cold dread. He clamped his eyes shut, not daring to breathe. Demio spread his wings and, as suddenly as it began, he stopped their descent, beating his wings furiously, and twisting his body in a powerful, lung-crushing motion, the muscles in his body rippling. Instantly they began to climb upward.

Solofaust was sure his vitals were somersaulting into the darkness below, and he was paralyzed by fear that the great carrion fowl's talons would open, releasing him to join the queasy rest of himself falling through the darkness. When at last he dared open his eyes, the steps were flying past, their constant spiraling shape giving them the illusion of screwing themselves madly into the castle's roots. They swept past the scum-thing which was running up the steps like some insect, laughing and singing in its shrill voice. It became a blot in the distance, then disappeared. After what seemed hours, but was really, he suspected, mere minutes, they reached the top of the shaft. But instead of depositing his passenger, Demio streaked over a nest of bones and shot through a great window and into the sky, his straight climb turning into a steady, circling ascent.

"My lord!" Solofaust gasped, seeing Ebon Bane grow tiny below him, and again he slammed his eyes shut against the sight.

"It iz a grand view!" Demio shrieked. "A zight rarely exzperienzed by zuch dirt-crawlerz az yourzelvh!"

"I prefer the dirt!"

"Ha ha ha ha haa!"

Below, the Dark Lord's aerie rose like a jagged needle from the bay, surrounded endlessly by slabs of brilliant ice, each grinding against or leaning over its frigid neighbors, their edges standing from inches to a hundred feet above the frigid water.

"Talk would be more sensible on the ground," Solofaust gasped, imagining the results of his body striking those jagged things.

"You do not like vlying?" the bird laughed. "Very well, we zhall talk on Ebon Bane." Demio banked and circled the castle, swooping closer and closer until he flew over the castle wall, dropping his passenger. Solofaust landed with a thump and rolled until he bumped into a wall. There he spread his arms frantically to balance himself and keep from going over the top. The Dark Lord came to rest a few yards away, where he watched as the badger regained his senses. The fowl's head tilted at the smaller animal, and soundlessly his beak opened, then snapped shut with a sharp crack. A strong wind ruffled his feathers, making a loud, rustling noise as he preened himself. His noxious odor nearly turned the counselor green.

"Welcome back to Demio Zway," the Dark Lord said at last.

"You . . . you wished to consult concerning the rebellion?" Solofaust asked, trying to sound indifferent.

"Ah! Never a moment vor zmall talk when your name iz Zolovauzt," came the mocking reply. Again the bird beast cocked his head, and the badger felt as if he were being sized up for the meat on his bones.

"You wish to know my progress?"

"I wizh to know the reason vhor your lack of it."

"I've taken the castle! The armies are mine! The subjects . . ."

"You do *not* have Quad. You do *not* have Gregor. And zo you have notvhing. When you do not have zem, you have notvhing."

"Them!" Solofaust scoffed. "They'll be ours soon enough: The entire kingdom is looking for them. Besides, what can that lone simpleton king and his bullying brother do to us?"

"They can do more harm than you know. Ezpezially Quad, zo long az he haz the Ruby Zion."

"If I'd known the Scion was so important, I'd have grabbed it before the coronation feast."

"THEN WHY DID YOU NOT DO ZO?" the bird shrieked, beating his wings furiously. Solofaust clung more tightly to the wall, and he shuddered as the great fowl paced toward him. "You knew the legends of the Zion! You zhould have grabbed it! You could have had them all, Zolovaust! The king! The prinze! The Zion! They are important! The kingdom cannot be mine without them! Why? Why have you vhailed?"

"I can't do everything, my lord! It was the fault of my general!" The bird stopped, and hardly daring to breathe, Solofaust spoke on. "He was careless and ungrateful. I seem to have chosen the general of my armies poorly."

"You are very talented, that way."

"This man obeys me when the whim strikes him, and even threatens to rebel against me."

"But vor him you would have the prinze and king?"

"Most certainly!"

"Then be rid of him." Demio's tone sounded as if he was explaining the existence of toes to a child.

"He's too popular with his soldiers."

"That was not a zuggeztion. It was a command, Zolovauzt. You are intelligent. You will vhind a way. And I zhall give you a general who I know will obey hiz commander blindly. I will even give you zome . . . advizorz who will keep ze zometimez unloyal men of Redaemus in line, hey? In the meantime you muzt vhind Quad and deal withvh that zituazion. You will accompliszh thiz bezt by remembering he will not be running vrom you zo much az he will be hunting zomeone out."

"Hunting? Who?"

"Vhind Quad, and you will never have to worry about that," Demio snapped. "Zo long az we take Quad and the Zion, we zhall have no problems wivh our greatezt enemy, and then your gloriouz dayz az my governor will begin in earnezt! Ah! But I am getting into a zubject which requirez much dizcourze. Come: Zcumwort haz prepared a little vheazt to eat while we talk of thingz coming. You will vhind vhine bugz, roazted and zeazoned, on your platter."

"Now you are speaking the language of a badger, my lord," Solofaust replied, allowing himself to laugh. "I'll even climb a few of those stairs for a treat such as that!"

11

riend Rat stared cross-eyed at the arrow tip touching his snout.

"I hope you are a bat, my furry fellow," his captor said, "for I can think of nothing else that has reason to be tumbling out of holes in caverns at the castle's roots."

"Flap, flap," the counselor whispered through his toes.

"I'll admit that you're the funniest rogue I'll ever kill."

"I wouldn't shoot me if I were you," the prisoner squeaked, still upside down. "A mighty warrior would avenge my death. Assuming, of course, he can ever squirm through that hole."

"What's going on! You rolled past the torch light and we can't see you!" Quad's voice called. The soldier looked up, his eyes alert.

"Have you gotten us into more trouble, you bumbling rat-pie?" another voice growled.

Suddenly the soldier grinned.

"Gregor!" he cried.

"Narramoore! By the stars and fields, is that you?"

"It is, my prince! Is the king with you?"

"He is, and that hairy bag of potatoes you're no doubt threatening is his counselor."

Narramoore glanced at the rat.

"At your service," Friend Rat offered.

"My good lord! I'm sorry!" the soldier said as he hastily unstrung his bow. "Let me help you up, if we can find which end of you is up."

Other voices spoke from the darkness.

"What is it?" one said.

"I tell you, it's Gregor! I'd know that bear growl any-where!" another called.

"Quit babbling and get me through this blasted hole!" Gregor roared from the other direction.

Soon the counselor was sitting head-side-up as other warriors came into the light, their uniforms, capes, and armor as torn and dented as Narramoore's. They gazed curiously down at the counselor. "It's a *rat*," one exclaimed.

"He's a friend, Arlan," Narramoore said.

"A rat is a friend?" Arlan huffed. "And where's Gregor?"

"He's . . ." Friend Rat began.

"*Raaarrrggghhh!*" came a shout from the hole above.

"Oh. Up there," Arlan said, and a smile traced his lips. He had a mischievous look about his dark, sparkling eyes. He was slender and of medium height, with delicate features and long, carefully oiled and—at points—braided hair. A fine, well-trimmed mustache highlighted his mouth and his clothing, in spite of its rips and tears, was colorful and clean. A shirt that fell to mid-thigh was cinched at his waist with a belt of tortoise shell. His breeches were of a rich dye, and boots of yellow-tinted leather extended to his thighs. His gloves were made of similar leather, decorated and finely cut, with their cuffs going two-thirds the way up his forearms. He grinned slightly as he climbed the slope and gazed at the warrior prince, whose head stuck through the opening like a hunting trophy hung on a wall.

"Are you stuck, my lord?" he asked innocently.

"I hope you like the taste of your own tongue, my poet-warrior," Gregor said, "for I intend to pull it out and feed it to you, once I'm out of here!"

"He's all his father's traits, hasn't he?" the counselor said.

"Indeed!" Arlan agreed.

"Go light a torch," Narramoore said as two others—a large, brooding man and the youth, Robin—joined them. "I'll see to our general, here."

The torch was lit quickly from a fire burning at the front of the cavern, but freeing Gregor from the hole wasn't easy. Its dimensions were too small for him and his shoulders were stuck fast. Narramoore pulled at his arms while Quad, in the passage, pushed from behind.

"Is all the Honor Guard here?" Gregor asked between huffs.

"Those that are left," Narramoore said.

"Those that are *left?*"

"The rebellion was better planned than you thought. We barely escaped the ramparts, and when we joined the others below, we were attacked from all sides by Artemus' men. I led a charge where their lines seemed thinnest, but only a few of us broke through . . . And then we ran into a force of peasants and soldiers on the road. In the end, only four of us survived."

"Four! Out of thirty?"

"Not much with which to turn back a rebellion, eh, General?" Arlan asked.

"'Tis a grave time for humor," Narramoore cautioned.

"But a grand time for graves," was Arlan's quick reply. "Twenty-six of our comrades have need of them. But, whether by the Oneking's grace or what, we've been spared and, to me, life is always a suitable reason for humor."

"Here! here!" Friend Rat applauded.

"Philosophers," Gregor groaned, "should be put to swords, not take them up."

"It's no use!" Quad called from the other side. "You're not going through like this."

"I fear he's right," Narramoore agreed.

"Bah!" Gregor said, sliding back into the passage. "Now what? Can we enlarge the hole?"

"We've only our swords to do it with," Narramoore said,

"and this rock is hard. Our weapons will be of little use once we've dulled them chopping at a wall."

"The problem isn't whether you'll fit through," the king said after a moment, sounding distant from behind his brother's bulk, "but whether you'll fit through wearing your armor. I think that chest plate and the shoulder pieces are too broad. Try taking them off."

"What? And go without my armor?"

"Go through without it, or stay here with it."

The prince swore and complained, but seeing no other option, he unfastened his armor and slid out of his chain mail. These he tried to push through the hole, but only the mail would fit. Even empty, the chest piece was too broad. He glared at the king, silhouetted beside him.

"I'm a warrior. My armor is my life."

"If you insist on keeping it, so is this cave."

"FAUGH!" the prince shouted, a cry that echoed through the passageway and made everyone jump. He hurled the chest piece blindly and it crashed against a wall. Then he slid his arms and head through the hole again, and pulled himself forward.

And stuck.

"BLAST!" Gregor roared.

"Really, Prince! All this shouting will bring down the whole castle guard! Tik! tik! tik!"

"Perhaps if you take off your clothes and oil your body, you could squeeze through," Quad said. The prince's face, already crimson, flushed deeper and Friend Rat broke into gales of laughter.

"You shut up!" Gregor snapped, trembling with fury, "or I'll oil you and roast you on a spit! And Quad, don't *you* be such an idiot!"

"It may be the only way," Narramoore said, throwing a warning glance at Arlan, who quickly covered his smile with a hand. "There's a stream outside you could wash in afterward, since it's dark. Hand your clothes to me, and let's get this unpleasant business done with."

"The kingdom's in rebellion and only you and I are still sane in it," Gregor muttered to his captain before backing into the passage again. "And if I find you laughing back there, you little turnip, I'll reshape that nose, king or not!"

The sword, cloak, and clothing fit through the hole rather easily. Narramoore lay them on the cavern floor where they were promptly picked up and put on by Friend Rat who paraded about, making it difficult for anyone to take Gregor's problem seriously.

"Here is some fatsoap I keep with my supplies," Arlan said, passing the bar through the hole. "I'll wager you won't be so snide about my 'obsessive bathing' from now on," he added with a grin.

"Shut up, or I'll feed your soap to you," Gregor replied. "It'll make your tongue slide down better." He greased his shoulders and hips and this time squeezed through at the price of only a little skin and blood. He stood on the slope by the hole until Quad climbed easily through, and the two slid to the bottom.

"This is Narramoore," Gregor said as he collected his clothes (which Rat had wisely abandoned before the prince caught him wearing them). "He's my captain, my best and most trusted soldier, and a man of honor. If you recognize him, it's because he was one of the men dancing about on the ramparts, fighting Solofaust's guards."

He was a large man with a square jaw and short-cropped, dark brown hair. Narramoore's clean-shaven face was tanned and his wide-set eyes had a brooding, serious look.

There is nobility in this man, Quad thought, seeing a fluid and dangerous grace in every movement he made.

"Aren't you going to say anything?" Gregor hissed to his brother as the captain dropped to one knee before him.

Quad cleared his throat. "You don't have to do that," he gulped.

With a groan Gregor seized Quad's wrist and dragged him aside.

"Do you know nothing of a king's decorum?" he whispered angrily. "At least show a little pride! These men have gone through terrible things to save your hide! There are twenty-six who died defending you! Show gratitude. Offer them courage, assuming you've any to give!"

"Who are these others?" Quad asked, hoping to change the subject.

"Ah! You've noticed them!" Gregor sneered. They approached Arlan, who avoided his general's angry eyes. "This man was also on the walls—Arlan of the Eastern Plains, where our own ancestors' hall lies in Yerushela. Some of his folk live in simple homes, but many live in Yerushela, which is built within a great cavern and lit by a system of mirrors and lights."

"I've read of it," Quad said.

"You've read of everything. It's high time you began to experience some of it. Yerushelites are poets and theologians and philosophers—worthless every one of them. They never know when to shut their mouths." Gregor broke into a smile then, and slapped Arlan on the back. "He makes sure we don't take ourselves too seriously, however, and I can think of no one I'd rather have beside me in times of trouble. As a warrior he's second only to Narramoore."

"And to yourself, my lord," Arlan protested. "Sire," he added, kneeling, "my sword and all I have are yours."

The king looked closely at this strange man, and wondered dimly why he would want his sword.

Next was a huge man with jet-black skin carrying a large, round shield of hide, elaborately decorated and slung over his back. His sword—so large Quad doubted he himself could lift it—hung bare at his thigh, and shining, five-pointed darts, called starbrands, poked from his belt.

"Nabo," Gregor said as the man knelt, "a man of thankfully few words. But don't think of his size and silence as signs of a weak mind. Nabo has no equal in lore of the field, survival, and tracking. He'll save us many times in the coming days, I'm sure."

Nabo gazed for a long moment at the king without speaking, his eyes gazing coolly from sockets set deep in his high forehead. His head was not shaven, but his kinky hair had more shadow than substance to it.

"My lord," he said at last with a slight nod. He did not, Quad noticed, bow.

"This last one is our boy," the prince laughed, roughing the hair of the fourth soldier. "His name is Robin and his worth is in his determination. We've tried to lose him a dozen times—bribed him, threatened and spanked him, even tied him up and left him at a pig farm once. He got loose and found his way back; so we finally accepted his company. He'll be a fine warrior one day."

"*One day!*" Robin protested. "Lord Gregor, you should have seen me at the castle! Cut down a man twice my size!"

Gregor smiled and glanced at Narramoore, who nodded his agreement.

"Your trial by fire, then," Gregor said, his hands on Robin's shoulders. "And what was the price of this victory?"

"Never touched me! He split my shield was all!" Robin said, his voice quivering with excitement.

"That's all! The one thing between a soldier and death, and you have it no longer. Well, I'm sure we'll have the chance to grab you another, courtesy of Solofaust and his grubby men."

"How old are you?" Quad asked.

"Eighteen."

"He's fifteen, except when he lies. Then he's only twelve," Gregor said, and Robin hung his head.

"Well, no matter," Quad replied, going to the boy. "I'm just eighteen myself, and it's good to be about someone who's actually younger than me."

Grinning, Robin raised his sword.

"To the king!" he shouted.

"The king!" the others cried, raising their swords. Gregor sat beside the counselor with a groan.

"Can you believe all this pomp for *him?*" he said, rolling his eyes.

"Tik! tik! tik!" the rat scolded.

Quad looked nervously at his admirers and their weapons, gleaming like the bars of a cage.

"Please lower those swords!" he begged. "I'm flattered by your attention, but we shouldn't shout so. We aren't that far from the castle highway.

"Well, I owe you my life and my apologies as well. I thought you were against me, the same as Solofaust. But it turns out you're all loyal, of course . . . and I . . . uh . . ."

He stopped. The words fled him (which was no matter, he realized: they hadn't been worth keeping, anyway). Swallowing hard, he tried to think of something more to say.

"Please, all of you stand. Or sit! Or . . . do something! You look so uncomfortable. Now then . . . I . . . well . . . oh, where is my scepter? Where's the Ruby Scion?"

The soldiers, obviously disturbed, settled around the fire. Gregor watched in disgust as the king found his scepter then hurried from the others. Their expressions grew more perplexed, but the king took no note as he stood hidden in the shadows, holding the scepter before him.

It was beautiful in its pure simplicity, a handle of gold-plated, gilt-leaf iron with fine, golden prongs securely holding the Scion in place. But the Scion—which had once been dazzling in its fiery brilliance, Quad imagined, had now grown so dark he had to reach out his hand to touch it before he was entirely sure it was still there. He gazed at the blackness and soon could pick out the tiny prick of light that lived deep within the Scion. *Oh, Father! Look at them: they expect me to lead them, to be their hope! And all I can do is babble nonsense! Why did you give me your crown! What can I do!* Slowly, he lost awareness of the things about him as the tiny speck within the gem locked his gaze, hypnotizing him with its subtle, rhythmic movement, until it seemed to climb into his soul.

Gregor watched his brother with embarrassed disbelief. Glancing away from the king, he caught the curious gazes of his men. *So this is what it's like to be humiliated,* he thought. Rather too loudly he said, "He's meditating. I've seen him do this before, when his spirit is troubled. I doubt he can even hear us!"

"That's an odd habit, stopping in mid-sentence to meditate," Arlan said, and Nabo nodded his agreement. Furious, Gregor strode to Friend Rat, who had been standing off by himself, and hoisted him from the floor.

"What's that fool doing? He just stands there, gaping like a scarecrow! Go do something!"

"Do what?" Friend Rat gasped.

"I don't know! But my men are beginning to suspect his sanity. Soon they'll abandon us and go home! If you can't rouse him, I'll do it with a stick!"

"Tik! tik! tik!" the counselor whispered. Still, he hurried to the young king.

"Sire!" he whispered desperately as he tugged on Quad's robe. "Snap out of it! Come about!"

Suddenly Quad's head snapped up and his shoulders squared.

"I am the king!" he said, his eyes wide as if the statement were a revelation.

"Yes! You are!"

"And the fate of Redaemus is in my hands."

"Indeed it is!"

Quad turned and walked to the circle of men, his step suddenly proud and his head high. A light danced in his eyes that took even his counselor off guard.

"My warriors!" he exclaimed. "Defenders of our land. Behold your king! A little man, now, in stature and in power. We know what the kingdom thinks of me: Quad the Untried. Quad the Frail and Sheltered, ignorant of the needs of his people. Yet destiny has given me this crown, and I cannot refuse it. We are caught in a vice of avarice and deception, rebellion and destruction. This is Redaemus' most difficult hour. At this moment the castle of my father is in the hands of the traitor Solofaust, whose mind is bent to the dark void of Demio's ways.

"And me? I am homeless. Hunted. Hated. Yet you alone have chosen to be loyal to me, to believe that destiny knows its own mind. What can I give you? Only this: that I will learn the subjects' needs, and see that they are met, and more.

"But first, there is a throne to regain and an enemy to overcome. If we march together, we will win. And when I sit in the Castle Pentatute, you'll know me to be a benevolent and grateful king, for then your rewards will know no bounds!"

"Bravo!" Friend Rat cried, leaping about. "Bravo! I guess he showed you a thing or two about honor and courage, my lord!" he added under his breath as he danced about Gregor's feet.

"Indeed he did," the prince said thoughtfully as the warriors cheered their king. "Perhaps there is an ounce of royalty in that sack, after all."

◆

"Counselor?" Robin gently shook his shoulder.

"What is it?" the rat asked, rousing from his slumber and poking his head from under his blankets.

"The king is outside and won't come in."

"What? Isn't it nearly dawn?"

"Yes," Robin said. "He's been there all night. We've tried to relieve him several times, but he keeps telling us to go away. Perhaps if you talk to him . . ."

"All right, I'll go," the counselor sighed.

Wringing his tail in one hand, Friend Rat started off in the direction Robin pointed, holding his free hand out into the blackness ahead to fend off bushes and trees. Outside the mouth of the cave was a natural wall of rock about three feet high, which hid the cave from all but the sharpest eyes. In addition, brambles and thornapple grew in a thick copse along the hillside. It was some thirty feet to the bottom of the mountain and another hundred yards or so to the road. The horses had been tethered in a natural pen of boulders below, and it was there that the king was sitting. Not wanting to startle him, the counselor called out softly, "Hallooo!"

"Go away!" a voice replied.

"Is that you, Sire?" the rat asked, squinting to make something of the specters and shadows of the night.

"Go away!" the voice hissed again.

"'Tis me! Friend Rat!"

"Friend Rat? Why didn't you say so? Come! I'm sitting underneath this horse!"

"Isn't that a dangerous place to sit, Sire? Beneath a horse?"

"That depends which end you sit under. He's good shelter if it rains, and assassins won't think to look for me here."

"Why do you keep telling the replacements we send to go away?" the counselor scolded as he found the king.

"Replacements? I thought they were enemies," Quad sighed. "Here. Stay with me a while."

They sat without speaking for a time. Friend Rat was silent, not wishing to disturb the deep and important thoughts and strategies his king must be mulling over. Quad, meanwhile, was recalling a warm feather bed and a scullery maid named Matty. Each kept his pensive silence as the gray curtain of dawn veiled the stars, while a trickle of breakfast colors slid upward into the sky. Finally, the counselor turned to the king.

"It was a brave speech you gave," he said.

"I know," the king replied, and for a moment he gazed quietly at the sunrise. Then he looked at his friend.

"Rat! For a moment I had courage. *Real* courage. I felt like a king is supposed to feel: I had visions, I had passion, I could've led them in a charge on the walls of Pentatute! But once I got out of the cavern, the courage left me as quickly as it came. I've been afraid to leave this spot. I can see how they'll write the chronicles now: 'At first there was King Pentatutinus, Ruler of a Thousand Years—Pentatutinus, the Law Giver!' Then you'll turn some pages and see, 'Then there was Quad, Ruler of a Thousand Seconds—Quad, the Wax-bound Volume of Ignorance!'"

"Tik! tik! tik! *I* think your memory will last much longer than your father's."

"Do you really?"

"Certainly," Rat said curtly. "Your name is easier to remember."

Their eyes turned back to the sunrise, and the king wondered if it was noble to whack a rat with the royal scepter.

◆

While the badger feasted in Ebon Bane, the king nibbled at berries and gnawed at a crust of dry bread, and Gregor, Nabo, and Narramoore sat at a large rock. Between them was a lantern and a sheepskin map so weathered its material had more hills and valleys and inlets than the geography it portrayed. They had been studying it most of the day. At last Gregor called his brother to join them.

"We must leave tonight," he said. "Sooner or later the guards will stumble on this cavern, and that'll be the end of us."

"Obviously we can't stay here forever, in any case," Quad agreed, hoping he sounded wise.

"Look," Gregor continued, ignoring him, "we are less than a two hour ride from Gregor Road. We can safely travel it for a while. I know how Artemus thinks: he sends out his patrols and search parties in one big wave, and by now that wave is a day's ride ahead of us. All we'll have to worry about, locally, is small patrols."

"And where shall we go?" Quad asked.

Gregor looked up, eyeing his brother irritably.

"We haven't decided," Narramoore volunteered. "We've few friends out there. . . . The bluebloods have been arrested or slain, and the common folk seem loyal to Solofaust."

"I'll vouch for that!" Friend Rat said, joining them.

"We've thought of riding north, to Sheolfrost," Gregor said. "The men there are more likely to be loyal, and that would give us an army for some kind of resistance. But there are problems with that idea."

"It's a long ride for folk not used to horses," Narramoore explained.

"We'd get used to it," Quad said hopefully. A loyal army sounded good to him.

"Not as hard as we'd have to ride," Gregor said, "and with patrols everywhere, it would be difficult to stay hidden. I'm sure the north-south roads will be well-guarded, for that's where they'll expect to find us. Even if we could all get there, and the army proved loyal, our situation wouldn't be much better than it is here. The Sheolfrost is right between Demio's armies and Solofaust's. They could simply attack us at the same time and crush us between them."

"Then you go there and bring any loyal men here," the king suggested.

"I wouldn't dare," Gregor said. "I said they were between Sheolfrost and Demio. They are all that keeps the Dark Lord out of your kingdom now. The moment we pull them out, he'll send his armies pouring through Whistler's Pass."

"'Tis a wonder he hasn't come through the pass already, from what I've heard of your men," Friend Rat said.

"I've wondered that myself," Narramoore agreed before Gregor could aim his boot to respond, "as has the prince. Certainly, with the kingdom in civil war, led by his own puppet, there's nothing to stop the Dark Lord."

"Wilgate said the armies have never kept him out," Quad mused. "Only his fear of Father and the laws did. So what does he fear now?"

"He may be waiting for an easier victory," Gregor guessed. "The passes will thaw in two months, and we could never adequately defend all three at once; by using them he could hit us at three points and destroy us more easily. Then again, we don't know that he isn't pouring through even now . . . and that's another reason why I can't take you."

"Then, for all purposes, you are the only army Redaemus has to turn back a rebellion?" Quad asked, referring to the five warriors present.

Gregor nodded.

"How depressing," Quad sighed. "What can we do?"

"You're the king," Gregor grinned. "Tell us!"

"So what if I'm king? What do you expect me to do?

Walk up to Solofaust, bop him on the head with the Ruby Scion, and say 'Go 'way!'?"

"You'll think of something," Narramoore assured him.

"How?"

"You turned such pretty words last night, we thought you'd have some wisdom for us still," Gregor said.

"Tik! tik! tik! You watch your tongue! He'll come up with something! You'll see!" Friend Rat scolded. "Quad will save the kingdom!"

"How?" the king shouted, tossing up his hands. He threw himself against the wall and sat there, gazing sadly at his scepter. "Perhaps it's hopeless."

"You can't give up hope!" Narramoore said. "You're our king. You must guide us."

Gregor choked back a groan, but Friend Rat jumped to his feet. "You see that, Sire! They believe in you! You see . . . ? Sire? Hello?"

"He's gone into another trance!" Gregor said, slapping himself in the head.

The counselor tip-toed to the king and, hoping to bring him around, touched his nose. "Beep!" he sang.

"The *Oneprince!*" Quad cried, spinning around. Friend Rat jumped back in surprise and tripped over his tail. Lying on the ground, he looked up at the king.

"The Oneprince? Are you on that again?" he sighed.

Gregor looked at Quad. "What did you say?"

"The Oneprince!" Quad repeated.

"The Oneprince?" Narramoore echoed.

"A magical prince from legends of old," Friend Rat explained. "Pentatutinus spoke of him, as did that crazy old high minister. I do believe Quad is delirious."

"No, I'm serious," Quad whispered.

"Is he still alive?" Gregor asked.

"Father said he is."

"That's enough for me."

"They're both delirious!" Rat shouted and, giving up, joined Arlan and Robin by the fire.

"Is he in the kingdom?" Gregor asked.

"I think so."

"Where?"

"I don't know! But if we can find him . . ."

The animation drained from Gregor's eyes. "No, if Solofaust were our only enemy, the Oneprince could help us. But our real enemy is Demio, and not even the Oneprince can stand against him."

"I think he can."

"Then why hasn't he?" Gregor shouted, storming about the cavern waving his arms. "Surely, if he's in the kingdom, he knows our plight! But what has he done about it? Where is he? If he were as powerful as you and Father think, this rebellion would never have happened!"

"But he made the spell that gave Father his long life!"

"And now Father is dead. No, there are two possibilities here. The Oneprince is alive, but too weak to help us—else he would, and Father would still be king—or the Oneprince is dead."

"But . . ."

"That's it! Not another word about him!" Gregor said, stopping at the map and bringing his fist down on it. "All of you! Come here," he ordered. While the others gathered, Quad and Gregor stood glaring at each other.

"Here is what we'll do," the warrior-prince said at last, his eyes never leaving Quad's. "I'll ride to Sheolfrost and see the situation. We must learn whether the army there is for us and what Demio is up to concerning them. Surely I'll find *some* loyal men."

"And what do we do with the king?" Arlan asked.

"Take him some place where I'll meet you, Arlan. Hide him in Yerushela. They are Father's people, and they'll befriend us. It's our best refuge."

"Humph!" Quad said. "And what will you do when you find these loyal men, Gregor?"

"Hide some in the forests, I suppose, or in the Eastern Plains. We'll conduct a hit-and-run war and hope the border situation improves."

"It won't," Quad said. "You know that. You've admitted it! Once the passes clear, Demio will slaughter your men.

And fighting a war in the woods is romantic nonsense."

Gregor spun on his brother, amazed. "*You* accuse *me* of romantic nonsense? All right, master strategist! Do you have a better plan?"

"I do," Quad said, raising his chin.

"Narramoore! Behold this little weed! He spends his life in castle books and scrolls while I oversee all the armies of the kingdom. Yet he thinks *he's* got the better plan!"

"Remember, my lord, there's something to be said for the wisdom of a bookish man," Narramoore said uncomfortably.

"Bookish man?" Quad asked the rat. "Have I just been insulted?"

"He is the king," Nabo said.

"Indeed!" Friend Rat chimed in.

Gregor sat with a huff on the rock. "All right. What's your plan, Sire?" he asked with barely concealed sarcasm.

"Only this: your plan is good to an extent—a hit-and-run war will at least buy us time. But it won't save the kingdom. Go. Seek your supporters. But don't hide me in a hut somewhere. Let me find the Oneprince. I know you doubt his existence, but if I'm right, he could be our only hope. If I'm wrong, we're no worse off, and at least I'll feel as if I'm accomplishing something. And, I'll be making myself a moving target, which you know is harder to catch."

"This Oneprince idea is grasping at straws, but no more so than my idea," Gregor admitted after a thoughtful pause. "How do you plan to find him?"

Quad opened his mouth to reply, but could not think of a thing to say.

"If the Oneprince is magical, why not employ a wizard?" Narramoore suggested.

"There are no wizards these days," Gregor said. "Father outlawed them."

"There's one," Arlan corrected him. "A wizardess, who's well-known by the superstitious folk of Yerushela. Her name is Iscara."

Friend Rat jumped up. "I've heard of her! She lives in the

enchanted forest of Magdalawood—performs minor charms and curses for wealthy men. And I hear she makes a grand cheese souffle!"

"Seeking a wizardess to find a wizard," Gregor sighed. "Father is rolling in his grave!"

"Of course, she isn't always friendly," Arlan added. "Many times folks have entered Magdalawood to find her and never returned."

"I'll risk that," Quad said, wondering why he was inviting such danger.

"Then here's what we'll do," Gregor said. "First, we'll need someone to keep watch of things at the castle. Narramoore, that'll be you. Stay to the woods and this cavern, and use the secret passages to eavesdrop on conversations there. Quad will draw you maps of where they go. Arlan: you, Robin and Nabo will go with Quad to Magdalawood, and I'll ride to Sheolfrost. When each has completed his task, he will make his way to Yerushela and wait for the others. We'll decide what to do about this rebellion then.

"Let's get ready! We'll part tonight."

The remaining Honor Guardsmen and Friend Rat were clustered together, one hundred feet west of a Gregor Road intersection. The soldiers sat uneasily in their saddles, listening for sounds of danger on the silent breeze. The counselor stood between them (for rats lost no fondness on horses), wringing his tail in his hands. Between them and Castle Pentatute to the west lay several miles of woods and fields and decaying farmers' huts. To the east, many days' ride through meadows, forests, and hills, lay Magdalawood; beyond to the south and east lay Yerushela, their eventual meeting place. The Sheolfrost beckoned Gregor on the north-bound King's highway which intersected Gregor Road, where the king and his brother were exchanging last words.

Quad sat on his horse, an animal far livelier than he liked, clinging to the saddle with one hand and keeping its mane knotted in the other. He wondered if they would ever meet again. *If we do*, he thought, *I wonder if we'll even know each other?*

"Do you think we'll all make it to Yerushela?" he asked.

"Perhaps," Gregor said. He looked north, and again Quad noticed how handsome and noble his brother appeared.

Gregor was every bit the king, *yet the crown has fallen to me, a gangly simpleton.*

"The way will be dangerous for both of us," Gregor said. "You can rely on the Honor Guard, but they alone won't save you in times like these. You must rely also on your wits." Quad began to protest, but the prince angrily cut him off. "You have brains, Quad, and you would find them if you'd just put away your little fears and paranoia long enough!"

"Paranoia seems a healthy thing to have, just now," Quad muttered.

"You have to trust somebody . . ." Gregor began angrily.

"I do!" Quad cut in.

"Besides that addled rat of a counselor, you little carp! People care for you, but you don't know it! You even thought *I* was out for your head. I don't want the crown! I can't handle that responsibility!"

"And *I* can?"

"Not now!" Gregor laughed, but his laugh lacked its usual sharpness, and his tone was unusually friendly. "You have it *in* you. I know, for I've seen it. Not often, for your courage fears the light, but you've shown it even recently: by getting us through the passage, in your speech, in standing up to me like you did in front of my men, though I'll admit I wanted to punch you when you did. Listen. I love my kingdom too much to let just anyone rule it, and if I thought you were as useless as you do, I'd never have come to help you. But see how easily you carry the Ruby Scion, and the effect it has on your spirit when you contemplate it. If you weren't truly a king, that wouldn't happen."

"I . . ."

"Quad—my lord—these coming days will bring deadly troubles without number. If you survive, and I think you can, you'll come out of it both a man and a king to rival Father. If I survive—and only time will tell us that—I know I shall be proud to serve you."

Quad looked away, his lower lip trembling, not knowing what to think of these words.

"Listen to me!" Gregor demanded. "Humility is not a cloak I like to wear, so you won't hear me say any of this again. You think you are an idiot, a coward, but it isn't true. All that is a mask. Beneath it lies manhood, courage, and power. Seek it out, and don't give up until you've found it. That alone can save us. I don't think this Oneprince can."

"Gregor, I . . ."

"'Tis time to part," Gregor said, cutting off the conversation. He listened quietly a moment, testing the wind for any sounds. Turning in his saddle, he prepared to ride off, but turned once more to his brother.

"My love and prayers are with you," he said, grasping Quad's arm. "May the Oneking guide you."

"And you," Quad replied, his voice sounding strange to his own ears.

Gregor turned again and urged his horse to canter. Quad watched him for several seconds before he called out.

"Gregor!"

The prince stopped and turned, the gentleness already faded from his eyes.

"What is it!" he said irritably.

"I don't wish to break the mood of our parting, but . . . I'm not used to horses! I want him to go slow until I'm used to him. How do I make him walk?"

The warrior looked over his brother with an impish grin.

"Kick his sides, Sire! Kick him hard!" Gregor said, a mischievous smile lighting his face.

Shortly, Narramoore, Arlan, Robin, Nabo, and Friend Rat watched in astonishment as Quad thundered past and out of sight, screaming and yowling as he bounced crazily, his face buried in his horse's mane.

◆

A sun dulled by rusting clouds lit the travelers as they picked their way through last year's fields, as pocked and stubbled as a smithy's face. Broken cornstalks, stone fences, and fingers of wood were their only cover. Still they found these safer than riding the dangerous road, and the gentle swells of the fields often gave them broad areas where they could lie low and watch when a patrol of Solofaust's men wandered by.

Toward the end of the first night, they came upon a stretch of scraggy hills, creased by a sparkling, lively stream. Arlan chose a ravine suitable for camp. Its bottom was carpeted in moss and divided by a rocky chute of the quick, cold water deep enough to dip a cooking pot in and narrow enough to jump across—if one had a running start and wasn't a clumsy rat. The counselor learned this to his chilly dismay. As each warrior took turns guarding from the crook of a nearby tree, the others tended a small, smokeless fire. They cheered one another with jokes and stories, each trying to outdo his fellows with tales of adventure. Nabo and Robin recounted their desperate fight on the day of the rebellion (Robin's foe had gained fifty pounds and six inches in height since the previous telling, and Nabo, laughing, suggested "Next time this soldier will have grown another arm!") while Arlan spoke of Yerushela, his people's city beneath the plains. "A great city of dazzling light," he proclaimed.

"A city underneath the plains has dazzling light?" Robin asked, unbelieving.

"It is provided by lamps, torches, and great mirrors," Arlan explained. "And the buildings and towers are built of alabaster and follow along the cavern's sweeping walls. And walkways cross the ceiling so high up you'll think you're in the sky."

Friend Rat followed this dreamy travelog by recounting his adventures at The Rasp & File when he'd pretended to be a rogue. Quad could think of no tales of himself worth telling at a camp fire, so finally he surprised everyone with legends of his father and the Oneprince.

"You will have me believing in this man soon," Arlan said at last, with a yawn. "But now 'tis time we got some sleep." He unhitched the brooch of his cape and, wrapping himself in his bedroll, added, "A song would be a pleasant way to end our day."

"I believe I have one," Quad volunteered.

"A bard, like your father?" the easterner asked with a smile.

"I wrote it today as we traveled. It's just a little one, of course, and tells no tale. It's more a mood, you see . . ."

"Let's hear it!" Robin said.

Nervous at having an audience, Quad gazed into the fire as he sang.

> Childhood is the best place to be.
> Let's run there, you and I,
> As if we've magic watchakeys
> To make the world go by!
>
> Let's hold hands in the berry patch
> Or skip stones at the pool,
> And fret about such horrid things
> As Master Juggs at school.
>
> Why bother with a'worrying?
> We'll draw kings in the sky
> If we can run to childhood
> And wave todays goodbye.

"'Tis odd," Quad admitted. "But I think we can all agree with its—" He stopped speaking suddenly, taking in each dumbfounded face. Finally he found himself locked in Arlan's glare.

"Very pretty, Sire. But your childhood is gone. You must be a man now, and your songs should be of victory and hope. When you've something we can march to, *then* sing to us again!" The king's face fell and Arlan, glancing at his comrades, rolled his eyes. He smiled and slapped Quad's shoulder. "In the meantime, come! Let's get some sleep—at least those of us who aren't on duty, for I see it's time I take my turn at playing rooster in the tree."

◆

Narramoore, his build more slender than Gregor's, found it simple to slip through the hole in the cavern's back wall. There he lit a torch and set about following the directions Quad had given him. Instead of explaining the way back to Castle Pentatute itself through the passages, the king had instructed Narramoore in how he would find a barracks chamber, complete with bunks, table, chairs, and maps. The maps, Quad said, would explain the secret passages far better than he could.

Is this passage such that it needs maps to be followed? the captain wondered as he picked his way along. Just how ambitious was this tunnel? He quickly found out. It was not simply one or two underground halls winding from the castle to a cave, but a veritable labyrinth. Soon he was passing tunnels that intersected with this main one or branched off to the right or left. At one point he reached a stairwell drilled into the rock, winding both up and down. He could hear rushing water below. *An underground river?* he wondered, making a mental note.

"Yerushela's caverns and tunnels have nothing on you but their width and trimmings," he murmured once, as he stood at the intersection of five different passages. He listened for sounds, but heard only the noises he made and the occasional distant patter of dripping water. He began to walk again and wondered with some consternation whether his torch would hold out until he found the chamber Quad had described. He was not concerned about losing his way, for it was not in Narramoore's make-up to doubt his abilities; still he had no strong faith in the torch, and the prospect of standing alone suddenly in darkness in the depths of a mountain, was not pleasing to him. Finally, just as his torch began to sputter and dance its last, he came upon the chamber in an area that widened out suddenly. There were doors of dark, musty wood with straps of metal to hold them together, their posts driven into the rock. There was a latch and keyhole as well, but this was of no

matter, for the lumber was so rotten with age and damp-
ness, the doors leaned like drunken sentinels. When Narramoore tapped at them with the hilt of his sword, they
buckled in upon themselves. With a slight smile, he
stepped in.

Holders were mounted on the walls, and in them there
were torches. He tried three before he found one that would
light and then he put his own in a holder.

"So this is my home for a few weeks," he said, looking
about.

The chamber was some thirty feet long and fifteen feet
wide, with bunks enough for thirty men along the side
walls and a chess table (its pieces, cracked with age, standing at attention, wrapped in cobwebs) leaning sullenly
against the far wall. Near it was a keg which, when he
turned its tap, rewarded him with dust. Blankets lay in
each bunk, and he even found a few that weren't riddled
with mildew. Beneath one bunk he found a great, sagging
chest in which, Quad had said, he would find the maps.

"A handsome home, indeed," he sighed, speaking his
thoughts for the simple company his own voice provided.
"Let's have a look at these maps and see how we shall find
the throne room." Squatting on his haunches, he examined
the chest. Like the door, it was locked, and the lock was
secure. But also like the door, the wood holding the lock
was soggy and weak. Breaking it apart required little more
than the thump of his fist.

The maps were in a water-tight sack, and much to his
relief, they were well preserved. There were at least a
dozen, and the warrior supposed that most were general
maps of the kingdom or plans of Castle Pentatute, itself,
from the days of its construction. One by one, Narramoore
removed them and spread them on the table. To his amazement, each leather scroll told of another and yet another
layer of passages or routes to and from a dizzying number of
locations about the castle, The Village, or the craggy hill on
which Pentatute sat.

Most of the passages threaded about the castle. They ran
along the inside of nearly every interior wall (sometimes

exterior walls as well), and virtually encircled the great throne room ("No wonder the place is so cold and drafty," Narramoore chuckled). One passage led to the kitchens; another ran alongside the dungeons, with spots marked where stones could be levered aside for entrance to the cells.

Other passages went past (or under or above) the stables, most of the bedchambers, and the servants' quarters. Only the most sensitive rooms did not have access to a passage: the king's bedchamber and the treasury, for instance. The Tomb of the Kings was also without a passage.

Below the castle were at least four main levels of the subterranean roads, leading to storage chambers where there were weapons, torches, furs, and sealed water kegs, and many leading to small caves or brushy ledges on Pentatute Hill. One also led to an underground river, Narramoore saw, but there was nothing indicating whether the river could be navigated from underground, or whether it surfaced anywhere before the sea.

There were passages into the village as well, although most of these were incomplete and none penetrated farther than a few hundred yards beyond the base of the hill.

He might have been overwhelmed, but Narramoore quickly spotted an invaluable clue to learning the many routes. Small stone and metal pads were mounted along the walls, according to the notes in the margins. Each panel identified a particular route by a series of rivets. If one wished to move quickly from the throne room to the stables, one followed the panels with three rivets driven into them at a diagonal, left upper corner to lower right corner.

The whole system had been masterminded and dug by a young and harried King Pentatutinus hundreds of years before—with the help of a loyal badger, no less (his scrawl, nearly illegible, was traced along one lower corner).

This would be Narramoore's work, then: That night he would go to one of the storage chambers and find enough oil and good torches to provide light in this chamber. Then he would clean the cask and fill it from the underground river, so that he would have water enough. Finally, for the next several hours he would commit most of the routes to memory—especially those going to the throne room, the kitchens, the armory, the stables, and the dungeons. He wasn't sure yet why he thought of the dungeons; but perhaps there would be something he could do quietly among the prisoners there. It might provide quite a bramble under Solofaust's saddle.

◆

For two days they easily avoided the roads, but then fog began to settle on the ground like fat sponges of mist, and the fingers of trees thickened into copses. The copses became large patches of young ash and maple, and soon they entered fields interlaced with the patches and granddaddy oak trees began to appear. Finally, on the fourth day, the acres of trees outnumbered the acres of fields, and the fog got so thick that the riders as often as not found themselves dismounted by low branches, while Friend Rat spent his time bumping into horse flanks and wading into briars.

"With all this fog," Arlan said at last, sprawled on the ground and pulling twigs from his hair, "the roads will give as much cover as these so-called trails, and they'll be easier to travel." And so a system was set up in which Robin rode a mile ahead as scout, and Arlan and Nabo rode on either side of Quad and the counselor. On occasion, Nabo dropped back to be sure no one was coming up from behind.

"But beware!" Arlan warned his companions. "Never speak above a whisper, and if I should stop and hold up my hand, then you stop as well, and don't make a sound!"

With the new plan of action they made better time, and the fog began to thin until it simply lay in patches. Still, the ban on speaking made the trip eerie and depressing. Quad and the rat both became despondent while even Robin's endless chatter at the campfire dwindled and died. On the sixth night, Nabo drew his horse to a sudden stop and froze. Instantly the others stopped, watching him.

"What is . . . ?" Quad began to say, but Arlan motioned for silence.

Nabo glanced at the others once, then edged his horse forward. He stopped again a dozen paces ahead and cocked his head in one direction, then the other. Finally he motioned for Arlan to come to him. The two leaned close together and made rapid motions with their hands and fingers.

"Can you hear what they're saying?" Friend Rat whispered to the king.

"They aren't saying anything—at least not with their voices," Quad replied. "I think . . . Yes! They're talking with their hands! A language of signs. How unique!"

"How silly," Rat huffed.

At that moment, Arlan looked angrily in their direction and they quickly shut their mouths with a double clack. The sign-talk continued some moments and then Arlan rode forward. He listened, too, cocking his head one way, then another, and turned back to Nabo. Again, they signed. Nabo watched uncertainly, then sighed heavily. Finally Arlan motioned for the king and rat to come along, and the travelers rode on.

"Was that a language you were using?" Quad asked.

"'Tis a language Gregor taught us. He learned it from cooks and attendants who are deaf and who learned it in turn from monks on the eastern coasts. I'll teach it to you and the rat, for you'll find it useful in the days to come. And again! Don't make a sound when I use that signal! Had there been trouble then, your whispers could've gotten us killed."

"We heard nothing. What danger did you—"

"You must learn to listen with more than your ears. We're losing time, your majesty!" Arlan said, cutting him off. He tapped his horse's flank with his heel, making it trot several paces ahead with Nabo, and Quad and the rat were left to each other's company again.

In an hour Nabo paused again, turning his head slowly this way and that. Arlan signaled a stop, then rode up to Nabo. Again they spoke in the silent language. The Easterner rode forward, listened, turned, and nodded.

It was not, Quad thought, a reassuring nod.

Silently, Arlan dismounted and, still looking cautiously about, led his horse to the side of the road. He motioned for the king to follow him. Nabo, going to the other side of the road, motioned to Friend Rat.

Quad followed Arlan into the shadows of low brush to the road's north. Fifty yards from the road, the soldier gently tugged at each horse's bridle. The animals dropped to their bellies and stretched their necks on the ground, each so motionless that anyone seeing them at this hour from the road would mistake them for rocks among the nettles. The men settled behind them and Arlan stroked his mount's belly.

"Is it the enemy?" Quad dared to ask.

"We shall see. Silence!"

They watched for endless minutes before Quad heard the barely audible hiss of Arlan's voice: "Now! Something's coming."

Quad felt a thrill of fear as he looked about. "How can you tell? I hear nothing."

"I can *feel* it!" the Easterner whispered, glancing his way. "And you can't?" Arlan turned his attention to the road and Quad strained all his senses trying to feel this approaching danger. He felt nothing, he was sure, yet he saw that Arlan's whole body began trembling in spite of the heavy cloak he wore. They sat there for some time—perhaps half an hour, Quad guessed by the moon, and Arlan's expression changed from one of mild apprehension to obvious fear, his tightly sealed lips parting to a silent snarl. When the king peeped over his horse and glanced toward the road, he still saw or felt nothing. From Arlan's reactions, he was glad he didn't.

A large figure appeared on the road. The king bit his own hand to avoid yelping, but relaxed as he realized it was Nabo, calling softly. "It has passed!"

"What's passed?" Quad gulped.

"I don't know," Arlan said. He clicked his tongue and the horses climbed to their feet. "Like you I saw nothing—with my eyes. But something was there, going right down that road, and I felt it as surely as I'd feel a net falling about me."

"All I felt was goose bumps," Quad said, following Arlan to the road. "And I've felt them since the day of the coronation."

"Your senses are dull, my King," Nabo said. "You will sharpen them, if you wish to see your throne again."

Friend Rat popped out of the underbrush, his eyes wide. "Did you feel anything?" the king asked him.

"No, but Nabo said he had a feeling in his stomach, thick as cheesy pudding."

"Thick as cheesy pudding!" Arlan laughed as Nabo sighed.

"He didn't use quite those words, but I'd never repeat the ones he did! Tik! tik! tik!"

"On you it settled in the bowels," Arlan said to Nabo. "On me, it circled in my head, like a cloud of hornets, and it made me dizzy. I don't like this. Terrible things are passing through the kingdom, all at the behest of our friend, Solofaust, no doubt."

"Solofaust!" Quad sighed. "How could things be worse?"

Suddenly Robin galloped around the bend, hunched low on his horse, swinging his arm in warning and shouting, "The foe! The foe!" As suddenly as he appeared, he disappeared again behind them, shouting as he galloped away.

"He'll ride a mile before he realizes he's passed us," Arlan said, looking after the receding form. "Come back to our hiding places! But this time let's stay together."

The travelers hurried off the road, farther than before, and hid. They waited and soon the sound of marching approached, distant and rhythmic, causing the ground to tremble as it came closer. Soon the rattling and banging of an army hastily on the march reached them on the breeze and not much later the figures appeared. The king had no trouble spying them this time: a large company of men, all heavily armed. Row after row passed, foot soldiers and mounted men, their armor dull in the light fog, their company banners drooping in the still night. Wagons manned by animal folk rolled by between the companies.

"I see Artemus's flag, and the flags of the eastern armies," Arlan said.

"Even Yerushela?"

"Yerushela has no army, outside of those she needs to guard entrances and halls. You can be sure, though, her flag is not among them. See there? Two flags of the Sheolfrost—that's bad, indeed. And look!" (A fine wagon rolled by and seated in it was Solofaust, apparently asleep, his paws and chin resting on his cane.) "You old curmudgeon! If I hadn't the king beside me, I would tickle your nose with an arrow or two!"

The armies passed and the travelers waited another ten minutes, then cautiously led their horses to the road. "I wonder if Robin is all right . . ." Friend Rat began.

"He is an Honor Guardsman," Nabo said, as if that settled the matter.

And the four stood silently, feeling the breeze build up.

"So many men! All of them against us!" Quad moaned, his face pale.

Arlan jumped into his saddle, unsheathing his sword.

"It grows cold and I feel a hint of rain in the sky. Let's find shelter before the dawn catches us. Within two nights we'll reach Magdalawood, and our adventure shall begin in earnest." He glanced at the king and threw him a confident smile. With that he thumped his heels against his mount and galloped away. The others hurried their steeds after him, Friend Rat climbing up reluctantly behind the king. As they rode they heard the pre-rain sizzle of the wind through the trees:

"*Wheeeeeeet!*"

13

elen sat in her chair, her nose buried in her knitting, keeping a careful count of each knit and purl. The tinny staccato of her needles sang a tiny antiphonal to the loud cracks to which she rocked in rhythm.

"There!" came a rough voice, and the sound of cracking stopped. She glanced up, looking annoyed. A hooded, bare-chested man stepped back, gathering his whip into coils as he smiled at his handywork.

Chained at the wrists and ankles to iron links forged into a beam overhead and the floor below, Nellie hung limply, her breath coming in sharp, painful gasps, her features soaked in sweat. Her dress was filthy and torn, her thick, blonde hair hung wet in her face, stinging her eyes, and one cheek and her arms were purple with bruises. For a moment there was only the labored sound of her breathing.

Helen smiled.

Rising to her feet, she lay the knitting down and walked over to Nellie, studying her face for any tell-tale expression. Then she stepped behind her to examine the torturer's work. Nellie's dress had been unlaced and torn open to her waist, where it draped about her hips in folds. Her narrow, firm back was streaked with snake-like welts, puffing and rising from her lightly tanned skin. Blood trickled from cuts on her ribs and shoulder blades, speckling her hanging clothes.

"A very nice job," Helen said. "Where did we ever find you, Darnion?"

"Thank'ee, my lady," the torturer said with a grin and a bow. He wiped a bulging arm across his sweaty brow.

"You've left no marks where they will show, except for welts. And they'll heal nicely enough," Helen was saying. She ran a claw along one welt and felt, with satisfaction, her victim shudder. She stepped in front of Nellie again and held her face in one paw, drawing aside the hair hanging over her eyes with the other. The prisoner's teeth were clenched against the pain and her eyes were red from a mixture of sleeplessness and tears. She had taken this beating soundlessly, determined not to give Helen the pleasure of hearing her scream. Beyond some gasps when the pain was almost overwhelming, she had succeeded. This little victory shone in her eyes.

"Smarts, I'll bet," Helen said, "that whip."

"I prefer its tender touch to yours, old thing," Nellie spat.

"It pains me to see you hurt," the other smiled sweetly. "Why must we continue? Make it easy on yourself. Sign the confession, little girl, and you'll be made comfortable and left alone until Solofaust returns."

"Confess to something I've not done?" Nellie replied with some difficulty. "I'll take my chances in a trial, thank'ee. Solofaust will hear me out and know your treachery. Ye've done this out of nothing but jealous spite."

Again that thin, smug, satisfied smile swept Helen's face. "The evidence I have against you is tight and will hang you, Nell. Why be humiliated in a trial and make things harder for poor Solofaust? Come now, sign the paper."

In answer Nellie spat at Helen and managed a smile.

The opossum stood gazing at her prisoner, her pink eyes brimming with hate, as Nellie's spittle ran down her snout. But when she spoke, her words were void of emotion.

"'Tis getting late, Darnion. I'm going to bed. I'll send some guards to take her to her cell. Give her a few more strokes to keep her company tonight, and rub some salt into those wounds when you're done. I'd hate to see such a pretty back get all infected."

Helen waddled away and Nellie felt Darnion's hand clamp painfully on her shoulder. She tensed herself to steel against the coming lashes. Like stinging demons they came.

With Helen no longer there to spite, the pain proved too much.

She released herself to the luxury of screaming.

Barely twenty feet away Narramoore listened from within the secret passage, his eyes stinging with angry, impassioned tears at every lash. He felt no love for Helen's victim; after all she was a traitor—cold and cunning, quick and slippery, the very one who'd delivered the death-dish to the king. From the ramparts he'd seen her standing idly as guests were butchered around her. She was Solofaust's pet, and for that alone he felt free of any responsibility to help her.

Crack! crack! crack! With each blow he wanted to crash through the wall and hack the torturer to pieces. And Helen? The desire to crush her skull beneath his fingers was strong. But, of course, he could do neither.

I am the Honor Guard—a complicated statement, an admission to the responsibility of difficult choices. Rescuing damsels in distress was a tradition to uphold, and the lore of the Honor Guard reeked of such tales, some of them silly and some of them true. But his duty to the king and the kingdom was stronger. As much as his conscience writhed against it, Narramoore had to tolerate Nellie's beatings.

And she was a traitor, after all.

Her fate was a case of true irony, he thought. She'd helped to plot the downfall of a king and then, through circumstances that were almost comical, had herself become the victim of a conspiracy put together by a friend. Whether that conspiracy worked against Nellie or not, it could only improve the king's situation.

In two days, Solofaust would return from a journey he'd made suddenly to Demio Sway. Helen would have a trumped-up trial awaiting him, and if her charges stuck, the governor would feel betrayed and Nellie would be delivered up to a hasty execution. If Helen's treachery were found out, however, she would be slain. In either case an enemy of the king would be eliminated, and the castle would be thrown into a swamp of confusion and rumor. Solofaust, known to form strong emotional ties to his associates, would likely lose much of his confidence.

And, however it turned out, Nellie's suffering would end. *If she can hang on.* And if *he* could hang on . . .

Narramoore's fingers closed on his sword as another shriek cut through him. This was followed by silence, then a jingling of chains. The beating had stopped, the salt applied, and she was being released. In a moment guards would arrive. Narramoore motioned to a rat crouching beside him, covering its ears. The fellow nodded his head and hurried away, thankful to escape this unpleasant spot. He would see that Nellie had something better than moldy soup tonight, at least. Each night that she had undergone Helen's hospitality, the warrior had made sure warm food was taken from the kitchen and left hidden in her cell. It was a penance of a sort . . . a way to make right his refusal to help her otherwise through her torments. Each day when the guards hauled her from the cell, he or one of his helpers slipped in cautiously and retrieved her empty platter, so obviously she was eating it. While she no doubt wondered from whence it came, at least she had enough sense not to inquire of the matter to her guards. She was a traitor, and he despised her for it. Still no one deserved this kind of torment. Have *compassion*, he reminded himself. *Do not hate.*

I am the Honor Guard.

He glanced at the little latch right in front of him that would cause the passage door to swing open. The torturer would be so surprised, and taking him out would be a pleasure. Narramoore's fingers brushed the latch, then pulled away, and he thought of the trouble this innocent-looking peasant girl had brought about.

For days he had operated a perfect war of harassment against the castle's superstitious staff: showing up in tattered rags in the halls before scullery maids and stable hands, scaring them into thinking ghosts of the rebellion's dead were haunting the palace; taking small weapons from the armory and placing them in other rooms to be discovered by the superstitious guards; invading the kitchen supplies and slipping into the wine cellar where he would open every tap. In the morning File arrived to find himself ankle-deep in a purple sea. He stood there and cried, and even Narramoore had to smile at the sight.

The passages had also given him access to the dungeons, and he had used them well, selecting a handful of the more able folk and positioning them at various listening posts. After several hours he would send them back to their cells where they would not be missed during the daily count. He had also been able to tend to the wounds and some of the hunger of many prisoners.

Things had gone quite well, despite the fact that he had been sharing the passages with Nellie. She had accidentally found an entrance in her room within a day of coming to the castle—only a day or so after his own return. Narramoore had worried at first, but he soon realized she had no intention of sharing her discovery with any of her compatriots. She used the passages only occasionally, and kept to the tunnels that connected the bedchambers, kitchens, stable, and throne room. This meant he could move quite freely in the lower levels and needed only a small amount of extra caution above. Because she assumed that only she was aware of them, Nellie's walk was careless and easily heard in the passages. Narramoore always had time to duck out of sight and watch as she scurried past, her hands full of mugs or platters and a lamp. He marveled at her quickness in figuring her way through the confusing twists and turns of the subterranean halls. She never suspected an Honor Guardsman was sharing her secret.

His plan of attack ran flawlessly until Nellie's discovery was discovered, in turn, by Helen. The opossum, far less trusting than the maid and quick to recognize a way to bring about Nellie's downfall, immediately began a systematic search. Shortly she located every passage on the ground level of the castle, as well as many of those between the walls in the floors above. Most of the lower levels were still unknown to the revolutionaries, including the routes leading to the dungeons, but how much longer would this be so? Narramoore had committed himself to waiting for the badger's return, so that he might learn something of Solofaust's trip and see the results of Nellie's trial. But after that, he would have to abandon Pentatute.

The gruff voices of guards reached his ears. Nellie gasped in pain. Had she been slapped? Thrown to the floor? Her arm violently twisted? He reminded himself not to react: it was a minor hurt, she would survive the incident. Many deaths could be laid at her feet, as well as many sufferings as bad or worse than she was suffering now.

Forget the girl. My duty is to the king.

I am the Honor Guard.

His face became placid. But his knuckles grew white and his hand twitched as it clamped tightly around the hilt of his sword.

Solofaust didn't sleep well. When he dreamed that infernal bat kept poking in, and when it didn't the wagon would discover a rut or a rock and with a merry jolt hauled him awake again. He had finally learned to snooze in spite of the banging and rattling when a rain began. It started as a tolerable drizzle but then became a torrent that he was certain would fill the wagon like a pool.

By noon the weather repented of its downpour and became a drizzle again, and at last it meekly retreated before an angry sun. Solofaust climbed out of the wagon and, shaking himself out, finished the journey on foot, cursing the puddles left by the rain and the horses.

Artemus was in his command tent, a great canvas thing littered with a cot, two stools, a table with a map and lamp, and a litter of dinner bones on a platter. He was wiping his whiskered chin on the sleeve of one arm and sucking the last of the after-dinner grease and juice from his fingers when the governor's horn sounded. With a grunt he rose from his table and wandered to the door. Solofaust, now dried out and looking perkier than usual, was walking toward him flanked by two guards. With a slight smile Artemus saluted.

"Your journey out of the kingdom was both unexpected and a pleasure," he said and after a pause added, "I assume."

"It was both," Solofaust agreed, ignoring Artemus' joke. "I visited our Lord Demio in Ebon Bane, and he advised me on how to handle various problems I've been dealing with." He smiled as he spoke and raised a brow.

Artemus brought his fist to his mouth and coughed, then squared his shoulders and spoke in a measured, cautious tone. "Was . . . uh . . . *I* brought up . . . at all?"

"Indeed! Demio commended our work and urged us to finish taking the land." The badger noticed that Artemus' tone became suddenly informal again but the mocking light in his eyes was gone.

"I'm surprised you didn't go straight from there to Castle Pentatute," the commander offered.

"Castle Nell," the governor corrected, and Artemus raised a brow. "I've renamed it, after my daughter."

"Nell? The fire-haired conspirator? Your daughter?" Artemus laughed. "Come, my lord! She's human!"

"She's like a daughter," Solofaust returned amiably.

"Now, are you going to stand there keeping me out in the weather, or will you invite me in to talk?"

"My tent is yours," the general replied. He called for an aide who quickly removed the remains of dinner, replacing them with mugs of golden mead. The man and the badger sat, clinked the mugs together, and drank in silence. Solofaust watched curiously as Artemus took three or four long draughts and let the mug clank onto the table, sloshing its contents about but not allowing them to spill.

The governor began to question him about the forces and at first Artemus volunteered only an affirmative grunt to the governor's inquiries. But Solofaust was in such high spirits and seemed so interested in Artemus' opinions that the commander's suspicions soon lifted. Before long the two were swapping plans and suggestions; then they broke out a chess board and played well into the night.

"Tell me more about your talk with Demio," Artemus said. "Did the recent—uhm—friction between us come up at all?"

"Ha! It most certainly did! Demio said it was obvious we weren't getting along and that it might be best if one of us were put out of the way. Can you believe it! I told him, 'Pride and animal stubbornness is our problem, and we're certainly big enough to overcome that.' After all, Artemus, I can't run this kingdom without an army to enforce my rule, while a general needs a statesman to give him purpose! The more I've thought, the more I've realized this. So, for our own survival, if nothing else, I've decided to give you more power, and to take you more seriously."

"I'll drink to that!" the general fairly sang.

Indeed you shall, Solofaust thought to himself with a smile. *Indeed, my friend, you shall.*

By morning Artemus was happily inebriated with wine. Solofaust smiled patiently as the general sang.

> Pretty little Maid, Maid in waiting,
> Skip like prunes, the girl I'm dating,
> What? Describe her? Glad to now!
> Graceful as an unmilked cow.

This was followed by a boom of laughter and he drained his mug again, the mead dripping from his mustache.

"A campfire song!" he roared. "My father taught me that as he bounced me on his knee!"

"A very different song."

"Ha ha! Differ'nt, indeed! Sing me a song of your cubhood, Gov'nor!"

"Badgers sing no songs but lullabies, and those are but grunts and gurbles."

"No wonder you're such stiff-headed old poops," Artemus sighed. "More mead?"

"I've had enough."

"Well, dandy for you. But I've just begun!" He tipped the mug to his lips again and stared with cross-eyed disappointment into its emptiness. A guard rapped at the door of the tent.

"Sirs!" he called. "Jerard of the highway patrol wishes to speak with the general."

"Well, show him in!" Artemus bellowed happily.

"This can wait," Solofaust said helpfully. "You're in no condition . . ."

"Nonsense! I'm sober as a tree in britches!"

"As you wish," the badger shrugged.

A moment later Jerard stepped in. A young man in officer's clothing, with blonde hair and alert, blue eyes, he was handsome, except for the numerous scratches and purplish bruises that covered his face. His shield arm and forehead were wrapped in bloody bandages. Seeing him, Artemus and Solofaust jumped to their feet.

"What is this!" the general cried.

"My lords! We've found one of the Honor Guard!" Jerard announced.

"Where? Did you catch him?"

"We have him . . . but we don't."

"What? Speak plain, boy! Can't you see I'm drunk as a rat's mother?" Artemus said.

"Perhaps we should let someone else handle this," Solofaust offered.

"Nonsense! I sober quicker than you think, badger! In a

moment, I'll be dry as a . . . a . . . well, as dry as *something*!
Go on, what d'ye mean you have him, but you don't?"

"Three miles from here, my patrol came upon six riders,
most of them villagers and farmers. There may have been a
deserter, too, I don't know. But one was Narramoore of the
Honor Guard."

"Gregor's captain," Solofaust said thoughtfully.

"I know that!" Artemus snapped.

"I didn't fall on him immediately, but called on him to
surrender."

"Foolish thing to do," Artemus growled.

"I know, my lord, and I'm at your mercy, for it led to disaster. As soon as I hailed him, the rabble who were with
him drew their bows. Before we could react, two of us were
dead and I, myself, was wounded. We charged them, but
Narramoore drew his bow and shot another man before we
could close ranks. Our own bowmen killed one of them,
but the rest broke and took to the woods. We followed, for
we knew if we could catch them we could ruin them in
close combat—you see, Narramoore is more an archer than
a swordsman."

"I know that!"

"And he and the deserter could hardly fight off a whole
patrol."

"Did you catch up with them, then?" Solofaust asked.

"Yes. But not before they holed up in Danes Mill."

"I know the place," Artemus said, tugging at his chin.
"Four miles from here. It's not used anymore and it's falling
apart, a building of stone and narrow windows, from which
one can shoot arrows. The only way in is through a single
door."

"We've surrounded it," Jerard said, "but we can't close in.
One of the walls rises from a river where the water is swift.
Its other sides are open to a field of two or three hundred
feet in any direction. I don't have enough men to storm it.
The few I have would be shot down before we got close to
the mill."

"I see," Artemus said, nodding. To Solofaust's surprise,
he really was sobering up.

"Still, he's in no better a spot, for leaving the mill would leave him just as open to us," Jerard said.

"Your wisdom in handling the mill has saved your rank, Jerard. Hmmm: from here the only way to that mill is through some old, beaten paths, and it's a good four hours' hike," Artemus said.

"This is disaster!" Solofaust jumped to his feet and began to pace. "It would take too long to get a large party there if there are only paths to it, for time is of the essence. Once dark, a man as crafty as Narramoore might slip away."

"Bah!" Artemus shouted. "I'll teach you how to be crafty, and use only my personal guard to do it! Jerard, come along, and I'll show you ways to make a fox flee his den. Are you coming, Badger?"

"I'd only slow you, for I won't ride horses. I'm sure you'll do well, General Artemus."

"Then wish me good hunting!" the general laughed, slapping the badger's back and knocking him onto the stool.

It was a difficult ride to the mill. The trees in these woods were scraggy and shrunken, capable of snagging any bit of cloth or weapon that passed and of whipping at any face. And the briars and thornapples were blessed with health and seemed pleased to dig their briars and thorns into any man's legs or horse's fetlocks. The way was so tangled it was barely a path at all. Artemus' horse picked its way along a surface of ingrown, knotted roots until finally the growth became so dense that Artemus and his official guard tied their horses' reins to the thornapples and walked the last mile on foot. After an unpleasant hike they reached a clearing where a patrolman met them.

"What's the situation?" Jerard demanded.

"Unchanged, sir," the man said, saluting sharply.

Artemus half-listened to the brief exchange, but his attention was primarily directed at the mill. It was a familiar

THE QUEST FOR THE ONEPRINCE   159

site. As a boy he had swum the river barely a mile below it, and when the shiny-headed old miller had shut the place down, young Artemus had brought village girls he aimed to conquer into its upper floors, baiting them with stories of a young soldier's daring. It had been well-sealed from the weather, but of course time had done its damage to the venerable old battle ground. The mill was not sizable in width and breadth, but it was a tall building, some thirty feet high—three stories, he recalled, full of gears and stones and drive shafts, and there was also a basement. *Assuming the river hasn't eroded the wall and flooded it,* he thought. Even from this distance, he could tell the old foundation's mortar was flaking and rotted. *Perhaps the wall has been washed away below the water level already. If so, our friend Narramoore is in a precarious situation at best: if he so much as jumps he could bring the whole thing down on himself.*

The roof was a wreck of beams and wooden shingles with peep-holes that admitted squawking, blue-black starlings. Artemus smiled on seeing this, for he knew he'd found the way to urge the king's band into the open.

"Have your men build a few good fires, and make them smoky enough that old Narramoore'll be sure to see them. Then bring me a flag of truce," he said. "I doubt I'll convince this dog to surrender, but at least a truce will get me close enough to study this 'fortress' better."

The flag was brought and Artemus stepped from the clearing, thrust his sword into the ground and marched slowly across the field, waving the white flag over his head. From the mill a voice cried out.

"That's far enough!"

"Narramoore! You see my flag. I'm an honorable man. Come out." There was no response. "Then, at least come to the door where I can see you."

The door opened and a figure stood, arms crossed, behind it. Artemus couldn't make him out well, but he thought he recognized the clothes and handsome lines of Narramoore's face.

"I've a deal to make with you," the general called. "You're

trapped, and you're smart enough to know it. Make things easy and surrender! We'll do nothing worse to your companions than banish them."

"And what of me?"

"I'm an honest man what won't lie to you. I'll see to it your death is quick and painless."

"Give me a few weeks to think this over!" the other laughed.

"I'll give you an hour, and I'm generous to do it."

"You already know my answer, I think."

"If you make me work to get you out, things won't go so easy for ye. You know I can easily drive you out."

"I also know that your promises are lies. We'll all die, and unpleasantly too, even if we surrender."

"In memory of Gregor I have given you my word! I'd have kept it, and not given a whit to the badger's thoughts! If you choose being broiled in this windbeaten mill, so be it!" Artemus roared. With an oath he broke the flag staff across his knee, threw it to the ground and, turning, stormed back to his sword. This he plucked from the ground and wiped clean on his hauberk.

"Take the best archers and shoot burning arrows through the windows and onto the roof," he ordered one of his personal guard. Turning back to the mill, he squinted to try and make out anyone within its narrow windows, and he pulled a cloth from his belt to polish his blade. "We'll turn this mill into an oven and cut down anyone who tries to escape!"

In minutes blazing shafts shot across the field like hawks of fire. About half bounced off the old walls, setting small blazes in the field or fizzling out in the river, but the rest lodged on the wood-shingled roof or slipped through the window slits.

These small fires fed and grew on the old lumber floors and supports. It wasn't long before flames licked out from the windows and smoke seeped through a million holes in the rotted mortar. The roof creaked and snapped, its charring beams finally buckling and sending the ceiling like a well-aimed comet through the floors below. A billion

crackling sparks shot like frenzied fireflies into the sky, spiraling crazily and dying in flight. Heated stones broke loose
and tumbled from their places. Soon whole sections of wall
collapsed. By midnight Danes Mill was a skeleton of glowing embers and Artemus watched with a frown.

"No one's fled," Jerard said uneasily, standing beside him,
"and we've heard no screams."

"Committed suicide, I suspect, as soon as we shot the
arrows," Artemus grumbled. "We'll poke about the ashes
for their carcasses to be sure when the ruins cool."

With dawn came another rain, this one light and misty.
Cautiously Artemus led the men to the old mill and stood
at the blackened maw where his enemy had mocked him
the night before. The charred remains of a wall still stood
and even most of the doorway was there, all of it giving the
impression of rotted, broken teeth in some dead thing's
lower jaw.

He stepped in. Charred, splintered stumps poked out of
the walls where beams had held floors, each now sweating
dewy beads of rain. The floor he stood on ended two steps
in and there gave way to jagged piles of burnt lumber and
stones in the basement. The hump of a scarred and worn
old millwheel poked through. The basement wall against
the river was puffed in by the surging water and the weight
of the now-skewed wheel. The stone wall had been lined
with boards for additional strength against collapse, and
these leaned heavily against a post. The boards were badly
charred and the post itself was loose in its socket from the
weight of stone and lumber falling against it. Muddy water
trickled through cracks between the boards.

There were no bodies.

Jerard stepped forward to draw attention to this fact, and
the general replied with a hostile look.

"They could well be buried under all this stuff," he
snapped. "If we find just one, I'll leave satisfied, and you
will win the pleasure of digging up the rest." Artemus
didn't like this whining, self-effacing officer and made a
mental note to strip him of his command. Then he turned
to his personal guard.

"Spread out in here and see what you find. Watch your step, men, and keep an eye on that wall against the river. It looks like the only thing holding it back is that one old post, and that could give without warning."

He climbed carefully into the basement and for the next half hour poked about, checking each cranny and nook. Jerard begged out of the search—which was no surprise to Artemus—and remained above at the door.

"Any bodies yet?" Jerard asked.

"None!" Artemus called back. "But I'm certain no one escaped; who could survive this?"

Barimor, the captain of the guard, looked out from beneath a beam and shouted, "Lord Artemus! Over here! I've found a tunnel!"

Jerard watched the searchers buzz about the tunnel entrance as a child might study ants before putting his heel to them. A figure slipped up and touched his shoulder.

"Helen!"

"The plan is working well," she said. "You're nearly a free man."

"I'll be right back in the dungeon, and you with me, if Artemus sees you!" he snapped. "Move out of sight, or I'll throttle you as sure as I did that baker!"

With a compliant grunt she stepped behind the wall, shielding herself from the men below.

"Have they found it?" she whispered to Jerard.

"Just now. Where is our actor?"

"At the far end of the tunnel, wondering why the exit's been sealed, I suspect."

"How efficient," Jerard smiled. "This is the pardon he earns?"

"He's too dangerous. His crime was greater than yours."

"Yes, I've seen him act. Well, I haven't earned my own pardon yet, so leave me." He walked through the door and, checking to be sure Helen was out of sight, called to the general. "Did I hear someone say 'tunnel,' my lord?"

"Indeed," Artemus growled in exasperation. "It seems Narramoore's escaped with all his villains."

"Perhaps they're still inside."

"Not unless they got confused in the smoke and heat, and if they did that, they're all dead. I've known this mill all my life, but I never knew the old man dug a tunnel below it. Where does it lead, I wonder?"

"I had an uncle who was a miller, and he had a tunnel going to a private dock where the grain could be loaded without interference from highwaymen. Perhaps this is such a tunnel."

"There's no dock near here."

"There's an inlet that could serve as one."

"Ah! That would be my old swimming hole, I'll wager. Then get me a torch. I'll take my men through to search for bodies or surprises. You take your patrol to the inlet, if you can do that much, and we'll see where we meet."

"What about the wall?" his captain asked, an edge of nervousness in his voice.

Artemus gazed at the bulging structure critically. "It will hold as long as we'll be gone, I think," he frowned. "Those boards are weak, but the beam will hold them long enough. Even if they do give way, we should be far enough along to outrun the waters to the end."

A torch was brought and the general led his guard into the dark tunnel, each man with his sword drawn. It was cold and clammy in there in spite of the inferno that had raged just a few feet above it. Artemus' skin crawled at the feel of the slimy green fungus that nearly covered the walls and set off a foul odor when singed by the torch's blaze. Kneeling in the muck, he held his torch low to the floor. It had been lined once, he saw, as evidenced by the occasional brick protruding, but the surface had been coated over the years by several inches of clay-like, sticky mud. And in the mud he saw footprints.

"Aye, our friend has been here," Barimor smiled.

"But only one friend," Artemus growled.

"What?" There are at least a half-dozen sets," his captain noted.

"Those are old and set—at least several hours old. Only one set is really fresh." Glancing back to the opening, he added, "Something ain't right."

"Perhaps Narramoore sent the others on ahead when he first found himself cornered in the tower. He's a grand bowman, and he may have thought he didn't need anyone other than himself to hold us at bay, so long's we thought he had others. Then, when we set fire to the mill, he ran through hisself."

Artemus grunted and wandered slowly forward, holding his torch ahead of him.

"'Tis dark as Demio's feathers in here," he growled.

Jerard sat cross-legged by the old door as the men below filed into the tunnel. Pursing his lips in a tight, self-satisfied smile, he signaled to a man sitting on a horse near the edge of the clearing. The rider came forward, unravelling a rope from the pommel of his saddle. When he and the horse had come within twenty feet of the mill's remains, the rider dismounted and led the horse to the doorway.

"There's your target," Jerard said sweetly, pointing to the support post. "Can you get it?"

"Blindfolded!" the man laughed. His rope looped neatly over its tip and he tied the other end to his saddle.

Toads, snakes, irritating, biting little black flies all revealed their presence as the soldiers worked their way through the narrow tunnel. Artemus' face brushed a sagging cobweb and was soaked by its heavy condensation. With an oath he wiped the strands from his face and examined the cocoon of what had apparently been a wasp, before it was trapped, stung, and sucked dry by its eight-legged foe.

A portent?

"Is something wrong, my lord?" Barimor asked.

"Nothin'. Move on. This tunnel has t'end someplace."

"Why can't we see the end?" someone called.

"Takes a bend, p'raps," Artemus muttered. "Let's move."

He listened to the *schlorp, schlorp, schlorp* of his boots pulling the muck, and felt a chill rush through him, more icy than he had ever known. *This dark ain't just black as Demio's feathers,* he thought. *It's thick as 'em, too.*

Jerard tugged on the rope to see that it would hold, then leaned pleasantly against the old doorpost.

"This should be quite a fine game," he chuckled.

Having secured the rope to the horse's saddle, the soldier leaned down toward Helen.

"Now?" he asked.

"No. Wait," she replied, holding her hand up and wandering lazily to the doorway beside Jerard. "We must wait for our actor to send his signal."

A sudden noise, a nervous squeak, and the flash of movement in the farthest reach of the torchlight.

"What's that!" a man cried.

"Who goes there!" Barimor shouted. "Narramoore! Surrender yourself!"

Artemus did not call out, but, clenching his torch tightly in his left fist and stabbing his broadsword with his right, he thrust his body forward. A figure stood before him, his body pressed against the moldy clay of the wall, his eyes wide and his face mushroom-pale in the flickering light, holding a tiny dagger out before him. The general stopped, amazed: this was not a warrior. He was, rather, a stringy, gangly man. His nearly bald pate, bugging eyes, and trembling, spindly limbs connected to an absurdly long torso and his long, feminine fingers interwoven in a prayerful plea, all made Artemus think of a praying mantis quivering uncertainly in a chilly breeze.

"Puh-puh-please!" the man whined as tears streamed down his hollow cheeks. "Oh please, mercy!"

With a growl of disgust Artemus drove his sword into the man's belly until its tip chunked into the wall behind. He twisted the blade and watched as the actor's mouth popped wide. For a moment the only sound from his throat was a frog-like croak. Then it transformed into a tormented scream.

"What's that!"

"Who goes there! Narramoore! Surrender yourself!"

Helen and Jerard looked at each other with satisfaction

as the voices echoed from the tunnel. Distorted and barely discernible they were followed a moment later by a startlingly clear scream.

"I believe our Narramoore look-alike has found the only exit," Jerard mused.

"Indeed. And Artemus and his men are realizing their mistake. Let's show them a similar escape for themselves, now," the opossum said and nodded to the rider. He spurred his horse. The animal strained forward and the rope went taut. The column trembled and shook.

Artemus watched the actor sink to the floor.

"That was one of Narramoore's men?" Barimor gasped.

"No," Artemus replied. "I don't know whose he was." Why had he just stood there, begging and whining? Why hadn't he escaped?

The general stopped cold. Everything tumbled into place. Suddenly trembling with fear and fury, he wrenched his sword free and stumbled over the actor, groping with his hands. The torch's flare illuminated a newly built wall of stone.

"This is the badger's work!" he shouted. "Turn back!"

The column leaned, heaved, and groaned, and the rope attached to it whined in the wind. "It's stronger than we thought," Jerard commented. "I told you we should have cut it part way through."

"Shut up," Helen growled. "It'll give quick enough. But her eyes trailed to the tunnel and she began to wonder.

They stumbled over one another, impeding their own escape. The floor seemed to cling to their soles, trying desperately to hold them back. Artemus' heart crashed in his chest as he stumbled forward, torch held outward. He cursed as he ran and imagined the miserly little badger dancing on the end of his sword. *What a pleasure it will be! If . . .*

The boards creaked and muddy water began to spill in torrents through the seams of the weakened wall. Swirling and rushing through the debris, it was sucked into its only place of escape, the tunnel. Helen watched the glowing embers and scarred chunks of wood wash into the darkness, and heard the cries and shouts growing worrisomely close.

"Pull harder!" she spat at the rider. "If they reach the entrance alive, your head will roll!"

The entrance was in sight, but struggling toward it became increasingly harder. Leading the way, Artemus strained against the sudden rush of angry water, feeling chunks of wood and stone bang painfully against his shins. A soldier yelped as his feet were swept out from under him and the torrent of water washed him away.

"Keep to your feet, men!" the general shouted. "Hang on to anything. Forward! Or we're lost!"

The horse screamed as the rider drove his spurs into its flanks, then lunged forward a final time. With a roar, a crack raced up the length of the beam. It began to splinter at its base.

If he could just reach the entrance, he would be able to climb up on the collapsed floors, and he would be able to pull his men to safety. Jerard and the handful of men who were overseeing this treachery would surrender their lives in a most unpleasant way.

Pull!" Helen shrieked. "Pull!"

The door loomed large and he thrashed through the now hip-deep flood water, grasping at the door frame with his hands. He pulled himself through the entrance. Free!

"My lord!" Barimor cried out behind him.

Artemus spun and grabbed the lunging hand of his captain, who had suddenly been swept from his feet. This sudden shock on his own body nearly tore him loose from his own handhold. He realized he could see none of his other men behind. Were they still coming? Had they been swept away? With a scream he turned and heaved his body forward, pulling himself through the doorway.

At the moment the column gave way, the sound of its ripping was overwhelmed by the thunderous shout of the river as it smashed the wall and raged into the little mill.

For a brief moment their eyes met—Helen's cold glare feasting on Artemus' realization that he was lost. He disappeared as the river banked about the lower walls and crashed upon him, sweeping him, along with piles of stone, soot, mortar, and lumber, back into the brooding hole from which he had nearly escaped.

"A grand show," Jerard commented, his eyes never leaving the fascinating scene. "And how do we follow this?"

Helen nodded silently to an onlooking soldier, who hefted a spear over his shoulder and threw it, impaling a surprised Jerard to the doorpost. Quickly he met Artemus in a traitor's otherworld, while frightened starlings made their raucous calls in the meadow, and the mist changed solemnly to driving rain.

"And so, Artemus . . . is dead!"

His voice choked with proud emotion, Solofaust concluded his speech. He spoke from a high platform made that day of stones and logs and draped with flags and banners. The wide, sloping fields before him were a bizarre mirror of the night sky. Numberless torches reflected off polished helmets and mocked the heavens. The soldiers listening silently were as numberless as the stars of the Milky Way.

"He was a hero of the highest order," Solofaust said, "for he died—and his personal guard with him—valiantly, fighting the enemies of our new kingdom!"

For the past hour he'd spoken, eloquently and profoundly as only a badger could, recounting the glorious history of the rebellion, embellishing here for effect and excluding details there for the sake of impression. He was especially generous toward Artemus' part in the war, playing up his role in the slaughter at the feast and describing, in a stirring account, his courageous advance into the enemy-held tunnel at the mill.

"It was a tragedy—a great tragedy—that the pillar gave way. You can be sure the man who allowed it to happen has been permanently relieved of his command.

"You mourn, for you have lost an excellent commander," he finished at last, tears in his eyes. "But I . . . have lost . . . a friend."

The soldiers responded with cheers, whistles, and shouts, stamping their feet. But as the minutes drew on, the steady drone changed pitch and the happy cries honoring Artemus' memory turned to wails of mourning at his death. Solofaust suppressed a smile. *You are gullible fools and mindless bullies*, he thought, *as willing a set of pawns as anyone could ask*. He stood patiently as the dirge rolled on, and after it had crested, he spoke again.

"Though we honor him tonight, we must remember that the quest to which he gave his life is still unfinished. Our enemy is free, while our greatest glory is yet to come. Artemus laid the groundwork. Now it is up to us to continue his plan by capturing the criminal king and the cutthroats who protect him. This will be accomplished swiftly and easily, for we have a new commander-general, generously sent by our friend, the Dark Lord of Demonia."

At the back of the stage, a tall, dark figure was waiting. It stepped boldly onto the platform and an audible gasp rose from the forces below, for the soldiers had never seen such an imposing figure. Nor had Solofaust, who found himself suddenly dwarfed in the pool of its immensity; even his spirit was somehow cowed by the thing's power, which seemed to emanate through its pores.

The commander-general was tall—nearly eight feet, and wore a tightly fitting black uniform over its great, muscular frame. About its shoulders, fastened by a brooch with the carrion symbol of Demio, was a cape of ebony velvet, whipping about as though it were at odds with the wind— except there was no wind this night. The lining of the cape was colorless. In fact, it possessed an absolute absence of light, as though it were a dark, consuming hole in the fabric of space. Solofaust did not doubt that, were he to throw a candle into the blankness, it would be sucked into some spirit-dimension and snuffed from existence.

While its clothes defined the shape of its body, the

commander-general's flesh was not exposed at any point. Perfectly formed gloves gave evidence of long, powerful fingers and leathery boots crackled and sparked whenever they touched down, as if the ground itself were in protest of the thing's existence. Most frightening of all was the vast emptiness that filled the cowled hood. During their conversations, Solofaust had found himself staring hard at that, and the creature seemed to enjoy his rude attention. The darkness within the hood was the same Solofaust had seen in the lining of the cape. And from deep within that blackness—seemingly miles away—two eyes glowed like hot embers with a mocking, unnatural light. This costume, the badger realized, held the creature's energy rather than any physical form. Were he to seize its glove and pull it off, he would find only empty air.

No, not empty air. But . . . what? The thing was not of this world, not even of another world. It was . . . what? A hole to another world? This was no physical being, but a walking portal, a door allowing access for the spirit-things Demio had fetched from his Ebon Trist. *Badger, old fool, what have you aligned yourself with now?*

"Thank you for your kindly introduction, Solo-faust," the commander-general said, as it stepped forward, its voice deep and hollow as if originating from within a cave. "I shall review my army."

"It is yours," Solofaust replied and stepped hurriedly aside.

It stood at the edge of the stage and gazed over the men, badgers, and rats that made up the forces. There was not so much as a whisper from anyone as they stared at this new thing.

"I am strange to you," it said, its voice filling the air with a bassy resonance. "You see that I am strong, but you do not understand me, and so you fear me. This is well, for anyone who betrays or disobeys me shall pay with far more than his life. I am your Commander-General!

"Obey me and love my master and all shall go well, for

with me you are invincible! Hear this!" it added with a shout that cracked like thunder, "I am your Commander-General, sent to protect your governor and to win your land! How shall that be done? We will crush every sign of the enemy, eliminating anyone or thing that threatens us! Some cities have not joined us. We shall storm them, then, and what is theirs will be your plunder, and every inhabitant will be sold or slain.

"Redaemus is your spoil, my brave children! We are at war with the remnants of an idiot king, a backward, moralistic maggot who enslaved you. Everything in the land carries his pollution but we will cleanse it. You'll claim for yourself its riches, its fields and villages, the shops and food, the beasts and women! Why? Because you are loyal and love the Dark Lord . . . and in this way he thanks you. Think of Quad. He would not serve Demio, nor would Prince Gregor. Where are they now? Cowering in some forest like hunted rabbits!

"But behold Solo-faust! He served the Dark Lord well and so he governs half a kingdom. Give me your oaths, your loyalty! Then Redaemus will be yours!"

The soldiers cheered wildly, and the commander-general basked in their exultation. It raised its arms and the crowd turned silent as stone.

"Do I have you?" it shouted.

"AYE!" The response was deafening.

"Then begin tonight! for the enemy is among us even now!" The soldiers grew quiet again, each looking at his neighbor, and the governor raised a curious brow. "Why, the human, rat, or badger standing beside you might be a friend of the idiot king! Yerushela has not sided with us. In fact, it has armed its entrances against us!"

The listeners responded with thunderous shouts of anger.

"They are criminals and despots who refuse the enlightenment of the new order! They are the ancestors and brethren of Quad and Gregor, and that cursed creator of the Laws, Pentatutinus! Can they ever change?"

The shouts turned to roars.

"Their brethren, the scum of the Eastern Plains, are just like them!"

The soldiers were consumed with righteous hysteria, and still the commander-general's voice rang out.

"Easterners are among you now. They are traitors wearing your very uniforms! They are Quad's puppets in your armor! Can we let this be?" it shouted. "You know who they are! Slay them, my warriors! Begin your heritage tonight! Deliver these enemies' heads to me and we shall hang them as trophies from the castle walls!"

A clatter of metal sounded as swords were drawn. The Easterners found themselves in a desperate fight as the host of soldiers became a writhing, agonized worm, gouging itself and emitting shrieks of agony and blood-lust. Appalled, Solofaust raced from the scene to his tent. Still, he couldn't avert his eyes from the carnage. The commander-general stood before its men, waving its hands about. Streams of fire trailed from its fingertips, bathing the night in a pulsing light. It laughed in wild euphoria as the field turned red with the sacrifice of men. The stage erupted into fire, and the commander-general stood unaffected in the withering heat.

◆

A day later the castle was decorated with the gore of Easterners' heads on poles. Solofaust sat upon his throne, listening to the commander-general as it paced back and forth before him.

"You see what a weapon words can be, Solo-faust? A word of passion here, a titillating promise there, and in a night I've driven love, fear, and respect into this army's soul."

"With a few ill-chosen words you've driven needless swords into many bellies," the badger muttered, looking away.

"Strange that you should complain of spilled blood."

"I've spilled blood a-plenty of late, Commander-General, but for a higher purpose. I killed so that a good end might be reached. You brought about a slaughter of innocent men, and there was no purpose in that."

"Bah! They were Easterners," the commander-general scoffed, waving its hand.

"Very few Easterners are from Yerushela—they live in the plains about that isolated city. Fewer still are for the king."

"Better we kill a thousand innocent than chance a guilty one going free, Solo-faust. Besides, a purge is good for morale and makes a fine warning to others who might otherwise be tempted to stir up trouble."

"You realize that many of them escaped," Solofaust said.

"They'll be caught. I've sent my spirit-guard after them, and any that are taken will be used for our nourishment. We don't lose our prey so easily, as you shall see when Quad is found."

"And you'll see he's found by my agents, not yours."

The commander-general snorted. A guard slipped cautiously into the great hall.

"A thousand pardons," he begged, his eyes never leaving the spirit-thing, "but there's someone says he must see you, Lord Solofaust."

"Send him in," the badger commanded, thankful for a distraction.

Wheeeeeeet! came a sound from the hall, and Solofaust laughed.

"I believe our king has been found!"

"You're so sure?" the spirit-thing said.

"That is my best spy now, the fates help me!"

The Rat Mugby came rushing in and, spying the commander-general, stopped suddenly, tripped over his tail, and landed with a splat on the floor.

"I can't believe how good it feels to see you!" Solofaust chuckled.

"Wheeeeet!" the Rat Mugby replied, gawking at the commander-general.

"Don't mind him. A friend. Commander-General, this is the Rat Mugby."

The commander-general bowed, and the rat did likewise, nearly banging his head on the stone flagging. Then he rushed to the throne, regaining the excited air he'd first entered with.

"Solofaust! Solofaust! I have a report for you! Great news! Gre*aaaaaaaat!*"

"You've found the king and Gregor?"

"Yes! I mean, no! I mean, maybe!"

"Make up your mind!"

"I know where they are! Sort of!"

"This is your best spy?" the commander-general laughed.

"He knows where the king is. He just doesn't know how to talk," the badger snapped. "Rat Mugby! Explain yourself before I smack you!"

"Wh*eeeet!* I followed them . . . I mean, I followed Quad and the counselor. Gregor wasn't with them. He went north. To Sheolfrost, I think. But Quad and the rat were with some of the Honor Guard. Which ones? Oh yes! There was Arlan and two others named Robin and Nabo. Or was it Nabo and two others named Arlan and Robin? 'Tis a thing of rank and should be said proper. It could have been Arlan and Nabo and . . ."

"On with it!"

"They were going east, and last I saw, they went into Magdalawood."

"Magdalawood!" Solofaust echoed. "They must plan to hide there."

"No," the commander-general said, "not hide. They seek someone."

"Who?"

"A certain Oneprince."

"Chasing after some character from a folktale?" Solofaust said with a smile. "This king is losing his mind if . . ." Suddenly his mouth dropped and his eyes lit up. With a victorious smile he turned slowly to the commander-general. "Or is he a folktale? Is this who Demio fears? Is this why he refuses to leave Ebon Bane?"

"He fears no one!" the spirit-thing shrieked, storming toward him. The Rat Mugby squealed and dropped behind the throne. The badger, though shaken, didn't move.

"Of course he doesn't," he confirmed, managing to keep his voice casual.

The spirit-thing stopped inches away, glaring. "Demio is merely cautious. Until the king is caught and the Ruby Scion seized there is . . . some danger, should Demio leave Ebon Bane."

"And this Oneprince?"

"Is no danger at all, so long as Quad doesn't find him."

"Could he be in Magdalawood?"

"No. I suspect they are seeking counsel of some sort. Magdalawood is, after all, enchanted."

"By a wizardess named Iscara," the Rat Mugby said.

"And they're already in the wood. We've great problems, Commander-General, if they've a wizardess on their side."

"Iscara, a wizardess?" the spirit-thing spat. "She's nothing but a bag of child's tricks and illusions. I'll collect the armies, Solo-faust. With a third I'll surround Magdalawood, with another build up the siege of Yerushela, and with the remainder cover the ground between. Sooner or later the king will come out, and when he does we'll take him. My own spirit-guard will return to you occasionally to be sure you're protected."

Or watched, Solofaust thought.

$\mathbb{T}$he week had been long and troublesome, and though his mound of pillows and blankets called yearningly, still Solofaust had a desire for wine and banter with a friend before he retired. He'd just gone to the bell ropes to ring for Nellie when a low figure appeared at the door.

"Solofaust," Helen said, her pink eyes darting nervously.

"Helen! I meant to congratulate you on your work at the mill, and to thank Jerard as well. Where is he?"

"He begged leave to go to his people, my lord. Now, you'd best come to the throne room. I've collected undeniable evidence of a traitor in our midst—and the creature must be dealt with now!" At that she turned and waddled down the dark hall, leaving Solofaust, his whiskers quivering, at the bell-pull.

While Artemus was singing ballads to an appalled badger in his tent, the fugitives came upon the foreboding rim of Magdalawood. Reaching open ground, they abandoned the roads and traversed the hilly fields. Cresting a last high, grassy hillock, the enchanted forest sprang into view.

It was a forest of immense trees, their formidable trunks towering to the sky. The king, awestruck, reined his horse to a sudden stop. Friend Rat, who came panting from behind, stopped as well and wrapped his tail about his nose—a sign of wonder for a rat—and gasped, "My goodness!"

"This is Magdalawood?" said the king.

"There's no wood like it," Arlan boasted, turning in his saddle and cocking his head with schoolboy pride. "It guards the way to the Eastern Plains!" He clicked at his horse and trotted after Nabo and Robin, who waited at the bottom of the hillock.

"You forgot something," Nabo said, grinning, and hitching his thumb over his shoulder. Arlan wheeled about; the king and his counselor were still above, staring into the wood.

"Blast!" Arlan spat. "Go ahead, you royal idiots; just stand up there like a pair of signal flags!" He waited a moment, his horse prancing nervously beneath him. "Sire!" he called. "You! Rat! Blast, they're under the looking spell."

"The looking spell?" Robin asked.

"If you look too long or too hard upon Magdalawood, you'll become as still as the trees. Old fishwives say you'll eventually become trees," Arlan explained. "Easterners' patrols have found a whole dozen folk at a time under the spell. Those two have never seen a forest that was more than toothpicks with branches. So of course Magdalawood would catch their attention!"

"You should waken them before a patrol comes," Nabo warned.

"Shall we wait for you?" Robin asked.

"No," Arlan sighed. "It would be disrespectful of someone your age to watch a king get his seat booted. Ride ahead, the two of you, on that path, there . . . Do you see it?"

Nabo scanned the forest edge, a wall of crabapple and thornwood guarding the great oaks beyond. The branches of the trees laced together in a thorny arch over a trail.

"There?" he asked, pointing.

"Yes. Go a mile or so and set up camp. We'll arrive sooner or later."

Arlan climbed the crest as Nabo and Robin disappeared into Magdalawood. Quad still sat on his horse with the counselor beside him, his tail looped about his snout and a bumble bee inspecting his nose. Arlan snapped his fingers before the king's eyes and waved his hand, but Quad continued staring. Arlan grabbed one spike of Quad's crown and gave it a royal shake. The king sneezed violently and clutched at the reins, looking wildly about.

"Ah! Oh! Arlan! What . . . ? Where is everyone?"

"Those fools are down in the wood where they think they won't be seen," the other replied, folding his arms and smiling slightly. "Of course, *we* know 'tis far wiser to hide in a more obvious place, since the enemy overlooks those—such as the top of this hill, which can be seen for five miles about."

"I don't know," Quad said slowly. "I wonder if perhaps Nabo and Robin have the better idea . . ."

At that Arlan cursed sharply and wheeled his horse about.

"Arlan!" Quad called to his retreating back, "I didn't mean to upset you . . . of course it was foolish to stand here like this! I don't know what came over me . . . I was . . . I don't know, surprised to see a wood looking like this. All those trees."

Arlan stopped and looked back.

"Yes, seeing all those trees in a wood is odd. Magdala-wood is unique in that it has trees. Of *course* it has trees! What did you expect? Corn stalks and ribbons?"

"I mean that there's something odd about this forest."

"'Tis enchanted, as were you," Arlan said, calming some. "Forgive my tongue, Sire. I should've warned you. Now, let's join the others."

"Let me rouse the counselor first," Quad said, grinning foolishly.

They heard a shriek and Friend Rat came bouncing between them, squealing and pinching his swollen nose as the bee buzzed away.

"It seems he's been roused already!" Arlan laughed. "Let's go!"

As they passed under the thorns, the king looked about, still amazed by the trees. Many climbed hundreds of feet, their trunks the size of houses. Vines as thick as a man clung lazily to their bark or hung in massive loops from high branches. Sunlight fell like shards of cathedral glass through the budding boughs, giving dismal green mosses a colorful hue and capping the dreary brown mushrooms with golden glory. In a few days the leaves would awaken, yawn, and stretch, spreading a spring canopy over this earthy shrine.

"I don't like this place," Friend Rat said.

"I doubt if it likes us," Arlan replied.

"Even I can feel it," Quad agreed. "'Tis beautiful but oppressive. The trees seem to be watching us."

"How ghastly!" The rat shuttered.

"You can be sure Iscara knows we're here," Arlan said. "I hope she'll take to us kindly."

"We've been riding for some time. Where are Robin and Nabo?" the king asked.

"I told them to ride a mile or so, which is deeper than any patrol will be willing to go in this wood."

"Certainly we've ridden *two* miles."

"You've *ridden* two miles, but I've *walked* a thousand," the counselor groaned.

"We've gone five, at least," Arlan agreed. "This is strange, indeed."

"Perhaps they turned down another path."

"Look about you, Sire. We've passed no turn-off." Arlan stopped his mount and jumped from the saddle. "But you know, I don't see their tracks, and the earth is soft enough that they would have left them."

"Could we have passed them?"

"They'd have been watching the road and stopped us."

Quad climbed gingerly from his horse.

"I'd say we have a problem, Arlan."

"I wouldn't," Friend Rat said. "That would be so depressing. Tik! tik! tik!"

Arlan glanced up at the sun.

"It'll be dark soon. There's no sense our going any further tonight. Let's set up camp and sleep on this matter. Perhaps it'll make sense in the morning.

"Gather some branches, Rat, and we'll get a good blaze going."

They took turns at watch, and when the trees became silhouettes against the rising sun, Quad shook Arlan, who sat up quickly.

"Something is wrong," Quad whispered. He saw Arlan's hand grasp his sword. "Not in that way—I don't mean as in enemies about. There's something wrong with the trees."

"What are you talking about?" Arlan asked irritably, looking about. *The trees? Has this cracker of a king been dreaming?* he wondered.

"I think they've moved," Quad whispered.

"I think your crown needs another good shake," Arlan replied.

"Look about."

"I am, and the trees look the same."

"These right here do. But look at the trees farther down the path. I think they've moved."

Arlan rose to his feet, mumbling poetic epitaphs, and nearly stumbled over Friend Rat who snored softly in an old oak's roots. Resisting an urge to give the furry fellow a boot, Arlan exchanged glances with the king and walked down the path, frowning. *I could be guarding the border, watching for Demio,* he thought. *Instead, I'm nursemaid to a king who sees trees walking like men.* He stopped abruptly at one tree and studied it, an uneasy chill running down his spine. His frown deepened. Turning around, he was startled to see Quad beside him.

"You know I'm right," the king said.

"I know that trees don't move, Sire. And these are so large that, if they did, we'd have heard them. And they would've left holes big enough to live in from dragging their roots about."

"Then what's wrong? There's *something* different about them. I can sense it."

"You couldn't sense things a few nights ago that left me shivering. Why can you now?"

"I don't know," the king replied, and glanced at the Ruby Scion. "At least, I don't think I do. But I do know something is wrong."

"So do I," Arlan reluctantly agreed.

"About the trees."

"Yes."

Arlan stepped back on the path and looked over his right shoulder at the rising sun, casting its palette of oranges and reds. Suddenly he shuddered and his face turned white.

"This path faces north!" Arlan said slowly.

"So?"

"Yesterday it faced east."

They looked at each other, a dark fear creeping up their spines.

Friend Rat wandered up, rubbing his eyes.

"Well, where is breakfast, you two?" he asked, then saw their expressions and looped his tail about his snout. "Oh dear! Now what?"

"I do believe our trees changed the path in the night," Arlan said.

"Rather unfriendly of them, don't you think?" the counselor commented.

"Then that's how we lost the others," Quad reasoned. "After they passed through, the trees shifted to make a different path for us. We could be miles apart!"

"Perhaps we'd best go back the way we came," Friend Rat said uneasily.

"If these trees can alter the path ahead, they can do the same behind," Arlan replied. "We could follow the sun to get out, but in such a dense forest, who knows what would happen? I'll ride back a little ways, to see how much the trees have changed things. If the path is still the same behind us, we'll take it to the edge of Magdalawood and see if Nabo thought to do the same." He climbed onto his horse. "You two wait here and start breakfast. I'll be back within the hour."

They started breakfast, and waited.

The hours passed, but Arlan didn't return. The worried king and his counselor found themselves watching the sun drop behind the trees.

"Do you think he's lost?" Friend Rat asked.

"No, I think he's met a fair maiden, married her, and that he'll return when the honeymoon ends."

"Sarcasm! Tik! tik! tik!"

"We're alone again!" Quad nearly wailed.

"Don't say that, Sire. Take courage! Something will come along, sooner or later."

"Yes, many things have, lately. A crown I don't want, a rebellion I don't need, an Unseen Presence I can't feel, an entire army out to kill me, and now these giant trees with nothing better to do than mix up the paths at night. I look forward to the next thing coming along. I really do."

"Around every cloud there's a silver lining."

"Inside every silver lining there looms a cloud."

"Oh! Stop feeling sorry for yourself. It isn't kingly! 'Tis a lovely forest, after all. The trees are mischievous, but at least they haven't stomped on us, or talked."

"So! What do we do now?"

"Why ask me? You're the king."

Quad looked sadly at his sceptor.

"Yes. I'm the king. You know, I always get such a feeling when I gaze at this. It seems to have a . . . a power about it."

"The Ruby Scion? I'm not surprised. 'Twas the key to your father's power. He always said your Oneprince gave it to him, long ago. There's never been another gem like it, and the only one even near its worth and magic is the Ebon Trist, which of course is held by Demio. When the Scion glowed crimson, Pentatutinus said, it alone held Demio in sway."

"Then why did it fade?"

Friend Rat shrugged. "We know only that it faded as the king did, and at the same time the folk of the kingdom started losing their respect and love for him. Whether the fading caused the sickness, or the sickness caused the fading, no one can say."

"And still it fades," Quad said, turning the scepter in his hand and trying to find the spark deep within. "Well, I'll unpack the bedrolls from Spindle Legs again and free him to graze. I'd tether him for the night, but the tree would probably walk off with him. As for us, we'd best get some sleep."

They awoke early the next morning, but neither had slept well. They'd both been too busy staring at the trees. They had a cold breakfast ("Make a fire," the king said, looking forward to a hot drink. "You make it!" the counselor retorted. "About the time I light a fire, one of these trees will use me to beat it out!"), then they gathered their bedrolls and tied them to Quad's horse, Spindle Legs.

"I wonder what's happened to the others?" Quad wondered wistfully as they walked down the path.

"Oh, I'm sure they're in no worse situation than we, and really I'm rather glad 'tis just the two of us again."

"Why?"

"With no boasting warriors about, 'tis like old times."

"We need their protection," Quad said.

"I'll admit they got us through dangers well enough, 'til now. But we won't need them once Iscara finds us, for her spells will protect us. In any case, a pocketful of warriors will be useless if we're found by a whole army."

"Still, I enjoyed their company."

"Hmph! All that stuff about honor and heroics. I'll take the company of rats anytime. Give me a tavernful of them, laughing and singing and telling their tales."

"You took me to such a place once," the king said, laughing. "I never heard such prattle and nonsense. The minstrel told stories without plots or endings."

"'Tisn't the plot that counts in rat-folk, but the feeling!" the counselor protested. "'Tis a feeling one rarely gets elsewhere."

"Not since I had the croup," the king agreed.

Friend Rat seemed not to hear him.

"I've scrutinized the works of the Rat Wugwart and once I even considered learning the rat-minstrel's trade. I'd have made a grand one!"

"I'm sure!"

Their conversation was stopped by a sudden voice. "Where do you think you're going?" it said.

The king and the rat looked at each other.

"Did you say that?" they asked together. Then both answered, "No! It wasn't me!" They dove into the bushes beside the path.

"Get out of here! Leaf!" the voice commanded.

"We're found out!" Friend Rat squealed, wrapping his tail about his snout. "I just know we're found out!"

"Not by Solofaust's men," Quad whispered. "Listen! That's no soldier. The voice is too high and strained."

"If you don't come out of there by the count of three," the voice called, "I'll stop believing in you. *Then* you'll be in a fine pickle!"

The companions exchanged glances.

"In fact, if you don't come out, I believe I'll chop you to ribbons!"

In spite of its threats, the voice seemed reassuringly harmless. And so, wielding his scepter like a club, the king stepped into the open.

"I'm in the path now, rogue!" he shouted, noticing how good it felt to be bold. "Now you step out! We'll see who chops who!"

"Who chops who! That's terrible. 'Tis 'Who chops *whom*,' you young yak."

"Show yourself!" Quad roared furiously.

"I am! I'm practically under your tree branch of a nose—"

"Aaaargh!"

"And why you haven't run is beyond me. I'm making a terrible face."

Livid with rage, the king looked about, seeing no one. Then the counselor poked his head out of his cover.

"Excuse me, Sire, but I believe you're conversing with this bush," Friend Rat said.

"Don't be ridiculous," Quad snapped. But, looking down, he realized that he was, indeed talking to the bush they'd been hiding behind.

"And a very furious bush at that!" the bush said. "Furthermore, I'm not a bush. I'm a tree, and I'm the Guardian of the Wood."

Seeing the scrubby fellow, Quad's anger drained away, and it was all he could do not to laugh. The Guardian of the Wood wasn't exactly a tree. It had a human look about it, with arms that were folded indignantly and fingers (though these were quite long and buds were growing out of the joints). The face was human-like, though it had a carved look about it, and a twig grew off the side of the nose. Still, from its arms down, it was definitely a tree, covered with bark and rooted to the ground. A shock of twigs instead of hair sprouted from the head.

"You . . . guard this forest?" the king asked, amazed.

"I believe I do."

"You aren't sure?"

"I said 'I believe I do,' didn't I? Just so. I believe I do. And believing makes it so."

"Who appointed you?"

"Iscara."

The king and counselor exchanged glances.

"It seems she'd choose someone a little, uhm, bigger," Quad said.

"Looks are deceiving. I can crush horses in my boughs."

Looking him over, the king doubted he could crush butterflies.

"Can you uproot yourself and move about?"

"Don't be ridiculous. Trees can't do that," the bush replied.

Quad thought of the larger trees that had been so much trouble, but chose not to argue the point.

"And Iscara has appointed you guardian."

"I believe that's true."

"You're not sure?" Quad said again.

"I *said* I believe so!" the bush shouted, "and believing makes it so! Don't you listen? Are those ears on your head, or gears to turn your eyeballs?"

"How does someone as small as you, rooted to the ground, guard this big forest?" Quad asked.

"I yell, 'Go away!' as folk walk by. And I make this terrible face. It scares them dead."

"It didn't scare us dead," Friend Rat pointed out.

"Well, I didn't believe it would."

"Yet it's scared everyone else dead?" Quad asked.

"I believe it has."

"No one else simply walks away without noticing your scary face?"

"If they do, I simply believe they never came by at all. That takes care of the matter."

"How?"

"The fact that anyone goes by is a fact only so long as I believe it. If I choose not to believe it, then 'tis a fact no longer. Reality is what you make it."

"And if we walk down this path, as if we hadn't heard you . . ." Quad began.

"You'd better not try, for I won't let you!" the bush said, putting its most terrifying expression on its face.

"But if we do?"

"I don't believe you will. So even if you do, you won't, and there's an end of it."

"Tik! tik! tik!" Friend Rat exclaimed. "What if we don't believe in you?"

"That's *your* problem."

"But you won't exist then, will you?" the counselor persisted.

"Of course I will. I believe I will."

"But we'll believe you won't, and believing makes it so!" Friend Rat began to wind his tail about his snout for extra security.

"I'll counter by believing otherwise!" the bush said, his broughs furrowed. " 'Tis my beliefs alone that matter. I believe that. I truly do."

"This is confusing," Quad said.

"I find it fascinating!" the rat replied.

"I'm not surprised. Guardian, why don't you believe yourself out of being a tree and become a man?"

"I don't believe I should."

"Why don't you?"

"I don't believe I should! And there's an end of it! Some things I do believe I should—and there's an end of that, too."

"You believe that, do you?" the king asked.

"I do," the guardian said thoughtfully, then confirmed itself. "Yes, I believe I do."

Quad broke out in a grin.

"This tree's got brambles on the brains. I believe that. And if we stand here much longer, we'll grow brambles in our brains. I believe that, too." He started up the path and

Friend Rat, after an apologetic shrug toward the Guardian, ran after him.

"Wait!" the Guardian shouted. "I told you I wouldn't let you go away like that! You're dead, the two of you! I believe you're going to drop dead in your tracks, right now! You idiots! Go ahead and walk on! You don't even know you're dead! Everybody I kill goes on like that! This world is full of folk who don't even know they're walking corpses! I believe that! I do!"

The night air turned cold while frost covered the forest floor like moss, its spidery lines glazing the bark and ferns under a clear, pale moon. Fearing the wrath of the trees, Quad and Friend Rat didn't light a fire, but sat huddled beneath the towering oaks. Quad shivered and contemplated his steamy breath while the counselor, looking cozy, rocked gently back and forth on his toes, crooning a ballad.

> Where is the rattie I love so dear?
> Far away tonight.
> Tell her I love her and bring her back
> So I may hold her tight.
>
> What is the use of love, I say,
> For a lonely rat?
> The only true love I ever did have
> Was lately et up by a cat.

"A haunting ballad," he sighed, daubing a tear. "And its tale is rather chilly."

"I'd think any rat's tail is chilly, hairless as it is," Quad growled. "How can you be so warm? Every muscle and bone I have is rattling with the cold!"

"You forget, Sire, that rats are equipped with fur. 'Tis that which keeps us warm, and saves us bundles of time on laundry to boot. I rather think humans would be better off with fur too—they wouldn't be so clammy to touch."

"It would take me all day to shave!" Quad said, "and I hate to shave!"

"How do you know if you hate shaving?" Friend Rat queried.

"What's that supposed to mean? I shave! I'm a man!"

"Tik! tik! tik!" the counselor sighed, gazing at the moon.

"Well, nearly so! I'm twenty, you know!"

"Eighteen!"

"Whatever!"

"Some men couldn't shave if they were thirty."

"What!" Quad shrieked.

"Listen to that. Are you sure you've passed puberty?" Friend Rat asked.

"Are you insinuating something? Why, just three days past I shaved, and now my chin feels rough as sandstone."

"Blackheads," the counselor suggested.

"Take that back!"

"Sire! I said nothing!"

"You always say nothing! You spend hours saying nothing! Now take it back! I, your king, command you!"

"Tik! tik! tik! That's right, you are the king. Now get a hold of yourself! A king must be mature. Think of your kingdom!"

"What kingdom? I'm monarch to a singing rat and mischievous trees. Here I sit in a castle of roots, with only four soldiers in an army of thousands willing to protect me—and they've all disappeared."

"Something will develop!" the counselor promised.

"Probably frostbite."

"Tik! tik! tik! Such a long face! So much pessimism! Things *could* be worse . . ."

"Hey!" a rasping voice interrupted them.

They jumped with a shout, for the harsh voice was not their own.

"W-who are you?" Quad called, trying to recapture the bravery he'd shown with the Guardian of the Wood. Friend Rat stepped quickly behind the king.

"What're ye doin' in my lay-dee's wood, hey? Hey!" the voice called again.

Its source was not far off, Quad thought, holding the Ruby Scion to his breast, but in the stark moonlight, he could see nothing. Suddenly a figure appeared, not three feet away, stepping from behind a tree. It was a bent and crooked old hag leaning heavily on a stick which she used to whack Quad across the shins.

"I asked ye a question, hey! Who are ye? Why're ye here?"

"Who are you?" Quad countered, taking two steps back. But with every step he took, nearly falling over Friend Rat as he did, the hag followed him and whacked some more.

"I'm me lay-dee's, that's who I am, hey!" she rasped. "She wants t' know who's in 'er wood, she do! Stand still!"

"Your lady—that's Iscara?" Quad asked.

"Aye! She saw ye enter, she did!" the hag said, then fell into a deep, lung-wrenching, hacking cough that continued several moments.

Peering at her closely, Quad decided that only her stick was dangerous, and it no more so than a schoolteacher's switch. She was not tall, although she was very round and bent, and her whole body seemed cockeyed. The hag's left shoulder was a good six inches lower than her right, and a hump swelled like a hill between them. Her gray, splotched skin was creased with warty folds of wrinkles, while hair, as fine as spider webs and as yellow as rotted corn silk, spilled in disarray from the hood of a heavy, monk-like robe. Her nose was squat, bumpy, and round, looking much like the tulip bulbs Quad planted each spring. Everything about her was repulsive save one. From deep within the wrinkles of her face, two eyes peered out like tiny green fires, dancing with a mocking, youthful light. They were the most beautiful he had ever seen, but they seemed especially strange and frightening set in such a withered face.

The hacking diminished, and everyone felt a little better with the passing of this storm. The hag thumped her stick on the ground as Quad half-danced to avoid having his toes crunched.

"I know ye, hey!" she gurgled. "Hey, I do! Ye're King Pentatutinus' son, ye are! What? Did he send ye here for a love potion? To find ye a lay-dee to fall in love wi' ye? Hey? Is that it?" (She poked Quad with each question, her sharp, lumpy nail rapping a staccato thump against his belly.) "Well, a potion'll cost ye."

The hag waited for a response, but the amazed king could give none. Taking this for an answer of another sort, her eyes widened until the jade pupils within them seemed like great, circular islands in a perfectly white sea.

"Aowww! I know it now! Ye're here t' seek me lay-dee's hand, hey? Hey? Hey!" And at that she crackled into gasping coughs and gales of laughter.

Quad's jaw dropped and his face turned crimson. From behind, Friend Rat was tapping his foot and wringing his tail. Finally, clicking his tongue angrily, he stepped from behind his king.

"Tik! tik! tik!" the rat scolded. "Why, you don't know a thing at all! We came to see Iscara on our own; no one sent us! What's more, Quad is king, not Pentatutinus. Pentatutinus is dead."

The hag abruptly stopped coughing. She looked quickly at the counselor, and then at Quad.

"Dead?" she whispered softly, the rasp strangely gone from her voice. Then, frantically, she jabbed her stick at the king, shouting venomously while her voice cracked like lightning.

"Dead, hey! Hey? Dead!"

Quad could only nod and back away.

Stopping her attack as quickly as she'd started it, the hag stared at the king and his counselor, then turned away and distractedly poked at the soft earth with her stick.

"La, I never knew," she muttered, and began a sing-song chant.

> The lay-dee, she weren't watchin'
> So the lay-dee never knew!

Time is gettin' late now, then,
An' Demio's comin' through.
The wood is full o' danger
An' there's danger in the wood,
The spirit-things is growin'
An' they'll feed upon the good!

"Come to me hut, then, so's I kin tell me lay-dee." The tone of her voice was urgent, and without another word, she hurried into the night. The king and counselor had to abandon their blankets, gear, and even Spindle Legs so as not to lose sight of her.

They ran more than they walked, chasing the old hag who hurried nimbly through brambles and thickets, up rocky ledges and across quick streams. She never paused or looked back, though once she stood at the top of a ridge, looking into the moonlit sky, . . . an eerie yet sweet-sounding hum escaping her throat. Quad could see her withered face in sharp detail, bathed by the full moon above her. Did he catch the sparkle of a tear running down her cheek?

She started off again and soon led them up a broad hillside littered with fallen timber. The logs were dry and brittle, shifting easily when leaned against, some so rotten Quad easily could put his foot into the aged, termite-ridden wood. Several times he and Friend Rat had to pause to haul each other over, around, or under such obstacles. At other times, panting, they wondered how such a grotesque old creature could move through this stuff so easily. At the top of the hill a broad hollow lay below them. Its trees were not oaks but saplings of slender ash, their flecked white bark ghostly looking in the darkness. In the clearing's center was a mound. No, on closer examination, it was a low, stone building, some forty feet long and twenty wide, with a thatched roof and a covering of ancient vines. Dark, carved shutters guarded its oddly shaped windows, and grass grew in patches across the thatching.

The hag began to whistle as she turned to them and motioned.

"We're here, hey? Hey!" she announced.

They walked along, Quad noticing there were a number of stunted, flowering fruit trees among the ash. He recognized apple and peach blossoms, but was unsure of some of the others in the dim light. He glanced at Friend Rat, who returned his gaze with a shrug. When they reached the old hut, the hag produced a long, rusty key and fitted it into a lock. Creaking, the door swung uneasily on its rust-caked hinges.

They entered, blinking. A small, cheerless fire produced the only light. A fat, gray cat lay on the hearth, its tail twitching, eyes half shut, and a pink tongue poking out slightly. Simple stools and heavy, plain blankets were scattered about. A low table stood in one corner, and at each wall was a doorway covered with a blanket or skins.

"What's in the rooms?" Friend Rat asked, unable to control his curiosity.

"Things t' keep yer snout out of!" the hag snapped. She paused, then added sweetly, "Things an old lay-dee needs t' git by in th' wood. Private things: a bed an' a pantry an' me frillies! I'll trust yer royal honors t' keep t' yer own business while I pays a visit t' me garden."

"And when will we see the wizardess?" Quad asked.

"Me lay-dee? In good time, hey. When—an' if—she's ready."

She left and Quad settled on the hearth, wondering about this strange woman and quietly scratching the cat's ears. Friend Rat, none too fond of cats, sat on a stool and rubbed his aching feet. At last the hag returned with carrots and potatoes, which she dumped into a pot of water and boiled with a handful of herbs. The resulting stew was memorably bland, but it filled their stomachs and warmed their insides.

The hag sat the rest of the evening, gazing at them through her large, unblinking eyes until they thought they'd go mad if she didn't stop. Quad tried to make conversation, asking about Magdalawood, the Guardian of the Wood, and Iscara, but the hag refused to banter. She simply tilted her head or twitched a cheek muscle or clucked her tongue. After what seemed hours she announced they should all go to sleep, and brought more blankets from another room. Piling them near the fire, she gave the counselor a final warning to stay out of the other rooms and went to bed.

"A strange old hag," Quad said.

"Very strange, indeed!" Friend Rat agreed.

He lay in his blankets listening for the sound of snoring. He was sure all hags snored, and especially this one, considering the route the wind would have to take to find its way out of her awful, twisted nose. But when he finally heard the sound of noisy slumber, it was Quad who made it.

Friend Rat curled up and tried to sleep, but found he couldn't. *Somehow*, he thought, *things aren't right! My king is here sleeping, unprotected, in a stranger's house!* He thought on this a while, then forced himself to smile. *Tik! tik! tik! What harm can that old sack of cowhide be? She's only a hag, after all, the slave of Iscara—she's hardly Iscara herself! Sleep, my good fellow. You'll need to be alert tomorrow to protect your king.*

At last he did sleep. But the cat found the rat's warm breath a comfort and so it wrapped itself around his snout. The counselor woke in a sneezing fit and pushed the cat away, only to have it come back and make itself a turban on his head. He woke, sneezing, again. Finally, in a fury, he flung the animal out the door and, curling up, dozed off in a decent sleep.

He awoke with a start.

"Frillies?" he said aloud. "Why would a hag have frillies?"

Friend Rat considered this a moment without satisfaction. He tried to roll over and just forget the matter, but the question kept creeping back into his mind.

"This is stupid," he told the ceiling. "Who cares why a hag has frillies?"

But the more he told himself how ridiculous the whole thing was, the more curious he became. *Oh, one peek into those rooms will do me no harm!* he thought at last. *Even if she catches me, what can she do? Whack me with her stick?*

He glanced at the king who slept with one hand wrapped tightly around the scepter. Crawling out of his blanket, the counselor tiptoed to the door leading to the hag's room and listened. There was no sound. *Then she's asleep,* he thought, *I hope.*

He sneaked to the next door and, holding his breath, slipped the curtain aside. It was a small room and, judging from the aroma of herbs and spices, served as a pantry. He squinted to see, but the room was pitch-black.

"A storage room," he sighed. "No frillies here."

Still, the aroma was exciting. He stepped in, his nose twitching. Basil, he thought, and rosemary. Peppers of some sort. Mustard and thyme. Coriander. And then there were scents he didn't recognize. He began to consider going to the fireplace and grabbing a burning stick so that he could see (and possibly try) these delights, when his shoulder bumped something.

"Excuse me!" he apologized, then clasped a hand over his mouth. With his other hand he reached out and felt for the thing he had bumped. There it was—large, dark, and heavy, swinging on a rope. *My goodness!* he thought, *she's hung a cow up in here!"*

Hurrying to the hearth, Rat selected a stick from the woodpile and held its end in the fire until it caught. Then he scurried back to the pantry. By the time he got there, the little blaze had gone out, but the stick's tip glowed red enough to provide a dim light. He slipped behind the blanket and held it up.

The long squeal of terror brought Quad instantly awake. He looked frantically about, saw the rat's empty bundle, and jumped to his feet. Wielding his scepter like a club, he scrambled through the curtain, calling, "Rat! Rat!"

He found his friend lying on the floor, the stick beside him and his eyes wide in its dying glow.

"We're undone! We're undone!" was all the rat could squeak.

"What are you talking about?" Quad demanded.

The rat only pointed in the air and continued squeaking. "We're undone!"

Quad looked around, shivering in fear, but could see only blackness. He bent down, picking up the still-glowing stick. *Do I really want to do this?* he wondered. *If something is going to kill us, I'd rather not see it.* The thought of assassination made him pale, and for a moment he considered simply scrambling through the curtain and out into the night. Instead he thrust the stick upward and gasped at what its glow revealed.

With a cry Quad stumbled back, crashing into a shelf that sent jars of herbs crashing and tumbling to the floor. From above Arlan stared back at him through wide, unseeing eyes, his body swinging from a hook like a slow, bloody pendulum. There were other shapes. Quad saw two. He quickly realized that one was Nabo, the other Robin. A furious rage swept him, and he tore out through the curtain, shouting.

"Hag! Where are you!"

"Right here," she replied sweetly, standing at the hearth. Beside her the fire blazed with a hungry brightness, its flames bathing her in a yellow glow. "So, ye've seen me frillies, hey?" she asked in a low, mocking tone. "I warned ye not t' look at me frillies, I did!"

"My friends . . ." Quad began angrily, his voice trembling.

"Have all met the wizardess of Magdalawood, they have," the hag cackled.

As she spoke, she brought her hands to her forehead, burying her claw-like fingers deep in the wrinkled skin and dragging her splintered nails down. The rotten skin parted in easy furrows. Quad shuddered with revulsion, and the fact that no blood poured from those gaping wounds made him tremble with fear. Still laughing, she pulled ribbons of skin from her skull. Quad sucked in a startled breath as he saw the perfect features of a youthful, olive face appear. The woman pulled the wispy clumps of hair from her head and let the whole mess fall to the floor. Smiling, her deep emerald eyes glittering, she peeled the same false skin from her wrists and hands to reveal slender, well-manicured fingers and shapely arms. Last she removed the hag's clothing, untying the stuffing that made the humps and rolls of fat. The clothing made an ugly pile on the floor as she stood before him, her supple, curving body dressed in firelight. She was the most beautiful woman Quad had ever seen. The scepter he held above his head slid from his wilting fingers and landed with a clunk on the floor beside him. His jaw fell nearly as far.

"Now 'tis time you found Iscara, Wizardess of Magdalawood." She smiled, her voice deep and melodic.

Quad stood trembling, not knowing what he felt. Fury, fear, and excitement rushed through him. Her smile was broad and knowing and kind, yet gently mocking, alluring, and full of threat—all those things at once. He took a step toward her then checked himself, remembering his friends. *Perhaps this nymph appeared to them in the same way,* he thought. With an effort he turned, mostly, away from her and picked up his scepter.

"Thank your fates, Wizardess, that I have no sword," he said unsteadily, "for as beautiful as you are, if I had one now I'd cut you in half."

Iscara laughed, a sound both haunting and cold.

"My little king," she said softly, "if you had a sword, I would turn it into a vine that would wrap itself about you, and you'd be in as tight a fix as your friends."

"What of my friends? If they're dead, you'll find this makes a good club, at least."

The woman blinked innocently.

"Your friends are enchanted, nothing more. I hung them in the pantry for lack of a better place. Now that you're here, I'll cut them loose and, once away from those herbs, they'll revive soon enough. As to the Ruby Scion in your hand, 'tis no simple club. You could fell a kingdom with it—certainly *I'm* helpless before it. But a confused little king such as you wouldn't know that, hey? Or how to use it? Come, sit by me. We must talk."

"My counselor . . .

"Is enchanted, like the others. And by now he's snoozing happily. You aren't afraid to come to me, are you? Here. Sit!" she said as she seated herself by the hearth.

Quad stepped toward her but stopped. She laughed again, a laugh that was both delightful and frightening.

"Little king! You've shown courage tonight, running unarmed, you thought, to help your friends. Now then, show a little more." She took his trembling hand and gently pulled him down, her eyes never leaving his. "What scares you most in me—the wizardess or the woman?"

Quad forced himself to hold her gaze. There was cruelty in it, he thought, but her smile was warm and overcame his doubts.

"You are beautiful," he said, the words catching in his throat.

"Thank you. You're no muscle-rippling warrior, I'm afraid, but Pentatutinus knew his mind. If he gave you the crown, there's good beauty in you."

"Did you know Father?"

"Since he was a little boy, and I a little girl!" she laughed. "We played together, and went through some bad times together. I was with him when he took the crown—no older than you, he was, though he was bigger and more arrogant. Oh, he was very arrogant! Short-tempered and ruthless. You were a gentle child, though, always playing in the flowers. And you're gentle now. How such a man of iron sired a boy of butterflies, I'll never know."

"How would you know about my childhood?"

"I'm a wizardess," she said, and the tone of her voice told him the subject was ended.

"You were crying as you led us here. Did you love him?"

Iscara raised one thick eyebrow as she studied Quad's face, and then looked away. She rose, going to a peg by the window where a tunic and fur cape hung. She dressed without speaking and, securing the cape with a gold-edged brooch so that one shoulder was bare, she leaned against the windowsill and gazed into the night.

"Tell me how he died, the great Pentatutinus. Tell me of

your coronation, why you came here, and everything that's happened in between. Like a fool, I've left off watching these past few years."

She spun around, her movements fluid and graceful, her body quivering and tense, barely able to hold in its energy. Her cheeks were flushed and excitement filled her eyes as she rushed to Quad, seized his hands and pulled him toward her until their faces nearly touched.

"Tell me!" she said, laughing. "I must know if there's still time!"

The king related, as best he could, everything that had happened from the day Friend Rat pounded on his door, demanding that the then-prince go to speak with the king. Iscara listened intently, interrupting occasionally with questions and having him repeat parts of the story, seeking further descriptions of this person or that one. She grew more animated as time passed, worriedly knitting her brows over the Unseen Presence and laughing at Quad's encounter with the Guardian of the Wood.

"And after Rat's ridiculous song, you came upon us," he finished. "You know the rest. Now you answer some questions for me."

"The Oneprince! His time has come!" she cried rapturously, her hands clasped over her breasts.

"What?"

Dragging him to his feet, Iscara swung Quad about in circles.

"'Tis the prophets, little king!" she laughed and, still swinging him, she sang.

One helper shall help
And another destroy!
One prince a brave one
And one but a boy!
A sorrow we feel
Though unseen through the land—
'Tis now! cries the Wise One,
My time is at hand!

Letting him go, she grabbed a tamborine and danced as she continued to sing. Weaving in and out of the room's deep shadows, she moved hypnotically before him and he watched in a near-trance. She was singing the poetry of the prophets, he knew—songs he himself had learned and pored over since his childhood. Had he not been so entranced by her spell, he could have sung each word with her. Yet her voice gave those ancient verses a new meaning he hadn't thought of. *Did the prophets*, he thought in wonderment, *speak of me?*

> The Dark One is reigning,
> His general goes
> Into the kingdom
> My children loved so!
> Treach'ry on treach'ry,
> Foe begets foe
> And the land in this shadow
> Knows nothing but woe!
> Fear not, little kingdom,
> The little king comes,
> And with him shall bring
> The Invincible One!
> And I shall ride with him
> However I may,
> And we'll be delivered
> By break of the day!

Quad found himself dancing and singing with her, for her joy was infectious. At dawn they collapsed on the floor and lay there, laughing.

"The kingdom is saved!" Quad shouted. "Long live the little king!"

"Long live the Oneprince!" Iscara cried.

His face fell and he stopped. Iscara jumped to her feet and whirled across the room where she leaned against a wall and, breathing heavily and wiping sweat from her brow, watched the king.

"How shall we find him?" Quad wondered.

"Through the gift he gave your father, silly thing!" she laughed.

"The Ruby Scion?"

"See that dark stone?" she asked, crossing the room and holding the scepter before him. He looked at the gem as she cupped it in her hands.

"When it comes close to its maker, the ruby will glow brighter than blood and hotter than fire!" she said, as her fingers danced about.

"As simple as that?" he murmured.

"As simple as that!" she answered.

"Then let's wake the others and tell them the news!" Quad jumped to his feet, excited anticipation growing inside him.

Together they cut his companions free and revived them outside in the early morning sun. The warriors grumbled at first and Friend Rat was suspicious, but Quad insisted they hear his tale. They were so amazed as he spoke, for the king sounded so happy and sure of himself, for once, that they couldn't help feeling the Oneprince was all but found.

The celebration began again, and this time the wizardess cooked up a feast that, to the weary travelers, was better than the coronation feast—and happier too!

eneral Norgrain, the second-in-command of the armies guarding the northern border, sipped his boiled mead and felt its steam thaw the frozen coating of his broomstick beard. It always happened at this latitude when one strained a hot drink through ice-caked whiskers. First his nose and beard would run like a waterfall; then he'd finish his drink in a gulp, and his beard and nose would freeze again. He ended up looking as though he'd soaked his head in a bag of wet salt and starch.

Duty at Sheolfrost wasn't grand, but it wasn't all bad either. The cold gnawed at your bones, but you got used to that. There was also a lack of women, but the hero's welcome the lasses gave when you went home on leave compensated nicely. There was always talk of war, but who was crazy enough to start one? Worst of all was an over-abundance of squeaky, obnoxious rats. *Irritating things*, Norgrain thought, but their thick, shaggy hides made them highly adaptable to duty on the Sheolfrost. And, at least, he could kick them.

There was one very big advantage to all this: his position as second-in-command and sounding board of Prince Gregor. Norgrain had only to lie on his bed, munching delicacies and tossing a "That's so!" or an "Of course not!" in Gregor's direction every so often as the prince discussed many things at length. That was, after all, what Gregor had always sought in his closest advisor—a yes-man who would sincerely admire his plots and plans, who would stare with boyish awe at his magnificent presence. And Norgrain was quite adept at the arts of nodding, agreeing, and gawking.

At present, however, things weren't so sweet. In the prince's prolonged absence Norgrain found himself with something he'd never thought he'd actually get: responsibility over the men. The warrior-prince had gone to Castle Pentatute to do something or other and stop a rebellion and save the kingdom. Thinking of that Norgrain laughed, spattering the tent post with his drool.

"Oh ho! You did that well, didn't you, my good lord!" The rebellion had succeeded in spite of Gregor, all but wiping out his pretty Honor Guard in the process. And the last Norgrain had heard, the prince, his foppish brother, and a court rat had hightailed it to the woods with that matted little badger's forces hot on their tails.

Norgrain turned on his heel and strode to the map table. The frozen ground crunched and even squeaked beneath his heel and he looked sadly down, examining the frosty toes of his boots.

"Ah! Gregor! what've ye done?" he said dramatically, waving his hand in a sweeping gesture. "For once I didn't agree with ye, and look what came of yer not heedin' my advice! I told ye, didn't I? What did I say? 'Gregor,' that's what I said, 'Gregor, the kingdom won't stand for a pin-headed runt like Quad bein' king. They want you. I ain't sayin' ye ought to kill the boy. Just banish 'im to some island. Heaven knows we've plenty of those things off the coast. Banish 'im, somewhere south where he can rule the monkeys, and take the crown for yerself. At least the kingdom won't fall apart then, an' Solofaust won't put up any fight with yuh, s'long as ye throw a favor his way now an' again.'

"But would ye believe me? No!" He unrolled a large map across the table, holding its sides flat with one hand and his mead mug.

"Look at this!" he muttered, pausing to spit. "Demio is here an' here an' here, just a-waitin' for the passes to clear. The flea-badger's here an' here an' everywhere else a-waitin' for ye to make one mistake. Ye're here or maybe here, or who knows where, hidin' out. An' me?" He hesitated dramatically, then stabbed the Sheolfrost Range with a hammy thumb and shouted, "I've got the responsibility of runnin' this misbegotten army of desertin' babies! What'm I supposed to do with 'em? I'm an advisor, not a warrior! When Demio comes a-sweepin' down Whistler's Pass, we won't last a minute . . . Half the army will be killed, half will desert, an' I'll be caught an' hauled to Ebon Bane in chains. An' then what'll become of happy ol' Norgrain?" He thought a second, and a tear came to his eye. "I'll be boiled alive for that bird as a sweet-meats pudding!" he wailed.

He looked up suddenly, his eyes shooting to the left and right.

"I've got t' do somethin'," he hissed. Lifting his mug he watched the ends of the map curl slowly together like a spider in a fire. "I've got to act quick-like. I've got t' be cunning! ruthless! alert for any opportunity! Hmmm . . . I think I'll go and sleep on 't."

The dribble in his beard was freezing again as he left the still cold of the war tent for the icy blasts of air outside. It was a hard hike of a hundred feet or so to his own tent, and there a pot-bellied stove would be burning red and raising the temperature to above-freezing, while blankets and pillows would be waiting to aid him in his plans. He passed a rat guard who was nodding off and kicked him a few times ("To get th' circulation goin'," he assured himself, "for th' both of us"). At the tent another rat stood, its back to him, oblivious of his approach.

"Wagrat!" Norgrain ordered.

"Sir! Sirrah! Sir!" it coughed, spinning around.

"I needs more wood."

"And I needs warn you, sirrah!" Wagrat said. "There is someone wants to see you."

"Well, I'll not see 'im now, tell 'im that," Norgrain said, and started for his tent.

"You can tell 'im yourself when you go in," the sentry suggested.

Norgrain stopped.

"What! Ye've let 'im in my tent?" he bellowed.

Wagrat hurried to his master's side and whispered conspiratorially.

"'Tis Gregor, sirrah!"

The general's eyes bulged at the same time as his fingers closed around the rat's neck, hoisting him to eye level.

"Gregor? In my tent?"

"'Tis his tent too!" the rat gagged.

Norgrain grunted and released his guard, who fell with a crash of baggy armor to the frozen ground.

"Opportunities," he muttered to himself as he pulled back the tent flap and went in. What he saw made him gasp.

The prince sat at a small table, his hair matted, his face and arms spotted with cuts and bruises, his clothes tattered, and his cloak streaming from his shoulders in ribbons. His eyes were dark, sullen, and accusing as they followed the assistant general's every move. Norgrain stared at him, shocked.

"Why, Gregor! Ye look a fright! What've ye done t' ye'self?"

"What do you think?" Gregor said, his voice tired and low.

"Ye look like a prospect for the asylum. Here, let me pour ye a good mug of mead. It's what ye'r needin' now."

"What I need is information. Every army to the south follows Solofaust. How does this one stand?"

"Not on its own two feet, I'll tell ye!" Norgrain laughed, filling two mugs from a cask. He glanced from the prince to the golden mead as it rose to the rim.

"That I knew. Is it loyal?"

"I'll tell ye," Norgrain said, setting a mug beside Gregor

and slurping at his own. "These men don't have life enough t' be loyal to their mothers, much less to you or that badger."

Gregor let out a long sigh. "That's what I thought," he said, and lay back on his bed.

"Now, there's an idea!" Norgrain told him, pointing. "That's just the thing. Ye look like ye could use some sleep. Come to think of it, so could I!"

"I could sleep for weeks. Ever since the coronation I've sat around pop-eyed, watching for my own skin or the king's . . ."

"Ye should've took th' crown yerself. I told ye that."

"It wasn't mine to take, nor do I want it. Besides, we've learned that Demio is the real mind behind this rebellion. He'd not let a son of Pentatutinus live—either Quad or myself."

"So what're ye goin' to do?"

"We'll get some of the better men together, and I'll take them with me to Yerushela," Gregor said wearily. "You keep the rest here. As soon as Demio makes a move to come across, ride hard to join us. I'll send a guide to show you a way into the city. Yerushela is built mostly in a cavern and has only a few gates to enter by. We could hold it for a while, I think, even against Demio."

"An' then what?"

"I don't know. Perhaps . . . help will come. Quad is looking for someone he thinks can stop this rebellion."

"Oh? And who is this miracle-worker?"

"I can't say just now."

"An' when will he come?"

"I don't know."

"Ye can't say who he is, and ye' can't say when he'll come. How about this: Is he coming at all?"

"Norgrain, I'll be honest. I don't even know if he exists. But I have to take the chance that he does. He's our only hope."

"Our only hope," Norgrain stressed as he crossed to the prince, "is to join the badger's side."

"Join Solofaust!" Gregor sputtered.

"Hear me out, Gregor! We're both good men, experienced. A team! If you renounce that stump of a brother, an' any interest in the crown—which ye've already done t' me—maybe they'd let ye live. Burn down a loyalist village or so to prove yer change of heart, and maybe they'd even give ye a command. It'd be like old times. Life'd be easy for both of us."

"Murder unarmed subjects and betray my own brother and king? You've never spoken like this before."

"'Tis never been healthy to. But now, 'tis fatal not to."

"Betray everything we know, just to stay alive?"

"Just, ye say! Gregor, me friend, stayin' alive is worth a better word than *just!* Stayin' alive is a very big thing, an' dyin' for love of a thought or a fool is 'just' silly. This noble stuff—it's wind, my friend! Wind, an' that's all."

He shouted the last phrase and spun his arms vigorously to illustrate, but the prince's scowl only grew deeper, showing an angry light that warned Norgrain he was storming down a dangerous path. Still, he plowed on.

"These are ugly times! Do ye know what the armies are doin' in the villages? Deflowerin' young ladies an' hangin' the men. Is burnin' one any worse? Ye'd be doin' 'em a favor, ye would. At least the folk'd die clean deaths."

"This is treachery. If you were any other man, Norgrain, I'd kill you for it."

"This is survival!" Norgrain screamed, the mead spilling from the corners of his mouth. "'Tis better to exist for tyranny than not to exist at . . ."

His words were cut off as Gregor's fist smashed into his jaw. Norgrain reeled back, shocked. Blood filled his mouth and his teeth wiggled loosely in their sockets. Gregor stood over him, rubbing a bruised and swelling hand.

"That's an end of it!" he ordered, breathing heavily.

"But, my lord . . ."

"No more!"

They stared at each other in silence and at last Norgrain climbed to his feet and used a towel to clean the blood from his lips and beard, then dabbed gingerly at his gums.

"I'm sorry, Gregor, I don't know what's come over me."

As he spoke, he lowered the towel to waist level, covering one hand and rubbing it vigorously. "Ye've been gone, an' I haven't known if you were alive or dead, and what I was t' do with all these men. I panicked."

"I'll let it go this once," Gregor said, sitting again. "But I'll not do so again. So steel yourself; our hard times have just begun."

"Just begun," Norgrain agreed, nodding his head slowly.

His fingers released the towel which fluttered to the floor as he jerked his arm up suddenly. Hidden from view, his hand had closed about a knife he kept tucked under his belt. With a quick, jerking motion, he let the weapon fly and Gregor leaped instinctively from the bed. It was a weapon Norgrain knew well, for he'd practiced with it often in the taverns he frequented. Gregor knew, as he stumbled awkwardly forward and to the side, that his failure to realize the situation should have cost him his life. However, Norgrain was drunk, and the knife flew high and to the left of its mark. The prince watched helplessly as it sank cleanly into his shoulder, its icy steel playing at his nerves like a sudden fire. Twisting about, his fingers clenching shut like a claw, he staggered forward and fell to his knees with a groan.

Norgrain snarled and seized a stool, raising it over his head. He staggered forward and brought it down on Gregor's skull once, twice, and again and again until the stool was a splintered and blood-splashed mess and the prince lay motionless on the floor. Throwing it aside, Norgrain spat blood and kicked the prince onto his back.

"For you, hard times are beginnin', but for me, they've just ended, Gregor, old friend."

The fight had been exhausting. He stood panting, feeling sobriety pump into his body with a dizzying dose of adrenaline. He pulled his knife free and wiped it clean on Gregor's coat, then held it just in front of his victim's parted lips. The blade misted, and Norgrain smiled.

"Ye've a head like a brick, prince of Redaemus," he said.

Shaking, he refilled his mug and sat on the edge of his

bed, panting and sipping at the mead, until his body relaxed and warmed up. Casually he walked to the door and called for his guard.

"Wagrat! Get me a wagon and a company to ride to Castle Pentatute! I've a gift for the governor there."

olofaust followed the muttering opossum down a series of winding stairs. She was moving quickly, more so than he chose to, for he was tired and felt strangely oppressed. Each step seemed enormous, the descent endless. The stairs at last led him to a great hall where he stood, taking things in. Helen was nowhere to be seen. Following the hall to the throne room, he paid no attention to the rich and beautiful tapestries and paintings adorning the walls he passed. Ordinarily he would have lingered, if only momentarily, to admire the deft and precise daubs of paint or threads of fabric which made Redaemus' history come alive. But not tonight.

He pushed open the door and stepped into the vast throne room. A few lamps and torches were lit, but their flames flickered sadly in a draft and cast erratic shadows across the flagging of the floor. *I am alone,* he thought, looking about. *Alone, facing the shadows. Drop that thought, you old fool! 'Tis an empty room, harmless as a pup.*

He glanced toward the great, vaulted ceilings, lost in the blackness above. Some simple pieces of furniture had been brought in, he noticed, but they were made insignificant by the heaving bulk of the throne in the room's center. Beside that seat of power (*Worthless power!* he laughed bitterly) an oakwood tray stood with a cup, a jug of wine, and a bowl heaped full of salted beetles. Before the throne and to the left was a low scribe's table neatly stacked with ink wells, quills, and a fat, glowing candle. *My nephew Laramy will sit there,* he thought. To the right of the throne was a prosecutor's table covered with notes and maps. Between the two tables, looking rough and uncomfortable, sat a prisoner's stool, surrounded by three iron rings set in the masonry of the floor. To these a prisoner's chains would be secured and to the chains, of course, a prisoner. Solofaust smiled for the first time as he climbed onto the throne.

"Now here is organization a badger can appreciate, and a situation I can do something about! Let us begin!" he called as he rapped the floor with his cane.

Laramy hurried in, dressed in a cloak and wearing a scribe's pendant. He bowed briefly and without a word sat at his table and quickly set about selecting a quill.

"Nephew," said Solofaust by way of greeting.

"Uncle," Laramy returned with another shy bow.

Helen entered, approached the throne, and bent her knee.

"Since I headed this investigation, I will act as a prosecutor, my lord."

"I assumed as much, and can ask for no better. Bring in the defendant."

She clapped her paws and the prisoner was led in by a large guard. Solofaust's jaw dropped to his chest and his eyes bulged. The prisoner stood, peering sadly at him from puffy eyes. Locks of her unkempt hair hung about her dirty face and clung at the corners of her chapped lips. Her chafed wrists, ankles, and throat were weighted with heavy chains. Her dress was whole, but looked as if she'd worn it dancing in the brambles.

"Nellie!" Solofaust gasped.

"My lord," she acknowledged, her voice an exhausted cough. "Forgive my failure to curtsy. I'm simply not in the mood." Then, a smile flitting her parched lips, she said, "May I beg your indulgence to let me sit?"

His whiskers quivered wildly, but he managed to nod and the guard led Nellie to the stool. Using locks, he connected her chains to the floor bolts. Solofaust's burning eyes fell on Helen.

"I trust you've good evidence, and much of it," he said, his voice heavy with threat.

"Even so," she nodded gravely.

"That is good," he replied, measuring his tone, "for, if you haven't, I'll have you sitting on that stool, wrapped to your muzzle in chains, and your neck will feel the bite of an ax."

"I know your fondness for the prisoner, for indeed, I like her myself. 'Tis with a heavy heart I bring Nellie before you."

"Of course 'tis heavy," Nellie muttered. "What would you expect of stone?"

Helen turned with a hiss and the guard, snapping "Silence!" gave the prisoner's chains a violent tug. Nellie cried out as she felt herself nearly pulled from the stool.

"Easy on her!" Solofaust growled. "I'll not have her abused before I've even heard proof of a crime. And Nellie, more respect from you. See where your quick tongue's got you now!"

He studied her carefully, his eyes narrowed, then addressed Helen.

"She looks poorly.

"Have you been tortured?" he asked Nellie.

"Of course not!" Helen said quickly before the other could reply. "I wouldn't harm her without your permission. Still, the dungeon's air and diet have an effect on folk. And, our being short-handed, I've exercised her by working her daily under guard. She's attended the spirit-things which arrived before you, as well."

Solofaust nodded, but he watched the opossum closely for some sign of betraying emotion. *Treachery from Nellie?* he wondered. *She's spirited, independent. It's possible, I suppose. And you've an enviable discernment, Helen. Still, I wonder—have you an ulterior motive?* Helen gazed back at him through expressionless, pink eyes. *If the face is a book to be read, Helen, yours is a tome of blank pages.*

"What is the charge, prosecutor?" he droned aloud.

"Treason."

Nellie blinked, and her gaze fell to the floor.

"Look at me!" Solofaust demanded. She glanced up and he added, "What is your response?"

"The noble prosecutor," Nellie replied, her voice a weary monotone, "is as mad as the deposed king's counselor."

"I hope so for your sake. I've loved you as though you were my child."

"You have been my father."

Helen made a huffing sound as she shuffled through the papers on her desk.

"I know my lord will not be prejudiced in matters vital to the security of the kingdom," she cautioned.

"If you know it, why remind me? Present your evidence."

"Even so! I suspected some time ago that Miss Nellie was, what? Divided in her loyalties. She told me in the kitchens, for instance, that she was glad the king and his brother escaped."

Solofaust raised his brows and turned to Nellie who shifted uncomfortably.

"Your response? Remember, I know when you lie."

"I said it seemed a good joke that he escaped, not that I was glad of it. Solofaust! You know my sense of humor!" Nellie's voice was even when she spoke.

"I know that it is dangerous," the governor said, then turned back to Helen. "But it is not treasonous."

"There's more, my lord," Helen answered coldly. "After one such talk I followed her out of the kitchen to find she'd disappeared, rather suddenly, from the hall. I wondered about this, for it was a long hall, with the only doors between its ends leading to the stables. She was bringing you a snack, so I knew she couldn't have gone out one of those, nor did she have time to cover the hall's distance. I watched for her for some time and questioned many folk about her. They will testify in a moment as to her words. Armed with such testimony I searched her room."

"And what did you find?"

"Only Nellie. Crawling out of her closet from a hidden passage."

"A hidden passage!" Solofaust repeated, clutching at his robe. He looked at Nellie with new severity, and she quickly turned her face away.

"We have yet to trace it all, but parts of this passage lead to the king's and prince's bedchambers, as well as to the stables, a tower, and a number of smaller rooms—including Nellie's. The main passage runs alongside the throne room . . . with an entrance here!" Dramatically, she took her stick and lifted a tapestry. Behind it the secret passage was exposed, a guard standing in it. The badger gasped.

"This is how Quad escaped!" Helen announced in a loud voice.

"I knew nothing of the king! I only used them as short-cuts, my lord!" Nellie cried out.

"How did she know of them, having never been in the castle before?" Helen charged.

"I found them by accident! I felt a draft in my closet and when I looked it over, careful-like, a door swung open to the passage."

"This simple village girl discovered a passage that the very Captain of the Guards knew nothing about!" Helen scoffed.

"Why didn't you report this passage, if you found it by accident?" Solofaust growled.

"I thought of it as my secret, my childish secret, that's all! My lord! 'Twas foolish, I know, but not treacherous!" Nellie burst into loud sobs, and Solofaust clamped his eyes shut against them.

"We learned just yesterday that the main passage goes down into the earth and ends at a cavern," Helen continued, her voice growing more harsh. "We found signs of people— an encampment some days old and, more recent, the tracks of a man. These were hard to pick up, and we never would have had I not had badgers in there who picked up the scent. The man does not wish to be known, but has apparently been stealing supplies and appearing before castle folk as though he were a ghost. He is a soldier, they say, and a guardsman reported he is Narramoore of the Honor Guard! Nellie hasn't been alone in there, 'twould seem."

Solofaust felt the blood drain from his face and a chill grip his spine. One paw clenched tightly at his chest, and the other closed, white, upon his cane.

"Lies!" the defendant screamed. "My lord! I'm loyal! Did I not bring the assassin to Quad's table?"

"As an agent of a young king known to fancy simple women, did you not knowingly carry poor Shrieker to his death!" Helen countered.

Helen brought in her witnesses, and Nellie sat in a near-daze as a score lined up to speak against her, many of them folk she'd considered to be friends. Guardsmen, cooks, and chambermaids in turn responded to Helen's questions and commands, telling of "traitorous" things Nellie had said. Some of their tales were simply distorted; others were outright lies. All were devastating to Nellie's cause. One frightened-looking, dark-eyed chambermaid named Matty even reported that, when she'd attended the room of then-prince Quad, she'd discovered Nellie with him, giggling and whispering romantic nonesuch. Even File addressed the court.

"The wine casks had been drained, all but one," he said, his mustache bristling, "and by that one I found a vial."

"It was full?" Helen asked.

"It was. I'd come into the cellar in time to interrupt the saboteur, for I heard someone running up the opposite stairs."

"And the defendant?"

"She avoided me all day, but when I saw her, her feet seemed stained, as though she'd stood in spilled wine. 'Tis hard stuff to wash off, let me say. I asked her about them feet, and she got all confused and hurried off."

"And the vial?"

"I tested a small bit on a prisoner, and it turned him green as a frog."

"Indeed!" Helen affirmed.

"Have you anything to add?" Solofaust asked the prisoner.

"Only that his lines are well-rehearsed," Nellie said. "File! You were me house and board!"

"It hurts me to speak it," File replied, and his eyes found interest in his feet.

Other conspirators spoke, and even one of Nellie's farm boys was brought in. She stared at him incredulously as he muttered or nodded to Helen's repeated questions. Once he looked at Nellie and exploded into heaving sobs.

"Take him out!" Helen spat at a guard.

"What have you done to him!" Nellie demanded. "That's Luke, and he'd never . . . What kind of threat did you . . . ?"

The guard yanked her chain and her voice was choked off. Solofaust looked sharply at the guard but he did not, Nellie realized with rising fear, reprimand the action.

Others spoke, including an architect who explained much of the passages' routes, displaying Helen's crude maps before the governor.

Finally Solofaust raised his hand for silence. He motioned Helen to approach.

"Is this your case?" he asked softly.

"There is some more, but that is the bulk of it."

"Return to your table."

She did, and Solofaust climbed down from the throne. There he stood, rocking slightly on his heels, leaning on his cane for support.

"Prisoner, rise."

Nellie struggled to her feet—the chains were long enough to allow a prisoner to stand for readings of verdict and sentence—and the three stood in silence, each alone and silent at a corner of their dark triangle. Beyond their world the guard scuffed restlessly at the flagstone. Laramy glanced up, overturning an inkpot which spilled across his manuscript. Hurriedly he set about dabbing it dry.

At last Solofaust uttered a long, throaty growl and, clutching his robe at its seams, he rent it apart.

"Guilty!" he cried.

"You can't believe that!" Nellie gasped.

"Indeed you are," he whispered. "And I must mourn. The one I called my daughter has turned her hand against me, and I must call her foe."

"No! I . . ."

"The verdict is high treason," he cut in, his voice an empty drone. "Justice must be served. At daybreak you will die."

"I will put her to torture until then," Helen said. "'Tis the only way she'll reveal her confederates."

"Until then you will leave her alone," Solofaust hissed. "You know as well as I she'll never reveal them. Take her to her cell. Let her contemplate her crime in solitude."

The guard loosened Nellie's chains and pulled her toward the door as Helen walked beside her, buzzing in her ear.

"Your severed head will look lovely on my mantel, dear. Perhaps I'll have it pickled so I can enjoy your silly countenance even longer!"

Nellie paled and the opossum waddled away. Her cheeks streaked by tears, the woman looked at the governor.

"Death is a cold and cruel master," she said softly, "but not near so cold nor cruel as my lord."

Solofaust glared at her, unmoving but for a twitch in his jowl. The guard pulled her reluctantly away as the scribe collected his papers and followed behind.

Their shadows had long receded, but still Solofaust stood before the throne, staring at the door. *What has happened?* he wondered. *My kingdom is crib-dead. My allies seek to rule me, my noblest plans have turned upon me, and my folk are in the grip of the spirit-things. And the one I loved most of all . . .*

He forced the thought to stop and stood, panting.

Suddenly he wheeled about and, with a snarl, smashed the bowl of beetles to the floor.

"What have I done?" he shouted.

Seizing the wine jug, he hurled it against a pastoral tapestry where it exploded with a bang, spattering its contents like a star burst whose bright red trails raced across the gentle hills and skies before the fabric absorbed them. Screaming guttural cries of fury, Solofaust drew the dagger from his walking stick and rushed at the tapestries, slashing and tearing them until he collapsed, panting, his heart pounding in the prison of his chest.

T he shock of the trial wore off before Nellie'd gone a hundred feet and her fury at Helen's betrayal welled up like a storm.

"What a fool I was!" she told the guard, "giving my time and spirit to that bug-eating bundle of mange! And trusting old, scheming, sour-pussed Helen! I hate 'em all. I do!"

"Watch your tongue!" the guard on her left warned. "Such words are treason."

"And what are ye going to do about 'em? Cut off my head twice?" Nellie shouted with a laugh. She wheeled about, her chains rattling, and shook her fist at the throne room. "A black widow in your beetles, Solofaust! And Helen! Another in your pouch!" One guard reprimanded her, nearly jerking her off her feet by snapping her chains, and she snapped, "Don't drag me so! I know the way to my cage!"

At last they reached the dungeon, a subterranean hall lined with twelve oak doors, aged and gray, flecked with wormholes and mildew. Each had a tiny window with a sliding panel just big enough to admit a hand. Used for passing food or keeping watch on prisoners, these were reinforced with strips of iron and lined with studs. Four of the cells were large, full of moldy hay and rotting prisoners. New folk were added almost daily but, since the arrival of the spirit-guards, the population had leveled off. Still they were sorely crowded.

Nellie's cell was one of the smaller, private ones. Built to house important prisoners or captives of war, these measured twelve paces by ten and afforded the luxury of a bed of boards and straw, a three-legged stool, a tiny table, and a candle. Past residents had dripped the wax onto the tables and stuck the candlesticks in the stuff to make holders, and the walls were scarred with the etchings of their diaries and calendars. Far from pleasant, Nellie at least found her new home bearable. Whenever she'd been put to her cell each night, she collapsed, exhausted, on the bed. When the dungeon door had slammed and she was sure no one would look in on her, she dug through the straw for her mysterious dinners. She was never disappointed and had noticed that the amount and quality of this food was always commensurate with the number of stripes and bruises she'd endured during the day. Whoever her friend was—probably a man, for men had easiest access to the dungeons—he was keeping up with her activities quite well.

She thought about him now. Would she receive a last meal? Was he aware of her sentencing? Would he take steps to save her? Remembering the chains hanging from her like vines and the determination of the possum who had brought this whole thing about, she suspected the chances of a dashing hero carrying her away were slim, indeed. *And why would he want to save me*, she thought, *looking as I do like a battered chicken on the block?*

She turned and stopped at the door of her cell, expecting the guards to wait there until someone could go and roust the snoozing turnkeep. Instead, they tugged her farther down the hall.

"That was my cell!" she protested.

"For tonight," the guard replied, "your cell is at the other end."

"That's the common dungeon!"

"'Tis Helen's orders," he shrugged.

"Can't I at least have privacy my last night alive?" she

wailed, her voice pleading, but neither of her escorts seemed moved.

"Mistress Helen wishes to guard you from any attempts at rescue by your loyalist friends," the man on the left said.

"I have no friends!"

"Then here's your chance to make some!" he laughed. Poking his companion, he added, "Here, watch our smelly guest. I'll go rap the turnkeep's toes and wake him up."

As Nellie waited, she felt her last dregs of hope wash away. What of the prisoners, many who'd looked at her pleadingly as they were dragged past her at the coronation feast? Would they remember her, she wondered? If so, they might literally tear her apart. *By morning, there won't be enough of me left for the ax-man.* Her face going white, she began to tremble and heave up wracking sobs.

The guard turned on her suddenly with an icy glare. Leaning close he snapped, "Be thankful that all are not as full of hate as you, Lady Nell! The friends you do not have are now your only hope."

She stared at him dumbly, then burst into laughter.

"Lady Nell! Why, all my life I've been nothing more than dirt from the gutters! Now I've a title to die with!" She laughed harder, squeezing her arms tightly to herself and gasping at the wrenching pain it brought her ribs.

It was the guard's turn to stare. He raised a brow curiously, then turned and shouted down the hall.

"Hey! Barton! Are you sleeping with that lazy turnkeep? I've a prisoner to turn in and a bed I want to turn into!"

From the end of the hall there came an explosive cough, followed by the unkempt turnkeep who'd delivered it. He came bowling up the hall with a yawn. He stopped before them, scratching lazily at an armpit and shaking himself like a dog.

"Wal, if it ain't the possum's own, back from courtin'!" he laughed, pulling a ring of keys from his belt. Nellie recognized this noxious man: Clepper, a gutter-minded and sometimes bullying patron of The Rasp and File whose fire she'd put out more than once with pitchers of ale poured in his lap.

"Open the door, then go back to bed," the guard snapped.

"Open th' door! Close th' door! Lock th' door! Open th' winder and toss in th' grool. Swear at the folk and shut th' winder! Takes talent to work a job like this," he laughed, winking at Nellie and leaning close to her. "Talent an' fine looks, too! Ah, if ye'd courted me, such fine things I'd a-done fer ye! Ye'd be in a cozy nice home now, a-warmin' my bath. They gived me a real blueblood's place, with iv'ry tiles on th' floor!" Reluctant tumblers responded to his key and the door gave way to his weight. It swung open to reveal a sea of prisoners—rats, men, and women, some chained to the damp walls and others lying about or sitting on the floor, staring vacantly ahead, seeing nothing. All looked undernourished, many seemed like breathing, coughing corpses. Some—even women, Nellie realized with revulsion—were missing fingers or hands. Some looked up, blinking, at the intruders.

Nellie wrinkled her nose. "I don't want to go in there!"

"You won't have to put up with 'em long!" Clepper laughed.

"Why are there torches? Since when is Helen so kind?"

"We usually let 'em play in the dark," Clepper said, "but this was done special so we could look out fer *you*." A broad, gap-toothed smile swept his face.

"Helen has ordered every precaution," Barton offered as he unlocked Nellie's chains.

She looked hesitantly into the dungeon and then at the guards. They gazed back at her, and she saw that one was a strong and handsome man, although his clear, gray eyes seemed old and weary and sad. Suddenly she began to cry, hating herself for her weakness.

"I don't want to go in! They'll hurt me!" she blurted.

One of the guards drew her to him, and she clung to him. After a moment he pushed her gently but firmly away.

"I have a daughter of my own, this age," he said to Clepper and Barton, who were gawking at him. He turned back to the prisoner. "Go! Things aren't always what they seem; those prisoners have neither the spirit nor the strength to harm you."

"Come on! Come on! B'fore I start to cry!" the turnkeep groaned. "You'd think you were sayin' so long to your mother!"

"At least I have one," Nellie countered, glaring at the turnkeep and gathering up the remains of her pride. She looked again through the door. The motley group inside wouldn't have the collective strength to squash a bug.

"If I must spend my last night with such as these," she said, squaring her shoulders and taking a long breath, "then I must. And I'll do it right proud, I will!"

With a swish of her skirts she paraded through the door and listened as it slammed shut behind her. An involuntary shudder ran down her spine, but she shook free of it, placed her fists on her hips, and studied her fellows.

"Give me your attention, you sorry fools!" she declared.

The prisoners looked up, their faces vacant and gaunt.

"For tonight," she told them undaunted, "I am your queen, and I name this dungeon Rasp & File, declaring it a kingdom of the folk! You shall be my treasurer," she said to one man in chains, "for I won't have to fear ye running off with the funds! And you," she pointed to a man who looked as if he could still walk about, "you are my general. You, sir rat, shall collect my taxes. Take twenty fleas from each one. We'll send them to Solofaust as a gift, since he likes bugs so." Chatting merrily, she gathered armfuls of straw and piled it below a torch. "Here! This is my throne. You may call me Queen Nell. No, Queen of the Dance!"

"Are you mad?" the rat asked sincerely.

"Mad?" the queen said, running to him and taking his hands in hers. "No indeed! I'm at the end of my rope, I am, and if I must dangle, the dangling will be dancing!"

Helen was mixing bad dreams with fitful sleep when a soldier knocked at her door. She poked her head out of the covers, her whiskers quivering, and sniffed the air.

"What is it!"

"A note, Mistress, from the dungeons."

With a grunt she pulled her night cap over her ears and scurried to the fireplace, where she'd be able to read.

"Come in," she called, then snatched the note and sent him away. It said:

𝔐istress.

𝔓risoners gone mad in ℭell 𝔖even. 𝔗hey're dancing and singing, carrying on. 𝔚hat shall 𝔍 do?

—ℭlepper, 𝔗urnkey

"Blazes!" she muttered, and with a hissing sound she crumpled the note and tossed it in the fire.

◆

How many hours left? Two? Three? Nellie didn't know, so she danced all the harder as the prisoners clapped and sang. She joked, strutted, and sang folk ditties to rouse their spirits. The effect was magical, for it not only made her feel better, but soon the men and rats were dancing with her.

"I'm too exhausted to dance any more," she said at last, "but continue, and I'll watch."

Fearing inaction would let her thoughts find her, Nellie wandered through her kingdom, listening to the ballads and bawdy songs and rubbing the cold, stiff joints of the prisoners in chains.

"I can see you are an angel," said a pale, trembling lord as she rubbed his hands.

"I can see you are touched in the head," she replied with a smile. *Before the rebellion,* she thought, *you'd have run me down with your carriage and not thought twice about it, old man.* She was surprised that this reflection didn't stir up her temper. Instead, looking at his wasted body, she felt the sad caress of pity. "If I had on more than this dress, I'd give it to you to warm you up," she told him. "This rebellion has been a disaster. The excesses of the governor are worse than the king's!"

"Then you're one of us?" the lord asked. He looked at her keenly, wondering if she was the wife of a friend from his own class.

Nellie thought a moment, chewing absently at her lip as she did.

"No," she said, "I'm a friend of neither the king nor the commoners. I'm by myself." She patted his hand and then stood.

Turning her head, she saw a prisoner she hadn't noticed before. His muscular back rested against the wall opposite the door; his knees were drawn up and his face hidden in his folded arms. He looked, and obviously felt, out of place as he tried to blend into his dingy surroundings. *Small chance of hiding in here,* she thought. As healthy as he was, he stood out like a bonfire in the midst of the half-starved, flea-bitten creatures.

"Hey, my fine fellow," she said, walking to him and tapping him with her foot. "Queen Nell allows no sadness in her kingdom, so up with ye!" The man ignored her and she set her hands on her hips, studying him more closely. "What! Do I have to take you through your first dance, myself? So be it!"

She seized his arm to pull him up. But, his steel-strong fingers closed about her wrist like a trap and pulled her to her knees. Nellie tried to twist herself free, until the prisoner looked up. She slapped a hand over her mouth and stifled a gasp. Looking quickly about the cell, she focused again on the man, cocking her head, her eyes wide.

"Well!" she said at last," we're not what we seem, any of us!"

He released her, motioning for silence. But she squealed and threw her arms about him.

"So! My tall, handsome guard is no guard at all! Who are you, then? My secret cook, perhaps?"

"My name," he whispered harshly, "is Narramoore."

"Narramoore!" she gasped, drawing away. "Of Gregor's Honor Guard?"

The warrior scowled. "I'll rescue you, but you must ask no questions, only obey. Do you understand?"

"'Tis a nice dream, you give me, my lord! But how . . . ?"

"No questions! Or I'll leave you to your death."

"All right," she agreed. "I'll do as you say."

"There will come a time to move, but I'll not know it 'til it arrives. When I do speak, you must be ready to flee for your life. You'll need all your strength, so until then, try to sleep."

"I'll obey you to the quick!" the queen said, flashing a sudden smile. "And I'll sleep—as soon as I see the stars over my head. But for now, my shining knight, I've reason to dance the more!"

"This is no time for celebrations," Narramoore warned, taking her arm again.

"We don't want fat Clepper wondering at our sudden silence, do we?" she countered.

In the hall a door groaned on its hinges. The rat ran up the steps and pressed his ear to the door, listening.

"My! my! They're coming! And a good many, too," he reported.

"A good many?" Nellie said, her face going ashen. "Can you save me, then? No! Not you alone!" Before Narramoore could react, Nellie kissed his forehead and spun around.

"Who'll give the queen her last dance? Hurry!"

"I, the Rat Boofer, would be delighted."

"Then I dub you Sir Rat Boofer," Nellie declared, "Taxrat extraordinaire! And you, Sir Narramoore! You are the noble knight of Rasp & File, for you brought your queen the courage she's needed most—futile though it be!"

At that she took the rat's hands. She was so much taller than he that, as they whirled about, his feet were in the air more often than on the floor.

> Silly little fellow, O so gray!
> Won't you dance with me today?

And please don't stomp my dainty feet
So we might dance when next we meet!
Raise your jug with a Ho! Ho! Hey!
We'll sing and dance this night away!

With a moan the dungeon door opened and Helen's bent figure waddled in, trailed by several armed men. Clepper stood at the door, grinning idiotically.

Looking about, the opossum hissed, "What is this!"

Nellie stopped, releasing the Rat Boofer, who retreated to Narramoore's side. The honor guardsman watched silently.

"Why, Helen," Nellie said, drawing herself up and feeling goosebumps prickling her skin, "welcome to the Kingdom of Rasp & File! 'Tis a kingdom built with you in mind!"

"A slut to the end," the castle mistress grunted.

"And now, an end to the slut?" Nellie asked, shuddering at her own grisly joke.

"Just so."

"Well then, I am ready for my last walk in the sun."

"No sense exposing yourself to the chill in that low-cut dress, child. I've arranged for the executioner to come to you."

She signaled and a monstrous man stepped through the door, his head hooded and his chest a mat of hair. In one burly arm he held a block of wood and slung over his shoulder was a great ax, its newly honed blade shimmering even in the dim torch light.

"You slug!" Nellie roared. "Why, you'll even deny me my last glimpse of daylight!"

With a scream she threw herself at the animal, burying her nails in its baggy throat. The possum hissed and gurgled, waving her arms. Narramoore watched, glowering, and his fingers stole beneath the straw until they touched his sword. He feared Nellie had denied herself her only chance, for now the guards were coming directly upon her. If he tried to rush into the fray, they'd kill her before he'd gone three steps.

"Oh my! My, my, my!" the Rat Boofer whispered, holding his toes and rocking back and forth. "What shall we do? Oh my, my my! What shall we do?"

Nellie continued shaking Helen, screaming oaths, digging her fingers deeper into the animal's bristly hide, until the executioner seized the back of her neck in a painful grip. His fist struck her above her kidney, and she cried out in pain, releasing her hold. He twisted her arm behind her and dragged her to her knees while she gasped painfully for air.

"Lay your head on the block!" he ordered, striking the back of Nellie's head with a rattling blow. Her face smacked against the block and a splinter gouged her chin. She saw an explosion of whiteness, and her temples throbbed with pain. Warm blood trickled along her throat as Helen drew close to her ear. Dazed, Nellie smelled the animal's foul breath.

"My mantel awaits your head, and the dogs are licking their lips at the thought of what's left!" Helen chuckled. "What? No more jokes? Your head too dizzy to think, girl? Let's solve that problem."

Turning to the executioner she shrieked, "Do it!"

Nellie's eyes focused on Narramoore so far away. There was desperation in his countenance as his body tensed. He knew, she realized, that he could never reach her in time. A freezing chill raced down her spine as she sensed the ax rising, arcing high over the executioner's head.

Glaring defiantly at Helen, Nellie gasped, "Long live King Quad!"

The opossum hissed.

The ax fell, slicing the air.

It clattered noisily on the landing, banging and crashing as it tumbled down each step. The executioner fell with a thud beside her. She stared, incredulous, at the hilt of a long knife quivering from between his ribs. Suddenly Clepper was there, grabbing her upper arm and yanking her to her feet. In his free hand was a broad, peasant's sword (she'd heard the guards refer to such weapons as idiot stickers), and a look of amazement was on his face. Nellie spat in his face and his jaw dropped in added surprise.

"Treachery!" Helen hissed. "Hold her, I'll do her in!"

She ran forward, holding out a short, jagged dagger, but the turnkey's foot shot out, catching the animal in the gut and sending her sprawling. As she lay there, writhing and sputtering, Clepper gave Nellie a shove toward the steps.

"Go, ye silly bug!"

Nellie staggered back, barely stopping herself from falling down the steps, shaking her head in an effort to clear the mental fog. She tried to take everything in, but events were happening so fast she simply couldn't.

The dungeon exploded with action. At the far end the Rat Boofer was dragging a stone from the wall, revealing a passage beyond. From within the passage there glowed the light of a torch. A blueblood woman was climbing out with jailer's keys in her trembling hands. Narramoore was on his feet, sword in hand, rushing toward the guards. He neatly put the first one away and turned his attention on the others. Nellie still stood frozen, the only immobile thing in the entire dungeon.

"Get to the passage!" Clepper was shouting. "Go!"

"Look out!" Nellie shouted back.

Clepper whirled about, bringing up his idiot sticker just in time to parry a blow as a soldier rushed him. He stepped backward to keep his balance but stumbled, instead, over the executioner's body, falling on his back on the landing and knocking Nellie to the floor. She lay sprawled, groping once more for her wits. Shouts and cries floated to her from both this dungeon and the others. The battle was apparently being repeated in other places where parties of soldiers had arrived to escort the doomed to their place of execution or to the spirit-things, but instead had met with armed resistance. Blades cracked against blades. Narramoore slashed fiercely with his sword, taking on the brunt of the guards, while Clepper lay on his back a few feet from her, desperately meeting the blows of his fear-driven enemy. Below the blueblood raced about with keys, unshackling prisoners, while the Rat Boofer helped them through the tiny passage entrance. Helen's shouts floated above the chaos.

"Kill the slut! Kill her!"

Clepper was weakening fast. He panted and gasped, his face and clothes soaked with sweat, and he screamed when his foe's deflected sword bit into his shoulder. Looking frantically about Nellie grabbed the executioner's block. Using all her strength she heaved it to her chest and hurled it into the guard's calves. With a startled cry he fell over backward, landing beside her. She tried to jump back but he grabbed her ankle while his other hand groped for the sword he'd dropped. Nellie took hold of the executioner's ax and, clutching it with both hands, drew in a painful breath and raised it above her head just as the guard's fingers closed on his sword hilt. In horror she watched his weapon glide in a deadly path toward her belly.

The ax completed its cycle first, cleaving his chest with a sickening *chunk!* The sword clattered harmlessly to the floor. Nellie stooped and plucked it up.

Narramoore had made himself a barrier between the guards and Nellie and Clepper. Chancing a glance back, he took in the situation: the Rat Boofer was pushing the last prisoner through the hole and Clepper was climbing, gasping, to his feet.

"You're too hurt to fight," Narramoore shouted. "Take Nellie to the passage. I'll hold these while I can!"

"But . . ." Clepper began.

"Go!"

Grabbing Nellie by the wrist he ran across the cell hauling her, protesting, behind him.

"We can't leave him!" she shouted.

"There's no other way!"

She looked wildly about and, as they passed the straw-pile throne, she twisted, trying to work free of his sweaty grip. He hung on and she pounded her fist into his wound. With a shriek he let go, then grabbed at her again as she ducked aside.

"What are you doing?" Clepper bawled. Already Narramoore was losing ground to a growing number of guards who pressed in at the door.

"I'll not leave him!" the queen of Rasp & File gasped,

holding the sword before her. "But if you touch me, your hand shall leave you! Go!"

Uncertainly, holding his shoulder, Clepper backed toward the hole where the Rat Boofer still stood, gasping "Oh my! Oh my, my, my!"

Nellie turned to the torch hanging above the straw-pile throne. Tensing herself and grunting from the strain, she swung her sword and sliced the torch in half. Its burning end tumbled into the bed of straw. Flames leaped up and she kicked the burning pile. It burst into a shower of sparks, setting off new blazes wherever they landed.

"Narramoore!" she shouted. Seeing the wall of smoke and flame, he jumped from the landing and, covering his face with one hand, ran through the flames. The three tumbled, crawled, and shimmied through the passage and the Rat Boofer climbed in behind them, pulling the stone shut by hauling on a rope anchored to it. He latched this shut with a draw bolt from inside and the four leaned against the fire-warmed wall, panting.

Helen's chest heaved as she stood at the top of the steps. "After them! After them, you fools!" she screamed.

"Mistress, we can't! The flames!"

"They won't get away!" she hissed. "Follow me!"

Sidestepping the fires that licked at her hungrily, smoke filling her lungs and eyes, the castle mistress charged across the dungeon. Coughing, choking, her eyes running, she pressed on, groping until she reached the wall. *Where is the passage? The passage!* She felt along, her sharp claws scraping at the flesh-blistering mortar as the flames closed in from behind.

"I'll find you!" she rasped, "I'll kill you! You stole Solofaust's affection, you slut, and you won't get away!"

Still screaming her fury, she was consumed by the flames.

"Now what?" Nellie asked in the darkness. "They know the main passage to the cavern, and the upper floors are guarded and blocked!"

"Move along," Narramoore commanded.

The Rat Boofer trotted ahead with his torch, stopping at intersecting tunnels to whisper passwords to mysterious figures. From behind her, Nellie could hear the scuffling, swaying steps and painful breath of Clepper, his gait seeming half-drunk as he clamped his wounded shoulder with his hand. Between them Narramoore half-led, half-pushed her along. While she often stumped her foot against fallen rocks, bricks, and stone, Narramoore's movements were unerring and cat-like. He seemed to know the tunnel and its obstacles as though he'd been raised there. Sounds of distant fighting floated like wind down every passage, meeting in echoey cacophanies at the intersections.

"There are ways out that the soldiers haven't found," Narramoore whispered. "Trickier passages that only I know."

"And what of the others?"

"We timed this so that all the prisoners would escape at the same time. Those who survive this battle will be taken to the forests and trained to raid Solofaust's patrols."

"And we will join them?"

"No," Narramoore said. "You will be escorted to the king."

"An' th' noble knights o' th' Rasp an' File will be yer guides," Clepper laughed.

"You're just leading me from one execution to another!" Nellie protested. "I won't go!"

"You will," Narramoore replied, his voice a whispered threat in the darkness. "You've deeds to answer for . . . and I suspect the king has many questions for the traitor-queen of Rasp & File."

scara reminded Quad of an excited child as she ran to this cupboard and that, pulling out one herb, changing her mind and replacing it with another, then putting that one back in favor of a third. As the afternoon passed, she busied herself at getting nowhere and chatted endlessly of the Oneprince.

"'Like stalks of corn battered and blown in a violent storm, that my tormentors shall be when the Mighty One comes!' That's from the book of Oedaeus," she added, grinding roots in a bowl. Quad smiled at her dreamily and she continued. "And, 'Against his wrath, their armies shall be Desolation!' That's . . ."

"Namath the Crier," Quad finished.

"Very good," she laughed, tapping a finger against his nose. "You know your prophets well."

"Father made sure of it: the Prophets, the Histories, and the Laws. I can tell the tales of the Oneprince forward, backward, and inside-out. But I never thought he still lived, or that I'd be searching for him to save my kingdom. I was never even sure if my father knew him, or if he'd merely made up legends in his own mind." He watched her a moment longer, admiring the way the sun lit up her hair.

"Actually, I never thought it would be my kingdom."

"'In the North the Warrior seeks his help; he finds it not. But to the east! Eastward goes my little one, and salvation is found!'"

"Oedaeus again."

"I like him most. His words stir my blood."

"I like the poems of the Ariel," Quad replied.

"The Ariel—a prophet of flowery visions! His words are droll, boring."

"His stuff is peaceful," Quad countered. "From what I've seen so far of action, peace will be excitement enough for me. He speaks of happiness, of years without war, a kingdom held together by love and not armies, a king who rules by understanding and concern for his people and not through threats and demands.

> Comes the Great One
> And with his coming, peace is coming,
> Swords are melting into earth
> And rising up as wheat:
> Their grain is golden,
> And my people are supplied!

"Hmph!" she huffed, scraping the ground root's paste into a little bag. "'Tis not a song to dance to, my little king."

"Must all dances leave you dizzy and stumbling into walls?"

"Of course!" she laughed, raising her head with a snap.

"Nonsense." He took her hands. "Let me show you."

Quietly singing another of the Ariel's verses, he pulled her from the table and led her slowly about the cluttered room. At first it was more battle than dance—he trying to restrain her steps, she trying to quicken them. Finally she succumbed and lay her head gently on his shoulder.

"You see?" he asked.

"Mmmmm."

"Peaceful, yet pleasant."

"I guess."

"Do you like it?"

"'Tis nice," she replied hesitantly.

THE QUEST FOR THE ONEPRINCE

In silence they continued, their steps bringing them toward the hearth. A burning log popped, its hot ember catching the wizardess' skirt. There it took to the fabric and, as they swayed, the burning skirt brushed her leg.

"I'm on fire!" she cried out, pulling violently away from the king. Her eyes shone with panic and she started to run. But Quad grabbed her by the shoulder and pulled her to the floor where he threw a blanket over her. In seconds the blaze was smothered.

"Are you burned?" he asked, leaning over her.

"A little . . . not badly . . ."

"Let me look."

"My lord!" Smiling, she drew her knees up, and pulled the blanket about her. "A man mustn't look on a lady's legs, even if he be a king! I'll tend my own wounds, thank you!" Quad drew back, blushing violently, and Iscara laughed. But then a harsh look chiseled itself back into her eyes.

"So this is what comes of slow dances. Ha! Peace is lovely, my lord, but love won't win your kingdom. 'Tis the cruelest emotion, I think, and the weakest as well. Not that I'm immune to it!" she added, seeing his stricken look, "but this is no time for tenderness. That comes later. Put away your poems! Take up a sword! Only that will save us now. The Oneprince will require it of you."

"Enough of this patriotic humbug!" came a laughing voice. "Let's forget that Redaemus lies in ruins. Continue the dance!"

They looked up, startled to see Arlan in the doorway, his feet set apart, one folded hand at his hip and the other resting on the door post. His usually pleasant face was twisted with a mock grin and his voice dripped sarcasm.

"A very fine party you're throwing, my king. The messenger must have gotten lost in the walking trees though, for he never got your invitation to my door."

"I don't know what this is about, but already you've gone far enough, Arlan," the king warned.

"Enough? Why, Sire, I've barely begun," Arlan said, bowing slightly. "I knew you wanted us all to enjoy your party, so I've invited Robin and Nabo, as well. I'd have invited your brother but he's out fighting—the fool!—to save your kingdom!"

He laughed again and turned to the door. Quad sputtered but could think of nothing to say, and Iscara glared, cat-like, at the intruder.

"Come in!" Arlan called to someone in the yard. "It's all right. You see? I told you we were invited!"

Nabo and Robin entered, the former looking uncomfortable and grim, the latter smiling broadly in anticipation.

"I've never been to a royal party!" Robin said.

Quad and Iscara simply stared, open-mouthed.

"I know the theme of the party is 'Your Favorite Prophet,'" Arlan continued with a flourish, "but, alas, my lord—and lady—I'm not so good at memorizing as you two. So I brought my favorite prophet with me! You've both heard, I'm sure, of the most famous court jester in history—the Rat Wugwart, who attended King Penta-tutinus' ill humors in the worst of times, hundreds of years ago. To me he was a prophet, for he spoke a language I understand, and his words are more stirring now than the greatest songs of—what is that name again? Odorous? And The Burial? In any case, for our entertainment, and to guide us on our way, I present the Rat Wugwart!"

He stepped aside, applauding, and Robin clapped wildly. Nabo's deep forehead creased into a frown and his eyes rolled hopelessly. A loud crash came from outside and suddenly Friend Rat appeared at the door. He wore a jester's wreath on his head and his foot was stuck in a bucket. "Tu-loo! Tuloo!" he announced, rolling his eyes in opposite directions. It was a performance he'd long wanted to try again: the Rat Wugwart was his favorite figure from history, a great hero to all rat-folk. He'd studied the jester's writings and biographies carefully until he'd mastered an impersonation that Pentatutinus said was perfect. With a galloping gait he ran to the center of the room, the bucket banging horridly. He bowed low, whumping his head on a stool, and jumped back with a squeal, tumbling over his tail and doing a noisy pratfall on the floor. Eyes rolling again, he called, "Tuloo! Tuloo! What did I do?"

Even Quad, despite his growing anger, couldn't stifle a laugh at the sight. Robin guffawed riotously while Arlan smiled, a look of mock rapture on his face. Nabo continued his frown, refusing to meet the king's eyes, and Iscara's whole persona blazed in fury.

"They are mocking me!" she breathed. Quad squeezed her hand.

"And now, my king, a poem for you!" the rat continued. He turned to the wizardess and broke character long enough to scold her. "All this dancing with so much to do! Tik! tik! tik!"

He held a finger up and sang in a falsetto voice—which was nonetheless most serious,

> The day shall come (and night will too!)
> But danger knocks. There's much to do!
> We've got to make a cheese soufflé
> While pig-dogs snarl in the bay.

He marched about, the bucket banging after him as he fell into everything in his path—and not a few things out of it. He kept his distance from the king and Iscara, however, for fear the former would whack him or that the latter might make him a rat-tree with leaves and apples sprouting from his nose.

> We've got to sing! We've got to dance!
> (That keeps the villains off our backs!)
> "And so I'll save you!" shouts the king.
> "I'll kill those villains as I sing!"

> And with his words so bold and bland
> He drove them back into their land
> Where they did wail, "Sire! Keep your throne
> And we shall swear we'll never roam,

> If you'll just grant us this one choice:
> To stop your mighty awful voice.
> And then, my lord, just one more thing:
> Please stop your naughty, dancing queen!

For she don't dance slow as she should.
Her feet fall hard in Magd'l'wood
And squashes all our visions so:
She'll squash us next, we fear, you know!"

Arlan and Robin burst into cheers. The king sat, trembling in a rage. Iscara's eyes were closed tight, her face white.

"I'm going to my garden," she said in a measured voice, looking as though she was avoiding violence only with the greatest of effort. "There's balms there for my leg."

As she left, there was an awkward silence. Quad glared at the others.

"All of you but Arlan, leave this room. Rat, I'll have words with you soon enough."

"Perhaps too soon," Friend Rat sighed as he banged out of the place. "Robin, come help me get this thing off my foot!"

"What's wrong?" Robin asked the king. "Wasn't it fun enough? I thought he was grand. Where's the food? Parties should have food."

Nabo took his hand and dragged him, protesting, from the room.

Only Quad and Arlan remained. The warrior turned and gazed out a window while the king remained by the fire.

"What's your problem?" Quad demanded. "Is this how you lead your men?"

"I was going to ask the same thing, myself," Arlan replied.

"Explain yourself."

With a sigh, Arlan turned and approached his king.

"Sire, we've been here, in this . . . shanty in the woods . . . three days now. Solofaust has tracked us by now, I'm certain. Nabo spent the night at the edge of Magdalawood and counted the fires of at least a dozen camps.

"We're safe here. The armies are superstitious and afraid to enter."

"They are, for now," Arlan admitted, "but they're not afraid to wait for us to come out. In another couple of days they'll have the whole wood surrounded. Sooner or later

Solofaust will send them in, or simply try to burn the forest down."

"We can't ride out of here without a plan!"

"In several days you haven't consulted me to help come up with one. You haven't even consulted your rat! The only one you've spoken to in any seriousness, in fact, is Iscara."

"You're jealous!"

"Of her!" Arlan scoffed. "A sultry hermit! What does she know?"

"She's a powerful wizardess! You saw what she does with trees . . ." Quad paused and a victorious smile swept his face. "I know what's going on! You're still upset about the spell!"

"I care nothing that she had me in one," Arlan said. "I've recovered from that, and the rest it gave me did wonders. I am concerned, however, about the spell she has on you."

"She's cast no spell on me!" the king said hotly.

"Not with her smelly weeds and roots," Arlan agreed, his voice softer now. "She's a beautiful woman, Sire. Desirable and intriguing. I see it in your eyes each time you look at her—you're in love."

"I am not!"

Arlan smiled.

"Well . . . so what if I am? Haven't you ever fallen in love with a beautiful woman? When this is over, I may make her my queen. Redaemus needs one with spirit, and with her spells, she'd be handy to have when the barons start pushing me around."

"I hope you'll have plenty of beds for when she charms them to sleep and good soil for when she turns them into trees."

"She's better than the snitty bluebloods I've seen about!"

"Your 'bluebloods' aren't about, anymore. Solofaust has killed or jailed every one of them, man, woman, or child. For all I know he may have my Jenna in chains."

"Jenna?"

"You asked if I've fallen in love before," Arlan said, and he pulled a red scarf from his collar. "You see? Her hair's like this—red and fine, and her kisses are life to me! Her father, the Farisae Cai, rules my city, Yerushela, the only city we know of that hasn't given in to follow the badger. As his daughter and as my betrothed, Jenna is Solofaust's enemy twice over."

Quad bowed his head, suddenly ashamed.

"I'm sorry," he said. "I'm forgetting how desperate the situation is. It's been too easy to forget these past couple of days."

"Love can do that, my lord, if you let it rule you untamed. 'Tis good you love, for you're a gentle king. So long as love rules you, you shall rule me. But you must master that emotion or it will master you. Go ahead, Sire. Let love feed your courage. Let it inspire you and stir you to action, but don't let it devour you. Mature love is a great servant. Untamed, 'tis but a monster."

"You're right, of course. Can you forgive me?"

"Forgive you for what? Were we arguing?" Arlan laughed. The two fell together, clasping each other. At last, they stepped back.

"One thing more," Arlan warned. "Guard your emotions, or you may bring more sorrow on yourself than you need."

"What do you mean?"

"I've seen the tender look you save for Iscara alone. But I've never seen that tender look reflected in her eyes." As quickly as it came, the serious demeanor left Arlan's face, and he lifted the Ruby Scion from where it had been, unattended, for three days past. "Our poet-king needs his club!"

Laughing, Quad took it and held it before him. Perhaps it was the reflection of the glowing fire, he would think on it later, but the crimson speck inside the ruby seemed to be growing, just a bit.

✦

In the midst of a song, the minstrel stopped, his fingers going dead on the lute and his voice catching suddenly in his throat. The rats, who had been swaying happily to his song, reacted with startled jumps as though they'd been awakened from slumber suddenly. File wiped his paws on a towel and walked up to the singer.

"Sirrah? Why've you stopped? We've listened to your teaching all day long, and have looked forward to this time of singing together!"

"He is coming."

"Who, sirrah?"

"The little king."

"Then, at last it *will* begin!" Snout said, clapping, and a murmur swept through the crowd.

"Indeed, it will. My father has told me my work shall begin now, in earnest."

"Then why aren't you smiling?" Snout wondered. "You should be happy, sirrah! You should be singing and laughing, you know."

"I am happy for you, my friends, and for what will be," the minstrel replied. "But I know what must happen before my little king arrives, and the road we must travel before this thing comes to an end, he and I. And the devastation . . ."

"Syncatus?" Snout asked, the pleasure falling from his face. "You told us that little town would be Desolation. Is this the time, then?"

"Even as we speak, the spirit-things are falling upon it."

"And can't you stop them? After all, you are . . ."

The minstrel cut him off emphatically.

"No," he said. "The little king's path must be laid before him. The prophecies must be fulfilled."

The travelers set out, and Iscara's hut faded behind them until it looked like a grassy hill in the midst of a clearing. The trees all around were swelling with welts of green buds.

They decided to spread out on the road: Nabo rode a half-mile to the rear, while Robin scouted ahead. He frequently rode back to give reports and, Arlan said with a laugh, to avoid being alone in the company of the walking trees he'd heard about too many times. A few yards behind Robin, Arlan rode with the king and wizardess, Quad on Spindle Legs, who had been retrieved from the woods, and Iscara rode her spirited pony. Friend Rat still preferred his feet to a saddle and trotted alongside. Toward noon, however, his feet grew sore and, when Robin appeared for a report, he hopped up behind him.

"I'm glad you're riding with me," the young warrior said when they'd galloped out of sight. "You accept me as your equal—unlike my so-called companions."

"Oh, I accept anybody," Friend Rat replied.

"I'm being serious!" Robin said angrily (and the rat said nothing, for he'd thought he was being serious, too). "I'm always left out! When plans are made, they send me for firewood! When battles are called, I'm left doing laundry and chopping meat. The only real fighting I've done was at the castle ambush, and then only because there wasn't any choice. Gregor keeps telling me I'm too young and inexperienced to do battle. So tell me, how can I become an experienced warrior if I never get to fight?"

"Whatever are you getting at?" Friend Rat asked.

"I mean, here we are!"

"Yes, we are," Friend Rat replied, looking about. "I certainly agree with you there."

"Six against a kingdom! One man's mistakes could be fatal for us all. But who tells me what's going on, so that I can avoid making them? Who tells me what our plan is?"

"I take it I'm to be your 'who.'"

"I was hoping so!" Robin laughed.

"'Tis simple enough. We follow the king."

"And what is his plan?"

"To follow his nose. An easy thing to do in his case, I might add."

"What do you mean?"

"I mean, his nose is rather large."

"No! What do you mean 'he'll follow his nose'?"

"The king reasons so: No one knows where the One-prince is, so 'tis no sense asking anyone how to find him."

Robin's brow wrinkled. "Then how will he be found?"

"There's magic in the Ruby Scion. At least the king thinks so. Iscara has convinced him that, sooner or later, it will draw him to the Oneprince, revealing him by glowing bright as a drunkard's nose."

"Do you believe that?"

"I believe there's magic in it, for how else could the last king have lived so long? But I also suspect that, if it does lead us to the Oneprince, then the place at which it stops will be a tomb."

"You believe he's dead?"

"If I believe in him at all. Remember, the tales of him are hundreds of years old and, for all we know, only legends after all."

"Then why don't you try to talk the king out of this?"

"Why? Quad has made up his mind. Tik! tik! tik! 'Tis so rare he makes a decision that when he does he clings to it for all he's worth, and I encourage him in it!" He shifted uneasily on the horse's back, trying to find a position that would not have him slipping at every stride.

"Well, if King Quad believes in the Oneprince, then so shall I!" Robin boasted. "Oneprince, here we come!"

"'Tis a blessing to have a simple mind," Friend Rat sighed.

That evening Nabo kept guard and Robin was sent— protesting loudly—to collect firewood. The others sat on the rocky bank of a stream, the king concentrating hard on his hands.

"You're picking up this sign-talk quickly," Arlan said. "I'm proud of you."

Iscara watched the lesson with fascination, while Friend Rat, Arlan's other student, carefully untangled his fingers.

"Tik! tik! tik! This just ties my knuckles in knots!"

"You'll get better," Arlan said. "Iscara, I want you to learn this, too."

"What's the sense of a language without a voice?" she asked.

"All the sense in the world if you cannot talk," Arlan replied. "Gregor learned it from deaf men who'd learned it at a monastery. He thought it would be useful for the Honor Guard when spying on enemy movements or communicating in a noisy battle. Well, I think we've done enough for tonight."

"Will we meet the enemy when we leave Magdalawood?" Quad asked.

"That depends on whether the badger has enough men to completely surround the wood and time to do it. If he has, we're as good as finished. If he hasn't it'll be a matter of luck whether we meet them."

"If we do?"

"We'll hope we find just a handful. Then we may be able to fight our way through. If there are many, your wizardess had best have some tricks up her sleeve."

Iscara smiled coolly. "Are you admitting I may be of some use?"

Arlan smiled back, but didn't speak.

"What lies beyond Magdalawood?" Quad wondered aloud.

Iscara shrugged. "My world ends with the trees. Beyond it lie the Eastern Lands."

"In which case I shall tell you what we'll see," Arlan said. "If I guess right, we'll come out a few hours' ride from Syncatus. 'Tis a village lying due east of the wood." He looked to Iscara, who nodded. "In that village, a road heads north and south. Northward is a colony of common folk, mostly rats. To the south lies my city, Yerushela."

"Then we'll ride south," Quad said. "If the Oneprince is anywhere about, he will be there with the other lords and scholars."

ellie had always loved her feather bed, but this night she found luxury lying on a mattress of grass and last year's leaves. She was alive! And everything she touched, heard, or saw was a wonder to behold. Wrapped in a blanket, she watched her breath rise— little gray puffs drifting upward on the cold night air.

Narramoore stood some ways off, his silhouette seeming thoughtful and impressive against the sky, while stars flickered in the night like candles at a royal wedding—a comparison that somehow made her tingle. Sleeping close at her left was Clepper, his rattling snore a rhapsody in phlegm, while the Rat Boofer snoozed on her right, rolled up in a ball with only the tips of his nose and tail protruding from his blanket.

Though she smiled, she was far from feeling cheery. *All these adventures and I'm not free yet*, she thought. *From a trumped-up treason trial to a real one still coming. And you,* her thoughts paused as she gazed wonderingly at the warrior, *I thought I had my freedom when we crawled through that passage together. Now I see I was only trading one dungeon-master for another!*

She had ached, body and soul, in that passage, but as Narramoore led them stumbling through the darkness, with Helen's awful howls and curses echoing in their ears, Nellie had quickly realized her aches had only begun.

For a quarter-mile they felt their way. Narramoore ducked deftly into passages with the Rat Boofer and Clepper easily following his lead—passages she couldn't even see but quickly found with her forehead.

"Ow!" she would cry.

"I'm sorry! Oh my!" came the rat's hurried reply.

"Sir Boofer," she said after the third such meeting of mind and doorpost, "things would go better if you'd say 'duck!' before we enter these holes instead of 'I'm sorry' after!"

"Then *duck!*" he said.

Whack!

"I'm sorry! Oh my!"

"Blast!" Nellie shouted. "Just leave me here to die!" Then she began to cry.

"We must keep moving," Narramoore urged, his voice soft yet severe. "This next passage is larger, and far enough from the main ones that we can light torches."

In a short time they reached a small chamber where bundles rested on small shelves along a wall. From these Narramoore removed torches and soaked their cloth wrappings in a jar of oil. He handed one to Clepper and kept the other for himself, and he lit them using flints.

"Where's mine?" Nellie ventured to ask.

"Two are enough," he replied.

"We don't want ye gettin' too adventurous, Nell," Clepper added with a grin. "Why, you might get the 'wanderies' an' get y'self lost somewheres!"

The torches' anemic, yellow light made her companions look ghostly, and Nellie shuddered to think how sad she must look herself, a mural of colorful bruises with trickles of blood spattering her skin and dress. For a moment they rested, and Narramoore tended to Clepper's wound, cleaning and binding it with supplies he had previously put in this room.

"'Tis not deep. It should heal well," he commented.

"It don't look deep, p'raps, but it feels like an almighty

mine shaft," Clepper replied with a grimace through clinched teeth. "Watch yer hands, Narry! Clean out th' dirt if ye must, but leave me some flesh!"

As the warrior worked, Nellie remained close to the passageway, listening to her own panting breath and the spectral sounds of distant battle. When he'd finished wrapping Clepper's shoulder, Narramoore took her by the hand and started forward again.

"Those cries," Nellie gasped, trying to keep pace and looking over her shoulder as Narramoore half-led, half-dragged her along, "they sound like prisoners being slaughtered."

"More so'diers are dyin' than pris'ners, if things are goin' right, Nell," Clepper chuckled.

"Which, of course, they never do," the Rat Boofer added. "Oh my!"

"However the battle is going, you can be sure prisoners are dying," Narramoore said, stopping suddenly to turn on her. "You weren't the only prisoner thinking today would be your last. Another dozen were marked for execution. Remember this, my lady: every killing since the day of the coronation comes from Solofaust, whom you helped bring to power. Therefore, every death falls on your silly head as well. Now then, down these stairs."

Nellie chewed her lip as his words sank in. "Out of the boiling pot, into the fire," she sighed, hurrying after him. "I guess I'll need a counselor for defense."

"You'll have to be your own defense," Narramoore called.

Clepper, his idiot-sticker clacking against the steps as he followed them down, chuckled.

"Ain't many loyers around. Ol' Solyfaust didn't like loyers much."

"To think I was studying to be one!" the Rat Boofer called from behind.

"Oh my!" he and Clepper said together.

"Solofaust is licensed. Perhaps I could hire him!" Nellie said, allowing herself to laugh. She stopped with a thud, as she bounced into Narramoore's suddenly rigid body and landed with a smack, sitting on the steps. The captain glared down at her, eyes flashing. The maid gasped, drawing up her hands, expecting to be run through. Instead, he turned again and continued his descent, holding so tightly to her wrist that she feared her bones would break.

"Does all the Honor Guard have a sense of humor as fine as yours?" she said, trying to ignore the pain. As an afterthought she added, "You're a real charmer!"

"My duty here isn't to charm you."

"And if it were?"

"I'd do so," came his serious reply.

"Ho! I love it!" Nellie said with a laugh.

"She'll stop laughing so hard, real quick now," Clepper whispered to the rat.

Turning, Nellie saw him respond with a vigorous nod and a knowing smile.

"What do ye mean by that?" she demanded, and again she banged into Narramoore, who had stopped.

"We've reached bottom," he said.

Looking down, her humor drained. The "bottom" she saw, was a dead end—there was no hall and no doorway. The walls were solid and slick, and the steps disappeared at her feet into a pool of black, still water. Panic washed over her and she jerked her hand back violently, freeing it from Narramoore's grip. With a cry she turned and rushed up the steps, straight into the hands of Clepper who, grinning, pushed her roughly back. She stumbled, landing soundly in Narramoore's waiting arms, and Clepper advanced a step toward her, drawing his sword.

"You'll assassinate me, right here!" she gasped.

"You ain't important enough for that!" Clepper sneered.

"Enough!" Narramoore ordered, then turned Nellie's face to his. "If your death was our intention, we'd have left you to the executioner," he said coldly. "This is not the dead end it appears to be. Seven feet under there's one last doorway."

She looked at the murky pool, its water so dark she couldn't see beneath the inky surface.

"You're crazy if you think I'm going into that," she said, her voice shaking.

"I'll walk with you until the water reaches your shoulders. There are pegs along the wall, and you can use them to pull yourself down to the doorway. More pegs on the other side will help you pull yourself to the surface. Hold tight to them, for this is an underground river, and the current beyond this wall is strong."

"And what then?"

"I'll tell you on the other side."

She looked at the others. Clepper seemed undisturbed at the thought of the river and pool, although the Rat Boofer bore a look of wide-eyed concern. He was tying a rope about his middle, which Clepper would use to haul him along.

"Rats float," he explained when he caught her eye, "like corks."

"And I float like stone," she replied, turning again to Narramoore. "You hold on to the pegs, my lord. I'm staying here."

With a sigh of resignation, Narramoore seized Nellie and dragged her, kicking and screaming, into the water as Clepper laughed uproariously. Nellie kicked the murky, still water into an angry foam, shuddering at its numbing cold stealing about her hips and then her waist, but Narramoore continued to carry her deeper. When only her head was still above the surface she heard his command.

"If you obey nothing else today, obey this: take a breath and hold it!"

She gulped in air as the icy water closed over her head and pounded in her ears. Narramoore dragged her under, clasping each peg with his free hand and feeling for the ridge of the arched, underwater door. Finding it, he firmly pushed her through and, feeling the sudden current hammer against her, she groped and found the pegs on the far side. The warrior let go and Nellie pulled herself frantically to the surface. There, spluttering and coughing, clinging to the wall for dear life, she looked about, letting her eyes adjust. A wide river stretched before her with a ceiling of limestone spanning no more than four feet above. Here and there a bit of surface light sliced through a crack in the earth and reflected off the fast-flowing water.

"Well!" she said through chattering teeth as Narramoore surfaced beside her, "what do we do now? Wait for the ferry?"

"Feel upstream. There's a rope stretching to a ledge on the other side, and that leads to another tunnel. Half a mile farther we'll climb a shaft that opens to a clump of rocks in a field."

Nellie reached ahead, tentatively, and found the rope. Hanging to it with all four limbs, she worked her way across. Narramoore stayed right behind her but, she thought, if he was doing so to guard her, he could have saved his effort. *I don't have the strength to run away no more.* She reached the far ledge and, with Narramoore's hand pushing from behind, hauled herself up onto the ledge.

"Watch where you lay your hand, my lord!" she managed to say between gasps for air, "or is it your duty to charm me now?" She thought his face flushed deeply at her words. At least she hoped it did. On the far side there came a splash and a popping sound as Clepper broke surface and hauled the Rat Boofer up behind.

"Is our queen still with us?" Clepper called.

"She is," Narramoore answered. "Hurry across!"

Water still dripped from her skirts when, sometime later, she stood gazing up the shaft.

"There's not room for a snake to slither up that hole," she said. But the sunshine beckoned at its far end and she climbed into it, almost greedily, ignoring the additional scraping her limbs took. Dragging herself through at last, blinking against her first sight of the sun in days, she collapsed, unceremoniously, on a rock.

There she lay, waiting for the others, feeling the warming caress of sun against her soaked, trembling body. Narramoore slipped easily out a moment later, followed by a grunting, straining Clepper who stuck fast in the opening and made such a fuss that Narramoore was reminded of Gregor's earlier difficulties in the cavern. A number of maneuvers were tried, with the Rat Boofer pushing and Narramoore pulling, while Nellie simply sat on the rock, her teeth chattering. Finally, Clepper retreated down the hole where he and the Rat Boofer used his idiot sticker to dislodge some stones. This time he squeezed through, though he nearly lost his breeches in the process. The Rat Boofer scampered out more easily, and Narramoore pulled Nellie, protesting, to her feet.

"We must continue," he said.

"The devil we must."

"Just to that copse of trees," he said, pointing toward the bottom of the hillside where they stood. "I'll build a fire. Shall I carry you?"

"I can walk, Lord Charming," she smiled disarmingly. She turned and led the way.

✦

Sitting close to the fire she examined her condition. Her dress was a tattered mess and her hair felt like birds had nested in it.

"I've got eggs in it, even!" she muttered, feeling the bumps there. Nothing felt broken, but she was spotted with bruises and cuts. Most noticeable was the gash on her chin and a fat bruise on her cheek, courtesy of the executioner and his block. A quick look at Clepper and the Rat Boofer showed they were in better shape than she, though not by much. Clepper's uniform was a collection of rips and holes held together with thread, and his hands, arms, and cheeks were scraped raw. The Rat Boofer's coat was matted with dirt and, she suspected, his shaggy hide masked a treasury of bumps and abrasions. Finally she looked at Narramoore, who sat on his haunches studying her. He was clean and neat, his light vest of chain mail dazzling, and every hair of his head was in place.

"I must say you're in fine shape!" Nellie growled.

"I'm trained to it. Are you in pain?"

"The dead feel no pain." She looked around, wondering

where they were. She knew the country about The Village well, but this place was unfamiliar. Perhaps, she thought, they were on the opposite side of Pentatute Hill.

"There's a hollow tree behind you," Narramoore said. "In it is a bundle of your clothes and a cloak, which Clepper took from The Rasp & File, as well as boots, soap, and towels. A spring lies beyond the tree for water, and a pot is here to heat it so that you can wash and clean your wounds. You may use my brush and mirror. The three of us will go and scout the area, and find some better clothes for Clepper and something to scrub the Rat Boofer's hide. We'll return in a couple of hours."

"You'll just go and leave me? What makes you so sure I'll be here when you return?"

"Where will you go?" Narramoore asked coolly. "To Solofaust?"

When they left she removed her clothes and wrapped herself in a blanket, then wandered to the pool where she inspected her reflection. She looked constantly about as she did. Narramoore didn't concern her—he was so noble, he seemed unreal. Sir Boofer was of no concern, either—he was, after all, a rat. But Clepper? *There's no danger in you, old Clep,* she thought, *but a lady needs to put a leash about your eyes.* Filling a pot, she let it heat a few minutes, then washed. The hot water felt good on her battered skin.

She finished without incident—for once—and dried. Then she went to the tree where she found a clean dress that was surprisingly practical (considering a man had chosen it), a brown, knitted shawl old Helen had made for her ages ago, and lest her faith in men be forever changed, uncomfortable, ill-fitting boots that weren't even hers. She dressed and warmed herself at the fire a few minutes, then began to feel hungry. Searching among the camp supplies she found some salted meat. This she sniffed carefully—it smelled like a dead thing proud of its condition. *Men!* she thought. *They'll eat anything, anything a t'all! Well, we'll need something better than this to hate each other by.* It would be some time before the others returned, so she set off to find some early spring plants that could make a more sensible meal and, just possibly, some tea.

◆

The others would go through Magdalawood, Narramoore knew, then head south to confer in the one stronghold of loyalists left in the kingdom—Yerushela. His own part in Quad and Gregor's plan had been to see how things fared at the castle. He had accomplished this, adding for himself the task of finding loyal officers among the dungeon prisoners and helping them organize an army of raiders to harass Solofaust's supply and communication lines. He might have, he mused, even taken control of Pentatute by strategic use of the passages if Helen hadn't discovered them. She had filled the larger corridors with soldiers and blocked up or collapsed the many smaller passages she didn't have time to explore.

Nellie's trial had come as a surprise, and when a spy told him of it, he'd disguised himself in a guard's uniform. Helen had given him an odd look when he showed up to escort the prisoner, but he explained he'd been transferred by request from the forces besieging Yerushela and she accepted him well enough. It had never occurred to her that an enemy could breach her system of security.

Watching the maid sleep, he wondered why he had rescued her. In a way, it had simply been logical—the moment of execution would make it easy to synchronize the escape of the other prisoners. While that exact moment wouldn't be known until the arrival of the execution squad, still the loyalists hidden in each cell could hear the unpleasant party marching past, for they did this with fanfare to keep the prisoners in terror. Since so much attention would be focused on Nellie's cell (thanks to Helen's strange and intense hatred of her), the prisoners in the other cells could be freed of their chains in advance. Some might even escape without having to battle. Some dungeons had no passage entrance, however, and their residents would have to battle their way across the hall to a dungeon that did. Finally, of course, there was the opportunity to slay Helen, whom the captain knew was one of the greatest threats to Quad's kingdom.

The girl could be useful for information on Solofaust's strategies, for who knew him better? And, her rescue would be a total surprise. Helen would hardly expect anyone to rescue a woman who was really opposed to Quad, and who, Helen knew, loyalists would be happy to see die. The charges against Nellie were, after all, trumped up.

Or were they?

Nellie had a decidedly rebellious attitude, he'd seen, but her spirit seemed to fall short of evil. While her devotion to the badger was strong (he had, after all, seen to much of her upbringing), she had always avoided direct participation in the violence and had shown compassion toward the prisoners who came under her care. At times she went about with a disturbed and haunted look in her eyes, as if she wondered whether she were really on the right side.

A lot of conclusions to make, he told himself, *and little evidence to support them.* Perhaps he should have left her in the forest with the raiders . . . but no, that would give her the opportunity to buy back Solofaust's trust by revealing their hideouts. And, with Helen apparently dead, it would be too easy for Solofaust to forgive his "little girl."

There were times, even when he was running down the passages with her and Clepper and the Rat Boofer, that he wanted for all the world to slay her. Who would have blamed him? Only two others would know how she died, and they'd seen enough of the suffering she'd brought about that they'd have kept quiet. They might even have applauded him!

Perhaps, he told himself, watching the beautiful woman who slept before him, head pillowed in her blood-drenched hands, he had refrained from killing her only because he couldn't stoop to the barbarism of Solofaust's regime.

Perhaps.

Solofaust's ward turned on her side and muttered in her sleep—Narramoore couldn't make out what. He turned his thoughts to how he might best rejoin the king's party. Most likely he could catch up with them on the west side of Magdalawood, possibly near or in the village of Syncatus, which guarded the north-south road to Yerushela. He'd already decided to leave behind Clepper and the Rat Boofer. Neither of them was in any condition for hard riding. They would return to the castle where they could oversee and develop the tiny opposition force.

Nellie would ride with him. She had spunk and strength and a wit that more than matched Clepper's and the Rat Boofer's. Should she so choose, she could give them the slip at any time. She had displayed endurance and strength in the tunnels and passages, and Narramoore thought she could hold up to a journey with him. He only hoped her unpredictable furies and humor didn't get them killed along the way.

The dawn was just beginning to draw the night aside when Nellie felt a boot tap against her ribs. She opened her eyes and rose on one elbow to find Narramoore stooping beside her.

"We're going," he said. "You'll do everything I say. If you obey and keep up, I'll treat you well. If you fall behind, I'll leave you. And if you try to run or expose us, I will kill you. Is that understood?"

"Yes."

She rolled up her blanket as he gathered supplies and tied them to his horse. The other two slept, undisturbed; they would wake in another hour, and go their way. Nellie climbed onto the horse behind her captor. As she rode, holding on to Narramoore's broad shoulders, she sensed in him a tension and exhaustion that his words and outward manner didn't display. She'd known such a man before, in The Rasp & File, and had watched him one day pull out a dagger and go crazy, slashing away as patrons and soldiers piled on him in frantic desperation. It was easy to believe this sullen, knightly man might somehow snap along the way, spin around, and take off her head.

Narramoore, sharply aware of her breath on the back of his neck, prayed he would not do just that.

◆

A slight mist rose, weaving itself into the fabric of another dawn. Nellie watched, fascinated, as Narramoore crept spider-like along a rocky ledge, his eyes never leaving the sentry who was unaware of his own peril. Leaning forward at a slight angle, his gloved hands closed about his spear, the foot soldier stared straight at where she lay hidden in a thicket of young ash. Yet he did not see her because of the night's darkness and his own lack of attention. Narramoore leapt from shadow to shadow, his cat-like movements flowing from bush to tree. Invisible in a boulder's shadow, he strung his bow and selected an arrow. In a moment the sentry lay dead. Narramoore went to the man, broke the shaft protruding from him, then looked over the ledge the sentry had been guarding. Satisfied, he signaled for Nellie to break cover.

"Why did you break the arrow?" Nellie asked, slipping toward him.

"So the enemy will not recognize my feathering on its shaft," he replied. "Now, take his cloak and valuables. Perhaps they'll think this was the work of deserters or marauders." Turning from her he walked again to the ledge. His attention was taken by whatever lay below as Nellie eyed the corpse distastefully.

"You want me to go about handling a dead man?" With a scowl she knelt beside it. "I'm a village girl, and superstitious. Haven't you heard? Ugh! What a face! Like the good gods were sleepy and they put it on him, inside-out. An' he's got a gold tooth. I hope ye don't expect me to pull that out."

Narramoore motioned distractedly for silence. Nellie rifled through the sentry's pockets.

"Ah! beefsticks! Want one?"

"No."

"Noble heroes don't eat breakfast, hey?" she smiled. "Well . . . your marauders an' deserters were fools, if they thought this man had much worth robbing." Dropping to her hands and knees she crept to the warrior, then slapped a beefstick into his hand. "Here, eat it anyway, Lord Valiant."

Silently, he took it.

Several minutes went by and the sun began to creep over the horizon. She grew restless and entertained herself by drawing in the dust with her toe.

"My feet hurt," she muttered. "Look. They're filthy! Hard as horses' feet and just as ugly, too."

Closing his eyes, Narramoore drew in a breath.

"I gave you boots. You threw them away."

"Those weren't boots. They were hooves for a cow. They were too big and hurt my feet."

"Oversized boots are better than none in situations like these."

Her lips broke into a smile and, turning her head to hide it, she said, "My head hurts, too."

Narramoore let loose a long, impatient sigh, despairingly clutching at his forehead. Watching, Nellie giggled.

At the sound, the warrior spun around.

"This is no time for a village girl's tricks and games!" he threatened through clenched teeth, grabbing her shoulders and rattling her. "Bridle your tongue or I'll bind and gag you and *carry* you about!"

"You're hurting me!" she cried, her voice rising.

"You'll be hurt far worse, and not by me, if you don't stop this noise! Look below!" He dragged her to the ledge. "Tell me! What do you see?"

She looked. The hill fell sharply away, an incline of loose rock and shale for several hundred feet, with scraps of pine and eager ferns poking testily from the cracks and soil. Beyond that, spreading like cancer, numberless tents filled the fields and woods, their eastern sides warming to the glow of the sun. With a gasp she dropped to her belly.

"There must be millions! It looks like all the armies of the kingdom!"

"Not all, but a fourth of them at least. If they hear your laughter, they'll all be clambering up this hill to find us."

"Whose is that?" she asked, pointing to a large tent halfway across the field. Solofaust's flag flapped in a slight breeze above it, a white scroll embossed on a scarlet field.

"The commander-general's tent?" Narramoore guessed aloud.

Suddenly Nellie brought her fist to her mouth and her eyes widened.

"Oh no! Look!" She pointed at two men who were being led, bound and flanked by guards, to the command tent.

"Prisoners?" Narramoore guessed.

"Spirit food!" Nellie gasped.

"What?"

He turned and saw she was trembling violently. She stumbled to her feet and, muttering distractedly, began to pace about, growing more hysterical with each step. The captain watched in astonishment.

"What's wrong?" he asked. His voice was calm and cool, but he felt a sensation of dread welling deep within him.

"The commander-general . . . and some of its men . . . they are spirit-things."

"Spirit-things!"

"That's what Helen called 'em. Creatures without a body, she said. At least, they've none you can see, though they have a man's shape when they're wrapped in clothes and under a hood." The words came streaming from her now, fast and soft, but filled with panic. "You can't see their faces in them hoods! Just their eyes! I've looked! Horrid, red eyes, hot as fire and full o' hate!"

"And they feed on people?"

Shuddering, she nodded.

"How do you know this?" Narramoore demanded.

"At the castle . . . they told me to bring young prisoners—

to be questioned and set free, they said. So I chose a couple of boys, not much more than kids. I scrubbed 'em an' took 'em to the spirit-thing, and then it bid me leave. The kids were cryin'—I didn't blame 'em, but I didn't think they'd come to harm. I told 'em so, left, an' closed the door. A minute later," she added, her whole body trembling, "the screaming began. I banged at the door an' shouted, but I was ignored. An' I banged and banged, an' they screamed an' . . ." She stopped a moment, as if to gather strength to go on, looking only at the ground as she spoke. "At last . . . the door opened and I saw their bodies taken out. Wrinkled, they were. And hard an' dry, an' . . . Not at all like boys no more . . . Poor things!"

She fell to her knees, tears running down her cheeks, wringing her skirts in her hands. Narramoore watched, amazed, and started toward her, his hands out. Glancing up at him, she jumped back with a hiss.

"Don't give me your pity! I'll not have it! Not when you're marchin' me off to a mock trial an' a traitor's dyin'! You're my guard, not my guardian! Stay away!"

"I'm doing only what must be done," Narramoore said confusedly. "These are difficult times for us all, and . . ."

"Don't tell me your troubles. You're doin' what you were born to do an' lovin' every minute, hacking your way through the rabble and slinkin' about for your noble cause. Soon you'll be fightin' with friends in exile, at least. But who's there for me? I've only enemies, whichever side I go. I even hate myself!"

The tears had dried, leaving long trails on her dirty cheeks, and her large, blue eyes stared vacantly. Knowing nothing else to say, feeling embarrassed to simply stare at her, Narramoore turned again and watched the camp below.

"I never meant to torture children," Nellie whispered.

He turned to her again. She was looking right at him, her expression that of a guilty child.

"My lord Narramoore, with silence or a shout, I can choose whose hands I'll fall into, yours or theirs. Theirs will be more brutal, perhaps, but with your king, my end will be the same. 'Tis a hard choice I'm makin'. Forgive me when I lose myself in tricks an' games."

They watched each other sadly. Narramoore felt a desire to go to her, to hold her, but something within held him back. *You're so close I could take you in my arms,* he thought, *yet we're whole worlds apart.*

He jerked his head up as the screaming began.

Hideous screams of terror and agony, long and loud and shrill carried to them on the wind. The shock of their sounds cut through the warrior and maiden like knives.

Nellie leaped from where she knelt and with an agonized cry ran toward the ledge. In desperation he dove for her as she passed, smothering her to the ground and pinning her, holding her flailing wrists, whispering meaningless sounds in an effort to comfort and calm her. She struggled, kicking and swearing oaths. With a violent jerk she freed her hands and instinctively Narramoore's own hands raised to his face, a defense against her flailing claws. But instead of attacking, she wrapped her arms about him, clinging frantically to his muscular frame, her body racked by sobs. Narramoore cradled her gently, his eyes swelling with tears. He was filled with a righteous loathing toward the spirit-things, a hatred he had never felt before.

He rocked the simple peasant girl in his arms, even after the screams had faded to a stifling silence, feeling her face wet against his neck, the soft, yet firm pressure of her vulnerable body and soul against him. Slowly it dawned on him that he had become as much prisoner to her as she was to him.

Narramoore, captain of the exalted Honor Guard, defender of the king, had fallen in love.

In spite of his growing optimism, leaving Magdalawood left Quad feeling as though he'd just built a huge bonfire on an inky night. Like a man in darkness, he was unable to continue his search for the Oneprince so long as they remained in the shadows of the enchanted wood. And like that same man who touched a spark to the pile of branches, leaves, and deadwood, he could not only see what he was about . . . the enemy could see him as well.

They reached the edge of Iscara's realm in the late afternoon with no sign of Solofaust's armies in the fields about.

"Apparently, they have yet to close their net," Arlan commented.

"But why tempt the fates?" Nabo said. "They're close, for I can sense them."

"Then let's move on," Arlan replied. "'Tis tempting to lie down and rest within Magdalawood just a few more hours, and then travel after dark. But if you sense the enemy coming, I've no doubt they are."

"There's a small wood not more than three or four hours' ride from here," Iscara suggested, "with a clearing in the midst of it large enough to sleep in for the night."

"What? And ride on in the morning? With all those monsters after us?" Friend Rat gasped.

"We seek the Oneprince, whose realm is daylight," she replied, tossing her head. "How will we find him, if we search only in darkness?"

"That makes sense!" Quad agreed.

"I hate to say you're right," Arlan said, "but you are. Not that finding this Oneprince makes a bit of sense to me, but if we're going to try, it only makes sense to do so in daylight. If this clearing is in the wood I'm thinking you mean, it'll put us an easy day's ride from Syncatus. Once there, we can nose about to see if anyone's heard of this fellow, and we can also pick up some news on the movements of Solofaust's armies."

"But they'll know we're Honor Guard!" Robin protested. "They'll turn us in for sure!"

"I'm not so sure," Arlan replied. "I suspect that by now our master badger has shown his true colors. There will be some folk, at least, who will do all they can to hide us. Besides, we look more the part of peasants than royalty and nobility now. Perhaps we'll pass a farm or an inn where we can get some peasant clothes for the king and this wizardess. As for us, if we can find some hide to stretch over our shields, they won't know us from any other soldiers or brigands. Sire, your face might be too well known. Perhaps we can wrap you and say you were wounded in fighting or something. And, Rat, you just act naturally. No one will suspect nobility in you then!"

"Tik! tik! tik!"

"What of the Ruby Scion?" Quad asked.

"Keep it under the cloak that we find you," Arlan said.

"And you expect me to put on some filthy peasant's dress?" Iscara sniffed.

"Or at least be more modest with the wrappings you're in," Arlan said, pointing his sword at her. "With your shoulder bare and your dress hung so low, every soldier and every man who's neither blind nor eighty will be gaping at you."

"Arlan!" Quad reprimanded.

"Do you deny it's the truth?"

"Let's go!" Nabo's rumbling voice interrupted.

Arlan pulled back on his reins, making his horse rear and whinny.

"On, then! We'll discuss these matters at camp! Ride quickly and in silence."

Robin reached down for Friend Rat, and the shaggy animal climbed up hesitantly behind.

"Hold tight!" the youth said with a laugh, and the party galloped away.

They reached the wood Iscara had described. It was thick with brambles and thorns and whispery ash, almost impossible to penetrate. Leading their horses carefully along a creekbed, however, they were able to get through and find the clearing. It was a broad, mossy spot, wide enough to tether the horses and for all to lie down in comfort, wrapped tightly in their blankets to ward off the chill. The last of the sun disappeared as they settled in. Deciding to hold off discussing their plans until morning, they fell quickly asleep.

But in the middle of the night a chill seized Quad and he awoke, drawing his cover more tightly about him. He blinked, gazing into the darkness. With a shudder he realized *something is watching me!*

There.

At the edge of the thicket, not twenty feet away.

He couldn't see it, but he felt it. Dread and loathing cut like an assassin's knife through his conscience. He told himself he was jumping at shadows. He tried—but failed—to laugh. For reassurance he touched the Ruby Scion, then cleared his throat.

"Arlan?" he whispered.

But Arlan was asleep.

"Iscara? Friend Rat? Nabo?"

None responded, though with each name his volume increased, until he was nearly shouting. From the dark came low, rumbling laughter—more a terrifying sensation than an audible sound.

"How can you sleep?" he cried. "The Presence is here, and it knows we are, too!"

Ha ha ha ha ha haaa!

And Quad realized that, while the sound was as real and sure to him as the bony clacking of the limbs in the trees, this thing was speaking from within his head, and only he could hear it.

They've had a hard day, simpering king. I doubt you'll wake them!

"What have you done to them!" Quad shouted.

They are . . . enchanted!

The word, harsh and sinister, made him reel.

All of them—forever! Even your precious wizardess!

The king scrambled to Iscara's side and shook her so violently, her teeth clacked in her head, but she remained limp in his hands. He ran to the rat and rattled him, too, even slapping his snout. Nothing. Arlan gave no response and Nabo lay immobile as a moody stone. Tears coming to his eyes, the king ran to the clearing's center.

"Robin! Where are you!"

The sentry? He is sleeping. They are all *sleeping!*

The laughter grew into dark thunderous sounds, building their strength from the swirling night air. As the wind built around him, Quad realized the spirit-thing's voice had grown, so that it was now outside him, as well as within.

"Why not me?" he shouted, "Why am I awake?"

"Because I have come for you!"

The king threw his arms wide as the sky tore apart around him. Hailstones as big as his fists rained down. Dropping his scepter, he scrambled on his hands and knees for the meager protection of the trees. For a moment he lay, pressed against the ghostly bark, his arms covering his face against the bruising ice. Then he remembered his friends.

Rushing headlong into the hail, he grabbed Iscara's wrists and dragged her to a tree. She was a bundle of sweet-smelling rags in his hands. Kissing her forehead, touching a hail-made bruise there, he drew the blanket over her. Then he rushed to the rat and half-rolled, half-dragged him to the recessed opening of a hollow tree. Arlan was next, but Nabo was so large he couldn't budge him. Pulling at the warrior's arm and trying to hide the panic rising in his voice, Quad shouted to the whirling, roaring deluge about him.

"Who are you!"

"*Who asks it!*" was the mocking reply.

"Your king!" Quad managed to gasp.

"*Darkness is my king!*" the voice said with laughter—numbing, insane laughter.

With a crack a branch tore loose from a tree and grazed his head. Half-dazed, Quad struggled to his feet and threw himself across Nabo, hoping at least his body would offer some protection. The hail hammered at his back and the wind shrieked in his ears. He heard a metallic clacking and reached out for the sound. It was the Ruby Scion, slick to the touch and coated in mud. Seizing it, he took courage.

"By this scepter I hold, I command you: *Who are you!*"

"*I am the Commander-General!*"

The answer was reluctant—but it came.

"How did you find me?"

"I am drawn to the Ruby Scion, idiot! So long as you carry it, I know right where you are!"

The wind built, the roar increased. A jagged branch struck Quad's shoulder, gouging deep and sending an agonizing spasm of pain down his arm. He heard the clatter of other branches raining on the ground, and he clung more tightly to the scepter and to Nabo.

"I was holding this scepter some days ago," he gasped, "and you walked right by me!"

"*What!*"

There was amazement in the response: he'd scored some kind of victory.

"*You hadn't carried it long enough, that is all. The bond was weak, but now it has betrayed you, and you are mine!*"

"Then kill me, but let the others go."

"*Perhaps*," the thought laughed, "*you're not worth my bother!*"

"Or perhaps!" Quad said in sudden revelation, his eyes wide, "you can't do it!"

In response, a thunderous roar seemed to tear open his skull. He clutched, screaming, at his head, and with an explosion of thorns, clodding mud, and branches, a writhing funnel cloud of dirt, loam, and wind smashed through the trees. It whirled drunkenly about, pulling up saplings by the roots and tossing his companions like dolls into the thicket as it performed its ugly dance. Quad himself, keeping a death grip on his scepter, was sucked effortlessly into the air. The whirling debris ripped his clothes and slashed him in a hundred places as it carried him along. He screamed in terror.

Through the thicket and the wood and into an open field he was carried, where still screaming Quad was thrown with crushing force to the ground. He lay there, stunned, panting, coughing up bile as his ribs and shoulder blazed with pain. The funnel cloud danced about, not twenty feet from him, before it flew off on a crooked eastward path, smashing stone fences and snapping gnarled old trees lying in its path.

"*Do you want to see power, little nothing? Then follow me!*"

Fury welled up inside the king, filling him with a desperate strength. He staggered to his feet and ran after the whirlwind, his heart crashing in his chest and the cold air burning as it filled his heaving lungs. The cloud danced always ahead, just within sight.

It veered suddenly to the right and climbed a small, round knoll, then skipped over the boughs of an apple grove crowning the top. Quad ran amidst the grizzled and groaning trees and stopped, gasping, too exhausted to follow the wind any more.

The wind doubled back.

He shouted, raising the scepter before him as if it were a sword and the whirlwind a flesh-and-blood foe. He was swept up and hurled like a stick as it passed, rolling hard and striking his head against a tree. His skull seemed to explode, and the world turned a dazzling white. For a moment he wondered if he was even alive. *I am,* he decided groggily, *for death couldn't hurt so much.* Everything was swimming, growing black. He bit his tongue and the exquisite pain and taste of blood brought him about. The writhing, living cloud was hovering, seeming to hesitate, at the eastern edge of the grove. Quad made a lunging dash for freedom out the western side, but the whirlwind swept around the grove and met him, hurling branches and even tree trunks in his way.

Still clinging to the Ruby Scion, the king crawled painfully to the grove's center and planted himself in a hollow made of heaved-up roots. There, with cold earth and a jagged roof of mangled trees to shelter him, he listened to the whirlwind shatter and splinter the grove in its fury. With this rest came pain and a wave of nausea. He didn't fight the oblivion which offered to swallow him whole.

✦

He awoke.

Sunrise sent its broken rays through the twisted branches, warming his face. He lay there, carefully flexing his joints to see if anything was broken: his fingers, wrists, then arms, working his way muscle by muscle to his toes. He was battered, but he was whole.

Painfully climbing from beneath the trees, he stood shakily, taking in the desolation that had been a canopy of blossoming flowers and honeybees. Now it was a circle of jagged splinters of trunks, branches, and twigs; even the grass was torn apart. But the whirlwind was gone.

"You are dangerous, my unseen friend," he whispered, "but me, at least, you cannot kill."

That thought brought a rush of hope and power. *Presence! I can beat you!* Giddily he spun around, his aching legs nearly giving out. He laughed and steadied himself, then spun again, singing the songs of the Ariel and weaving about the hilltop, working his way to the grove's edge. There, the song was snatched from his throat.

He gasped.

The village of Syncatus lay below, bodies littering its streets. Corpses, bound and torn open, hung from every post and tree. Moldering ruins sent watery trails of smoke into the sky.

"My people!"

He ran, stumbling headlong down the hill, forgetting his own wounds as this newest horror filled his eyes. Below the village opened to him. Charred posts and caved-in chimneys were all that was left of many homes. Every building had been gutted and burned. The smoking shells of wagons littered the bloody roads.

Worst of all was the sight of his subjects, their corpses bristling with arrows: tiny children, old men, and women; humans, rats and badgers. The king shouted in fury as he raced blindly down one street after another, inebriated with horror. Dangling corpses gaped crazily from the trees; each yawning, broken mouth crying of atrocities. At the village square, where Syncatus' roads merged like spokes in a wheel, he walked dazedly about.

"What have you done!" he moaned. "Solofaust! Is this how you save your people from an ignorant king?"

He tripped over something and fell. Scrambling up he saw the remains of a mother, her bloodied arms clinging to a butchered child. Nearby a badger lay dead. With a shriek Quad raised the Ruby Scion high above his head and brought it down on the creature, smashing and pounding until nothing badger-like remained. But still he swung, his arms and shoulders aching with the effort. When he could swing no more, he stood over the mutilated thing, panting and wild-eyed. His trembling fingers relaxed. The Ruby Scion, spattered with blood and fur, fell from his hands.

And the king began to think. *This creature is not Solofaust. Nor is it his work.*

Not even Solofaust could do this to his own kind.

Who hates us this much?

Who can bring spirit-things on us from the very realms of the dead? Can Solofaust? No.

Only Demio.

Demio and the Ebon Trist.

For a moment Quad wondered if Solofaust himself still survived.

"You've taken my friends, Demio," he hissed, turning his face north. "My subjects, you've slaughtered and enslaved. My lords, you've seduced and turned against me, and I've little doubt you killed my father. But you don't have me.

"So long as I live I'll fight. And anyone who has anything to do with you shall die.

"I swear it!"

His oath echoed up and down the smoldering streets, but no one heard. He sank to his knees and cried for his people, great sobs shaking his body and soul.

"*S*ire! Sire! Are you awake?"

Quad sat upright, his eyes wide.

"My people!"

"Tik! tik! tik! 'Tis what you've been saying since we found you!"

"Friend Rat?"

The counselor smiled and dabbed the king's forehead with a cold, wet cloth.

"How good it is to see you!" Quad said. "I thought you were under a spell."

"I don't know about any spells," Rat said, "but you certainly put us in a fright—waking up and finding you gone, with the only clue to your where-abouts a path of uprooted trees."

"Where is Iscara? And the others?"

"They're burying the dead, and Robin is scouting about," the counselor said, frowning at the sound of Iscara's name.

"How did you find me?"

"I trailed you while the others broke camp. 'Twas easy enough when all I had to do was follow ditches and giant toothpicks. We found you here, among these poor souls." The counselor smiled. "The place is deserted. We've found no enemies."

Seeing Quad's anxious look, Friend Rat added, "And, I fear, no survivors. Many in the village were carried away. The rest, as you've seen, were slaughtered."

"Rat, why has this happened? I only wanted peace for my kingdom! More than that, I didn't want the kingdom. I wanted to be left alone!"

"'Twould seem that Fate's decided otherwise."

"So! You're awake, little wanderer!"

Quad turned to see Iscara, a most becoming smile on her lips.

"Good. My medicines revived you."

"Revived you, my nephew's tailbone!" the rat muttered to himself, stepping back. "All she did was slap a weed on you that smelled like baby doop."

"You don't know how good it is to see that you're all right!" Quad said, ignoring the counselor's remarks. "Have you seen what Demio's done?"

She nodded and kissed his forehead.

"'Tis sad, I know.

> Beware! They take our children!
> Cry! For our sons and daughters are
> Made to serve them in every way.
> Our old! Our leaders!
> Women with child are murdered—
> They lie dead on their doorsteps.
> What shall I do?
> Love those who took them?
> Shall mercy outweigh justice?
> Am I the King?

"That," she concluded, "is from your Ariel."

The two looked at each other as Arlan and Nabo strode up.

"How are you feeling?" Arlan asked.

"Tired, stiff, and sore. I think I've cracked some ribs. And I'm not sure my shoulder won't fall off. Where's my scepter?"

"Here!" Friend Rat said. "I cleaned it for you. It was quite a mess."

Quad took the Ruby Scion and handed it to Iscara.

"Put this in Spindle Leg's pack," he said.

"But why?" Friend Rat asked.

"Because I can't hold both it and a sword," Quad answered.

"You can't . . ." Arlan began.

"I must," the king replied, his voice low and harsh. "I'm sick with loathing at this violence to my people. I will avenge them."

"'Tis a mistake, Sire," Arlan said warily. "You're not a man of blood."

"Swordplay is no easy thing," Nabo warned.

"I doubt you can even lift one," Rat added, rolling his eyes.

"Nevertheless, I want one," Quad insisted, his eyes hard.

Arlan noticed a victorious smile sweep across Iscara's face.

"Open your eyes, warrior!" she said. "His enemies are wasting the land! It seems strange to me that a man so good at killing should want a milksop for a king."

"The chaos about us is in part because we could no longer bear an ungentle one," Arlan said.

"Ha! You've a milkmaid's nobility, Arlan! Go to Ebon Bane if you will, and tell Demio he must be a good old bird and take his men home. Say to Solofaust, 'Please give back the throne! 'Tis the noble thing to do!'" Iscara said.

"I'll fight my king's battles, but he must not take a sword, himself!" Arlan insisted, his face red. "That is not the answer!"

"Then what is?" the wizardess challenged.

Arlan trembled with anger, but gave no response.

"You have another sword, haven't you?" Quad demanded, turning to Nabo.

"Use mine, Sire," Arlan sighed. "It's lighter and more suited to your strength." ("A butter knife would be more suited, yet," Friend Rat muttered to Nabo, who nodded his assent.) "I think you're wrong; still you are king."

From up the road there came a clattering of hooves and Robin's cry.

"Alert! Alert! The enemy is coming! They're coming!"

The boy galloped through the group, which flew in all directions to escape his charging horse, and Arlan shook his fist as Robin galloped past, still crying his call.

"You little idiot! Come back and report!" Arlan shouted, still shaking his fist.

Robin's horse reeled to a stop, burying its hooves in the road and dropping its head. The rider sailed over with a cry and landed with a thud. Robin's face burned as he heard Arlan's sudden laugh, and he stumbled, swearing wickedly, to his feet. But a movement down a narrow road caught his eye, and he reeled around, pulling out his sword. Arlan, seeing this, stopped laughing abruptly and rushed up the road, stringing his bow as he went. The others ran along behind him.

Just as they reached the youth, however, Robin's sword arm went limp and his eyes grew wide. From up the alley a large, dark figure, its cape floating in the breeze, called out.

"So! You've found your wizardess. And the king, I see, is still alive."

"Narramoore!" Arlan cried. "You old war horse! Narramoore!"

They clasped and pounded each other's backs in greeting as Quad arrived. Narramoore's gaze fell fleetingly on the sword in his hand, but he kept his peace.

"I thought surely they'd get you at the castle!" Arlan laughed.

"They nearly did, and I've a hundred stories to tell," Narramoore smiled. "But there's no time, for the badger's forces aren't far behind."

"Behind you?" Arlan asked, then turned in the direction from which Robin had ridden. "Then the enemy is closing in from two sides, at least."

As they spoke, Friend Rat, Nabo, and Iscara arrived. Robin was still looking past everyone, down the road.

"What are you staring at?" Nabo ordered.

"Who's she?" Robin asked, pointing to a beautiful, golden-haired woman, dressed in a commoner's skirts and seated on Narramoore's horse.

"She's from the castle," Narramoore said. "Nellie, come here."

Quad looked up and met her eyes.

She was surprised, for the king was not only more bruised and battered than she, he was also more robust than when she'd seen him last, and his bearing revealed a newfound pride. The boy had become a man. His color was good and muscles were developing on his arms and legs. There was determination and nobility in his bearing, where before there had only been giddy fear. Something else was new, too, that made her turn uncomfortably away.

Unlike Robin, Quad didn't see her beauty, the curves of her body, or the flashing azure in her eyes. What he saw was a laughing maid at a coronation feast nervously announcing "a special roast for the king!"

ellie sat on Narramoore's horse, gazing down, hoping she looked defiant. Quad glared back.

"You're one of Solofaust's women," he said at last.

"I was," Nellie began, trying to word some defense.

"But she is no longer, Sire," Narramoore said quickly. "Her spirit was too free for some, and they made up charges against her. I saved her from an executioner's axe and" (he tilted a slight smile at her) "she saved me from an execution of swords."

"You should've let the ax fall," Iscara growled.

Arlan groaned in exasperation.

"More than axes will fall, and our heads will be wondering where our bodies went, if we don't get out of here!" He grabbed Quad by the shoulders and looked into his brooding face. "May I remind you, Sire, that armies approach from two directions, and neither will sing us songs when they find us here!"

Quad's eyes slowly focused on the handsome face before him, then unfocused, retraining on the woman. Rolling his eyes, Arlan released the king and went to his horse, pulling his second sword from its pack.

"Narramoore, I've never seen a group so eager to bicker

when trouble's afoot as this one is. How strong is the enemy behind you?"

"They looked like a quarter of the armies of the land," Narramoore said, and Arlan whistled in amazement.

"That's an exaggeration, I hope!" Friend Rat put in.

"Counselor, I fear not. Exaggeration is not one of his strengths," Arlan said. "Tell me, Narramoore, are they encamped?"

"They were moving out when we passed them, but they're keeping with their supply trains. It'll take them several hours to get here. Still, there's a small advance force not far behind me, and it could arrive any time."

"How small?" Friend Rat asked, suspecting he wouldn't like the answer.

"Perhaps two hundred."

The counselor wrapped his tail about his snout and groaned.

"How many did you spot, Robin?" Narramoore asked.

"Hundreds!" the youth said, then added, "Hundreds of hundreds!" ("He, at least, exaggerates well," Arlan whispered to the rat, who by now had drawn his tail so tight his nose paled from lack of circulation.) "They're coming from the east. They'll be here soon, I'm sure!"

"Sire! Come here! We could use your input!" Narramoore called.

"I'm listening now," Quad said, coming up. Still, he kept one eye on Nellie, as if fearful she would get away.

"Enemies in two directions. What are our options?" Arlan asked.

"They're coming from the east and south," Narramoore replied quickly. "That leaves north or west."

"Let's ride to Yerushela," the king replied. "We'll be safe there for a while, at least, since they're loyal and strong."

"Yerushela is south," Arlan reminded him.

Quad paled.

"That means our way to your people, where the Oneprince will most likely be, is cut off!"

"I suggest we go west," Arlan offered. "We can double

back south before we meet up with any large forces and outflank them."

"Then let's do it, and quickly," Friend Rat squeaked, twisting his beloved tail, "before more than just our routes are cut off."

Breathing a loud sigh, Nabo turned and started off.

"Where are you going?" Narramoore demanded.

"To get the king's horse," Nabo replied. "There are enough of you stirring this soup already. You don't need me."

"You're right," the captain agreed. "Too many cooks over one pot, and it's boiling over into our laps as we debate its ingredients!" Turning to the others, he shouted, "West, then! To your horses, and have your bows at the ready. If we're pursued, Arlan and I will turn to draw them off. Nabo and Robin, it will be your responsibility, then, to see your king around these forces and into Yerushela."

"What about her?" Iscara demanded.

Everyone looked at Nellie.

"I'm sure no one's forgot me," Nellie said, giving the wizardess a shrug and a pretty smile.

"She'll ride with me," Narramoore said.

"What? And lose the benefit of your marksmanship?" Arlan snapped. "You won't shoot so well with a rider clinging to your back! And if we have to turn and fight, what will become of her?"

"He has a point," Quad said. "She'll ride with Friend Rat."

"So she can knock him off his horse and run?" Iscara spat.

"She won't run. Our enemy is hers now, too," Narramoore said. "They'd kill her."

"Or reward her!" Iscara huffed.

Arlan's lip turned up in a sneer.

"Would you have us slay her on the spot?"

"She is a traitor, and this is a war!" Iscara said.

"She will have a trial," Quad decided.

"When, little king? As we gallop along in flight?"

"Let her ride with me!" Friend Rat shrieked. "Let her do headstands in the breeze, if it'll get us out of here!"

"*Alert! Alert!*" Robin called.

They turned to see Robin, bent low on his horse as he galloped toward them, and again they scattered for cover as he thundered by, his words trailing after.

"They're coming! They're coming! They're coming from the west as well! Alert! Alert!"

"I do hope he stops before he reaches the ones coming from the east," Friend Rat said, peeking from behind a fallen wall. "Tik! tik! tik!"

Nabo ran up, leading the horses. "Let's go!" he shouted, and everyone ran for their mounts. Narramoore lifted Nellie from his own horse and strung his bow while the animal pawed the ground, its nostrils flaring. The counselor grabbed the maid and dragged her toward his own horse— then stopped suddenly.

"Wait! In the excitement we forgot: I don't have a horse! I ride with Robin! You shall have to ride with the king!"

"The king! Have you lost your little mind?" Nellie nearly shrieked.

"Oh, fear not, he likes you."

"Stretched and yowling on a rack, perhaps!"

"Tik! tik! tik! Don't I know him! He's upset now, is all. And you're just his type, too: simple, crude . . . Why, I'll bet he falls in love with you before we're done. Assuming he doesn't execute you, first."

Before she could reply, Friend Rat shoved her unceremoniously toward the king and into his arms.

"What am I supposed to do with her?" Quad asked.

"That's your problem!" Rat called as he scurried up a fallen wall. "She's your subject!"

Quad scowled at the rat, who stood atop a heap, tail looped in his hands, waiting for Robin's return. Already the others were mounted and waiting, Narramoore and Arlan with their bows strung, Nabo holding a sword in one hand and a starbrand in the other. Iscara waited, her head turned south, seeming to listen to the distant enemy's advance. Finally the king sighed and climbed onto his mare.

"Well, come on!" he said, and Nellie, looking reluctantly about as if hoping a horse of her own might materialize out of nothing, climbed up behind him. She sat there, nervously chewing her lip, her hands around the king's waist. Robin came galloping back and, seeing the rat wave frantically, pulled to a stop before him. The counselor joined him and, at last, they hurried at a gallop down the road.

"At the village center we'll turn north, ride a ways and cut to the east," Narramoore said. That way, he hoped, they could stay well clear of the advancing armies, skirting the large force and regaining the Yerushela Road south of the warbands.

Galloping into the hub, Narramoore saw the clouds of dust marking the approach of soldiers from south and west. Listening carefully, he could already hear their clattering approach.

"Ride like you've never ridden before!" he shouted, turning his horse hard about.

"I've barely ever ridden before!" Friend Rat gasped, shutting his eyes and clinging to Robin, his tail looped about the boy's head so that Robin had to drag it from his eyes. They broke into a gallop, although Quad hesitated kicking Spindle Legs, remembering that night with Gregor. Nellie hindered by no such memories, kicked the horse for him. They charged around a bend that led north, stone and dust churning beneath the animals' hooves, nearly storming right into the arms of an advance patrol.

No one had expected this. The fugitives dragged their horses to a halt, with Quad's ramming into Arlan's and nearly knocking both to the ground in a tangle of legs and cursing. But the advance patrol was no less surprised and, meeting this unforeseen apparition of armed men, they scattered with cries and screams. Narramoore managed to fire three arrows as they fled, but struck only one man, who fell over screaming at the sight of an arrow in his forearm. Another soldier dropped behind a wall, sat down hard, and leveled a distress blast from his horn.

"Turn about!" Narramoore shouted, but even as he spoke he saw, through the ruins, soldiers hurrying into Syncatus' western side, clambering for position. The din of their clattering armor and shouts rose up in everyone's ears.

"Follow me!" Narramoore called again, spurring his horse back to the crossroads.

"He'll take us right to their arms!" Nellie cried.

"'Tis our only chance," Arlan said as he pulled alongside. "We must reach the hub and grab the road due east!"

But they quickly discovered the enemy had already spread to cover that exit.

"We're surrounded!" Friend Rat gasped.

"We've been in worse situations!" Robin called.

"Really?" Friend Rat asked, hopefully.

"No!"

"You should have said yes, at least I'd have felt better!"

"I should lie and not see heaven?" Robin demanded. With a motion that was quick if not graceful, he drew his sword from its scabbard, nearly relieving the rat of some fingers in the process.

"You get down, and use my bow," Robin said. "I can't shoot it, anyway."

Friend Rat was reluctant to jump, but he had the uneasy feeling he would be riding into that growing throng if he didn't. He stood with the bow unstrung, gaping.

Quad looked about, his face grim. He raised his own sword, clutching the hilt with both hands, marveling at how awkward and impossible the weapon seemed. He doubted he would have a chance to use it.

Still he swallowed, and said, "If this is our end, then I'm ready to fight them, here. We'll go down gloriously, and minstrels will sing of this battle one day!"

"If we go down now," Friend Rat sighed, "we'll go down forgotten. Minstrels don't sing ditties for the losers."

Arlan cast a sharp eye on the wizardess.

"If ever there was a good time for magic," he said, "'tis now."

"What do you expect me to do with a whole army?" she asked, her voice edged with panic.

"Anyone who makes trees walk can certainly stop an army!" Robin said frantically.

"Yes!" Quad added. "You can get us out of here!"

"With what!" Iscara cried. "Shall I fly us out like birds?"

"Yes! You're a wizardess!"

"Little king! You don't understand! I don't have that kind of magic!"

"But the trees!"

"I did nothing to 'em! They never moved!" She looked at each of her companions and found them no more shocked to hear it than she was to tell it. "It was your *mind* I played tricks on. Don't look at me to save you here!"

"A fine time to tell us you're useless!" Arlan roared.

"I can find the Oneprince!" she protested.

"Not unless he's here among Solofaust's men!"

Nellie found herself laughing. That her captors could find time to argue, even as hundreds of armed men converged on them, was ludicrously funny. Yet within her laugh was a sound of hopeless desperation, too.

"My merry heroes!" she shouted, "if there's something up anyone's sleeves, you'd best pull it out, and quick!"

Iscara shot her a venomous look, but suddenly her face brightened.

"Quad! Put down your sword!"

"What? And face them unarmed?"

"No! Arlan was right! You aren't a sword-king. This is your weapon!"

She pulled the scepter from its bag.

"The Ruby Scion?" He doubted its worth, for none of those approaching would likely bend a knee to it. *Still, it's lighter than that sword, and I can use it for bashing if nothing else,* he thought. He handed the sword to the rat and took the Ruby Scion. As always it felt comforting in his hands.

"Hold it before me!" Iscara said. "Hurry!"

He did, staring at its gem, darker now than ever. Iscara chanted softly, her long fingers caressing the stone.

"What's she up to?" Arlan demanded.

"Your father would have slain her for that . . ." the rat protested.

"Let her be," Narramoore interrupted. "She's our only hope."

The soldiers were close now—close enough to make out their faces, almost within range of bowmen. The foremost men to the east pulled arrows from their quivers and strung them against their bows.

"They won't give us the honor of a fight!" Robin cried.

Friend Rat rubbed his tail.

"Oh, I just know this is going to smart!"

Even as they spoke a string of mist began to trail from the Ruby Scion. It curled about them, snake-like, then congealed and grew, spreading like a fog. Iscara's chant grew louder and mixed with the cries of surprise from her companions and the enemy. Horses pawed nervously at the ground, tossing their heads and snorting while the riders pulled tight on the reins to control them. Foot soldiers who'd been closing in turned as though they would run, but officers flanking them swore and clubbed them until they turned again to face the travelers—who were now enveloped in the Ruby Scion's fog. They started to approach, but arrows sprang suddenly from the heavy mist, clattering about like deadly hail and bringing down three men. The rest shrieked, turned, and ran, ignoring their officers' threats. The enchanted fog oozed outward until the entire village was lost to it.

Pale and trembling, Iscara fell forward on her horse.

"'Tis all I can do!" she gasped. "This will hide us, and we'll be able to see if we drop to our hands and knees. 'Tis not so thick close to the ground, I think, and there we can slip away. But hurry! I sense great evil . . . coming from the south. When it arrives this fog will be worthless."

"The spirit-things!" Nellie gasped.

"We'll have to abandon the horses," Quad called. "Narramoore! Lead the way!"

Even on their hands and knees Quad could see no more than twenty feet. He hoped Narramoore's sense of direction was better than his. The frantic cries and oaths of soldiers, whose superstitious minds had given the fog a mind-numbing power, grew close. Narramoore gave directions, speaking with his hands and fingers. Nellie grabbed Friend Rat's tail and, when he looked back, gave a quizzical look toward the captain.

"Narramoore?" he whispered. "He's using sign-talk! He wants us to follow him, but I'm not so good at this, so I don't know where."

Narramoore chose his way quickly, flashing signs each time he changed direction, weaving around this ruin or through that one, evading the most impassable clusters of the enemy. The fog was so dense, some inches above the ground, that the soldiers were unaware their quarry was among them. The fugitives had to roll quickly to avoid the stamping hooves, and countless soldiers tripped over or stepped on them, mistaking them for the village dead or their own companions. What few soldiers who fell among the travelers or looked to see what they'd struck found themselves getting stuck on the end of a dagger or sword.

Soon, beneath the fog the sound of battle reached them. Swords rang against shields and the wounded cried out. In the confusion the enemy had begun battling with itself, as captains screamed in a useless attempt to stop the fighting.

At last the fugitives reached an end of the fog—and of the village and soldiers, too—and climbed the hill of the ruined grove. They sat panting, collecting their thoughts and their breath, listening to the noise rising from the fog below.

"It should be colorful down there when the fog clears," Friend Rat observed.

"Is everyone all right?" Narramoore asked.

"Everyone but those dunder-brains below!" Robin laughed.

"I wish I were back at The Rasp & File," Nellie sighed.

"I've never been kicked and walked over so much in my life," the king said between puffs.

"I feel like a rug," the counselor added.

"You look like a rug," Arlan muttered.

"Some fat slug nearly ground my fingers to mush," Iscara growled, rubbing them together.

"At least we're alive, thanks to you," Quad said.

Arlan smiled slightly. "I hate to say it, but I agree."

"No! 'Tis thanks only to the scepter of the Oneprince!" Iscara replied. "I . . ."

"We've trouble," Nabo interrupted. "Look below!"

They did, and saw with a gasp that the billowing fog was turning from white to a sickly green. A long, dark blotch grew on the horizon and the travelers felt an icy chill as they realized it was another army, far larger than the one defeating itself below.

"How far off?" Arlan asked.

"An hour at most," Nabo said, shading his eyes with a hand.

"Then we must hurry away!" Narramoore said, standing up. "The way that fog is changing, I'd guess the spirit-things are coming, too, and we'd best not be around when they arrive. We've no horses, and only the time it will take the spirit-things to reach this group and untangle them to put distance between us!"

"But the spirit-things won't need to wait for the army to catch us!" Nellie protested.

"They will so long as I carry this scepter," Quad said confidently.

"Even so, how long can we run from so many?" Looking about, Nellie saw that her thought was echoed in every mind.

"Then it's hopeless," Iscara whispered.

"No. We're still alive," the king insisted, rising and holding the Ruby Scion close. "And so long as we are, we may yet find the Oneprince. So long as we may find him, there's hope for the kingdom.

"Lead on, Narramoore. Our quest continues to the end."

They had no horses, but their fear carried them well enough as they ran from the grove at a gallop.

Keeping at first to patches of woods and fields, the travelers picked up the northward road, calling to one another for courage and strength. Quad and the rat found it difficult to keep up, for although they'd developed muscle and stamina these past days, they were still castle-bred and couldn't match the others who'd spent their lives at physical labor. Frequently Narramoore had to stop and wait for them, his eyes scanning the horizon, his bow drawn and ready.

"Come, little king!" Iscara shouted. "Look at that village girl, how she runs! Can't you keep up with *her* at least?" The taunts were cold, but the sound of her laughing, singsong voice drew him on.

Just as it seemed his lungs would burst, he crested a hill and a lone tavern popped into view; carefree laughter erupted from within. The sound was so out of place that the travelers stopped cold and stared at one another.

"What are they so happy about?" the king wondered.

The counselor's face lit up.

"Why, I'd know a sound like that anywhere! 'Tis a tavern full of rats!"

"Acting like that with the spirit-things about?" Robin asked. "'Tis a tavern full of idiots."

"Same difference," Arlan sighed.

"Tik! tik! tik!" Friend Rat scolded. "'Tis just the medicine for us now!" With a happy squeal he ran toward it, but Arlan grabbed his tail as he passed and the counselor found himself running furiously and getting nowhere at the same time.

"Where do you think you're going?"

"A drink would be a nice thing," Nellie said. "So would some food, about now, enemy or not. How long can we run without it?"

"That's true," Quad said. "And we don't know when we'll have a chance to get food again. We could stop long enough to get supplies and pay for them with some of mine and Arlan's finery."

"That's cruel, Sire," the warrior said, looking sadly at his rings.

"Oh, let's go! I'd like to see some rats again," the counselor urged.

Narramoore scowled uncertainly. "Can we enter a tavern that might be full of Solofaust's fellows? Remember, that wheezy one the counselor spoke of is about."

"Then let's send Rat and Nellie first," Robin suggested. "They'd both look at home in a rat tavern."

"Forget it," Nellie countered. "The Rat Mugby knows me, and he's already tried to kill your counselor."

"Indeed!" Friend Rat agreed.

"Then we'll all go in together," the king decided. "If they're unfriendly, we'll be strong enough to fight them off. If they are friendly, we'll grab supplies and be off quick, and send them off as well. I doubt they'll get any better treatment than those poor folk in Syncatus when the enemy arrives here."

"Your idea is good," Narramoore said, nodding. "And you, Sire, shall be the first one in."

"Me?" Quad gulped. "It was peasants who nearly did me in once before!"

"And so you'll announce yourself here, unafraid, as the peasants' king."

"I like that!" Arlan said, looking up.

"Sounds grand to me!" the counselor said.

"'Tis your chance!" Iscara agreed.

Quad did not agree. Still, the idea made sense. And, after all, help would be just outside the door if things got ugly. He shrugged—to hide a shiver—and started down the road.

Prominent on the low, mud-brick building was a sign hung on ropes. It was colored green, with a fat, yellow slab of cheese painted on. Heavy lettering identified this place as "The Fettid Cheese." The letters were crooked and smeared, and the cheese was identifiable only by the name of the establishment and the fact it was painted with holes. The artist who'd done the work must have received a hefty payment of drink in advance, Quad thought with amusement. The door below was also green and not very large. He'd have to duck to enter, and he wondered whether Nabo and Narramoore could even get through. From within there came the sounds of clinking mugs, laughter, high-pitched shouting, and the lively, nonsensical sounds of rat music.

He squared his shoulders, straightened his drooping crown, pushed open the door, and strode in.

"I am the king! Quad, the son of Pentatutinus, come to claim his kingdom!" he announced loudly.

He stood waiting for a reaction and was surprised to find he was ignored.

Flustered, he announced himself again.

A plump rat at the bar turned and smiled through a thick pair of spectacles.

"So! You are the king, sirrah, or should I say, '*If* you are the king,' sirrah, of Redaemus . . . But I suppose you are, for you hold the Ruby Scion just as we've been told! Well, then, bring your fellows in and sit! 'Tis about time you arrived, we were getting impatient and ready to send someone out to find you. 'Tis an honor you're here, sirrah, and don't be so late again! Sit down and join us!"

"We've little time, good Tavern-keep," Quad said, flustered. *They've been expecting me!* "We wish only to purchase supplies and be quickly on our way. You must all leave, as well, for . . ."

"No, no, sirrah! You'll eat here!" The rat's eyes had grown wide behind his glasses. "There's plenty to dish out and we can always make more room!"

The tavern-keep, who called himself Snout, dragged the protesting king to a table and plopped him down. While several rats dumped huge portions of meat and fruit in front of Quad, Snout hurried to the door. Blinking into the sunlight, he grinned at the others.

"The king says to come in, sirrahs, and to do so quickly."

"There's trouble!" Narramoore said.

"Indeed no, sirrah! There's fun!"

With that Snout disappeared into the tavern. The travelers looked at one another in amazement, and Friend Rat scrambled happily toward the door. At a loss, the others followed him inside, drinking in the sight of more than two dozen rats merry-making while the king sat hidden behind a pile of food. Rat servants bustled about him, calling and whistling as they slapped great dippers full of mashed potatoes and gravy as much on the king as on his plate.

"I don't believe this!" Arlan shouted.

"Neither do I!" Quad replied. "But they won't let me go!"

"I'll clear you a path," Nabo growled, raising his sword.

"No! Don't harm them!" Quad pleaded, waving his arms. "Let's just eat quickly to satisfy them, then hurry away. Please! Sit!"

Muttering angrily, but obedient both to their king and the tempting smell of the food, the travelers found places to sit. Narramoore kept a firm hand on Nellie's wrist, fearing to trust her good behavior when she was among her own. She turned her head sharply from him and found Friend Rat climbing onto a chair beside her.

"I think Narramoore likes you," the counselor whispered. "Do you like him?"

"You're a hairy little cupid, aren't you?" she whispered back.

Friend Rat grinned. "I was hoping you and the king would like each other, but he's so wrapped up in the wizardess' charms—I thought maybe you'd settle for someone with courage, instead."

"Oh, this one's courageous, all right," Nellie sighed, her voice low, "but he's as much fun as a pumpkin after the frost."

"Compared to a turnip, a pumpkin is fun. Have you ever worn one on your head?"

Nellie grinned. "A castle counselor seems hardly the type to take part in October foolery!"

"If it's fun you wish, you might like Quad after all. He's Narramoore turned around—a funny man with the courage of a pumpkin!"

"You're a strange little thing!" Nellie laughed.

The food was brought on, much of it actually making it from the counter to the tables, even though a good amount landed on the floor. What succeeded in covering that distance was divided among their plates, laps, and the table itself. The servers sang all the while, a sound Friend Rat described as like beautiful ravens warbling in the morning (and Arlan suggested the ravens must be having their heads twisted off while singing to achieve such interesting notes). As they ate hurriedly, the fugitives discussed possible escape routes and places where the rats might hide. Finally they finished, but they couldn't rise to leave because of the close quarters they were keeping with their hosts.

"Move out of our way!" Quad shouted. "Your king demands it!"

"If they don't move soon, we'll have to use our swords," Arlan whispered. "Better we chop off a couple of tails than be here when the spirit-things arrive."

"They're my subjects, and they've shown us kindness!" Quad argued. "How can I just start chopping off tails?"

Arlan sighed. "Soon they'll face a chopping that's worse! Do *something*! We could all die here!"

"I can think of worse places to die!" Friend Rat said.

Narramoore turned to Nellie. "They're your kind. Speak to them! They'll listen to you!"

Nellie rose—with a firm prod from her guardian—and rapped the table.

"All of you! We have to flee! There's a huge army of cruel men coming, and when they arrive they'll kill us all . . . or worse!"

The rats responded only with good-natured laughter.

"It's useless!" Quad told his friends. "I've warned them over and over. All they do is giggle!"

Snout climbed onto a table and clapped his hands for silence.

"A fine speech, sirrah!" he told the king. "A fine speech! And now, to return the favor, sirrah, we'll favor you with entertainment!"

"We must flee!" Quad cried in near-anguish. He wanted to seize the crazy rat and rattle sense into him, but couldn't reach him through the others. "Are you going to force us to hurt . . ."

His words died in his throat as from out of the kitchen stepped a minstrel, the same one who'd badgered Solofaust at the coronation!

"So, a noble guest, indeed!" the minstrel laughed. "Sire Quad, how *did* you find that covered dish?"

"A bit rare," he answered weakly. "'Twas a rare feast, all around."

"And one not ended till now . . . for you've arrived at The Fettid Cheese. All feast to their fill when they enter my kingdom!"

Arlan's hand shot to his sword, but Narramoore clasped his wrist. "Wait," the captain whispered.

Arlan's face turned hot. "But he said . . ."

"I know!"

"And we've got to get . . ."

"I know!"

"This makes no sense! Why wait?" Arlan whispered through clenched teeth.

Narramoore wondered himself, but his instincts warned him to let things continue for now.

"A song! A ballad for myself and Nell!" blurted out Friend Rat, who'd been inside the castle the day of the coronation and, therefore, didn't recognize the minstrel.

"There's no time!" Quad blurted again.

The minstrel bowed to the counselor. "I shall play, and you shall sing!"

And so, regardless of the loud protests of the king, the minstrel strummed his lute and Friend Rat began to sing, making up the words as he went along.

> He loved a rat, she loved him too,
> They drank of fetid, cheesy goo
> And clasping tails, said "I love you!"
> It was the rat-like thing to do!

The patron-rats applauded wildly. Furious, Quad jumped to his feet, bowling over several, and seized the minstrel.

"This is insane!" he shouted. "*You're* insane!" Finally, he realized, he was getting through to the rats, for they fell silent and looked at him, shocked at his words.

"Listen!" the king begged. "There are soldiers—thousands of them. Evil powers you can't comprehend are coming this way! Snout, I've warned you over and over—we have to flee! Yet all you do is laugh and sing."

Iscara shut her eyes tightly and suddenly began to chant.

> The end is near! they said to me,
> Evil's coming on a wing,
> And all you do is die to sing,
> You die to sing of mad'ning things!

"Oedaeus," Quad said automatically, identifying the prophet without realizing he'd done so. The minstrel placed his hands—surprisingly strong, Quad thought, for a man who lived by tickling a lute—upon the king's shoulders and smiled.

"They've no reason for fear and anger," the minstrel said. "There's trouble about, but I am here, and thus they're happy."

"Then they're fools and you're a murderer!" Quad shouted, throwing his scepter onto the table and seizing the minstrel with both hands. "What's the matter with you! Don't you know what happened at Syncatus? Don't you know the folk are being enslaved and murdered?"

"We all know that," Snout assured him.

"They do," the minstrel agreed. "I've told them. They've mourned for them, but they also rejoice, for they know it's only temporary and that justice will soon have its way."

"What makes them think so?"

"Because they are with me, here, in my kingdom," the minstrel smiled.

"That's twice!" Arlan roared, pushing forward, and now even Narramoore's hand went to his sword.

"No! This isn't treason," Quad said, holding up his hand to them. " 'Tis madness. This lunatic means his 'kingdom' of The Fettid Cheese!"

"My lord!" Iscara cried, her voice deep with rapture. Everyone turned to see she was speaking not to Quad, but to the minstrel. Trembling and on her knees, she clung to his legs. Whispers rippled through the tavern, and Friend Rat tugged frantically at the king's sleeve.

"Sire! The Ruby Scion!" he squealed. "Look at the Ruby Scion!"

All eyes turned to the scepter lying on the table. Deep within its gem, something throbbed and grew. A tiny, crimson speck soon became a blot. Then it spread and swallowed the stone's blackness, and not only filled the whole gem, but washed the tavern with a crimson glow. Slowly, Quad turned to the minstrel.

"You . . ." he managed to say, "are *him*! You are the Oneprince!"

And the minstrel smiled. "Yes."

"Wh-where have you been?" the king stammered. "Why didn't you come?"

"My little king!" he laughed. "You've sought so long. You've walked through caves and tunnels and fields and woods and all the time you've carried this scepter, my sign among men! If only you'd quit seeking with man's blindness, and called upon me as a king should do, I'd have heard you as plainly as I do now.

"And I'd have been there by your side . . . any time . . . all along!"

They stood together, the minstrel's smile both sad and wise, the king's uncertain and confused.

"You really *are* the Oneprince?"

"What do you think?"

Quad sighed. "I wish I knew. I expected a man full of thundering words, keeping company with scholars and priests. Instead I've found a minstrel in a floppy cap, telling folk tales to rats. Still, Iscara believes in you, and the Ruby Scion has no doubts. How can I?"

"Your heart speaks true, little king. But your mind can't quite agree," the minstrel said patiently. "Your friends accept me even less—except the wizardess, who has no doubts at all." He took her hand and gently raised her to her feet, tenderly kissing her forehead, then lowered her to the table, pillowing her cheek on her folded arms.

"My name is Josiah," he said, turning back to them, and added decisively, "I am the Oneprince! The scepter itself says this is true! You've risked every danger, just to seek my help. But for what purpose if you won't believe?"

"Understand how we feel!" Arlan said, rising. "We've nearly been butchered only to find our 'savior' takes himself no more seriously than to loaf in the company of . . . of *rats!*"

The minstrel laughed. "You're a true son of Yerushela, Arlan of the East! Your own prophet Ariel said the Oneprince is the prince of *all* the folk. Why, blue-bloods such as you are but a drop in a peasants' sea. Why shouldn't I be found among the commoners, enjoying their ways?"

"Bah!" Arlan snapped, stabbing a finger at him. "If you are the Oneprince, prove it. Show me a sign."

"A sign," Josiah echoed, amazed. "You've seen the Ruby Scion. Do you need more? The simple folk believe, and they've seen no signs at all!"

"Simple folk believe anything," Arlan coughed.

"And educated fools believe nothing!" the minstrel replied coolly. "Before this day has ended you'll have your proof—evidence beyond doubt that I am who I say. Then what excuse will you use?"

Iscara, recovering, clung to him. He gazed sadly into her eyes.

"You alone, among these humans, know me?"

"You're my lord and master!"

"Yet, even you . . ." he began, shaking his head sadly.

"What will you do?" Nabo suddenly asked the king. "The enemy is closing fast."

"Indeed!" Friend Rat agreed, raising a mug of mead frothing with cheddar.

"Give me a moment to myself!" Quad begged. "Let me think!"

"Tik! tik! tik!" his counselor scolded. "For years a thought to think never entered your head. Now you're so excited by the idea, you do it at the worst of times."

Ignoring him, Quad wormed his way through the pandemonious rats and his protesting fellow travelers to the kitchen. There Snout pulled aside a curtain, uttering a cheerful, "There 'e go, sirrah!" as the king passed.

This room was as cheerily disrupted as the last. Black cauldrons, kettles, pots, and pans dangled from hooks and pegs above, and a long wooden table featured cheeses coated in orange and red and yellow wax. A long carving knife was buried to its hilt in a particularly fat blue one. Loaves of bread frosted with glazes and cinnamon glittered on another table, their fluffy white dough spackled with plump raisins. A friendly fire licked at a huge kettle in which an aromatic broth of beef bits and vegetables bubbled and stewed.

"*Snnnffff!* Ah! 'Tis just like the kitchens at Pentatute!" sighed Friend Rat, who had slipped up behind him. "The very air says, 'peace at last!'"

"And so do your rats and that singer in the other room," Quad responded.

"So what do you think?"

"That, suddenly, I feel like that ignorant prince again, the one who wants nothing more than to go home."

"Indeed! But you've no home to go to."

"Nor will I, so long as Solofaust infests the kingdom." Quad chuckled tiredly. "It's strange. A few hours ago our lives were nearly snuffed out. We were surrounded by rebels and almost slaughtered. We ran for our lives and stumbled onto this little inn where everything is at peace, where the rats themselves sing and dance in spite of knowing the enemy is nearly at the door."

"Like the eye of a storm," Friend Rat allowed, carving himself a slice of bleu cheese.

"And the storm is fast closing in. I have to decide what we will do."

"You've two choices. Go with Arlan and run the rats away—assuming they'll go, of course, or turn this whole affair over to the Oneprince."

"The minstrel?" Quad said, as though just remembering him.

"So says Arlan. So I would agree. But you saw how Iscara flopped about, and even I have a hard time dismissing the Ruby Scion and how it glows!"

"But you don't believe he's who he says?"

"I don't know," Friend Rat admitted. "All reason and intelligence denies it. But what is reason and intelligence to such as you and me? I am a rat, and you are Quad. Go with your heart, my lord."

"My heart says he is the Oneprince," Quad sighed. "My head tells me that my heart lies. Look at him! I fully expected to find a warrior in armor, or at the very least, a sage in a room full of scrolls, wearing embroidered robes and oil in his hair. I thought he would be in Yerushela, awaiting us in the Hall of the King. I believed, and Arlan did as well, that if we found him, he would rise up and build an army for us, and then lead us through incredible campaigns to a victory and a peace that would never end. What kind of campaign will this weaver of songs put together? And where is his army? Rats!"

"Tik! tik! tik!"

"I'm sorry," the king apologized, "but you have to admit rats are not warring creatures. If we handed you swords, you'd simply cut off your fingers and toes."

"Josiah has the Honor Guard," Friend Rat pointed out. "Arlan and Narramoore and Nabo and Robin, and your brother too—should he ever show up again."

"Yes, I wonder how he's fared?" Quad mused. "I thought he was wrong in what he did, and then I thought, perhaps, he would find a loyal army on which the Oneprince might build. But such a small force of five or six men against the thousands that are marching against us . . ."

"Which will be battering down the door soon enough," Friend Rat pointed out. "This debate is fine, but you must make a decision, and quick, my lord."

They stood in silence and listened to the commotion beyond the kitchen door. Above the din Quad could pick out the angry voice of Arlan and could almost feel the brooding silence of Nabo. But the rats chatted merrily, and he remembered Iscara's rapture. The room was still awash in the Ruby Scion's cherry glow.

The Oneprince!

Quad's father had often spoken of him as the kingdom's eventual and only hope. Doddering old Wilgate had agreed, his ludicrous face strangely setting itself with assurance and power whenever he spoke the name.

The Oneprince. One man. Against hundreds of thousands.

Your only hope.

"I believe," Quad said at last. "I don't know why; there's no sense to it. But I know Josiah is who he says. We will follow him."

Two arms wrapped around him from behind and squeezed him tight, nearly sweeping him off the floor. The king would have shouted in startled fear, had the strong embrace not forced the air from his lungs. He was set down and spun about, and there stood Josiah, grinning broadly.

"I knew you would believe!" he beamed. "I could see your faith wanting to come through, little king!"

"Yes," Quad agreed, squaring his shoulders. He wondered how Josiah had managed to creep up on him so quietly, and why Friend Rat had not given warning of his approach. "Come, I had better announce this decision to my friends."

As the three left the kitchen, Friend Rat grabbed two pans which he banged together to gain attention. The crowd quickly quieted and watched the pair of men.

"Well," Arlan snorted in the silence, "have you made up your mind, my lord . . . or lost it?"

"I have reached a decision," Quad said, ignoring the inference, "if you will allow me the honor of stating it."

Arlan huffed, but Narramoore's hand closed on his wrist in warning. Friend Rat, satisfied that all were listening, plopped himself down beside Nellie. Thankfully, she took his paw in her hand.

"What's he going to do?" she whispered.

"You'll see," Rat whispered back. "I suggest you watch Arlan's face. 'Twill be interesting to see which glows more, him or the Scion, when the king's decision is heard!"

Quad cleared his throat. He wasn't anxious to speak, for what he had to say sounded clearly insane.

"We have traveled weeks to find the Oneprince," he began, "and faced hundreds of dangers in a hopelessly lop-sided war. Only you few and Gregor were willing to follow me, and we all know that isn't enough to win, or even to survive, Solofaust's rebellion. And so we agreed to seek the Oneprince, for my father, King Pentatutinus himself, had warned us that only the Oneprince could redeem our kingdom. Iscara told us of the Scion's ability to identify the Oneprince, and in Syncatus we all saw an example of that scepter's power. Now it has identified this man beside me. I believe in my heart he is the Oneprince. We will do as he says."

"This is madness!" Arlan sputtered (and his face did glow). His consternation was reflected in the face of every man, and even Nellie wondered at the thought.

"You expect us to follow this rat balladeer?" the Easterner demanded.

"I not only expect it; as your king I command it," Quad declared. "Remember, you have sworn to obey me, to a man."

Turning to the minstrel, he said, "I don't know how you'll do it, Josiah, but I believe the prophecies, and I know this war has reached its end."

The minstrel smiled.

"Little king," he sighed, "an army marches against us and we shall meet and defeat it, yes—and do so this very day. But that is only the beginning of our trials together, for such an army is no threat at all. The real enemy we must fight lies in a frozen castle to the north, and the greatest battleground shall be within this field," he tapped Quad's chest, "and the battle will be long and bitter in the heart of every man and woman here."

Turning to the others he announced, "You think the war is nearly over, but it isn't. In fact, until Quad acknowledged me in your presence, it hadn't begun."

ABOUT THE AUTHOR

Bill Hand received the B.A. degree in English and theater from Geneva College, Beaver Falls, Pennsylvania, where he was awarded the Andrew Metheny Writers Award. He has published a collection of skits with Contemporary Drama Service, entitled *Aesop's Fables,* and *Power Plays for Youth* with Baker Book House.

Hand describes himself as a writer, playwright, and actor who passes the time impersonating Mark Twain and writing about talking rats and badgers. He lives in Greenville, Pennsylvania, with his wife, Roberta, and their infant daughter, Rachael Elizabeth.